Winston listened to the sound of the British artillery echoing over the Point. "It'll be the first time a settlement in the Americas has ever fired on an English ship," he said. "I guess that's the price you're going to have for staying your own master."

Canninge and the men had finished turning the guns towards the RAINBOWE. "How does it look?" Winston asked.

"I know these eighteen-pounders, Cap'n like I was born to one. At this range I could line-of-sight these whoresons any place you like."

"How about just under the lower gun deck? At the water line? The first round better count."

"Aye, that's what I've set them for." Canninge grinned and reached for a burning linstock. "I didn't figure we was up here to send a salute."

CARIBBEE

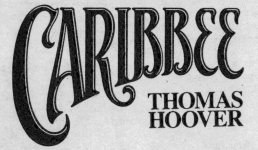

CARIBBEE

THOMAS HOOVER

ZEBRA BOOKS

KENSINGTON PUBLISHING CORP.

ZEBRA BOOKS

are published by

Kensington Publishing Corp.
475 Park Avenue South
New York, NY 10016

First Zebra Books Printing: December 1987

Printed in the United States of America

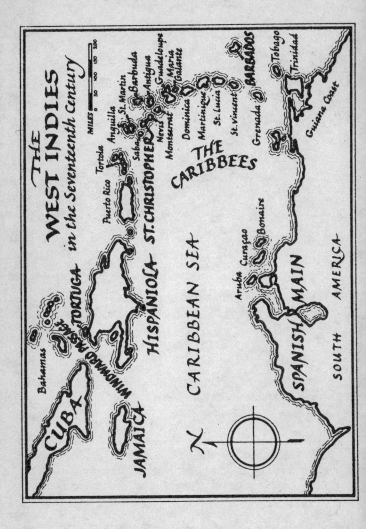

AUTHOR'S NOTE

By the middle of the seventeenth century, almost a hundred thousand English men and women had settled in the New World. We sometimes forget that the largest colony across the Atlantic in those early years was not in Virginia, not in New England, but on the small eastern islands of the Caribbean, called the *Caribbees*.

Early existence in the Caribbean was brutal, and at first these immigrants struggled merely to survive. Then, through an act of international espionage, they stole a secret industrial process from the Catholic countries that gave them the key to unimagined wealth. The scheme these pious Puritans used to realize their earthly fortune required that they also install a special new attitude: only certain peoples may claim full humanity. Their profits bequeathed a mortgage to America of untold future costs.

The Caribbean shown here was a dumping ground for outcasts and adventurers from many nations, truly a cockpit of violence, greed, drunkenness, piracy, and voodoo. Even so, its English colonists penned a declaration of independence and fought a revolutionary war with their homeland over a hundred years before the North American settlements. Had they respected the rights of mankind to the same degree they espoused them, the face of modern America might have been very different.

The men and women in this story include many actual and composite individuals, and its scope is faithful to the larger events of that age, though time has been compressed somewhat to allow a continuous narrative.

To Liberty and Justice for all.

The Caribbean
1638

The men had six canoes in all, wide tree trunks hollowed out by burning away the heart, Indian style. They carried axes and longbarreled muskets, and all save one were bare to the waist, with breeches and boots patched together from uncured hides. By profession they were roving hunters, forest incarnations of an older world, and their backs and bearded faces, earth brown from the sun, were smeared with pig fat to repel the swarms of tropical insects.

After launching from their settlement at Tortuga, off northern Hispaniola, they headed toward a chain of tiny islands sprawling across the approach to the Windward Passage, route of the Spanish *galeones* inbound for Veracruz. Their destination was the easterly cape of the Grand Caicos, a known Spanish stopover, where the yearly fleet always put in to reprovision after its long Atlantic voyage.

Preparations began as soon as they waded ashore. First they beached the dugouts and camouflaged them with leafy brush. Next they axed down several trees in a grove back away from the water, chopped them into short green logs, and dragged these down to the shore to assemble a pyre. Finally, they patched together banana leaf *ajoupa* huts in the cleared area. Experienced woodsmen, they knew well how to live off the land while waiting.

The first day passed with nothing. Through a cloudless sky the sun scorched the empty sand for long hours, then dropped into the vacant sea. That night lightning played across thunderheads towering above the main island, and around midnight their *ajoupas* were soaked by rain. Then, in the first light of the morning, while dense fog still mantled the shallow banks to the west, they spotted a ship. It was a single frigate, small enough that there would be only a handful of cannon on the upper deck.

Jacques le Basque, the dense-bearded bear of a man who was their leader, declared in his guttural French that this was a historic moment, one to be savored, and passed a dark onion-flask of brandy among the men. Now would begin their long-planned campaign of revenge against the Spaniards, whose infantry from Santo Domingo had once burned out their settlement, murdered innocents. It was, he said, the start of a new life for them all.

All that remained was to bait the trap. Two of the hunters retrieved a bucket of fat from the *ajoupas* and ladled it onto the green firewood. Another scattered the flask's remaining liquor over the top of the wood, then dashed it against a heavy log for luck. Finally, while the men carefully checked the prime on their broad-gauge hunting muskets, le Basque struck a flint to the pyre.

The green wood sputtered indecisively, then crackled alive, sending a gray plume skyward through the damp morning air. Jacques circled the fire triumphantly, his dark eyes reflecting back the blaze, before ordering the men to ready their dugouts in the brushy camouflage along the shore. As they moved to comply, he caught the sleeve of a young Englishman who was with them and beckoned him back.

"Anglais, *attendez ici*. I want you here beside me. The first shot must count."

The young man had been part of their band for almost five years and was agreed to be their best marksman, no slight honor among men who lived by stalking wild cattle in the forest. Unlike the others he carried no musket this morning, only a long flintlock pistol wedged into his belt. In the flickering light, he looked scarcely more than twenty, his face not yet showing the hard desperation of the others. His hair was sandy rust and neatly trimmed; and he alone among them wore no animal hides—his doublet was clearly an English cut, though some years out of fashion, and his sweat-soiled breeches had once been fine canvas. Even his boots, now weathered and cracked from salt, might years before have belonged to a young cavalier in Covent Garden.

He moved to help Jacques stoke the fire and pile on more green limbs. Though the blaze and its plume should have been easily visible to the passing frigate by now, the sleepy lookout seemed almost to fail to notice. The ship had all but passed them by before garbled shouts from its maintop finally sounded over the foggy waters. Next came a jumble of orders from the quarterdeck, and moments later the vessel veered, its bow turning into the wind, the mainsail quickly being trimmed.

As it steered into the bay, Jacques slapped at the buzzing gnats around them and yelled out a Spanish plea that they were marooned seamen, near death. As he examined the frigate through the morning fog, he grunted to himself that she was small, barely a hundred tons, scarcely the rich prize they'd braved the wide Caribbean in dugouts for.

But now a longboat had been launched, and two seamen in white shirts and loose blue caps were rowing a young mate toward the pair of shadowy figures huddled against the smoky pyre at the shore. Le Basque laughed quietly and said something in a growl of French about allowing the ship's officers to die quickly, to reward their hospitality.

The younger man wasn't listening. Through the half-light he was carefully studying the longboat. Now he could make out the caps of the seamen, woolen stockings loosely flopping to the side. Then he looked back at the ship, seamen perched in its rigging to stare, and thought he heard fragments of a

3

familiar tongue drifting muffled over the swells. Next a crowd of passengers appeared at the taffrail, led by a well-to-do family in ruffs and taffetas.

They weren't Spanish. They couldn't be.

The man wore a plumed hat and long curls that reached almost to his velvet doublet, London fashions obvious at hundreds of yards. The woman, a trifle stout, had a tight yellow bodice and long silk cape, her hair tied back. Between them was a girl, perhaps twelve, with long chestnut ringlets. He examined the rake of the ship once more, to make doubly sure, then turned to Jacques.

"That ship's English. Look at her. Boxy waist. Short taffrail. Doubtless a merchantman out of Virginia, bound for Nevis or Barbados." He paused when he realized Jacques was not responsive. Finally he continued, his voice louder. "I tell you there'll be nothing on her worth having. Wood staves, candle wax, a little salt fish. I know what they lade."

Jacques looked back at the ship, unconcerned. *"Cela n'a pas d' importance,* Anglais. There'll be provisions. We have to take her."

"But no silver. There's no English coin out here in the Americas, never has been. And who knows what could happen? Let some ordnance be set off, or somebody fire her, and we run the risk of alerting the whole Spanish fleet."

Now le Basque shrugged, pretending to only half understand the English, and responded in his hard French. "Taking her's best. If she truly be Anglaise then we'll keep her and use her ourselves." He grinned, showing a row of blackened teeth. "And have the women for sport. I'll even give you the pretty little one there by the rail, Anglais, for your *petite amie.*" He studied the ship again and laughed. "She's not yet work for a man."

The younger man stared at him blankly for a moment, feeling his face go chill. Behind him, in the brush, he heard arguments rising up between the English hunters and the

4

French over what to do. During his years with them they had killed wild bulls by the score, but never another Englishman.

"Jacques, we're not Spaniards. This is not going to be our way." He barely heard his own words. Surely, he told himself, we have to act honorably. That was the unwritten code in the New World, where men made their own laws.

"Anglais, I regret to say you sadden me somewhat." Le Basque was turning, mechanically. "I once thought you had the will to be one of us. But now. . . ." His hand had slipped upward, a slight motion almost invisible in the flickering shadows. But by the time it reached his gun, the young man's long flintlock was already drawn and leveled.

"Jacques, I told you *no.*" The dull click of a misfire sounded across the morning mist.

By now le Basque's own pistol was in his hand, primed and cocked, a part of him. Its flare opened a path through the dark between them.

But the young Englishman was already moving, driven by purest rage. He dropped to his side with a twist, an arm stretching for the fire. Then his fingers touched what he sought, and closed about the glassy neck of the shattered flask. It seared his hand, but in his fury he paid no heed. The ragged edges sparkled against the flames as he found his footing, rising as the wide arc of his swing pulled him forward.

Le Basque stumbled backward to avoid the glass, growling a French oath as he sprawled across a stack of green brush. An instant later the pile of burning logs suddenly crackled and sputtered, throwing a shower of sparks. Then again.

God help them, the young man thought, they're firing from the longboat. They must assume . . .

He turned to shout a warning seaward, but his voice was drowned in the eruption of gunfire from the camouflage along the shore. The three seamen in the boat jerked backward, all still gripping their smoking muskets, then splashed into the bay. Empty, the craft veered sideways and in moments was drifting languorously back out to sea.

5

Many times in later years he tried to recall precisely what had happened next, but the events always merged, a blur of gunfire. As he dashed for the surf, trailed by le Basque's curses, the dugouts began moving out, muskets spitting random flashes. He looked up to see the stout woman at the rail of the frigate brush at her face, then slump sideways into her startled husband's arms.

He remembered too that he was already swimming, stroking toward the empty boat, when the first round of cannon fire from the ship sounded over the bay, its roar muffled by the water against his face. Then he saw a second cannon flare . . . and watched the lead canoe dissolve into spray and splinters.

The others were already turning back, abandoning the attack, when he grasped the slippery gunwale of the longboat, his only hope to reach the ship. As he strained against the swell, he became dimly aware the firing had stopped.

Memories of the last part were the most confused. Still seething with anger, he had slowly pulled himself over the side, then rolled onto the bloodstained planking. Beside him lay an English wool cap, its maker's name still lettered on the side. One oar rattled against its lock. The other was gone.

He remembered glancing up to see seamen in the ship's rigging begin to swivel the yards, a sign she was coming about. Then the mainsail snapped down and bellied against a sudden gust.

Damn them. *Wait for me.*

Only a hundred yards separated them now, as the longboat continued to drift seaward. It seemed a hundred yards, though for years afterward he wondered if perhaps it might have been even less. What he did remember clearly was wrenching the oar from the lock and turning to begin paddling toward the ship.

That was when the plume of spray erupted in front of him. As he tumbled backward he heard the unmistakable report of the ship's sternchaser cannon.

He could never recollect if he had actually called out to them. He did remember crouching against the gunwale, listening to the volleys of musket fire from seamen along the ship's taffrail.

Several rounds of heavy lead shot had torn through the side of the longboat, sending splinters against his face. When he looked out again, the frigate was hoisting her lateen sail, ready to run for open sea.

The line of musketmen was still poised along the rail, waiting. Beside them was the family: the man was hovering above the stout woman, now laid along the deck, and with him was the girl.

Only then did he notice the heat against his cheek, the warm blood from the bullet cut. He glanced back at the fire, even more regretful he hadn't killed Jacques le Basque. Someday, he told himself, he would settle the score. His anger was matched only by his disgust with the English.

Only one person on the ship seemed to question what had happened. The girl looked down at the woman for a long, sad moment, then glanced back, her tresses splayed in the morning wind. His last memory, before he lapsed into unconsciousness, was her upraised hand, as though in farewell.

TEN YEARS LATER . . .

Book One

BARBADOS

Chapter One

No sooner had their carriage creaked to a halt at the edge of the crowd than a tumult of cheers sounded through the humid morning air. With a wry glance toward the man seated opposite, Katherine Bedford drew back the faded curtains at the window and craned to see over the cluster of planters at the water's edge, garbed in their usual ragged jerkins, gray cotton breeches, and wide, sweat-stained hats. Across the bay, edging into view just beyond the rocky cliff of Lookout Point, were the tattered, patched sails of the *Zeelander,* a Dutch trader well known to Barbados.

"It's just rounding the Point now." Her voice was hard, with more than a trace of contempt. "From here you'd scarcely know what their cargo was. It looks the same as always."

As she squinted into the light, a shaft of Caribbean sun candled her deep-blue eyes. Her long ringlet curls were drawn back and secured with a tiara of Spanish pearls, a halfhearted attempt at demureness spoiled by the nonchalant strands dangling across her forehead. The dark tan on her face betrayed her devotion to the sea and the sun; although twenty-three years of life had ripened her body, her high cheeks had none of the plump, anemic pallor so prized in English women.

"Aye, but this time she's very different, Katy, make no mistake. Nothing in the Americas will ever be the same again. Not after today." Governor Dalby Bedford was across from her in the close, airless carriage, angrily gripping the silver knob of his cane. Finally he bent forward to look too, and for a moment their faces were framed side by side. The likeness could scarcely have been greater: not only did they share the same intense eyes, there was a similar high forehead and determined chin. "Damned to them. It's a shameful morning for us all."

"Just the same, you've got to go down and be there." Though she despised the thought as much as he did, she realized he had no choice. The planters all knew Dalby Bedford had opposed the plan from the beginning, had argued with the Council for weeks before arrangements were finally made with the Dutch shippers. But the vote had gone against him, and now he had to honor it accordingly.

While he sat watching the *Zeelander* make a starboard tack, coming about to enter the bay, Katherine leaned across the seat and pulled aside the opposite curtain. The hot wind that suddenly stirred past was a sultry harbinger of the coastal breeze now sweeping up the hillside, where field after identical field was lined with rows of tall, leafy stalks, green and iridescent in the sun.

The new Barbados is already here, she thought gloomily. The best thing now is to face it.

Without a word she straightened her tight, sweaty bodice, gathered her wrinkled skirt, and opened the carriage door. She waved aside the straw parasol that James, their Irish servant and footman, tried to urge on her and stepped into the harsh midday sun. Dalby Bedford nodded at the crowd, then climbed down after.

He was tall and, unlike his careless daughter, always groomed to perfection. Today he wore a tan waistcoat trimmed with wide brown lace and a white cravat that matched the heron-feather plume in his wide-brimmed hat. Over the years, the name of Dalby Bedford had become a byword for freedom in the Americas: under his hand Barbados had been made a democracy, and virtually independent of England. First he had convinced the

14

king's proprietor to reduce rents on the island, then he had created an elected Assembly of small freeholders to counter the high-handed rule of the powerful Council. He had won every battle, until this one.

Katherine moved through the crowd of black-hatted planters as it parted before them. Through the shimmering glare of the sand she could just make out the commanding form of Anthony Walrond farther down by the shore, together with his younger brother Jeremy. Like hundreds of other royalists, they had been deported to Barbados in the aftermath of England's Civil War. Now Anthony spotted their carriage and started up the incline toward them, and for an instant she found herself wishing she'd thought to wear a more fashionable bodice.

"Your servant, sir." A gruff greeting, aimed toward Dalby Bedford, disrupted her thoughts. She looked back to see a heavyset planter riding his horse directly through the crowd, with the insistent air of a man who demands deference. Swinging down from his wheezing mount, he tossed the reins to the servant who had ridden with him and began to shove his way forward, fanning his open gray doublet against the heat.

Close to fifty and owner of the largest plantation on the island, Benjamin Briggs was head of the Council, that governing body of original settlers appointed years before by the island's proprietor in London. His sagging, leathery face was formidable testimony to twenty years of hard work and even harder drink. The planters on the Council had presided over Barbados' transformation from a tropical rain forest to a patchwork of tobacco and cotton plantations, and now to what they hoped would soon be a factory producing white gold.

Briggs pushed back his dusty hat and turned to squint approvingly as the frigate began furling its mainsail in preparation to drop anchor. "God be praised, we're almost there. The years of starvation are soon to be over."

Katherine noted that she had not been included in his greeting. She had once spoken her mind to Benjamin Briggs concerning his treatment of his indentures more frankly than he cared to hear. Even now, looking at him, she was still amazed that a man once a small Bristol importer had risen to so much power in the Americas. Part of that success, she knew, derived from his practice of lending money to hard-pressed freeholders at generous rates but short terms, then foreclosing on their lands the moment the sight bills came due.

"It's an evil precedent for the English settlements, mark my word." Bedford gazed back toward the ship. He and Benjamin Briggs had been sworn enemies from the day he first proposed establishing the Assembly. "I tell you again it'll open the way for fear and divisiveness throughout the Americas."

"It's our last chance for prosperity, sir. All else has failed," Briggs responded testily. "I know it and so do you."

Before the governor could reply, Anthony Walrond was joining them.

"Your servant, sir." He touched his plumed hat toward Dalby Bedford, conspicuously ignoring Briggs as he merged into their circle, Jeremy at his heel.

Anthony Walrond was thirty-five and the most accomplished, aristocratic man Katherine had ever met, besides her father. His lean, elegant face was punctuated by an eye-patch, worn with the pride of an epaulette, that came from a sword wound in the bloody royalist defeat at Marston Moor. After he had invested and lost a small fortune in support of the king's failed cause, he had been exiled to Barbados, his ancestral estate sequestrated by Parliament.

She still found herself incredulous that he had, only four weeks earlier, offered marriage. Why, she puzzled, had he proposed the match? He was landed, worldly, and had distinguished himself during the war. She had none of his style and polish. . . .

"Katherine, your most obedient." He bowed lightly, then stood back to examine her affectionately. She was a bit brash, it was true, and a trifle—well, more than a trifle—forward for her sex. But underneath her blunt, seemingly impulsive way he sensed a powerful will. She wasn't afraid to act on her convic-

16

tions, and the world be damned. So let her ride her mare about the island daylong now if she chose; there was breeding about her that merely wanted some refinement.

"Sir, your servant." Katherine curtsied lightly and repressed a smile. No one knew she had quietly invited Anthony Walrond riding just two weeks earlier. The destination she had picked was a deserted little islet just off the windward coast, where they could be alone. Propriety, she told herself, was all very well, but marrying a man for life was no slight matter. Anthony Walrond, it turned out, had promise of being all she could want.

He reflected on the memory of that afternoon for a moment himself, delighted, then turned back to the governor with as solemn an air as he could manage. "I suppose this island'll soon be more in debt than ever to the Hollanders. I think it's time we started giving English shippers a chance, now that it's likely to be worth their bother."

"Aye, doubtless you'd like that." Briggs flared. "I know you still own a piece of a London trading company. You and that pack of English merchants would be pleased to charge us double the shipping rates the Hollanders do. Damn the lot of you. Those of us who've been here from the start know we should all be on our knees, thankin' heaven for the Dutchmen. The English settlements in the Americas would've starved years ago if it hadn't been for them." He paused to spit onto the sand, just beside Anthony's gleaming boots. "Let English bottoms compete with the Dutchmen, not wave the flag."

"Your servant, Katherine." Jeremy Walrond had moved beside her, touching his plumed hat as he nodded. A cloud of perfume hovered about him, and his dark moustache was waxed to perfection. Though he had just turned twenty, his handsome face was still boyish, with scarcely a hint of sun.

"Your most obedient." She nodded lightly in return, trying to appear formal. Over the past year she had come to adore Jeremy as though he were a younger brother, even though she knew he despised the wildness of Barbados as much as she gloried in it. He was used to pampering and yearned to be back

17

in England. He also longed to be thought a man; longed, in truth, to be just like Anthony, save he didn't know quite how.

They all stood awkwardly for a moment, each wondering what the ship would signify for their own future and that of the island. Katherine feared that for her it would mean the end of Barbados' few remaining forests, hidden groves upland where she could ride alone and think. Cultivated land was suddenly so valuable that all trees would soon vanish. It was the last anyone would see of an island part untamed and free.

Depressed once more by the prospect, she turned and stared down the shore, toward the collection of clapboard taverns clustered around the narrow bridge at the river mouth. Adjacent to the taverns was a makeshift assemblage of tobacco sheds, open shops, and bawdy houses, which taken together had become known as Bridgetown. The largest "town" on Barbados, it was now all but empty. Everyone, even the tavern keepers and Irish whores, had come out to watch.

Then, through the brilliant sunshine she spotted an unexpected pair, ambling slowly along the water's edge. The woman was well known to the island—Joan Fuller, the yellow-haired proprietor of its most successful brothel. But the man? Whatever else, he was certainly no freeholder. For one thing, no Puritan planter would be seen in public with Mistress Fuller.

The stranger was gesturing at the ship and mumbling unhappily to her as they walked. Abruptly she reached up to pinch his cheek, as though to dispel his mood. He glanced down and fondly swiped at her tangled yellow hair, then bade her farewell, turned, and began moving toward them.

"God's life, don't tell me he's come back." Briggs first noticed the stranger when he was already halfway through the crowd. He sucked in his breath and whirled to survey the line of Dutch merchantmen anchored in the shallows along the shore. Nothing. But farther down, near the careenage at the river mouth, a battered frigate rode at anchor. The ship bore no flag, but the word *Defiance* was crudely lettered across the stern.

"Aye, word has it he put in this morning at first light." Edward Bayes, a black-hatted Council member with ruddy jowls, was squinting against the sun. "What're you thinking we'd best do?"

Briggs seemed to ignore the question as he began pushing his way through the crowd. The newcomer was fully half a head taller than most of the planters, and unlike everyone else he wore no hat, leaving his rust-colored hair to blow in the wind. He was dressed in a worn leather jerkin, dark canvas breeches, and sea boots weathered from long use. He might have passed for an ordinary seaman had it not been for the two Spanish flintlock pistols, freshly polished and gleaming, that protruded from his wide belt.

"Your servant, Captain." Briggs' greeting was correct and formal, but the man returned it with only a slight, distracted nod. "Back to see what the Hollanders've brought?"

"I'm afraid I already know what they're shipping. I picked a hell of a day to come back." The stranger rubbed absently at a long scar across one cheek, then continued, as though to himself, "Damn me, I should have guessed all along this would be the way."

The crowd had fallen silent to listen, and Katherine could make out that his accent was that of a gentleman, even if his dress clearly was not. His easy stride suggested he was little more than thirty, but the squint that framed his brown eyes made his face years older. By his looks and the uneasy shuffle of the Council members gathered around them, she suddenly began to suspect who he might be.

"Katy, who the devil?" Jeremy had lowered his voice to a whisper.

"I'm not sure, but If I had to guess, I'd say that's probably the smuggler you claim robbed you once." Scarce wonder Briggs is nervous, she thought. Every planter on the shore knows exactly why he's come back.

"Hugh Winston? Is that him?" Jeremy glared at the newcomer, his eyes hardening. "You can't mean it. He'd not have the brass to show his face on English soil."

"He's been here before. I've just never actually seen him. You always seem to keep forgetting, Jeremy, Barbados isn't part of England." She glanced back. "Surely you heard what he did. It happened just before you came out." She gestured toward the green hillsides. "He's the one we have to thank for all this. I fancy he's made Briggs and the rest of them rich, for all the good it'll ever do him."

"What he's done, if you must know, is make a profession of stealing from honest men. Damned to their cane. He's scarcely better than a thief. Do you know *exactly* what he did?"

"You mean that business about your frigate?"

"The eighty-tonner of ours that grounded on the reefs up by Nevis Island. He's the one who set our men ashore—then announced he was taking the cargo in payment. Rolls of wool broadcloth worth almost three thousand pounds sterling. And several crates of new flintlock muskets. He smuggled the cloth into Virginia, sold it for nothing, and ruined the market for months. He'd be hanged if he tried walking the streets of London, I swear it. Doesn't anybody here know that?"

She tried to recall what she did know. The story heard most often was that he'd begun his career at sea on a Dutch merchantman. Then, so word had it, he'd gone out on his own. According to tales that went around the Caribbees, he'd pulled together a band of some dozen runaway indentures and one night somehow managed to sail a small shallop into the harbor at Santo Domingo. He sailed out before dawn at the helm of a two-hundred-ton Spanish square-rigger. After some heavy refitting, it became the *Defiance*.

"They probably know he robbed you, Jeremy, but I truly doubt whether they care all that much."

"What do you mean?"

"He's the one Benjamin Briggs and the others hired to take them down to Brazil and back."

That voyage had later become a legend in the English Caribbees. Its objective was a plantation just outside the city of Pernambuco—capital of the new territory in Brazil the Dutch

20

had just seized from the Portuguese. There Barbados' Council had deciphered the closely guarded process Brazilian plantations used to refine sugar from cane sap. Thanks to the friendly Dutch, and Hugh Winston, Englishmen had finally cracked the centuries-old sugar monopoly of Portugal and Spain.

"You mean he's the same one who helped them get that load of cane for planting, and the plans for Briggs' sugarmill?" Jeremy examined the stranger again.

"Exactly. He also brought back something else for Briggs." She smiled. "Can you guess?"

Jeremy flushed and carefully smoothed his new moustache. "I suppose you're referring to that Portuguese mulatto wench he bought to be his bed warmer."

Yes, she thought, Hugh Winston's dangerous voyage, outsailing several Spanish patrols, had been an all-round success. And everybody on the island knew the terms he had demanded. Sight bills from the Council, all co-signed at his insistence by Benjamin Briggs, in the sum of two thousand pounds sterling, payable in twenty-four months.

"Well, sir"—Briggs smiled at Winston as he thumbed toward the approaching ship—"this is the cargo we'll be wanting now, if we're to finish converting this place to sugar. You could be of help to us again if you'd choose. This is where the future'll be, depend on it."

"I made one mistake, helping this island." Winston glanced at the ship and his eyes were momentarily pained. "I don't plan to make another." Then he turned and stared past the crowd, toward the green fields patchworked against the hillsides inland. "But I see your cane prospered well enough. When do we talk?"

"Why any time you will, sir. We've not forgotten our debts." Briggs forced another smile. "We'll have a tankard on it, right after the auction." He turned and motioned toward a red-faced Irishman standing behind him, wearing straw shoes and a long gray shirt. "Farrell, a moment of your valuable time."

"Yor Worship." Timothy Farrell, one of Briggs' many indentured servants, bowed sullenly as he came forward, then

21

doffed his straw hat, squinting against the sun. His voice still carried the musical lilt of his native Kinsale, where he had been offered the choice, not necessarily easy, between prison for debt and indentured labor in sweltering Barbados. He had finally elected Barbados when informed, falsely, that he would receive a grant of five acres of land after his term of servitude expired— a practice long since abandoned.

Katherine watched as Briggs flipped him a small brass coin. "Fetch a flask of kill-devil from the tavern up by the bridge. And have it here when I get back."

Kill-devil was bought from Dutch shippers, who procured it from Brazilian plantations, where it was brewed using wastes from their sugarworks. The Portuguese there employed it as a cheap tonic to rout the "devil" thought to possess African slaves at the end of a long day and render them sluggish. It retailed handily as a beverage in the English settlements of the Americas, however, sometimes being marketed under the more dignified name of "rumbullion," or "rum."

Briggs watched as Farrell sauntered off down the shore. *"That's* what we'll soon hear the last of. A lazy Papist, like half the lot that's being sent out nowadays." He turned to study the weathered Dutch frigate as it eased into the sandy shallows and the anchor chain began to rattle down the side. "But we've got good workers at last. By Jesus, we've found the answer."

Katherine watched the planters secure their hats against a sudden breeze and begin pushing toward the shore. Even Anthony and Jeremy went with them. The only man who held back was Hugh Winston, still standing there in his worn-out leather jerkin. He seemed reluctant to budge.

Maybe, she thought, he doesn't want to confront it.

As well he shouldn't. We've got him to thank for this.

After a moment he glanced back and began to examine her with open curiosity, his eyes playing over her face, then her tight bodice. Finally he shifted one of the pistols in his belt, turned, and began strolling down the sloping sand toward the bay.

Well, damn his cheek.

All along she had planned to go down herself, to see firsthand what an auction would be like, but at that instant the shifting breeze brought a sudden stench from the direction of the ship. She hesitated, a rare moment of indecision, before turning back toward the carriage. *This,* she now realized, marked the start of something she wanted no part of.

Moving slowly toward the shore, Winston found himself puzzling over the arch young woman who had been with Governor Bedford. Doubtless she was the daughter you heard so much about, though from her dress you'd scarcely guess it. But she had an open way about her you didn't see much in a woman. Plenty of spirit there . . . and doubtless a handful for the man who ever got her onto a mattress.

Forget it, he told himself, you've enough to think about today. Starting with the *Zeelander.* And her cargo.

The sight of that three-masted *fluyt* brought back so many places and times. Brazil, Rotterdam, Virginia, even Barbados. Her captain Johan Ruyters had changed his life, that day the *Zeelander* hailed his bullet-riddled longboat adrift in the Windward Passage. Winston had lost track of the time a bit now, but not of the term Ruyters had made him serve in return for the rescue. Three years, three miserable years of short rations, doubled watches, and no pay.

Back when he served on the *Zeelander* her cargo had been mostly brown *muscavado* sugar, ferried home to Rotterdam from Holland's newly captive plantations in Brazil. But there had been a change in the world since then. The Dutch had seized a string of Portuguese trading fortresses along the coast of West Africa. Now, at last, they had access to a commodity far more profitable than sugar.

He reflected on Ruyters' first axiom of successful trade: sell what's in demand. And if there's no demand for what you've got, make it.

New sugar plantations would provide the surest market of all for what the Dutch now had to sell. So in the spring of 1642 Ruyters had left a few bales of Brazilian sugarcane with Benjamin Briggs, then a struggling tobacco planter on Barbados, suggesting that he try growing it and refining sugar from the sap, explaining the Portuguese process as best he could.

It had been a night over two years past, at Joan's place, when Briggs described what had happened after that.

"The cane grew well enough, aye, and I managed to press out enough of the sap to try rendering it to sugar. But nothing else worked. I tried boiling it in pots and then letting it sit, but what I got was scarcely more than molasses and mud. It's not as simple as I thought." Then he had unfolded his new scheme. "But if you'll take some of us on the Council down to Brazil, sir, the Dutchmen claim they'll let us see how the Portugals do it. We'll soon know as much about sugar-making as any Papist. There'll be a fine fortune in it, I promise you, for all of us."

But how, he'd asked Briggs, did they expect to manage all the work of cutting the cane?

"These indentures, sir. We've got thousands of them."

He'd finally agreed to accept the Council's proposition. And the *Defiance* was ideal for the run. Once an old Spanish cargo vessel, he'd disguised her by chopping away the high fo'c'sle, removing the pilot's cabin, and lowering the quarterdeck. Next he'd re-rigged her, opened more gunports in the hull, and installed new cannon. Now she was a heavily armed fighting brig and swift.

Good God, he thought, how could I have failed to see? It *had* to come to this; there was no other way.

So maybe it's time I did something my own way for a change. Yes, by God, maybe there's an answer to all this.

He thought again of the sight bills, now locked in the Great Cabin of the *Defiance* and payable in one week. Two thousand pounds. It would be a miracle if the Council could find the coin to settle the debt, but they did have something he needed.

And either way, Master Briggs, I intend to have satisfaction, or I may just take your balls for a bell buoy.

Now a white shallop was being lowered over the gunwales of the *Zeelander*, followed by oarsmen. Then after a measured pause a new figure, wearing the high collar and wide-brimmed hat of Holland's merchant class, appeared at the railing. His plump face was punctuated with a goatee, and his smile was visible all the way to the shore. He stood a long moment, dramatically surveying the low-lying hills of Barbados, and then Captain Johan Ruyters began lowering himself down the swaying rope ladder.

As the shallop nosed through the surf and eased into the sandy shallows, Dalby Bedford moved to the front of the receiving delegation, giving no hint how bitterly he had opposed the arrangement Briggs and the Council had made with the Dutch shippers.

"Your servant, Captain."

"Your most obedient servant, sir." Ruyters' English was heavily accented but otherwise flawless. Winston recalled he could speak five languages as smoothly as oil, and shortchange the fastest broker in twice that many currencies. "It is a fine day for Barbados."

"How went the voyage?" Briggs asked, stepping forward and thrusting out his hand, which Ruyters took readily, though with a wary gathering of his eyebrows.

"A fair wind, taken for all. Seventy-four days and only some fifteen percent wastage of the cargo. Not a bad figure for the passage, though still enough to make us friends of the sharks. But I've nearly three hundred left, all prime."

"Are they strapping?" Briggs peered toward the ship, and his tone sharpened slightly, signaling that social pleasantries were not to be confused with commerce. "Remember we'll be wantin' them for the fields, not for the kitchen."

"None stronger in the whole west of Africa. These are not from the Windward Coast, mark you, where I grant what you get is fit mostly for house duty. I took half this load from Cape Verde, on the Guinea coast, and then sailed on down to Benin, by the Niger River delta, for the rest. These Nigers make the

25

strongest field workers. There is even a chief amongst them, a Yoruba warrior. I've seen a few of these Yoruba Nigers in Brazil, and I can tell you this one could have the wits to make you a first-class gang driver." Ruyters shaded his eyes against the sun and lowered his voice. "In truth, I made a special accommodation with the agent selling him, which is how I got so many hardy ones. Usually I have to take a string of mixed quality, which I get with a few kegs of gunpowder for the chiefs and maybe some iron, together with a few beads and such for their wives. But I had to barter five chests of muskets and a hundred strings of their cowrie-shell money for this Yoruba. After that, though, I got the pick of his boys."

Ruyters stopped and peered past the planters for a second, his face mirroring disbelief. Then he grinned broadly and shoved through the crowd, extending his hand toward Winston. "By the blood of Christ. I thought sure you would be hanged by now. How long has it been. Six years? Seven?" He laughed and pumped Winston's hand vigorously, then his voice sobered. "Not here to spy on the trade I hope? I'd best beware or you're like to be eyeing *my* cargo next."

"You can have it." Winston extracted his hand, reflecting with chagrin that he himself had been the instrument of what was about to occur.

"What say, now?" Ruyters smiled to mask his relief. "Aye, but to be sure this is an easy business." He turned back to the planters as he continued. "It never fails to amaze me how ready their own people are to sell them. They spy your sail when you're several leagues at sea and build a smoke fire on the coast to let you know they've got cargo."

He reached for Dalby Bedford's arm, to usher him toward the waiting boat. Anthony Walrond said something quietly to Jeremy, then followed after the governor. Following on their heels was Benjamin Briggs, who tightened his belt as he waded through the shallows.

Ruyters did not fail to notice when several of the oarsmen smiled and nodded toward Winston. He was still remembered as the best first mate the *Zeelander* had ever had—and the only seaman anyone had ever seen who could toss a florin into the air and drill it with a pistol ball better than half the time. Finally the Dutch captain turned back, beckoning.

"It'd be an honor if you would join us, sir. As long as you don't try taking any of my lads with you."

Winston hesitated a moment, then stepped into the boat as it began to draw away from the shore. Around them other small craft were being untied, and the planters jostled together as they waded through the light surf and began to climb over the gunwales. Soon a small, motley flotilla was making its way toward the ship.

As Winston studied the *Zeelander*, he couldn't help recalling how welcome she had looked that sun-baked afternoon ten years past. In his thirsty delirium her billowing sails had seemed the wings of an angel of mercy. But she was not angelic today. She was dilapidated now, with runny patches of tar and oakum dotting her from bow to stern. By converting her into a slaver, he knew, Ruyters had discovered a prudent way to make the most of her last years.

As they eased into the shadow of her leeward side, Winston realized something else had changed. The entire ship now smelled of human excrement. He waited till Ruyters led the planters, headed by Dalby Bedford and Benjamin Briggs, up the salt-stiff rope ladder, then followed after.

The decks were dingy and warped, and there was a haggard look in the men's eyes he didn't recall from before. Profit comes at a price, he thought, even for quick Dutch traders.

Ruyters barked an order to his quartermaster, and moments later the main hatch was opened. Immediately the stifling air around the frigate was filled with a chorus of low moans from the decks below.

Winston felt Briggs seize his arm and heard a hoarse whisper. "Take a look and see how it's done. It's said the Dutchmen've learned the secret of how best to pack them."

"I already know how a slaver's cargoed." He pulled back his

27

arm and thought again of the Dutch slave ships that had been anchored in the harbor at Pernambuco. "A slave's chained on his back, on a shelf, for the whole of the voyage, if he lives that long." He pointed toward the hold. "Why not go on down and have a look for yourself?"

Briggs frowned and turned to watch as the quartermaster yelled orders to several seamen, all shirtless and squinting in the sun, who cursed under their breath as they began reluctantly to make their way down the companionway to the lower deck. The air in the darkened hold was almost unbreathable.

The clank of chains began, and Winston found himself drawn against his will to the open hatchway to watch. As the cargo was unchained from iron loops fastened to the side of the ship, their manacled hands were looped through a heavy line the seamen passed along the length of the lower deck.

Slowly, shakily, the first string of men began to emerge from the hold. Their feet and hands were still secured with individual chains, and all were naked. As each struggled up from the hold, he would stare into the blinding sun for a confused moment, as though to gain bearings, then turn in bewilderment to gaze at the green beyond, so like and yet so alien from the African coast. Finally, seeing the planters, he would stretch to cover his groin with manacled hands, the hesitation prompting a Dutch seaman to lash him forward.

The Africans' black skin shone in the sun, the result of a forced diet of cod liver oil the last week of the voyage. Then too, there had been a quick splash with seawater on the decks below, followed by swabbing with palm oil, when the *Zeelander*'s maintopman had sighted the low green peaks of Barbados rising out of the sea. They seemed stronger than might have been expected, the effect of a remedial diet of salt fish the last three days of the voyage.

"Well, sir, what think you of the cargo?" Ruyters' face was aglow. Winston winced. "Better your vessel than mine."

"But it's no great matter to ship these Africans. The truth is we don't really even have to keep them fettered once we pass sight of land, since they're too terrified to revolt. We feed them twice a day with meal boiled up into a mush, and every other day or so we give them some English horsebeans, which they seem to favor. Sometimes we even bring them up topside to feed, whilst we splash down the decks below.'' He smiled and swept the assembled bodies with his eyes. ''That's why we have so little wastage. Not like the Spaniards or Portugals, who can easily lose a quarter or more to shark feed through overpacking and giving them seawater to drink. But I'll warrant the English'll try to squeeze all the profit they can one day, when your ships take up the trade, and then you'll doubtless see wastage high as the Papists have.''

''English merchants'll never take up the slave trade.''

Ruyters gave a chuckle. ''Aye but that they will, as I'm a Christian, and soon enough too.'' He glanced in the direction of Anthony Walrond. ''Your London shippers'll take up anything we do that shows a florin's profit. But we'll give you a run for it.'' He turned back to Briggs. ''What say you, sir? Are they to your liking?''

''I take it they're a mix? Like we ordered?''

''Wouldn't load them any other way. There's a goodly batch of Yoruba, granted, but the rest are everything from Ibo and Ashanti to Mandingo. There's little chance they'll be plotting any revolts. Half of them are likely blood enemies of the other half.''

The first mate lashed the line forward with a cat-o'-nine-tails, positioning them along the scuppers. At the head was a tall man whose alert eyes were already studying the forested center of the island. Winston examined him for a moment, recalling the haughty Yoruba slaves he had seen in Brazil.

''Is that the chief you spoke of?''

Ruyters glanced at the man a moment. ''They mostly look the same to me, but aye, I think that's the one. Prince Atiba, I believe they called him. A Niger and pure Yoruba.''

''He'll never be made a slave.''

''Won't he now? You'll find the cat can work wonders.'' Ruy-

29

ters turned and took the cat-o'-nine-tails from the mate. "He'll jump just like the rest." With a quick flick he lashed it against the African's back. The man stood unmoving, without even a blink. He drew back and struck him a second time, now harder. The Yoruba's jaw tightened visibly but he still did not flinch. As Ruyters drew back for a third blow, Winston reached to stay his arm.

"Enough. Take care or he may prove a better man than you'd wish to show."

Before Ruyters could respond, Briggs moved to begin the negotiations.

"What terms are you offering, sir?"

"Like we agreed." Ruyters turned back. "A quarter now, with sight bills for another quarter in six months and the balance on terms in a year."

"Paid in bales of tobacco at standing rates? Or sugar, assuming we've got it then?"

"I've yet to see two gold pieces keeping company together on the whole of the island." He snorted. "I suppose it'll have to be. What do you say to the usual exchange rate?"

"I say we can begin. Let's start with the best, and not trouble with the bidding candle yet. I'll offer you a full twenty pounds for the first one there." Briggs pointed at the Yoruba.

The Dutch captain examined him in disbelief. "This is not some indentured Irishman, sir. This is a robust field hand you'll own for life. And he has all the looks of a good breeder. My conscience wouldn't let me entertain a farthing under forty."

"Would you take some of my acres too? Is there no profit to be had in him?"

"These Africans'll pay themselves out for you in one good year, two at the most. Just like they do in Brazil." Ruyters smiled. "And this is the very one that cost me a fortune in muskets. It's only because I know you for a gentleman that I'd even think of offering him on such easy terms. He's plainly the pick of the string."

Winston turned away and gazed toward the shore. The price

would be thirty pounds. He knew Ruyters' bargaining practices all too well. The sight of the *Zeelander*'s decks sickened him almost as much as the slaves. He wanted to get to sea again, to leave Barbados and its greedy Puritans far behind.

But this time, he told himself, you're the one who needs *them*. Just a little longer and there'll be a reckoning.

And after that, Barbados can be damned.

"Thirty pounds then, and may God forgive me." Ruyters was slapping Briggs genially on the shoulder. "But you'll be needing a lot more for the acres you want to cut. Why not take the rest of this string at a flat twenty-five pounds the head, and make an end on it? It'll spare both of us time."

"Twenty-five!"

"Make it twenty then." Ruyters lowered his voice. "But not a shilling under, God is my witness."

"By my life, you're a conniving Moor, passing himself as a Dutchman." Briggs mopped his brow. "It's time for the candle, sir. They're scarcely all of the same quality."

"I'll grant you. Some should fetch well above twenty. I ventured the offer thinking a gentleman of your discernment might grasp a bargain when he saw it. But as you will." He turned and spoke quickly to his quartermaster, a short, surly seaman who had been with the *Zeelander* almost as long as Ruyters. The officer disappeared toward the Great Cabin and returned moments later with several long white candles, marked with rings at one-inch intervals. He fitted one into a holder and lit the wick.

"We'll begin with the next one in the string." Ruyters pointed to a stout, gray-bearded man. "Gentlemen, what am I bid?"

"Twelve pounds."

"Fifteen."

"Fifteen pounds ten."

"Sixteen."

As Winston watched the bidding, he found his gaze drifting more and more to the Yoruba Briggs had just purchased. The man was meeting his stare now, eye to eye, almost a challenge.

31

There were three small scars lined down one cheek—the clan marks Yoruba warriors were said to wear to prevent inadvertently killing another clan member in battle. He was naked and in chains, but he held himself like a born aristocrat.

"Eighteen and ten." Briggs was eyeing the flickering candle as he yelled the bid. At that moment the first dark ring disappeared.

"The last bid on the candle was Mr. Benjamin Briggs." Ruyters turned to his quartermaster, who was holding an open account book, quill pen in hand. "At eighteen pounds ten shillings. Mark it and let's get on with the next one."

Winston moved slowly back toward the main deck, studying the first Yoruba more carefully now—the glistening skin that seemed to stretch over ripples of muscle. And the quick eyes, seeing everything.

What a fighting man he'd make. He'd snap your neck while you were still reaching for your pistol. It could've been a big mistake not to try and get him. But then what? How'd you make him understand anything? Unless . . .

He remembered that some of the Yoruba in Brazil, still fresh off the slave ships, already spoke Portuguese. Learned from the traders who'd worked the African coast for . . . God only knows how long. The Portugals in Brazil always claimed you could never tell about a Yoruba. They were like Moors, sharp as tacks.

His curiosity growing, he edged next to the man, still attempting to hold his eyes, then decided to try him.

"Fala português?"

Atiba started in surprise, shot a quick glance toward the crowd of whites, then turned away, as though he hadn't heard. Winston moved closer and lowered his voice.

"Fala português, senhor?"

After a long moment he turned back and examined Winston.

"Sim. Suficiente." His whisper was almost buried in the din of bidding. He paused a moment, then continued, in barely audible Portuguese. "How many of my people will *you* try to buy, senhor?"

"Only free men serve under my command."

"Then you have saved yourself the loss of many strings of money shells, senhor. The *branco* here may have escaped our sword for now. But they have placed themselves in our scabbard." He looked back toward the shore. "Before the next rainy season comes, you will see us put on the skin of the leopard. I swear to you in the name of Ogun, god of war."

Chapter Two

Joan Fuller sighed and gently eased herself out of the clammy feather bed, unsure why she felt so oddly listless. Like as not it was the patter of the noonday shower, now in full force, gusting through the open jalousies in its daily drenching of the tavern's rear quarters. A shower was supposed to be cooling, so why did she always feel hotter and more miserable afterwards? Even now, threads of sweat lined down between her full breasts, inside the curve of each long leg. She moved quietly to the window and one by one began tilting the louvres upward, hoping to shut out some of the salty mist.

Day in and day out, the same pattern. First the harsh sun, then the rain, then the sun again. Mind you, it had brought to life all those new rows of sugar cane marshalled down the hillsides, raising hope the planters might eventually settle their accounts in something besides weedy tobacco. But money mattered so little anymore. Time, that's the commodity no purse on earth could buy. And the Barbados sun and rain, day after day, were like a heartless cadence marking time's theft of the only thing a woman had truly worth holding on to.

The tropical sun and salt air would be telling enough on the face of some girl of twenty, but for a woman all but thirty—well, in God's own truth some nine years past—it was ruination. Still, there it was, every morning, like a knife come to etch deeper those telltale lines at the corners of her eyes. And after she'd frayed her plain brown hair coloring it with yellow dye, hoping to bring out a bit of the sparkle in her hazel eyes, she could count on the harsh salt wind to finish turning it to straw. God damn miserable Barbados.

As if there weren't bother enough, now Hugh was back, the whoremaster, half ready to carry on as though he'd never been gone. When you both knew the past was past.

But why not just make the most of whatever happens . . . and time be damned.

She turned and glanced back toward the bed. He was awake now too, propped up on one elbow, groggily watching. For a moment she thought she might have disturbed him getting up—in years past he used to grumble about that—but then she caught the look in his eyes.

What the pox. In truth it wasn't always so bad, having him back now and again. . . .

Slowly her focus strayed to the dark hair on his chest, the part not lightened to rust by the sun, and she realized *she* was the one who wanted *him*. This minute.

But she never hinted that to Hugh Winston. She never gave him the least encouragement. She kept the whoreson off balance, else he'd lose interest. After you got to know him the way she did, you realized Hugh fancied the chase. As she started to look away, he smiled and beckoned her over. Just like she'd figured . . .

She adjusted the other shutters, then took her own sweet time strolling back. Almost as though he weren't even there. Then she casually settled onto the bed, letting him see the fine profile of her breasts, and just happening to drape one long leg where he could manage to touch it.

But now she was beginning to be of two minds. God's life, it was too damned hot, Hugh or no.

He ignored her ankle and, for some reason, reached out

and silently drew one of his long brown fingers down her cheek. Very slowly. She stifled a shiver, reminding herself she'd had quite enough of men in general, and Hugh Winston in particular, to do a lifetime.

But, still . . .

Before she realized it, he'd lifted back her yellow hair and kissed her deeply on the mouth. Suddenly it was all she could manage, keeping her hands on the mattress.

Then he faltered, mumbled something about the heat, and plopped back onto the sweat-soaked sheet.

Well, God damn him too.

She studied his face again, wondering why he seemed so distracted this trip. It wasn't like Hugh to let things get under his skin. Though admittedly affairs were going poorly for him now, mainly because of the damned Civil War in England. Since he didn't trouble about taxes, he'd always undersold English shippers. But after the war had disrupted things so much, the American settlements were wide open to the cut-rate Hollanders, who could sell and ship cheaper than anybody alive. These days the Butterboxes were everywhere; you could look out the window and see a dozen Dutch merchant-men anchored right in Carlisle Bay. Ever since that trip for the Council he'd been busy running whatever he could get between Virginia and some other place he hadn't said—yet he had scarcely a shilling to show for his time. Why else would he have paid that flock of shiftless runaways he called a crew with the last of his savings? She knew it was all he had, and he'd just handed it over for them to drink and whore away. When would he learn?

And if you're thinking you'll collect on the Council's sight bills, dear heart, you'd best think again. Master Benjamin Briggs and the rest of that shifty lot could hold school for learned scholars on the topic of stalling obligations.

He was doubtless too proud to own it straight out, but he needn't trouble. She already knew. Hugh Winston, her lover in times past and still the only friend she had worth the bother, was down to his last farthing.

She sighed, telling herself she knew full well what it was like. God's wounds, did she know what it was like. Back when Hugh Winston was still in his first and only term at Oxford, the son of one Lord Harold Winston, before he'd been apprenticed and then sent packing out to the Caribbees, Joan Fuller was already an orphan. The hardest place you could be one. On the cobblestone streets of Billingsgate, City of London.

That's where you think you're in luck to hire out in some household for a few pennies a week, with a hag of a mistress who despises you for no more cause than you're young and pretty. Of course you steal a little at first, not too much or she'd see, but then you remember the master, who idles about the place in his greasy nightshirt half the day, and who starts taking notice after you let the gouty old whoremaster know you'd be willing to earn something extra. Finally the mistress starts to suspect—the bloodhounds always do after a while—and soon enough you're back on the cobblestones.

But you know a lot more now. So if you're half clever you'll take what you've put by and have some proper dresses made up, bright colored with ruffled petticoats, and a few hats with silk ribands. Then you pay down on a furnished lodging in Covent Garden, the first floor even though it's more than all the rest of the house. Soon you've got lots of regulars, and then eventually you make acquaintance of a certain gentleman of means who wants a pert young thing all to himself, on alternate afternoons. It lasts for going on two years, till you decide you're weary to death of the kept life. So you count up what's set by—and realize it's enough to hire passage out to Barbados.

Which someone once told you was supposed to be a paradise after London, and you, like a fool, believed it. But which you discover quick enough is just a damned sweltering version of hell. You're here now though, so you take what

37

little money's left and find yourself some girls, Irish ones who've served out their time as indentures, despise having to work, and can't wait to take up the old life, same as before they came out.

And finally you can forget all about what it was like being a penniless orphan. Trouble is, you also realize you're not so young anymore.

"Would you fancy some Hollander cheese, love? The purser from the *Zeelander* lifted a tub for me and there's still a bit left. And I'll warrant there's cassava bread in back, still warm from morning." She knew Hugh always called for the local bread, the hard patties baked from the powdered cassava root, rather than that from the stale, weevily flour shipped out from London.

He ran a finger contemplatively across her breasts—now *they* at least were still round and firm as any strutting Irish wench half her age could boast—then dropped his legs off the side of the bed and began to search for his boots.

"I could do with a tankard of sack."

The very brass of him! When he'd come back half drunk in the middle of the night, ranting about floggings or some such and waving a bottle of kill-devil. He'd climbed into bed, had his way, and promptly passed out. So instead of acting like he owned the place, he could bloody well supply an explanation.

"So how did it go yesterday?" She held her voice even, a purr. "With that business on the *Zeelander?*"

That wasn't the point she actually had in mind. If it hadn't been so damned hot, she'd have nailed him straight out. Something along the lines of "And where in bloody hell *were* you till all hours?" Or maybe "Why is't you think you can have whatever you want, the minute *you* want it?" That was the enquiry the situation called for.

"You missed a fine entertainment." His tone of voice told her he probably meant just the opposite.

"You're sayin' the sale went well for the Dutchmen?" She

watched him shrug, then readied herself to monitor him sharply. "And after that I expect you were off drinking with the Council." She flashed a look of mock disapproval. "Doubtless passing yourself for a fine gentleman, as always?"

"I *am* a gentleman." He laughed and swung at her with a muddy boot, just missing as she sprang from the bed. "I just rarely trouble to own it."

"Aye, you're a gentleman, to be sure. And by that thinking I'm a virgin still, since I was doubtless that once too."

"So I've heard you claim. But that was back well before my time."

"You had rare fortune, darlin'. You got the rewards of years of expertise." She reached to pull on her brown linen shift. "And I suppose you'll be telling me next that Master Briggs and the Council can scarcely wait to settle your sight bills."

"They'll settle them in a fortnight, one way or another, or damned to them." He reached for his breeches, not the fancy ones he wore once in a while around the Council, but the canvas ones he used aboard ship, and the tone of his voice changed. "I just hope things stay on an even keel till then."

"I don't catch your meaning." She studied him openly, wondering if that meant he was already planning to leave.

"The planters' new purchase." He'd finished with the trousers and was busy with his belt. "Half of them are Yoruba."

"And, pray, what's that?" She'd thought he was going to explain more on the bit about leaving.

"I think they're a people from somewhere down around the Niger River delta."

"The Africans, you mean?" She examined him, still puzzled. "The slaves?"

"You've hit on it. The slaves. Like a fool, I didn't see it coming, but it's here, all right. May God curse Ruyters. Now I realize this is what he planned all along, the bastard, when he started telling everybody how they could get rich with cane. Save none of these Puritans knows the first thing about working Africans. He's sold them a powder keg with these Yoruba.'' He rose and started for the door leading into the front room of the tavern. "And they're doing all they can to spark the fuse.''

"What're you tryin' to say?'' She was watching him walk, something that still pleased her after all the years. But she kept on seeming to listen. When Hugh took something in his head, you'd best let him carry on about it for a time.

"They're proud and I've got a feeling they're not going to take this treatment.'' He turned back to look at her, finally reading her confusion. "I've seen plenty of Yoruba over the years in Brazil, and I can tell you the Papists have learned to handle them differently. They're fast and they're smart. Some of them even come off the boat already knowing Portugee. I also found out that at least one of those Ruyters sold to Briggs can speak it.''

"Is that such a bad thing? It'd seem to me . . .''

"What I'm saying is, now that they're here, they've got to be treated like men. You can't starve them and horsewhip them the way you can Irish indentures. I've got a strong feeling they'll not abide it for long.'' He moved restlessly into the front room, a wood-floored space of rickety pine tables and wobbly straight chairs, plopping down by the front doorway, his gaze fixed on the misty outline of the river bridge. "I went on out to Briggs' plantation last night, thinking to talk over a certain little matter, but instead I got treated to a show of how he plans to break in his slaves. The first thing he did was flog one of his new Yoruba when he balked at eating *loblolly* corn mush. That's going to make for big trouble, mark it.''

She studied him now and finally realized how worked up he was. Hugh usually noticed everything, yet he'd walked straight through the room without returning the groggy nods of his men, two French mates and his quartermaster John

Mewes—the latter now gaming at three-handed whist with Salt-Beef Peg and Buttock-de-Clink Jenny, her two newest Irish girls.

She knew for sure Peg had noticed *him*, and that little sixpenny tart bloody well knew better than to breathe a word in front of her mistress.

"Well, settle down a bit." She opened the cabinet and took out an onion-flask of sack, together with two tankards. "Tell me where you're thinking you'll be going next." She dropped into the chair opposite and began uncorking the bottle. "Or am I to expect you and the lads'll be staying a while in Barbados this time?"

He laughed. "Well now, am I supposed to think it's *me* you're thinking about? Or is it you're just worried we might ship out while one of the lads still has a shilling left somewhere or other?"

She briefly considered hoisting the bottle she'd just fetched and cracking it over his skull, but instead she shot him a frown and turned toward the bleary-eyed gathering at the whist table. "John, did you ever hear the likes of this one, by my life? He'd have the lot of you drink and play for free."

John Mewes, a Bristol seaman who had joined Hugh years ago after jumping ship at Nevis Island, stared up groggily from his game, then glanced back at his shrinking pile of coins—shrinking as Salt-Beef Peg's had grown. His weathered cheeks were lined from drink, and, as always, his ragged hair was matted against his scalp and the jerkin covering his wide belly was stained brown with spilled grog. Inexplicably, women doted on him in taverns the length of the Caribbean.

"Aye, yor ladyship, it may soon have to be. This bawd of yours is near to takin' my last shilling, before she's scarce troubled liftin' her skirts to earn it." He took another swallow of kill-devil from his tankard, then looked imploringly toward Winston. "On my honor, Cap'n, by the look of it I'm apt to be poor as a country parson by noontide tomorrow."

41

"But you're stayin' all this week with me, John." Peg was around the table and on his lap in an instant, her soft brown eyes aglow. "A promise to a lady always has to be kept. Else you'll lose your luck."

"Then shall I be havin' your full measure for the coin of love? It's near to all that's left, I'll take an oath on it. My purse's shriveled as the Pope's balls."

"For love?" Peg rose. "And I suppose I'm to be livin' on this counterfeit you call love. Whilst you're off plyin' your sweet talk to some stinkin' Dutch whore over on the Wild Coast."

"The damned Hollander wenches are all too sottish by half. They'd swill a man's grog faster'n he can call for it." He took another pull from his tankard and glanced admiringly at Peg's bulging, half-laced bodice. "But I say deal the cards, m'lady. Where there's life, there's hope, as I'm a Christian."

"And what was it you were saying, love?" Joan turned back to Winston and poured another splash into his tankard. "I think it was something to do with the new slaves?"

"I said I don't like it, and I just might try doing something about it. I just hope there's no trouble here in the meantime." His voice slowly trailed off into the din of the rain.

This bother about the slaves was not a bit like him, Joan thought. Hugh'd never been out to right all the world's many ills. Besides, what did he expect? God's wounds, the planters were going to squeeze every shilling they could out of these new Africans. Everybody knew the Caribbees and all the Americas were "beyond the line," outside the demarcation on some map somewhere that separated Europe from the New World. Out here the rules were different. Hugh had always understood that better than anybody, so why was he so out of sorts now that the planters had found a replacement for their lazy indentures? Heaven can tell, he had wrongs enough of his own to brood about if he wanted to trouble his mind over life's little misfortunes.

"What is it really that's occupying your mind so much this trip, love? It can't just be these new slaves. I know you too well for that." She studied him. "Is't the sight bills?"

"I've been thinking about an idea I've had for a long, long time. Seeing what's happened now on Barbados, it all fits together somehow."

"What're you talking about?"

"I'm wondering if maybe it's not time I tried changing a few things."

This was definitely a new Hugh. He never talked like that in the old days. Back then all he ever troubled about was how he was going to manage making a living—a problem he still hadn't worked out, if you want the honest truth.

She looked at him now, suddenly so changed, and recollected the first time she ever saw him. It was a full seven years past, just after she'd opened her tavern and while he was still a seaman on the *Zeelander*. That Dutch ship had arrived with clapboards and staves from Portsmouth, Rhode Island, needed on Barbados for houses and tobacco casks. While the *Zeelander* was lading Barbados cotton for the mills in New England, he'd come in one night with the other members of the Dutch crew, and she'd introduced him to one of the girls. But, later on, it was her he'd bought drinks for, not the plump Irish colleen he'd been with. And then came the questions. How'd she get on, he wanted to know, living by her wits out here in the New World? Where was the money?

She'd figured, rightly, that Hugh was looking for something, maybe thinking to try and make his own way, as she had.

After a while he'd finally ordered a tankard for the pouting girl, then disappeared. But there he was again the next evening, and the one after that too. Each time he'd go off with one of the girls, then come back and talk with her. Finally one night he did something unheard of. He bought a full flask of kill-devil and proposed they take a walk down to look at the ship.

43

God's life, as though she hadn't seen enough worn-out Dutch frigates. . . .

Then she realized what was happening. This young English mate with a scar on his cheek desired her, was paying court to her. He even seemed to *like* her. Didn't he know she no longer entertained the trade herself?

But Hugh was different. So, like a fool, she lost sight of her better judgment. Later that night, she showed him how a woman differed from a girl.

And she still found occasion to remind him from time to time, seven years later. . . .

"I want to show you how I came by the idea I've been working on." He abruptly rose and walked back to the bedroom. When he returned he was carrying his two pistols, their long steel barrels damascened with gold and the stocks fine walnut. He placed them carefully on the table, then dropped back into his chair and reached for his tankard. "Take a look at those."

"God's blood." She glanced at the guns and gave a tiny snort. "Every time I see you, you've got another pair."

"I like to keep up with the latest designs."

"So tell me what's 'latest' about these."

"A lot of things. In the first place, the firing mechanism's a flintlock. So when you pull the trigger, the piece of flint there in the hammer strikes against the steel wing on the cap of the powder pan, opening it and firing the powder in a single action. Also, the powder pan loads automatically when the barrel's primed. It's faster and better than a matchlock."

"That's lovely. But flintlocks have been around for some time, or hadn't you heard?" She looked at the guns and took a sip of sack, amused by his endless fascination with pistols. He'd always been that way, but it was to a purpose. You'd be hard pressed to find a marksman in the Caribbees better or faster than Hugh—a little talent left over from his time with the Cow-Killers on Tortuga, though for some reason he'd as soon not talk about those years. She glanced down again. "Is

44

it just my eyes, or do I see two barrels? Now I grant you this is the first time I've come across anything like *that*."

"Congratulations. That's what's new about this design. Watch." He lifted up a gun and carefully touched a second trigger, a smaller one in front of the first. The barrel assembly emitted a light click and revolved a half turn, bringing up the second barrel, ready to fire. "See, they're double-barreled. I hear it's called a 'turn-over' mechanism—since when you pull that second trigger, a spring-loaded assembly turns over a new barrel, complete with a primed powder pan." He gripped the muzzle and revolved the barrels back to their initial position. "This design's going to be the coming thing, mark it." He laid the pistol back onto the table. "Oh, by the way, there's one other curiosity. Have a look there on the breech. Can you make out the name?"

She lifted one of the flintlocks and squinted in the half-light. Just in front of the ornate hammer there was a name etched in gold: "Don Francisco de Castilla."

"That's more'n likely the gunsmith who made them. On a fine pistol you'll usually see the maker's name there. You ought to know that." She looked at him. "I didn't suppose you made them yourself, darlin'. I've never seen that name before, but God knows there're lots of Spanish pistols around the Caribbean. Everybody claims they're the best."

"That's what I thought the name was too. At first." He lifted his tankard and examined the amber contents. "Tell me. How much do you know about Jamaica?"

"What's that got to do with these pistols?"

"One thing at a time. I asked you what you know about Jamaica."

"No more'n everybody else does. It's a big island somewhere to the west of here, that the Spaniards hold. There's supposed to be a harbor and a fortress, and a little settlement they call Villa de la Vega, with maybe a couple of thousand planters. But that's about all, from what I hear, since the

Spaniards've never yet found any gold or silver there.'' She studied him, puzzling. ''Why're you asking?''

''I've been thinking. Maybe I'll go over and poke around a bit.'' He paused, then lowered his voice. ''Maybe see if I can take the fortress.''

'' 'Maybe take the fortress,' you say?'' She exploded with laughter and reached for the sack. ''I reckon I'd best put away this flask. Right now.''

''You don't think I can do it?''

''I hear the Spaniards've got heavy cannon in that fortress, and a big militia. Even some cavalry. No Englishman's going to take it.'' She looked at him. ''Not wishing to offend, love, but wouldn't you say that's just a trifle out of your depth?''

''I appreciate your expression of confidence.'' He settled his tankard on the table. ''Then tell me something else. Do you remember Jackson?''

''The famous 'Captain' Jackson, you mean?''

''Captain William Jackson.''

''Sure, I recall that lying knave well enough.'' She snorted. ''Who could forget him. He was here for two months once, while you were out, and turned Barbados upside down, recruiting men to sail against the Spaniards' settlements on the Main. Claiming he was financed by the Earl of Warwick. He sat drinking every night at this very table, then left me a stack of worthless sight drafts, saying he'd be back in no time to settle them in Spanish gold.'' She ___ ___ed him for a moment. ''That was four years past. The ___ I know he was never heard from since. For sure *I* never heard from him.'' Suddenly she leaned forward. ''Don't tell me you know where he might be?''

''Not any more. But I learned last year what happened back then. It turns out he got nothing on the Main. The Spaniards would empty any settlement—Maracaibo, Puerto Cabello—he tried to take. They'd just strip their houses and disappear into the jungle.''

''So he went back empty-handed?''

"Wrong. That's what he wanted everybody to *think* happened. Especially the Earl of Warwick. He kept on going." Winston lowered his voice again, beyond reach of the men across the room. "I wouldn't believe what he did next if I didn't have these pistols." He picked up one of the guns and yelled toward the whist table. "John."

"Aye." Mewes was on his feet in an instant, wiping his hand across his mouth.

"Remember where I got these flintlocks?"

"I seem to recall it was Virginia. Jamestown." He reached down and lifted his tankard for a sip. Then he wiped his mouth a second time. "An' if you want my thinkin', they was sold to you by the scurviest-lookin' whoreson that ever claim'd he was English, that I'd not trust with tuppence. An' that's the truth."

"Well . . ." She leaned back in her chair.

"Along with the pistols I also got part of the story of Jackson's expedition. It seems this man had been with them—claimed he was first mate on the flagship—but he'd finally jumped ship when Jackson tried to storm a fortress up on the coast of Spanish Florida, then made his way north to Virginia. He stole these pistols from Jackson's cabin the night he swam ashore."

"Then I've half a mind to confiscate them here and now as payment for my sight drafts." She inspected the guns. "But I still don't follow what that's got to do with Jamaica."

He picked up one of the pistols again and traced his finger along the flintlock. "The name. Don Francisco de Castilla. I kept thinking and thinking, and finally I remembered. That's not a pistol maker. That's the name of the Spanish governor of Villa de la Vega. *Jamaica.*"

"But then how did Jackson get them? I never saw these pistols when he was here, and I'd have remembered them, you can be sure." She was staring skeptically at the guns.

"*That's* what I began to wonder. So I tracked down the seller and found out what *really* happened." He lowered his voice again. "Jackson got them from de Castilla's personal strongbox. In the fortress. William Jackson *took* Jamaica. He got the idea the Spaniards'd never be expecting an attack that far from the Main, and he was right. So after Maracaibo, he made way straight for Jamaica. He raised the bay at dawn, brought the fleet together and put in for the harbor. The fortress, the town, all of it, was his in a morning."

"But how could he hold the place? As soon as the Spaniards over on the Main got word, they'd be sure to send a . . ."

"He didn't bother. He delivered the town back in return for provisions and a ransom of twenty thousand pieces of eight. Split the money with his men and swore them to secrecy. But he kept these pistols." Winston smiled. "Except now they're mine."

"*Hold* a minute. I'm afraid I'm beginning to see what you're thinking." She leaned forward, alarm in her eyes. "So let me tell *you* a few things. About that little expedition of Jackson's. That fast-talking rogue put in here with three armed frigates. He raised over five hundred men and God knows how many muskets. I saw them all off, holding my valuable sight drafts, the day he set sail out of Carlisle Bay."

"But what if I got more men?"

"In God's name, who from?"

"Who do you think?" He ran his fingers through his hair and looked away. "I've been thinking it over for months. Well, now I've made up my mind. What the hell are the Americas for? Slavery?" He looked back. "I'm going to take Jamaica, and keep it. It'll be the one place in the New World where there'll be no indentures. No slaves. Just free men. The way it was on Tortuga."

"Christ on a cross, you've totally taken leave of sense!" She looked at him dumbfounded. "You'd best stop dreaming about Jamaica and put your deep mind to work on how you're going to collect those sight bills from the Council. You've got to make a living, love."

"The sight bills are part of my plan. As it happens, I expect to settle that very item next Friday night."

"Best of luck." She paused, then pushed back from the table. "God's blood, were you invited?"

He looked up from his tankard. "How do *you* know where I'm going?"

"There's only one place it could be. The fancy ball Master Briggs is holdin' for the Council. In his grand new estate house. It's the reason there's not a scrap of taffeta left in the whole of Bridgetown. I was trying to buy some all yesterday for the girls."

"I have to go. It's the perfect time to see them all together."

"And I suppose Miss Katherine Bedford'll be there as well?" Her voice had acquired an unmistakable edge. "In her official capacity as 'First Lady'?"

"Oddly enough, I neglected to enquire on that point."

"Did you now?" She sniffed. "Aye, her highness'll be in attendance, and probably wearin' half the taffeta I wanted to buy. Not that it'll be made up properly. She'll be there, the strumpet, on my honor. . . ."

"What if she is? It's no matter to me." He drank again. "I just want my sight bills paid, in coin as agreed, not in bales of their damned worthless tobacco."

She seemed not to hear. ". . . when she's too busy ridin' that mare of hers to so much as nod her bonnet to an honest woman who might have need to make a living. . . ."

"All right." He set down his tankard. "I'll take you."

"Pardon?"

"I said I'll *take* you."

"Now you've gone *totally* daft." She stared at him, secretly overjoyed he'd consider asking. "Can you fancy the scene? *Me*, in amongst all those dowdy Puritan sluts! Stuffing their fat faces whilst arguing over whether to starve their indentures completely to death. Not to mention there'd be general heart seizure in the ranks of the Council, the half of

49

which keep open accounts here on the sly. Only I'm lucky to get paid in musty tobacco, let alone the coin *you're* dreaming of.'' She laughed. ''And I warrant you'll be paid with the same, love. That's assuming you're ever paid at all.''

''As you will.'' He took a sip of sack. ''But since you're so worried about the women, don't forget who else'll probably be there.''

''Who do you mean?''

''Remember what the Portugals say: *'E a mulata que e Mulher.'* ''

'' 'It's the mulatto who's the *real* woman.' '' She translated the famous Pernambuco expression, then frowned. ''I suppose you mean that Portuguese mulatto Master Briggs bought for himself when you took them all down to Brazil. The one named Serina.''

''The very one. I caught a glimpse of her again last night.''

''I know her, you rogue. Probably better than you do. Briggs is always sending her down here for bottles of killdevil, sayin' he doesn't trust his indentures to get them home. She's a fine-featured woman of the kind, if I say it myself.''

''Finer than Briggs deserves.''

''Did you know that amongst the Council she's known as his 'pumpkin-colored whore'? Those hypocritical Puritan whoremasters. I always ask her to stay a bit when she comes. I think she's probably lonely, poor creature. But I can tell you one thing for certain—she takes no great satisfaction in her new owner. Or in Barbados either, come to that, after the fine plantation she lived on in Brazil.'' She laughed. ''Something not hard to understand. I'm always amazed to remember she's a slave. Probably one of the very first on this island.'' She looked away reflectively. ''Though now she's got much company.''

''Too much.''

''You may be right for once. It's a new day, on my faith, and I don't mind telling you it troubles me a bit. There're apt to be thousands of these Africans here soon. There'll be

50

nothing like it anywhere in the Americas.'' She sighed. ''But the Council's all saying the slaves'll change everything, make them all rich.'' Her voice quickened as she turned back. ''Do you suppose it's true?''

''Probably. That's why I plan to try and change a few things too.'' He looked out at the bay, where a line of brown pelicans glided single file across the tips of waves. The horizon beyond was lost in mist. ''My own way.''

Chapter Three

Katherine gazed past the pewter candlesticks and their flickering tapers, down the long cedar table of Briggs' dining hall, now piled high with stacks of greasy wooden plates spilling over with half-finished food. The room was wide and deep, with dark oak beams across the ceiling and fresh white plaster walls. Around the table were rows of grim men in black hats and plump Puritan women in tight bodices and starched collars. For all its surface festivity, there was something almost ominous about the evening. Change was in the air, and not change for the better.

At the head of the table were the most prominent members of the Council, the owners of Barbados' largest plantations. She knew the wealthiest ones personally: Edward Bayes, his jowls protruding beneath his whisp of beard, owned the choicest coastal lands north around Speightstown; Thomas Lancaster, now red-cheeked and glassy-eyed from the liquor, had the largest plantation in the rolling plains of St. George's parish, mid-island; Nicholas Whittington, dewlapped and portly, was master of a vast acreage in Christ's Church parish, on the southern coast.

Anthony Walrond had not been invited, nor any other of the new royalist émigrés—which she should have *known* was exactly what was going to happen before she went to all the

52

bother of having a new dress and bodice made up. No, tonight the guests were the rich planters, the old settlers who arrived on Barbados in the early years and claimed the best land. They were the ones that Dalby Bedford, now seated beside her, diplomatically sipping from his tankard, liked to call the "plantocracy." They had gathered to celebrate the beginnings of the sugar miracle. And the new order.

The room was alive with an air of expectancy, almost as palpable as the smoke that drifted in through the open kitchen door. Benjamin Briggs' banquet and ball, purportedly a celebration, was in truth something more like a declaration: the Assembly, that elected body created by Dalby Bedford from among the small freeholders, would soon count for nothing in the face of the big planters' new wealth and power. Henceforth, this flagship of the Americas would be controlled by the men who owned the most land and the most slaves.

The worst part of all, she told herself, was that Briggs' celebration would probably last till dawn. Though the banquet was over now, the ball was about to commence. And after that, Briggs had dramatically announced, there would be a special preview of his new sugarworks, the first on the island.

In hopes of reinforcing her spirits, she took another sip of Canary wine, then lifted her glass higher, to study the room through its wavy refractions. Now Briggs seemed a distorted, comical pygmy as he ordered the servants to pass more bottles of kill-devil down the table, where the planters and their wives continued to slosh it into their pewter tankards of lemon punch. After tonight, she found herself thinking, the whole history of the Americas might well have to be rewritten. Barbados would soon be England's richest colony, and unless the Assembly held firm, these few greedy Puritans would seize control. All thanks to sugar.

Right there in the middle of it all was Hugh Winston, looking a little melancholy and pensive. He scarcely seemed to notice as several toasts to his health went round the table—

salutes to the man who'd made sugar possible. He obviously didn't care a damn about sugar. He was too worried about getting his money.

As well he should be, she smiled to herself. He'll never see it. Not a farthing. Anybody could tell that Briggs and the Council hadn't the slightest intention of settling his sight bills. He didn't impress them for a minute with those pretty Spanish pistols in his belt. They'd stood up to a lot better men than him. Besides, there probably weren't two thousand pounds in silver on the whole island.

Like all the American settlements, Barbados' economy existed on barter and paper; everything was valued in weights of tobacco or cotton. Metal money was almost never seen; in fact, it was actually against the law to export coin from England to the Americas. The whole Council together couldn't come up with that much silver. He could forget about settling his sight bills in specie.

"I tell you this is the very thing every man here'll need if he's to sleep nights." Briggs voice cut through her thoughts. He was at the head of the table, describing the security features of his new stone house. "Mind you, it's not yet finished." He gestured toward the large square staircase leading up toward the unpainted upper floors. "But it's already secure as the Tower of London."

She remembered Briggs had laid the first stone of his grand new plantation house in the weeks after his return from Brazil, in anticipation of the fortune he expected to make from sugar, and he had immediately christened it "Briggs Hall." The house and its surrounding stone wall were actually a small fortress. The dining room where they sat now was situated to one side of the wide entry foyer, across from the parlor and next to the smoky kitchen, a long stone room set off to the side. There were several small windows along the front and back of the house, but these could all be sealed tight with heavy shutters—a measure as much for health as safety, since the planters believed the cool night breeze could induce dangerous chills and "hot paroxysms."

Maybe he thought he needed such a house. Maybe, she told herself, he *did*. He already had twenty indentures, and he'd just bought thirty Africans. The island now expected more slave cargos almost weekly.

As she listened, she found herself watching Hugh Winston, wondering what the Council's favorite smuggler thought of it all. Well, at the moment he looked unhappy. He seemed to find Briggs' lecture on the new need for security either pathetic or amusing—his eyes were hard to make out—but she could tell from his glances round the table he found something ironic about the need for a stone fort in the middle of a Caribbean island.

Briggs suddenly interrupted his monologue and turned to signal his servants to begin placing trenchers of clay pipes and Virginia tobacco down the table. A murmur of approval went up when the planters saw it was imported, not the musty weed raised on Barbados.

The appearance of the tobacco signaled the official end of the food. As the gray-shirted servants began packing and firing the long-stemmed pipes, then kneeling to offer them to the tipsy planters, several of the more robust wives present rose with a grateful sigh. Holding their new gowns away from the ant-repellent tar smeared along the legs of the table and chairs, they began retiring one by one to the changing room next to the kitchen, where Briggs' Irish maidservants could help loosen their tight bodices in preparation for the ball.

Katherine watched the women file past, then cringed as she caught the first sound of tuning fiddles from the large room opposite the entryway. What was the rest of the evening going to be like? Surely the banquet alone was enough to prove Briggs was now the most powerful man in Barbados, soon perhaps in all the Americas. He had truly outdone himself. Even the servants were saying it was the grandest night the island had ever seen—and predicting it was only the first of many to come.

The indentures themselves had all dined earlier on their usual fare of *loblolly* cornmeal mush, sweet potatoes, and hyacinth beans—though tonight they were each given a small allowance of pickled turtle in honor of the banquet. But for the Council and their wives, Briggs had dressed an expensive imported beef as the centerpiece of the table. The rump had been boiled, and the brisket, along with the cheeks, roasted. The tongue and tripe had been minced and baked into pies, seasoned with sweet herbs, spices, and currants. The beef had been followed by a dish of Scots collops of pork; then a young kid goat dressed in its own blood and thyme, with a pudding in its belly; and next a sweet suckling pig in a sauce of brains, sage, and nutmeg mulled in Claret wine. After that had come a shoulder of mutton and a side of goat, both covered with a rasher of bacon, then finally baked rabbit and a loin of veal.

And as though that weren't enough to allow every planter there to gorge himself to insensibility, there were also deep bowls of potato pudding and dishes of baked plantains, prickly pear, and custard apples. At the end came the traditional cold meats, beginning with roast duck well larded, then Spanish bacon, pickled oysters, and fish roe. With it all was the usual kill-devil, as well as Canary wine, Sherry, and red sack from Madeira.

When the grease-stained table had been cleared and the pipes lighted, Briggs announced the after-dinner cordial. A wide bowl of French brandy appeared before him, and into it the servants cracked a dozen large hen eggs. Then a generous measure of sugar was poured in and the mixture vigorously stirred. Finally he called for a burning taper, took it himself, and touched the flame to the brandy. The fumes hovering over the dish billowed into a huge yellow blossom, and the table erupted with a cheer. After the flame had died away, the servants began ladling out the mixture and passing portions down the table.

Katherine sipped the sweet, harsh liquid and watched as two of the planters sitting nearby, their clay pipes billowing, rose unsteadily and hoisted their cups for a toast. The pair smelled strongly of sweat and liquor. They weren't members of the Council, but both would also be using the new sugarworks—for a percentage—after Briggs had finished with his own cane, since their plantations were near Briggs' and neither could afford the investment to build his own. One was Thomas Lockwood, a short, brooding Cornwall bachelor who now held a hundred acres immediately north of Briggs' land, and the other was William Marlott, a thin, nervous Suffolk merchant who had repaired to Barbados with his consumptive wife ten years before and had managed to accumulate eighty acres upland, all now planted in cane.

"To the future of sugar on Barbados," Lockwood began, his voice slurred from the kill-devil. Then Marlott joined in, "And a fine fortune to every man at this table."

A buzz of approval circled the room, and with a scrape of chairs all the other men pulled themselves to their feet and raised their cups.

Katherine was surprised to see Hugh Winston lean back in his chair, his own cup sitting untouched on the boards. He'd been drinking all evening, but now his eyes had acquired an absent gaze as he watched the hearty congratulations going around.

After the planters had drunk, Briggs turned to him with a querulous expression.

"Where's *your* thirst, Captain? Will you not drink to the beginnings of English prosperity in the Caribbees? Sure, it's been a long time coming."

"You'll be an even longer time paying the price." It was virtually the first time Winston had spoken all evening, and his voice was subdued. There was a pause, then he continued, his voice still quiet. "So far all sugar's brought you is

57

slavery. And prisons for homes, when it was freedom that Englishmen came to the Americas for. Or so I've heard claimed.''

"Now sir, every man's got a right to his own mind on a thing, I always say. But the Caribbees were settled for profit, first and foremost. Let's not lose sight of that.'' Briggs smiled indulgently and settled his cup onto the table. "For that matter, what's all this 'freedom' worth if you've not a farthing in your pocket? We've tried everything else, and it's *got* to be sugar. It's the real future of the Americas, depend on it. Which means we've got to work a batch of Africans, plain as that, and pay mind they don't get out of hand. We've tried it long enough to know these white indentures can't, or won't, endure the labor to make sugar. Try finding me a white man who'll cut cane all day in the fields. That's why every spoon of that sweet powder an English gentlewoman stirs into her china cup already comes from a black hand in chains. It's always been, it'll always be. For sure it'll be the Papist Spaniards and Portugals still holding the chains if not us.''

Winston, beginning to look a bit the worse for drink, seemed not to hear. "Which means you're both on the end of a chain, one way or another.''

"Well, sir, that's as it may be.'' Briggs settled back into his chair. "But you've only to look at the matter to understand there's nothing to compare with sugar. Ask any Papist. Now I've heard said it was first discovered in Cathay, but we all know sugar's been the monopoly of the Spaniards and Portugals for centuries. Till now. Mind you, the men in this room are the first Englishmen who've ever learned even how to plant the cane—not with seeds, but by burying sections of stalk.''

Katherine braced herself for what would come next. She had heard it all so many times before, she almost knew his text by heart.

"We all know that if the Dutchmen hadn't taken that piece of Brazil from the Portugals, sugar'd be the secret of the

Papists still. So this very night we're going to witness the beginning of a new history of the world. English sugar.''

"Aye," Edward Bayes interrupted, pausing to wipe his beard against his sleeve. "We've finally found something we can grow here in the Caribbees that'll have a market worldwide. Show me the fine lord who doesn't have his cook lade sugar into every dish on his table. Or the cobbler, one foot in the almshouse, who doesn't use all the sugar he can buy or steal." Bayes beamed, his red-tinged eyes aglow in the candlelight. "And that's only today, sir. I tell you, only today. The market for sugar's just beginning."

"Not a doubt," Briggs continued. "Consider the new fashion just starting up in London for drinking coffee, and chocolate. There's a whole new market for sugar, since they'll not be drunk without it." He shoved aside his cup of punch and reached to pour a fresh splash of kill-devil into his tankard. "In faith, sugar's about to change forever the way Englishmen eat, and drink, and live."

"And I'll wager an acre of land here'll make a pound of sugar for every pound of tobacco it'll grow." Lockwood rose again. "When sugar'll bring who knows how many times the price. If we grow enough cane on Barbados, and buy ourselves enough of these Africans to bring it in, we'll be underselling the Papists in five years' time, maybe less."

"Aye." Briggs seconded Lockwood, eyeing him as he drank. It was common knowledge that Briggs held eighteen-month sight drafts from the planter, coming due in a fortnight. Katherine looked at the two of them and wondered how long it would be before the better part of Lockwood's acres were incorporated into the domain of Briggs Hall.

"Well, I kept my end of our bargain, for better or worse." Winston's voice lifted over the din of the table. "Now it's time for yours. Two thousand pounds were what we agreed on, in coin. Spanish pieces-of-eight, English sovereigns—there's little difference to me."

It's come, Katherine thought. But he'll not raise a shilling.

Briggs was suddenly scrutinizing his tankard as an uneasy quiet settled around the table. "It's a hard time for us all just now, sir." He looked up. "Six months more and we'll have sugar to sell to the Dutchmen. But as it is today . . ."

"That's something you should've thought about when you signed those sight drafts."

"I'd be the first one to grant you that point, sir, the very first." Briggs' face had assumed an air of contrition. "But what's done's done." He placed his rough hands flat down on the table, as though to symbolize they were empty. "We've talked it over, and the best we can manage now's to roll them over, with interest, naturally. What would you say to . . . five percent?"

"That wasn't the understanding." Winston's voice was quiet, but his eyes narrowed.

"Well, sir. That's the terms we're prepared to offer." Briggs' tone hardened noticeably. "In this world it's the wise man who takes what he can get."

"The sight bills are for cash on demand." Winston's voice was still faint, scarcely above a whisper. Katherine listened in dismay, realizing she'd secretly been hoping he could stand up to the Council. Just to prove somebody could. And now . . .

"Damn your sight bills, sir. We've made you our offer." Briggs exchanged glances with the other members of the Council. "In truth, it'd be in the interest of all of us here to just have them declared worthless paper."

"You can't rightfully do that." Winston drank again. "They have full legal standing."

"We have courts here, sir, that could be made to take the longer view. To look to the interests of the island."

"There're still courts in England. If we have to take it that far."

"But you'll not be going back there, sir. We both know it'd take years." Briggs grinned. "And I'll warrant you'd get

60

more justice in England than you bargained for, if you had the brass to try it."

"That remains to be seen." Winston appeared trying to keep his voice firm. "But there'll be no need for that. I seem to recall the terms give me recourse—the right to foreclose. Without notice."

"Foreclose?" Briggs seemed unsure he had caught the word.

"Since you co-signed all the notes yourself, I won't have to bother with the rest of the Council," Winston continued. "I can just foreclose on you personally. Remember you pledged this plantation as collateral."

"That was a formality. And it was two years past." Briggs laughed. "Before I built this house. And the sugarworks. At the time there was nothing on this property but a thatched-roof bungalow."

"Formality or not, the drafts pledge these acres and what's on them."

"Well, damn you, sir." Briggs slammed down his tankard. "You'll not get . . ."

"Mind you, I don't have any use for the land," Winston interjected. "So why don't we just make it the sugarworks? That ought to about cover what's owed." He looked back. "If I present the notes in Bridgetown tomorrow morning, we can probably just transfer ownership then and there. What do you say to that arrangement?"

"You've carried this jest quite far enough, sir." Briggs' face had turned the color of the red prickly-pear apples on the table. "We all need that sugarworks. You'll not be getting your hands on it. I presume I speak for all the Council when I say we'll protect our interests. If you try foreclosing on that sugarworks, I'll call you out. I've a mind to anyway, here and now. For your damned impudence." He abruptly pushed back from the table, his doublet falling open to reveal the handle of a pistol. Several Council members shoved back also. All had flintlock pistols in their belts, the usual precaution in an island of unruly indentures.

61

Winston appeared not to notice. "I see no reason for anyone to get killed over a little business transaction."

Briggs laughed again. "No sir, I suppose you'd rather just try intimidating us with threats of foreclosure. But by God, if you think you can just barge in here and fleece the Council of Barbados, you've miscalculated. It's time you learned a thing or two about this island," he continued, his voice rising. "Just because you like to strut about with a pair of fancy flintlocks in your belt, don't think we'll all heel to your bluff." He removed his dark hat and threw it on the table. It matched the black velvet of his doublet. "You can take our offer, or you can get off my property, here and now."

Katherine caught the determined looks in the faces of several members of the Council as their hands dropped to their belts. She suddenly wondered if it had all been planned. Was this what they'd been waiting for? They must have known he'd not accept their offer, and figured there was a cheaper way to manage the whole business anyway. A standoff with pistols, Winston against them all.

"I still think it'd be better to settle this honorably." Winston looked down and his voice trailed off, but there was a quick flash of anger in his bloodshot eyes. Slowly he picked up his tankard and drained it. As the room grew silent, he coughed at the harshness of the liquor, then began to toy with the lid, flipping the thumb mechanism attached to the hinged top and watching it flap open and shut. He heaved a sigh, then abruptly leaned back and lobbed it in the general direction of the staircase.

As the tankard began its trajectory, he was on his feet, kicking away his chair. There was the sound of a pistol hammer being cocked and the hiss of a powder pan. Then the room flashed with an explosion from his left hand, where a pistol had appeared from out of his belt. At that moment the lid of the tankard seemed to disconnect in midair, spinning sideways as it ricocheted off the post of carved mastic wood at the top of the stairs. The pistol clicked, rotating up the

62

under-barrel, and the second muzzle spoke. This time the tankard emitted a sharp ring and tumbled end over end till it slammed against the railing. Finally it bounced to rest against the cedar wainscot of the hallway, a small, centered hole directly through the bottom. The shorn lid was still rolling plaintively along the last step of the stairs.

The entire scene had taken scarcely more than a second. Katherine looked back to see him still standing; he had dropped the flintlock onto the table, both muzzles trailing wisps of gray smoke, while his right hand gripped the stock of the other pistol, still in his belt.

"You can deduct that from what's owed." His eyes went down the table.

Briggs sat motionless in his chair staring at the tankard, while the other planters all watched him in expectant silence. Finally he picked up his hat and settled it back on his head without a word. Slowly, one by one, the other men closed their doublets over their pistols and nervously reached for their tankards.

After a moment Winston carefully reached for his chair and straightened it up. He did not sit. "You'll be welcome to buy back the sugarworks any time you like. Just collect the money and settle my sight bills."

The room was still caught in silence, till finally Briggs found his voice.

"But the coin's not to be had, sir. Try and be reasonable. I tell you we'd not find it on the whole of the island."

"Then maybe I'll just take something else." He reached out and seized the motley gray shirt of Timothy Farrell, now tiptoeing around the table carrying a fresh flask of kill-devil to Briggs. The terrified Irishman dropped the bottle with a crash as Winston yanked him next to the table. "Men. And provisions."

Briggs looked momentarily disoriented. "I don't follow you, sir. What would you be doing with them?"

"That's my affair. Just give me two hundred indentures,

owned by the men on the Council who signed the sight drafts.'' He paused. ''That should cover about half the sum. I'll take the balance in provisions. Then you can all have your sight bills to burn.''

Now Briggs was studying the tankard in front of him, his eyes shining in the candlelight. ''Two hundred indentures and you'd be willing to call it settled?''

''To the penny.''

In the silence that followed, the rasp of a fiddle sounded through the doorway, followed by the shrill whine of a recorder. Briggs yelled for quiet, then turned back.

''There may be some merit in what you're proposing.'' He glanced up at Farrell, watching the indenture flee the room as Winston released his greasy shirt. ''Yes sir, I'm thinking your proposal has some small measure of merit. I don't know about the other men here, but I can already name you a number of these layabouts I could spare.'' He turned to the planters next to him, and several nodded agreement. ''Aye, I'd have us talk more on it.'' He pushed back his chair and rose unsteadily from the table. The other planters took this as a signal, and as one man they scraped back their chairs and began to nervously edge toward the women, now clustered under the arches leading into the dancing room. ''When the time's more suitable.''

''Tomorrow, then.''

''Give us till tomorrow night, sir. After we've had some time to parlay.'' Briggs nodded, then turned and led the crowd toward the sound of the fiddles, relief in his eyes.

Katherine sat unmoving, dreading the prospect of having to dance with any of the drunken planters. She watched through the dim candlelight as Winston reached for an open flask of kill-devil, took a triumphant swig, then slammed it down. She suddenly realized the table had been entirely vacated save for the two of them.

The audacity! Of course it had all been a bluff. Anyone

64

should have been able to tell. He'd just wanted the indentures all along. But why?

"I suppose congratulations are in order, Captain."

"Pardon?" He looked up, not recognizing her through the smoke and flickering shadows. "Forgive me, madam, I didn't catch what you said."

"Congratulations. That was a fine show you put on with your pistol."

He seemed momentarily startled, but then he laughed at his own surprise and took another swig of kill-devil. "Thank you very much." He wiped his mouth, set down the bottle, and glanced back. "Forgive me if I disturbed your evening."

"Where did you learn to shoot like that?"

"I used to do a bit of hunting."

"Have you ever actually shot a man?"

"Not that I choose to remember."

"I thought so. It really *was* a bluff." Her eyebrows lifted. "So may I enquire what is it you propose doing now with your two hundred men and provisions?"

"You're Miss Bedford, if I'm not mistaken." He rose, finally making her out. "I don't seem to recall our being introduced." He bowed with a flourish. "Hugh Winston, your most obedient servant." Then he reached for the flask of kill-devil as he lowered back into his chair. "I'd never presume to address a . . . lady unless we're properly acquainted."

She found the hint of sarcasm in his tone deliberately provoking. She watched as he took another drink directly from the bottle.

"I don't seem to recall ever seeing you speak with a lady, Captain."

"You've got a point." His eyes twinkled. "Perhaps it's because there're so few out here in the Caribbees."

"Or could it be you're not aware of the difference?" His insolent parody of politeness had goaded her into a tone not entirely to her own liking.

"So I've sometimes been told." Again his voice betrayed his pleasure. "But then I doubt there is much, really." He grinned. "At least, by the time they get around to educating me on that topic."

As happened only rarely, she couldn't think of a sufficiently cutting riposte. She was still searching for one when he continued, all the while examining her in the same obvious way he'd done on the shore. "Excuse me, but I believe you enquired about something. The men and provisions, I believe it was. The plain answer is I plan to take them and leave Barbados, as soon as I can manage."

"And where is it you expect you'll be going?" She found her footing again, and this time she planned to keep it.

"Let's say, on a little adventure. To see a new part of the world." He was staring at her through the candlelight. "I've had about enough of this island of yours, Miss Bedford. As well as the new idea that slavery's going to make everybody rich. I'm afraid it's not my style."

"But I gather you're the man responsible for our noble new order here, Captain."

He looked down at the flask, his smile vanishing. "If that's true, I'm not especially proud of the fact."

At last she had him. All his arrogance had dissolved. Just like Jeremy, that time she asked him to tell her what *exactly* he'd done in the battle at Marsten Moor. Yet for some reason she pulled back, still studying him.

"It's hard to understand you, Captain. You help them steal sugarcane from the Portugals, then you decide you don't like it."

"At the time it was a job, Miss Bedford. Let's say I've changed my mind since then. Things didn't turn out exactly the way I'd figured they would." He took another drink, then set down the bottle and laughed. "That always seems to be the way."

"What do you mean?"

"It's something like the story of my life." His tone waxed

slightly philosophical as he stared at the flickering candle. "I always end up being kicked about by events. So now I've decided to try turning things around. Do a little kicking of my own."

"That's a curious ambition. I suppose these indentures are going to help you do it?" She was beginning to find him more interesting than she'd expected. "You said just now you learned to shoot by hunting. I know a lot of men who hunt, but I've never seen anything like what you did tonight. Where exactly did you learn that?"

He paused, wondering how much to say. The place, of course, was Tortuga, and these days that meant the Cow-Killers, men who terrified the settlers of the Caribbean. But this wasn't a woman he cared to frighten. He was beginning to like her brass, the way she met his eye. Maybe, he thought, he'd explain it all to her if he got a chance someday. But not tonight. The story was too long, too painful, and ended too badly.

His memories of Tortuga went back to the sultry autumn of 1631. Just a year before, that little island had been taken over by a group of English planters—men and women who'd earlier tried growing tobacco up on St. Christopher, only to run afoul of its Carib Indians and their poisoned arrows. After looking around for another island, they'd decided on Tortuga, where nobody lived then except for a few hunters of wild cattle, the Cow-Killers. Since the hunters themselves spent a goodly bit of their time across the channel on the big Spanish island of Hispaniola, Tortuga was all but empty.

But now these planters were living just off the northern coast of a major Spanish domain, potentially much more dangerous than merely having a few Indians about. So they petitioned the newly formed Providence Company in London to swap a shipment of cannon for a tobacco contract. The

Company, recently set up by some Puritan would-be privateers, happily agreed.

Enter Hugh Winston. He'd just been apprenticed for three months to the Company by his royalist parents, intended as a temporary disciplining for some unpleasant reflections he'd voiced on the character of King Charles that summer after coming home from his first term at Oxford. Lord Winston and his wife Lady Brett, knowing he despised the Puritans for their hypocrisy, assumed this would be the ideal means to instill some royalist sympathies. As it happened, two weeks later the Providence Company posted this unwelcome son of two prominent monarchists out to Tortuga on the frigate delivering their shipment of guns.

No surprise, Governor Hilton of the island's Puritan settlement soon had little use for him either. After he turned out to show no more reverence for Puritans than for the monarchy, he was sent over to hunt on Hispaniola with the Cow-Killers. That's where he had to learn to shoot if he was to survive. As things turned out, being banished there probably saved his life.

When the Spaniards got word of this new colony, with Englishmen pouring in from London and Bristol, the Audiencia of Santo Domingo, the large Spanish city on Hispaniola's southern side, decided to make an example. So in January of 1635 they put together an assault force of some two hundred fifty infantry, sailed into Tortuga's harbor, and staged a surprise attack. As they boasted afterward, they straightaway put to the sword all those they first captured, then hanged any others who straggled in later. By the time they'd finished, they'd burned the settlement to the ground and killed over six hundred men, women and children. They also hanged a few of the Cow-Killers—a mistake that soon changed history.

When Jacques le Basque, the bearded leader of Hispaniola's hunters, found out what had happened to his men, he vowed he was going to bankrupt and destroy Spain's New

68

World empire in revenge. From what was heard these days, he seemed well on his way to succeeding.

Hugh Winston had been there, a founding member of that band of men now known as the most vicious marauders the world had ever seen. That was the piece of his life he'd never gotten around to telling anyone. . . .

"I did some hunting when I was apprenticed to an English settlement here in the Caribbean. Years ago."

"Well, I must say you shoot remarkably well for a tobacco planter, Captain." She knew he was avoiding her question. Why?

"I thought I'd just explained. I also hunted some in those days." He took another drink, then sought to shift the topic. "Perhaps now I can be permitted to ask *you* a question, Miss Bedford. I'd be interested to know what you think of the turn things are taking here? That is, in your official capacity as First Lady of this grand settlement."

"What exactly do you mean?" God damn his supercilious tone.

"The changes ahead. Here on Barbados." He waved his hand. "Will everybody grow rich, the way they're claiming?"

"Some of the landowners are apt to make a great deal of money, if sugar prices hold." Why, she wondered, did he want to know? Was he planning to try and settle down? Or get into the slave trade himself? In truth, that seemed more in keeping with what he did for a living now.

"Some? And why only some?" He examined her, puzzling. "Every planter must already own a piece of this suddenly valuable land."

"The Council members and the other big landowners are doubtless thinking to try and force out the smaller freeholders, who'll not have a sugarworks and therefore be at their mercy." She began to toy deliberately with her glass, uncomfortable at the prospect she was describing. "It's really quite simple, Captain. I'm sure you can grasp the basic principles of commerce . . . given your line of work.''

''No little fortunes? just a few big ones?'' Oddly, he refused to be baited.

''You've got it precisely. But what does that matter to you? You don't seem to care all that much what happens to our small freeholders.''

''If that's true, it's a sentiment I probably share with most of the people who were at this table tonight.'' He raised the empty flask of kill-devil and studied it thoughtfully against the candle. ''So if Briggs and the rest are looking to try and take it all, then I'd say you're in for a spell of stormy weather here, Miss Bedford.''

''Well, their plans are far from being realized, that I promise you. Our Assembly will stand up to them all the way.''

''Then I suppose I should wish you, and your father, and your Assembly luck. You're going to need it.'' He flung the empty flask crashing into the fireplace, rose, and moved down the table. The light seemed to catch in his scar as he passed the candle. ''And now perhaps you'll favor me with the next dance.''

She looked up, startled, as he reached for her hand.

''Captain, I think you ought to know that I'm planning to be married.''

''To one of these rich planters, I presume.''

''To a gentleman, if you know what that is. And a man who would not take it kindly if he knew I was seen with you here tonight.''

''Oh?''

''Yes. Anthony Walrond.''

Winston erupted with laughter. ''Well, good for him. He also has superb taste in flintlock muskets. Please tell him that when next you see him.''

''You mean the ones you stole from his ship that went aground? I don't expect he would find that comment very amusing.''

"Wouldn't he now." Winston's eyes flashed. "Well, damned to him. And if you want to hear something even less amusing than that, ask him sometime to tell you *why* I took those muskets." He reached for her hand. "At any rate, I'd like to dance with his lovely fiancée."

"I've already told you . . ."

"But it's so seldom a man like me is privileged to meet a true lady." His smile suddenly turned gracious. "As you were thoughtful enough to point out only a few moments ago. Why not humor me? I don't suppose you're his property. You seem a trifle too independent for that."

Anthony would doubtless be infuriated, but she found herself smiling back. Anyway, how would he ever find out? None of these Puritans even spoke to him. Besides, what else was there to do? Sit and stare at the greasy tankards on the table? . . . But what exactly had Hugh Winston meant about Anthony's muskets?

"Very well. Just one."

"I'm flattered." He was sweeping her through the archway, into the next room.

The fiddles were just starting a new tune, while the planters and their wives lined up facing each other, beginning the country dance Flaunting Two. As couples began to step forward one by one, then whirl down the room in turns to the music, Katherine found herself joining the end of the women's line. Moments later Winston bowed to her, heels together, then spun her down the makeshift corridor between the lines. He turned her away from him, then back, elegantly, in perfect time with the fiddle bows.

The dance seemed to go on forever, as bodies smelling of sweat and kill-devil jostled together in the confinement of the tiny room. Yet it was invigorating, purging all her misgivings over the struggle that lay ahead. When she moved her body to her will like this, she felt in control of everything. As if she were riding, the wind hard against her cheek. Then, as now, she could forget about Anthony, the Council, about everything. Why couldn't all of life be managed the same way?

When the dance finally concluded, the fiddlers scarcely paused before striking up another.

"Just one more?" He was bending over, saying something.

"What?" She looked up at him, not hearing his words above the music and noise and bustle of the crowd. Whatever it was he'd said, it couldn't be all that important. She reached for his hand and guided him into the next dance.

A loud clanging resounded through the room, causing the fiddles to abruptly halt and startling Katherine, who found herself alarmed less by the sound than by the deadening return of reality. She looked around to see Benjamin Briggs standing in the center of the floor, slamming a large bell with a mallet.

"Attention gentlemen and ladies, if you please." He was shouting, even though the room had gone silent. "All's ready. The sugarworks start-up is *now.*"

There was general applause around the room. He waited till it died away, then continued, in a more moderate tone.

"I presume the ladies will prefer to retire above stairs rather than chance the night air. There's feather beds and hammocks ready, and the servants'll bring the candles and chamber pots."

Winston listened in mock attentiveness, then leaned over toward Katherine.

"Then I must bid you farewell, Miss Bedford. And lose you to more worthy companions."

She looked at him dumbly, her blood still pumping from the dance. The exhilaration and release were the very thing she'd been needing.

"I have no intention of missing the grand start-up." She

tried to catch her breath. "It's to be history in the making, don't you recall?"

"That it truly will be." He shrugged. "But are you sure the sugarworks is any place for a woman?"

"As much as a man." She glared back at him. "There's a woman there already, Captain. Briggs' mulatto. I heard him say she's in the boiling house tonight, showing one of the new Africans how to heat the sap. She supposedly ran one once in Brazil."

"Maybe she just told him that to avoid the dance." He turned and watched the planters begin filing out through the wide rear door. "Shall we join them, then?"

As they walked out into the courtyard, the cool night air felt delicious against her face and sweltering bodice. At the back of the compound Briggs was opening a heavy wooden gate in the middle of the ten-foot-high stone wall that circled his house.

"These Africans'll make all the difference, on my faith. It's already plain as can be." He cast a withering glance at Katherine as she and Winston passed, then he followed them through, ordering the servants to secure the gate. The planters were assembled in a huddle now, surrounded by several of Briggs' indentures holding candle-lanterns. He took up his place at the front of the crowd and began leading them down the muddy road toward the torch-lit sugarworks lying to the left of the plantation house.

Along the road were the thatched cabins of the indentured servants, and beyond these was a cluster of half-finished reed and clay huts, scarcely head high, that the Africans had begun constructing for themselves.

"They're sound workers, for all their peculiar ways." Briggs paused and pointed to a large drum resting in front of one of the larger huts. It was shaped like an hourglass, and separate goatskins had been stretched over each mouth and laced together, end to end. "What do you make of that contrivance? The first thing they did was start making this drum.

73

And all this morning, before sunup, they were pounding on it. Damnedest racket this side of hell.''

"Aye, mine did the very same," Lancaster volunteered. "I heard them drumming all over the island."

Briggs walked on. "They gathered 'round that Yoruba called Atiba, who's shaking some little seashells on a tray and chanting some of their gabble. After a time he'd say something to one of them and then there'd be more drumming." He shook his head in amazement. "Idolatry worse'n the Papists."

"I've a mind to put a stop to it," Whittington interjected. "The indentures are already complaining."

"It's a bother, I grant you. But I see no harm in their customs, long as they put in a day's work. The place I drew the line was when they started trying to bathe in my pond every night, when any Christian knows baths are a threat to health. But for it all, one of them will cut more cane than three Irishmen." He cast a contemptuous glance backward at Timothy Farrell, who was following at a distance, holding several bottles of kill-devil. "From sunup to sundown. Good workers, to the man. So if they choose to beat on drums, I say let them. It's nothing from my pocket."

Katherine watched Winston shake his head in dismay as he paused to pick up the drum, turning it in his hands.

"You seem troubled about their drumming, Captain. Why's that?"

He looked up at her, almost as though he hadn't heard. "You've never been to Brazil, have you, Miss Bedford?"

"I have not."

"Then you probably wouldn't believe me, even if I told you." He looked back at the huts and seemed to be talking to himself. "God damn these Englishmen. They're fools."

"It's surely some kind of their African music."

"Obviously." His voice had a sarcastic cut, which she didn't particularly like. But before she could reply to him in kind, he had set down the drum and moved on, seeming to

74

have forgotten all about whatever it was that had so distressed him the moment before. Then he turned back to her. "May I enquire if you yourself play an instrument, Miss Bedford?"

"I once played the spinet." She reached down and picked up a small land crab wandering across their path. She examined it, then flung it aside, its claws flailing. "But I don't bother anymore."

He watched the crab bemusedly, then turned back. "Then you do know something about music?"

"We're not without some rudiments of education here on Barbados, Captain."

"And languages? Have you ever listened to these Yoruba talk? Theirs is a language of tones, you know. Same as their drums."

"Some of these new Africans have a curious-sounding speech, I grant you."

He stared at her a moment, as though preoccupied. "God help us all."

He might have said more, but then he glanced after the crowd, now moving down the road. Ahead of them a gang of blacks could be seen through the torchlight, carrying bundles of cane in from the field and stacking them in piles near the new mill, situated atop a slight rise. A group of white indentured workers was also moving cane toward the mill from somewhere beyond the range of the torchlight, whipping forward a team of oxen pulling a large two-wheeled cart stacked with bundles. She noticed Winston seemed in no great hurry, and instead appeared to be listening absently to the planters.

"Would you believe this is the very same cane we brought from Brazil?" Briggs was pointing toward a half-cut field adjacent to the road. "I planted October a year ago, just before the autumn rains. It's been sixteen months almost to the day, just like the Dutchmen said." He turned back to the crowd of planters. "The indentures weeded and dunged it, but I figured the Africans would be best for cutting it, and I was right. Born field workers. They'll be a godsend if they can be trained to run the sugarworks." He lowered his voice. "This is the last we'll need of these idling white indentures."

They were now approaching the mill, which was situated inside a new thatched-roof building. Intended for crushing the cane and extracting the juice, it would be powered by two large white oxen shipped down specially from Rhode Island.

The mill was a mechanism of three vertical brass rollers, each approximately a foot in diameter, that were cogged together with teeth around their top and bottom. A large round beam was secured through the middle of the central roller and attached to two long sweeps that extended outward to a circular pathway intended for the draft animals. When the sweeps were moved, the beam would rotate and with it the rollers.

"We just finished installing the rollers tonight. There was no chance to test it. But I explained the operation to the indentures. We'll see if they can remember."

An ox had been harnessed to each of the two sweeps; as Briggs approached he signaled the servants to whip them forward. The men nodded and lashed out at the animals, who snorted, tossed their heads, then began to trudge in a circular path around the mill. Immediately the central roller began to turn, rotating the outer rollers against it by way of its cogs. As the rollers groaned into movement, several of the indentures backed away and studied them nervously.

"Well, what are you waiting for?" Briggs yelled at the two men standing nearest the mill, holding the first bundles of cane. "Go ahead and try feeding it through."

One of the men moved gingerly toward the grinding rollers and reached out, at arm's length, to feed a small bundle consisting of a half dozen stalks of cane into the side rotating away from him. There was a loud crackle as the bundle began to gradually disappear between the rollers. As the crushed cane stalks emerged on the rear side of the mill, a second indenture seized the flattened bundle and fed it back through the pair of rollers turning in the opposite direction. In moments a trickle of pale sap began sliding down the sides of the rollers and dripping into a narrow trough that led through the wall and down the incline toward the boiling house.

Briggs walked over to the trough and examined the running sap in silence. Then he dipped in a finger and took it to his lips. He savored it for a moment, looked up, triumph in his eyes, and motioned the other men forward.

"Have a taste. It's the sweetest nectar there could ever be." As the planters gathered around the trough sampling the first cane juice, indentures continued feeding a steady progression of cane bundles between the rollers. While the planters stood watching, the trough began to flow.

"It works, by Christ." Marlott emitted a whoop and dipped in for a second taste. "The first English sugar mill in all the world."

"We've just witnessed that grand historic moment, Miss Bedford." Winston turned back to her, his voice sardonic. "In a little more time, these wonderful sugarmills will probably cover Barbados. Together with the slaves needed to cut the cane for them. I'd wager that in a few years' time there'll be more Africans here than English. What we've just witnessed is not the beginning of the great English Caribbees, but the first step toward what'll one day be the great African Caribbees. I suggest we take time to savor it well."

His voice was drowned in the cheer rising up from the cluster of planters around Briggs. They had moved on down the incline now and were standing next to the boiling house, watching as the sap began to collect in a tank. Briggs scrutinized the tank a moment longer, then turned to the group. "This is where the sap's tempered with wet ashes just before it's boiled. That's how the Portugals do it. From here it runs through that trough,"—he indicated a second flow, now starting—"directly into the first kettle in the boiling house." He paused and gestured Farrell to bring the flasks forward. "I propose we take time to fortify ourselves against the heat before going in.''

"Shall we proceed?" Winston was pointing down the hill. Then he laughed. "Or would you like some liquor first?"

"Please." She pushed past him and headed down the incline. They reached the door of the boiling house well before the planters, who were lingering at the tank, passing the flask. Winston ducked his head at the doorway and they passed through a wide archway and into a thatched-roof enclosure containing a long, waist-high furnace of Dutch brick. In the back, visible only from the light of the open furnace door, were two figures: Briggs' new Yoruba slave Atiba and his Portuguese mistress, Serina.

Katherine, who had almost forgotten how beautiful the mulatto was, found herself slightly relieved that Serina was dressed in perfect modesty. She wore a full-length white shift, against which her flawless olive skin fairly glowed in the torchlight. As they entered, she was speaking animatedly with Atiba while bending over to demonstrate how to feed dry cane tops into the small openings along the side of the furnace. When she spotted them, however, she pulled suddenly erect and fell silent, halting in mid-sentence.

The heat in the room momentarily took away Katherine's breath, causing her to stand in startled disorientation. It was only then that she realized Hugh Winston was pulling at her sleeve. Something in the scene apparently had taken him completely by surprise.

Then she realized what it was. Serina had been speaking to the tall, loincloth-clad Yoruba in an alien language that sounded almost like a blend of musical tones and stops.

Now the planters began barging through the opening, congratulating Briggs as they clustered around the string of copper cauldrons cemented into the top of the long furnace. Then, as the crowd watched expectantly, a trickle of cane sap flowed down from the holding tank and spattered into the first red-hot cauldron.

The men erupted with a cheer and whipped their hats into the air. Again the brown flask of kill-devil was passed appreciatively. After taking a long swallow, Briggs turned to Serina, gesturing toward Atiba as he addressed her in pidgin Portuguese, intended to add an international flavor to the evening.

"*Êle compreendo?*"

"*Sim. Compreendo.*" She nodded, reached for a ladle, and began to skim the first gathering of froth off the top of the boiling liquid. Then she dumped the foam into a clay pot beside the furnace.

"She's supposed to know how fast to feed the furnaces to keep the temperature right. And when to ladle the liquor into the next cauldron down the row." He stepped back from the furnace, fanning himself with his hat, and turned to the men. "According to the way the Portugals do it in Brazil, the clarified liquor from the last cauldron in the line here is moved to a cistern to cool for a time, then it's filled into wooden pots and moved to the curing house."

"Is that ready too?" A husky voice came from somewhere in the crowd.

"Aye, and I've already had enough pots made to get started. We let the molasses drain out and the sugar cure for three or four months, then we move the pots to the knocking house, where we turn them over and tap out a block of sugar. The top and bottom are brown sugar, what the Portugals call *muscavado*, and the center is pure white." He reached again for the bottle and took a deep swallow. "Twenty pence a pound in London, when our tobacco used to clear three farthings."

"To be sure, the mill and the boiling house are the key. We'll have to start building these all over the island." Thomas Lancaster removed his black hat to wipe his brow, then pulled it firmly back on his head. "And start training the Africans in their operation. No white man could stand this heat."

"She should have this one trained in a day or so." Briggs

thumbed toward Atiba, now standing opposite the door examining the planters. "Then we can have him train more."

"I'll venture you'd do well to watch that one particularly close." Edward Bayes lowered his voice, speaking into his beard. "There's a look about him."

"Aye, he's cantankerous, I'll grant you, but he's quick. He just needs to be tamed. I've already had to flog him once, ten lashes, the first night here, when he balked at eating *loblolly* mush."

"Ten, you say?" Dalby Bedford did not bother to disguise the astonishment in his voice. "Would you not have done better to start with five?"

"Are you lecturing me now on how to best break in my Africans?" Briggs glared. "I paid for them, sir. They're my property, to manage as I best see fit."

Nicholas Whittington murmured his assent, and others concurred.

"As you say, gentlemen. But you've got three more Dutch slavers due within a fortnight. I understand they're supposed to be shipping Barbados a full three thousand this year alone." Bedford looked about the room with a concerned expression. "That'll be just a start, if sugar production expands the way it seems it will. It might be well if we had the Assembly pass Acts for ordering and governing these slaves."

"Damn your Assembly. We already have laws for property on Barbados."

Again the other planters voiced their agreement. Bedford stood listening, then lifted his hand for quiet. Katherine found herself wishing he would be as blunt with them as Winston had been. Sometimes the governor's good manners got in the way, something that hardly seemed to trouble Hugh Winston.

"I tell you this is no light matter. No man in this room knows how to manage all these Africans. What Englishman has ever been responsible for twenty, thirty, nay perhaps even a hundred slaves? They've to be clothed in some manner, fed, paired for offspring. And religion, sir? Some of the

Quakers we've let settle in Bridgetown are already starting to say your blacks should be baptized and taught Christianity."

"You can't be suggesting it? If we let them be made Christians, where would it end?" Briggs examined him in disbelief. "You'd have laws, sir, Acts of your Assembly. Well there's the place to start. I hold the first law should be to fine and set in the stocks any of these so-called Quakers caught trying to teach our blacks Christianity. We'll not stand for it."

Katherine saw Serina's features tense and her eyes harden, but she said nothing, merely continued to skim the foam from the boiling surface of the cauldron.

"The Spaniards and Portugals teach the Catholic faith to their Negroes," Bedford continued evenly.

"And there you have the difference. They're not English. They're Papists." Briggs paused as he studied the flow of cane sap entering the cauldron from the holding tank, still dripping slowly from the lead spout. "By the looks of it, it could be flowing faster." He studied it a moment longer, then turned toward the door. "The mill. Maybe that's the answer. What if we doubled the size of the cane bundles?"

Katherine watched the planters trail after Briggs, out the doorway and into the night, still passing the flask of kill-devil.

"What do *you* think, Captain? Should an African be made a Christian?"

"Theology's not my specialty, Miss Bedford." He walked past her. "Tell me first if you think a Puritan's one." He was moving toward Serina, who stood silently skimming the top of the first cauldron, now a vigorous boil. She glanced up once and examined him, then returned her eyes to the froth. Katherine just managed to catch a few words as he began speaking to her quietly in fluent Portuguese, as though to guard against any of the planters accidentally overhearing.

"Senhora, how is it you know the language of the Africans?"

She looked up for a moment without speaking, her eyes disdainful. "I'm a slave too, as you well know, senhor." Then she turned and continued with the ladle.

"But you're a Portugal."

"And never forget that. I am not one of these *preto*." She spat out the Portuguese word for Negro.

Atiba continued methodically shoving cane tops into the roaring mouth of the furnace.

"But you were speaking to him just now in his own language. I recognized it."

"He asked a question, and I answered him, that's all."

"Then you *do* know his language? How?"

"I know many things." She fixed his eyes, continuing in Portuguese. "Perhaps it surprises you Inglês that a *mulata* can speak at all. I also know how to read, something half the *branco* rubbish who were in this room tonight probably cannot do."

Katherine knew only a smattering of Portuguese, but she caught the part about some of the *branco*, the whites, not being able to read. She smiled to think there was probably much truth in that. Certainly almost none of the white indentures could. Further, she suspected that many of the planters had never bothered to learn either.

"I know you were educated in Brazil." Winston was pressing Serina relentlessly. "I was trying to ask you how you know the language of this African"

She paused, her face a blend of haughtiness and regret. She started to speak, then stopped herself.

"Won't you tell me?"

She turned back, as though speaking to the cauldron. "My mother was Yoruba."

"Is that how you learned?" His voice was skeptical.

"I was taught also by a *babalawo*, a Yoruba priest, in Brazil."

"What's she saying?" Katherine moved next to him, shielding her eyes from the heat.

"Desculpe, senhora, excuse me." Winston quickly moved forward, continuing in Portuguese as he motioned toward Katherine. "This is . . ."

"I know perfectly well who Miss Bedford is." Serina interrupted him, still in Portuguese.

Katherine stared at her, not catching the foreign words. "Is she talking about me?"

"She said her mother was a Yoruba." Winston moved between them. "And she said something about a priest."

"Is she some sort of priest? Is that what she said?"

"No." Serina's English answer was quick and curt, then she said something else to Winston, in Portuguese.

"She said she was not, though the women of her mother's family have practiced divination for many generations."

"Divination?" Katherine studied him, puzzled. Then she turned back to Serina. "What do you mean by that?"

Serina was looking at her now, for the first time. "Divination is the way the Yoruba people ask their gods to tell the future."

"How exactly do they go about doing such a thing?"

"Many ways." She turned back to the cauldron.

Winston stood in the silence for a moment, then turned to Katherine. "I think one of the ways is with shells. In Brazil I once saw a Yoruba diviner shaking a tray with small seashells in it."

Serina glanced back, now speaking English. "I see you are an Inglês who bothers to try and understand other peoples. One of the few I've ever met. *Felicitacao,* senhor, my compliments. Yes, that is one of the ways, and the most sacred to a Yoruba. It's called the divination of the sixteen cowrie shells. A Yoruba diviner foretells the will of the gods from how the shells lie in a tray after it has been shaken—by how many lie with the slotted side up. It's the way the gods talk to him."

"Who are these gods they speak to?" Katherine found herself challenged by the mulatto's haughtiness.

Serina continued to stir the cauldron. "You'd not know them, senhora."

"But I would be pleased to hear of them." Katherine's voice was sharp, but then she caught herself and softened it. "Are they something like the Christian God?"

Serina paused, examining Katherine for a moment, and then her eyes assumed a distant expression. "I do not know much about them. I know there is one god like the Christian God. He is the high god, who never shows his powers on earth. But there are many other gods who do. The one the Yoruba call on most is Shango, the god of thunder and lightning, and of fire. His symbol is the double-headed axe. There also is Ogun, who is the god of iron." She hesitated. "And the god of war."

Katherine studied her. "Do you believe in all these African deities yourself?"

"Who can say what's really true, senhora?" Her smooth skin glistened from the heat. She brushed the hair from her eyes in a graceful motion, as though she were in a drawing room, while her voice retreated again into formality. "The Yoruba even believe that many different things can be true at once. Something no European can ever understand."

"There's something *you* may not understand, senhora," Winston interjected, speaking now in English. "And I think you well should. The Yoruba in this room also knows the language of the Portugals. Take care what you say."

"It's not possible." She glanced at Atiba contemptuously, continuing loudly in Portuguese. "He's a saltwater *preto.*"

Before Winston could respond, there was an eruption of shouts and curses from the direction of the mill. They all turned to watch as Benjamin Briggs shoved through the doorway, pointing at Atiba.

"Get that one out here. I warrant he can make them understand." The sweltering room seemed frozen in time, except for Briggs, now motioning at Serina. "Tell him to come out here." He revolved to Winston. "I've a mind to flog all of them."

"What's wrong?"

"The damned mill. I doubled the size of the bundles, the very thing I should've done in the first place, but now the oxen can't turn it properly. I want to try hooking both oxen to one of the sweeps and a pair of Africans on the other. I've harnessed them up, but I can't get them to move." He motioned again for Atiba to accompany him. "This one's got more wit than all the rest together. Maybe I can show him what I want."

Serina gestured toward Atiba, who followed Briggs out the door, into the fresh night air. Katherine stared after him for a moment, then turned back. Winston was speaking to Serina again in Portuguese, but too rapidly to follow.

"Will you tell me one thing more?"

"As you wish, senhor." She did not look up from the cauldron.

"What was going on last night? With the drums?"

She hesitated slightly. "I don't know what you mean."

Winston was towering over her now. "I think you know very *well* what I mean, senhora. Now tell me, damn it. What were they saying?"

She seemed not to hear him. Through the silence that filled the room, there suddenly came a burst of shouts from the direction of the mill.

Katherine felt fear sweep over her, and she found herself seizing Winston's arm, pulling him toward the doorway. Outside, the planters were milling about in confusion, vague shadows against the torchlight. Then she realized Atiba was trying to wrench off the harness from the necks of the two blacks tied to the sweeps of the mill, while yelling at Briggs in his African language.

She gripped Winston's arm tighter as she watched William Marlott, brandishing a heavy-bladed cane machete, move on Atiba. Then several other planters leapt out of the shadows, grabbed his powerful shoulders, and wrestled him to the ground.

"You'd best flog him here and now." Marlott looked up, sweat running down his face. "It'll be a proper lesson to all the rest."

Briggs nodded toward several of the white indentures and in moments a rope was lashed to Atiba's wrists. Then he was yanked against the mill, his face between the wet rollers. One of the indentures brought forward a braided leather horse-whip.

Katherine turned her face away, back toward the boiling house, not wanting to see.

Serina was standing in the doorway now, staring out blankly, a shimmering moistness in her eyes.

Chapter Four

For almost a month now, any night he could manage, Atiba had slipped unseen from the compound and explored the southern coast of the island, the shore and the upland hills. Now he was sure they could survive after the island became theirs. The *branco,* the white English, were savages, who destroyed all they touched, but there were still traces of what once had been. Between the fields of sterile cane he had found and tasted the fruits of the sacred earth.

There were groves of wild figs, their dark fruit luscious and astringent, and plump coconuts, their tender core as rich as any in Yorubaland. Along the shore were stands of sea-grape trees, with a sweet purple fruit biting to the tongue. He had also found palmlike trees clustered with the tender papaya, and farther inland there were groves of banana and plantain. He had discovered other trees with large oranges, plump with yellow nectar, as well as pomegranates and ta-marind just like those he had known in Ife, his home city. The soil itself gave forth moist melons, wild cucumbers, and the red apples of the prickly cactus. There also were cala-bash, the hard, round gourds the Inglês had already learned could be hollowed out for cups and basins. The only thing wanting was that staple of the Yoruba people, the yam.

But they would not have to survive from the soil alone. In the thickets he had heard the grunts and squeals of the wild hogs, fat sows foraging nuts, leading their litters. Along the shore he had seen flocks of feeding egrets in the dawn light, ready to be snared and roasted, and at his feet there had been hundreds of land crabs, night prowlers as big as two hands, ripe for boiling as they scurried back to their sand burrows along the shore.

He could not understand why the *branco* slaves who worked alongside the Yoruba allowed themselves to be fed on boiled corn mush. A natural bounty lay within arm's reach.

The Orisa, those forces in nature that work closest with man, were still present on the island. He could sense them, waiting in the wood of the trees. This ravished place had once been a great forest, like the one north of Ife, and it could be again. If the hand of the Inglês was taken from it, and the spirit of the Orisa, its rightful protectors, freed once more.

The first cooing of the wood dove sounded through the thatched hut, above the chorus of whistling frogs from the pond, signaling the approach of day. Atiba sat motionless in the graying light, crosslegged, at the edge of the mud seat nearest the door, and studied the sixteen cowrie shells as they spun across the reed tray that lay before him. As he watched, eight of the small ovals came to rest mouth up, in a wide crescent, the remainder facing down.

The tiny room was crowded with the men of the Yoruba, their cotton loincloths already drenched with sweat from the early heat. Now all eyes narrowed in apprehension, waiting for this *babalawo*, the priest of the Yoruba, to speak and interpret the verses that revealed the message in the cowries.

Bi a ko jiya ti o kun agbon
If we do not bear suffering that will fill a basket,

A ko le jore to kun inu aha
We will not receive kindness that will fill a cup.

He paused and signaled the tall, bearded drummer waiting by the door. The man's name was Obewole, and he had once been, many rains ago, the strongest drummer in the entire city of Ife. He nodded and shifted the large drum—the Yoruba *iya ilu*—that hung at his waist, suspended from a wide shoulder strap. Abruptly the small wooden mallet he held began to dance across the taut goatskin. The verses Atiba had just spoken were repeated exactly, the drum's tone changing in pitch and timbre as Obewole squeezed the cords down its hourglass waist between his arm and his side. Moments later there came the sound of more drums along the length of the southern coast, transmitting his verses inland. In less than a minute all the Yoruba on Barbados had heard their *babalawo*'s exact words.

Then he said something more and shook the tray again. This time five cowries lay open, set as a star. Again he spoke, his eyes far away.

> *A se'gi oko ma we oko*
> The tree that swims like a canoe,
>
> *A s'agada ja'ri erin*
> The sword that will cut iron.

Once more the drum sent the words over the morning quiet of the island.

Atiba waited a few moments longer, then slowly looked up and surveyed the expectant faces around him. The shells had spoken, true enough, but the message of the gods was perplexing. Seemingly Shango had counseled endurance, while Ogun foretold war.

He alone was priest, and he alone could interpret this contradictory reading. He knew in his heart what the gods wanted, what they surely *must* want. Still, the realization brought painful memories. He knew too well what war would mean. He had seen it many times—the flash of mirrored steel in the sunlight, the blood of other men on your hands, the deaths of wise fathers and strong sons.

The worst had been when he and his warriors had stood shoulder to shoulder defending the ancient royal compound at Ife with their lives, when the Fulani from the north had breached the high walls of the city and approached the very entrance of the ruling Oba's palace, those huge sculptured doors guarded by the two sacred bronze leopards. That day he and his men had lost more strong warriors than there were women to mourn them, but by nightfall they had driven out the worshippers of other gods who would take their lands, pillage their compounds, carry away their seed-yams and their youngest wives.

He also knew there could be betrayal. He had seen it during the last season of rains, when the drums had brought news of strangers in the southeastern quarter of the world that was Yorubaland. He and his men had left their compounds and marched all day through the rain. That night, among the trees, they had been fallen upon by Benin slavers, men of black skin who served the *branco* as a woman serves the payer of her bride-price.

But the men of the Yoruba would never be made to serve. Their gods were too powerful, their ancestors too proud. The Yoruba were destined to rule. Just as they had governed Yorubaland for a thousand years. Theirs was an ancient and noble people, nothing like the half-civilized Inglês on this island. In the great metropolis of Ife, surrounded by miles of massive concentric walls, the Yoruba had lived for generations in wide family compounds built of white clay, their courtyards open to light and air, walking streets paved with brick and stone, wearing embroidered robes woven of finest cotton, sculpting lost-wax bronzes whose artistry no Inglês could even imagine. They did not swelter in patched-together log huts like the Inglês planters here, or in thatched hovels like the Inglês planters' servants. And they paid reverence to

90

gods whose power was far greater than any *branco* had ever seen.

"The sky has no shadow. It reaches out in all directions to the edge of the world. In it are the sun, the moon, all that is." He paused, waiting for the drums, then continued. "I have gone out into the dark, the void that is night, and I have returned unharmed. I say the Orisa are here, strong. We must make war on the *branco* to free them once more." He paused again. "No man's day of death can be postponed. It is already known to all the gods. There is nothing we need fear."

After the drums had sent his words across the island, the hut fell quiet. Then there came a voice from a small, wizened man sitting on Atiba's left, a Yoruba older than the rest, with sweat pouring down the wrinkles of his long dark face.

"You are of royal blood, Atiba. Your father Balogun was one of the sixteen royal *babalawo* of the Oba of Ife, one of the great Awoni. It was he who taught you his skills." He cleared his throat, signifying his importance. "Yet I say you now speak as one who has drunk too many horns of palm wine. We are only men. Ogun will not come forth to carry our shields."

"Old Tahajo, you who are the oldest and wisest here tonight, you know full well I am but a man." Atiba paused, to demonstrate deference. He was chagrined that this elder who now honored his hut had to sit directly on the mud seat, that there was no buffalo skin to take down off the wall for him as there would have been in a compound at Ife. "Though the gods allow me to read their words in the cowries, I still eat the food a woman cooks."

"I know you are a man, son of Balogun, and the finest ever sired in Ife. I knew you even before you grew of age, before you were old enough to tie a cloth between your legs. I was there the day your clan marks were cut in your cheek, those three proud lines that mark you the son of your father. Be his son now, but speak to us today as a man, not as *babalawo*. Let us hear your own voice."

Atiba nodded and set aside the tray. Then he turned back to the drummer and reached for his gleaming machete. "Since Tahajo wishes it, we will wait for another time to consult more with Ogun and Shango. Now I will hold a sword and speak simply, as a man."

Obewole nodded and picked up the mallet.

"This island was once ruled by the Orisa of the forest. But now there is only cane. Its sweetness is bitter in the mouths of the gods, for it has stolen their home. I say we must destroy it. To do this we will call down the fire of lightning that Shango guards in the sky."

"How can we call down Shango's fire?" The old man spoke again. None of the others in the cramped hut dared question Atiba so boldly. "No man here is consecrated to Shango. We are all warriors, men of Ogun. His power is only over the earth, not the skies."

"I believe there is one on this island whose lineage is Shango. A woman. Perhaps she no longer even knows it. But through her we will reach him." He turned and signaled Obewole to ready the drum. "Now I will speak. Hear me. Shango's spirit is here, on this island. He will help us take away the strength of the Inglês." He paused for the drums, then continued, "I learned on the ship that before the next new moon there will be many more of us here. The other warriors who were betrayed by the Benin traitors will be with us again. Then we will take out the fire of Shango that the Inglês hold prisoner in the boiling house and release it in the night, among the fields of cane. We will burn the compounds of the Inglês and take their muskets. Then we will free the white slaves. They are too craven to free themselves, but they will not stand with their *branco* masters."

He turned again to Obewole and nodded. "Send the words."

Winston shifted uneasily in his sleep, then bolted upright, rubbing the slight ache of his scar as he became aware of the distant spatter of drums. They were sporadic, but intense. Patterns were being repeated again and again all down the coast.

He slipped from the bed and moved quietly to the slatted window, to listen more closely. But now the drums had fallen silent. The only sounds left in the sweltering predawn air were the cooing of wood doves and the harsh "quark" of egrets down by the bridge, accompanied by Joan's easy snores. He looked back and studied her face again, realizing that time was beginning to take its toll. He also knew he didn't care, though he figured she did, mightily.

She'd never concede he could take Jamaica. Maybe she was right. But odds be damned. It was time to make a stand.

Jamaica. He thought about it again, his excitement swelling. Enough cannon, and the Spaniards could never retake it, never even get a warship into the harbor. It was perfect. A place of freedom that would strike a blow against forced labor throughout the New World.

Not a minute too soon either. The future was clear as day. The English settlers in the Caribbees were about to install what had to be the most absolute system of human slavery ever seen. Admittedly, finding sufficient men and women to work the fields had always been the biggest impediment to developing the virgin lands of the Americas, especially for settlements that wanted to grow money crops for export. But now Barbados had discovered Africans. What next? If slavery proved it could work for sugar in the Caribbees, then it probably would also be instituted for cotton and tobacco in Virginia. Agricultural slavery had started here, but soon it would doubtless be introduced wholesale into North America.

Christians, perpetrating the most unspeakable crime against humanity possible. Who knew what it would someday lead to?

He no longer asked himself why he detested slavery so much, but there was a reason, if he'd wanted to think about it. A man was a man. Seeing Briggs horsewhip his Yoruba was too similar to watching Ruyters flog his seamen. He had tasted the cat-o'-nine-tails himself more than once. In fact, whipping the Yoruba was almost worse, since a seaman could always jump ship at the next port. But a slave, especially on a small island like Barbados, had nowhere to go. No escape.

Not yet. But come the day Jamaica was his . . .

"Are you all right, love?" Joan had awakened and was watching him.

"I was listening to the drums. And thinking." He did not turn.

"Those damned drums. Every morning. Why don't the planters put a halt to it?" She raised up and swabbed her face with the rough cotton sheet. "God curse this heat."

"I'm tired of all of it. Particularly slavery."

"I fancy these Africans are not your worry. You'd best be rethinking this daft scheme of yours with the indentures."

"That's on schedule. The Council agreed to the terms, drew up a list of men, and I picked the ones I wanted."

"What're you thinkin' to do about ordnance?" Skepticism permeated her groggy voice.

"I've got a batch of new flintlocks on the *Defiance*. Generously supplied to me by Anthony Walrond's trading company." He laughed. "In grateful appreciation for helping out that frigate of theirs that went aground up by Nevis Island."

"I heard about that. I also hear he'd like those muskets back."

"He can see me in hell about that." He was strolling back toward the bed, nude in the early light. She admired the hard ripple of his chest, the long, muscular legs. "Also, I've got the boys at work making some half-pikes. We've set up a forge down by the bay."

"And what, pray, are you expectin' to use for pikestaffs?"

"We're having to cut palm stalks." He caught her look. "I know. But what can I do? There's no cured wood to be had on this short a notice."

94

"Lo, what an army you'll have." She laughed wryly. "Do you really think all those indentures will fight?"

"For their freedom, yes." He settled onto the bed. "That's what I'm counting on."

"Well, you're counting wrong, love. Most of them don't care a damn for anything, except maybe drinkin' in the shade. Believe me, I know them."

"I'll give them something to fight for. It won't be like here, where they're worked to death, then turned out to starve."

"I could tell you a few stories about human nature that might serve to enlighten you." She stretched back and pulled up her shift to rub a mosquito bite on her thigh. "If it was me, I'd be trying to get hold of some of these Africans. From the scars I've seen on a few of them, I'd say they've done their share of fighting. On my faith, they scare the wits half out of me."

"They make me uneasy too."

"How do you mean, darlin'?"

"All these drums we've been hearing. I found out in Brazil the Yoruba there can talk somehow with a special kind of drum they've got, one that looks like a big hourglass. I figure those here can do it too, only nobody realizes it. Let me tell you, Joan, there was plenty of Yoruba talk this morning. So far, the Africans here are considerably outnumbered, but if they start a revolt, the indentures might decide to rise up too. Then . . ."

"Some indentures here tried a little uprising once, a couple of years back. And about a dozen got hanged for their pains. I don't fancy they'll try it again soon."

"Don't be so sure. Remember how the Irish indentures went over to the Spaniards that time they attacked the English settlement up on Nevis Island? They swam out to the Spaniards' frigates, hailed them as fellow Papists, and then told them exactly where all the fortifications were."

"But how many of these Africans are there here now? Probably not all that many."

"Maybe not yet. With the Dutch slavers that've come so far, I'd guess there're no more than a couple of thousand or so. But there're more slave ships coming every week. Who knows what'll happen when there're three or four thousand, or more?"

"It'll not happen soon. How can it?" She slipped her arms around his neck and drew him down next to her. "Let's talk about something else. Tell me how you plan to take Jamaica. God's life, I still don't know why you'd want to try doing it at all."

"You're just afraid I *can't* do it." He turned and kissed her, then pulled down the top of her shift and nipped at one of her exposed breasts. "Tell me the truth."

"Maybe I will someday. If you get back alive." She took his face in her hands and lifted it away. "By the bye, I hear you had a fine time at the ball. Dancin' with that jade."

"Who?"

"You know who, you whoremaster. The high and mighty Miss Bedford."

"I'd had a bit to drink. I don't precisely recall what all happened."

"Don't you now? Well, some of the Council recall that evening well enough, you can be sure. You weren't too drunk to scare the wits out of them with those Spanish pistols. It's the talk of the island." She watched as he returned his mouth to her breast and began to tease the nipple with his tongue. "Now listen to me. That little virgin's no good for you. For one thing, I hear she's supposed to be marryin' our leading royalist, Sir Anthony, though I swear I don't know what he sees in her. She's probably happier ridin' her horse than being with a man. I warrant she'd probably as soon be a man herself."

"I don't want to hear any more about Miss Bedford." He

slipped an arm beneath her and drew her up next to him. "I've got something else in mind."

She trailed her hand down his chest to his groin. Then she smiled. "My, but *that's* promisin'."

"There's always apt to be room for improvement. If you set your mind to it."

"God knows, I've spoiled you." She leaned over and kissed his thigh, then began to tease him with her tongue. Without a word he shifted around and brushed the stubble of his cheeks against her loins. She was already moist, from sweat and desire.

"God, *that's* why I always let you come back." She moved against him with a tiny shudder. "When by rights I should know better. Sometimes I think I taught you too well what pleases me."

"I know something else you like even better." He seized a plump down pillow and stationed it in the middle of the bed, then started to reach for her. She was assessing her handiwork admiringly. He was ready, the way she wanted him.

"Could be." She drew herself above him. "But you can't always be havin' everything your own way. You've got me feelin' too randy this mornin'. So now I'm going to show you why your frustrated virgin, Miss Bedford, fancies ridin' that horse of hers so much."

Serina was already awake before the drums started. Listening intently to catch the soft cadence of the verses, she repeated them silently, knowing they meant the cowrie shells had been cast.

It was madness.

Benjamin Briggs sometimes called her to his room in the mornings, but she knew there would be no call today. He had ordered her from his bed just after midnight, drunk and cursing about a delay at the sugarmill.

Who had cast the cowries? Was it the tall, strong one named Atiba? Could it be he was also a Yoruba *babalawo?*

She had heard the verses for the cowries once before, years ago in Brazil. There were thousands, which her mother had recited for her all in one week, the entire canon. Even now she still remembered some of them, just a few. Her mother had never admitted to anybody else she knew the verses, since women weren't supposed to cast the cowries. The men of the Yoruba always claimed the powers of the cowries were too great for any save a true *babalawo,* and no woman would ever be permitted to be that. Women were only allowed to consult the gods by casting the four quarters of the kola nut, which only foretold daily matters. Important affairs of state were reserved for the cowries, and for men. But her mother had secretly learned the verses; she'd never said how. She'd even promised to explain them one day, but that day never came.

When she was sure the drums had finished, she rose slowly from the sweltering pallet that served as her bed and searched the floor in the half-dark till she felt the smooth cotton of her shift. She slipped it on, then began brushing her long gleaming hair, proud even now that it had always been straight, like a Portuguese *donna*'s.

She slept alone in a small room next to the second-floor landing of the back stairway, the one by the kitchen that was used by servants. When she had finished with her hair and swirled it into a high bun, Portuguese style, she slowly pushed open the slatted jalousies to study the clutter of the compound. As always, she found herself comparing this haphazard English house to the mansion she had known in Brazil, on the large plantation outside Pernambuco.

Now it seemed a memory from another world, that dazzling white room she had shared with her mother in the servants' compound. The day the *senhor de engenho,* the master of the plantation, announced that she would go to the black-robed Jesuits' school, instead of being put to work in the fields like most of the other slave children, her mother had begun to cry. For years she had thought they were tears of joy. Then the next day her mother had started work on their room. She had whitewashed the walls, smeared a fresh layer of hard clay on the floor, then planted a small frangipani tree by the window. During the night its tiny red blossoms would flood their room with a sweet, almost cloying fragrance, so they woke every morning to a day bathed in perfume. Years later her mother had confessed the beautiful room and the perfume of the tree were intended to always make her want to return there from the foul rooms of the *branco* and their priests.

She remembered those early years best. Her mother would rise before dawn, then wake the old, gnarled Ashanti slave who was the cook for the household, ordering the breakfast the senhor had specified the night before. Then she would walk quietly down to the slave quarters to waken the gang driver, who would rouse the rest of the plantation with his bell. Next she would return to their room and brush her beautiful *mulata* daughter's hair, to keep it always straight and shining, in preparation for the trip to the mission school the priests had built two miles down the road.

Serina still recalled the barefoot walk down that long, tree-lined roadway, and her mother's command, repeated every morning, to never let the sun touch her light skin. Later she would wander slowly back through the searing midday heat, puzzling over the new language called Spanish she was learning, and the strange teachings of the Christians. The priests had taught her to read from the catechism, and to write out the stories they told of the Catholic saints—stories her mother demanded she repeat to her each night. She would then declare them lies, and threaten her with a dose of the purgative physic-nut to expel their poisons.

Her mother would sometimes stroke her soft skin and explain that the Christians' false God must have been copied from Olorun, the Yoruba high god and deity of the cosmos.

99

It was well known he was the universal spirit who had created the world, the only god who had never lived on earth. Perhaps the Christians had somehow heard of him and hoped to steal him for their own. He was so powerful that the other gods were all his children—Shango, Ogun, all the Yoruba deities of the earth and rivers and sky. The Yoruba priests had never been known to mention a white god called Jesu.

But she had learned many things from Jesu's priests. The most important was that she was a slave. Owned by the *senhor de engenho*. She was his property, as much as his oxen and his fields of cane. That was the true lesson of the priests. A lesson she had never forgotten.

These new saltwater Yoruba were fools. Their life and soul belonged to the *branco* now. And only the *branco* could give it back. You could never take it back yourself. There was nothing you could do to make your life your own again.

She recalled a proverb of the Ashanti people. "A slave does not choose his master."

A slave chose nothing.

She found herself thinking again of her mother. She was called Dara, the Yoruba name meaning "beautiful." And she *was* beautiful, beyond words, with soft eyes and delicate skin and high cheekbones. Her mother Dara had told her how she had been taken to the bed of her Portuguese owner after only a week in Brazil. He was the *senhor de engenho,* who had sired *mulata* bastards from the curing house to the kitchen. They were all still slaves, but her mother had thought her child would be different. She thought the light-skinned girl she bore the *branco* would be made free. And she had chosen a Yoruba name for her.

The *senhor de engenho* had decided to name her Serina, one night while drunk.

A slave chose nothing.

Dara's *mulata* daughter also was not given her freedom. Instead that daughter was taken into the master's house: taught to play the lute and dance the galliards of Joao de Sousa

Carvalho when she was ten, given an orange petticoat and a blue silk mantle when she was twelve, and taken to his bed the day she was fourteen. Her own father. He had used her as his property for eight years, then sold her to a stinking Englishman. She later learned it was for the princely sum of a hundred pounds.

A slave chose nothing.

Still, something in the defiance of Atiba stirred her. He was bold. And handsome, even though a *preto*. She had watched his strong body with growing desire those two days they were together in the boiling house. She had begun to find herself wanting to touch him, to tame his wildness inside her. For a moment he had made her regret she had vowed long ago never to give herself to a *preto*. She was half white, and if ever she had a child, that child would be whiter still. To be white was to be powerful and free. She also would make certain her child was Christian. The Christian God was probably false, but in this world the Christians held everything. They owned the Yoruba. The Yoruba gods of her mother counted for nothing. Not here, not in the New World.

She smiled resignedly and thought once more of Atiba. He would have to learn that too, for all his strength and his pride, just as she had. He could call on Ogun to tell him the future, but that god would be somewhere out of hearing if he tried to war against the *branco*. She had seen it all before in Brazil. There was no escape.

A slave chose nothing.

Could he be made to understand that? Or would that powerful body one day be hanged and quartered for leading a rebellion that could only fail?

Unsure why she should bother, yet unable to stop herself, she turned from the window and quietly headed down the creaking, makeshift rear stair. Then she slipped past the kitchen door and onto the stone steps leading out into the back of the compound. It was still quiet, with only the occasional cackle of Irish laughter from the kitchen, whose chimney now threaded a line of wood smoke into the morning air.

The gate opened silently and easily—the indenture left to guard it was snoring, still clasping an empty flask—and she was out onto the pathway leading down the hill to the new thatched huts of the slaves.

The path was quiet and gray-dark. Green lizards scurried through the grass around her and frogs whistled among the palms, but there was no sign the indentures were awake yet. In the distance she could hear the low voice of Atiba, lecturing courage to his brave Yoruba warriors.

The *preto* fools.

She knew a woman would not be welcome, would be thought to "defile" their solemn council of war. Let them have their superstitions. This was the New World. Africa was finished for them. They weren't Yoruba warriors now. Here they were just more *preto* slaves, for all their posturing. Once more she was glad she had been raised a Portuguese, not a Yoruba woman bound to honor and revere whatever vain man she had been given to as wife.

As she neared the first hut, she stopped to look and shake her head sadly. What would the slaves in Brazil think of these thatched hovels? She knew. They would laugh and ridicule the backwardness of these saltwater *preto*, who knew nothing of European ways.

Then she noticed a new drum, a small one only just finished, that had been left out for the sun to dry. She had heard once what these special drums were for. They were used in ceremonies, when the men and women danced and somehow were entered and possessed by the gods. But there were no Yoruba women on Briggs' plantation. He had not bothered to buy any yet, since men could cut cane faster. She wanted to smile when she realized the Yoruba men here had to cook their own food, a humiliation probably even greater than slavery, but the smile died on her lips when she realized the drum was just a sad relic of a people torn apart.

She examined the drum, recalling the ones she had seen in Brazil. Its wood was reddish and the skins were tied taut with new white cords. She smoothed her hand against her shift, then picked it up and nestled it under her arm, feeling the coolness of the wood. She remembered the goat skin could be tuned by squeezing the cords along the side. Carefully she picked up the curved wooden mallet used to play it and, gripping the drum tightly against her body, tapped it once, twice, to test the fluctuation in pitch as she pressed the cords.

The sharp, almost human sound brought another rush of memories of Brazil, nights when she had slipped away to the slave quarters and sat at the feet of a powerful old *babalawo*, an ancient Yoruba priest who had come to be scorned by most of the newly baptized slaves. She was too young then to know that a *mulata* did not associate with black *preto*, that a *mulata* occupied a class apart. And above.

She had listened breathlessly night after starry night as he spun out ancient Yoruba legends of the goddess Oshun—who he said was the favorite wife of Shango. Then he would show her how to repeat the story back to him using just the talking drum.

She looked toward the gathering in the far hut, thinking again of the verses of the cowries. Holding the drum tightly, she began to play the curved stick across the skin. The words came easily.

> *A se were lo nko*
> You are learning to be a fool.
>
> *O ko ko ogbon*
> You do not learn wisdom.

She laughed to herself as she watched the startled faces of the Yoruba men emerging from the thatched hut. After a moment, she saw Atiba move out onto the pathway to stare in her direction. She set the drum onto the grass and stared back.

He was approaching now, and the grace of his powerful stride again stirred something, a desire she had first felt those nights in the boiling house. What would it be like, she wondered again, to receive a part of his power for her own?

Though his face declared his outrage, she met his gaze with defiance—a *mulata* need never be intimidated by a *preto*. She continued to watch calmly as he moved directly up the path to where she stood.

Without a word he seized the drum, held it skyward for a moment, then dashed it against a tree stump. Several of the partly healed lash marks on his back opened from the violence of the swing. He watched in satisfaction as the wood shattered, leaving a clutter of splinters, cords, and skin. Then he revolved toward her.

"A *branco* woman does not touch a Yoruba drum."

Branco. She had never heard herself referred to before as "white." But she had always wanted to. Always. Yet now . . . now he spat it out, almost as though it meant "unclean."

"A *branco* woman may do as she pleases." She glared back at him. "That's one of the first things you will have to learn on this island."

"I have nothing to learn from you. Soon, perhaps, you may learn from me."

"You've only begun to learn." She felt herself turning on him, bitterly. She could teach him more than he ever dreamed. But why? "You'll soon find out that you're a *preto*. Perhaps you still don't know what that means. The *branco* rule this island. They always will. And they own you."

"You truly are a *branco*. You may speak our tongue, but there is nothing left of your Yoruba blood. It has long since drained away."

"As yours will soon. To water the cane on this island, if you try to rise up against the *branco*."

"I can refuse to submit." The hardness in his eyes aroused her. Was it desperation? Or pride?

"And you'll die for it."

"Then I will die. If the *branco* kills me today, he cannot kill me again tomorrow. And I will die free." He fixed her with his dark gaze, and the three Yoruba clan marks on his cheek seemed etched in ebony. Then he turned back toward the hut and the waiting men. "Someday soon, perhaps, I will show you what freedom means."

Chapter Five

Katherine held on to the mizzenmast shrouds, shielding her eyes against the glitter of sun on the bay, and looked at Hugh Winston. He was wearing the identical shabby leather jerkin and canvas breeches she remembered from that first morning, along with the same pair of pistols shoved into his belt. He certainly made no effort to present a dignified appearance. Also, the afternoon light made you notice even more the odd scar across one weathered cheek. What would he be like as a lover? Probably nothing so genteel as Anthony Walrond.

Good God, she thought, what would Anthony, and poor Jeremy, say if they learned I came down here to the *Defiance*, actually sought out this man they hate so much. They'd probably threaten to break off marriage negotiations, out of spite.

But if something's not done, she told herself, none of that's going to matter anyway. If the rumor from London is true, then Barbados is going to be turned upside down. Hugh Winston can help us, no matter what you choose to think of him.

She reflected on Winston's insulting manner and puzzled why she had actually half looked forward to seeing him again. He certainly had none of Anthony's breeding, yet there was something magnetic about a man so rough and careless. Still, God knows, finding him a little more interesting than most of the dreary planters on this island scarcely meant much.

Was he, she found herself wondering, at all attracted to *her?*

Possibly. If he thought on it at all, he'd see their common ground. She finally realized he despised the Puritans and their slaves as much as she did. And, like her, he was alone. It was a bond between them, whether he knew it now or not. . . .

Then all at once she felt the fear again, that tightness under her bodice she had pushed away no more than half an hour past, when her mare had reached the rim of the hill, the last curve of the rutted dirt road leading down to the bay. She'd reined in Coral, still not sure she had the courage to go and see Winston. While her mare pawed and tugged at the traces, she took a deep breath and watched as a gust of wind sent the blood-red blossoms from a grove of cordia trees fleeing across the road. Then she'd noticed the rush of scented air off the sea, the wide vista of Carlisle Bay spreading out below, the sky full of tiny colored birds flitting through the azure afternoon.

Yes, she'd told herself, it's worth fighting for, worth jeopardizing everything for. Even worth going begging to Hugh Winston for. It's my home.

"Do you ever miss England, living out here in the Caribbees?" She tried to hold her voice nonchalant, with a lilt intended to suggest that none of his answers mattered all that much. Though the afternoon heat was sweltering, she had deliberately put on her most feminine riding dress—a billowing skirt tucked up the side to reveal a ruffle of petticoat and a bodice with sleeves slashed to display the silk smock beneath. She'd even had the servants iron it specially. Anthony always noticed it, and Winston had too, though he was trying to pretend otherwise.

"I remember England less and less." He sipped from his tankard—he had ordered a flask of sack brought up from the Great Cabin just after she came aboard—and seemed to be studying the sun's reflection in its amber contents. "The

107

Americas are my home now, for better or worse. England doesn't really exist for me anymore.''

She looked at him and decided Jeremy had been right; the truth was he'd probably be hanged if he returned.

He paused a moment, then continued, ''And you, Miss Bedford, have you been back?''

''Not since we left, when I was ten. We went first to Bermuda, where father served for two years as governor and chief officer for the Sommers Island Company. Then we came down here. I don't really even think of England much anymore. I feel I'm a part of the Americas now too.'' She shaded her face against the sun with one hand and noticed a bead of sweat trickling down her back, along the laces of her bodice. ''In truth, I'm beginning to wonder if I'll ever see England again.''

''I'd just as soon never see it again.'' He rose and strolled across the deck, toward the steering house. Then he settled his tankard on the binnacle and began to loosen the line securing the whipstaff, a long lever used for controlling the rudder. ''Do you really want to stay aboard while I take her out?''

''You've done it every day this week, just around sunset. I've watched you from the hill, and wondered why.'' She casually adjusted her bodice, to better emphasize the plump fullness of her breasts, then suddenly felt a surge of dismay with herself, that she would consider resorting to tawdry female tricks. But desperate times brought out desperate measures. ''Besides, you've got the only frigate in the bay now that's not Dutch, and I thought I'd like to see the island from offshore. I sometimes forget how beautiful it is.''

''Then you'd best take a good, long look, Miss Bedford,'' he replied matter-of-factly. ''It's never going to be the same again, not after sugar takes over.''

''Katherine. You can call me Katherine.'' She tried to mask the tenseness—no, the humiliation—in her voice. ''I'm sufficiently compromised just being down here; there's scarcely any point in ceremony."

"Then Katherine it is, Miss Bedford." Again scarcely a glimmer of notice as he busied himself coiling the line. But she saw John Mewes raise his heavy eyebrows as he mounted the quarterdeck companionway, his wide belly rolling with each labored step. Winston seemed to ignore the quartermaster as he continued, "Since you've been watching, then I suppose you know what to expect. We're going to tack her out of the harbor, over to the edge of those reefs just off Lookout Point. Then we'll come about and take her up the west side of the island, north all the way up to Speightstown. It's apt to be at least an hour. Don't say you weren't warned."

Perfect, she thought. Just the time I'll need.

"You seem to know these waters well." It was rhetorical, just to keep him talking. Hugh Winston had sailed up the coast every evening for a week, regardless of the wind or state of the sea. He obviously understood the shoreline of Barbados better than anyone on the island. That was one of the reasons she was here. "You sail out every day."

"Part of my final preparations, Miss Bedford . . . Katherine." He turned to the quartermaster. "John."

"Aye." Mewes had been loitering by the steeringhouse, trying to stay in the shade as he eyed the opened flask of sack. Winston had not offered him a tankard.

"Weigh anchor. I want to close-haul that new main course one more time, then try a starboard tack."

"Aye, as you will." He strode gruffly to the quarterdeck railing and bellowed orders forward to the bow. The quiet was broken by a slow rattle as several shirtless seamen began to haul in the cable with the winch. They chattered in a medley of languages—French, Portuguese, English, Dutch.

She watched as the anchor broke through the waves and was hoisted onto the deck. Next Mewes yelled orders aloft. Moments later the mainsail dropped and began to blossom in the breeze. The *Defiance* heeled slowly into the wind, then began to edge past the line of Dutch merchantmen anchored along the near shoreline.

Winston studied the sail for a few moments. "What do you think, John? She looks to be holding her luff well enough."

"I never liked it, Cap'n. I've made that plain from the first. So I'm thinkin' the same as always. You've taken a fore-and-aft rigged brigantine, one of the handiest under Christian sail, and turned her into a square-rigger. We'll not have the handling we've got with the running rigging."

Mewes spat toward the railing and shoved past Katherine, still astonished that Winston had allowed her to come aboard, governor's daughter or no. It's ill luck, he told himself. A fair looker, that I'll grant you, but if it's doxies we'd be taking aboard now, I can think of plenty who'd be fitter company. He glanced at the white mare tethered by the shore, wishing she were back astride it and gone. Half the time you see her, the wench is riding like a man, not sidesaddle like a woman was meant to.

"If we're going to make Jamaica harbor without raising the Spaniards' militia, we'll have to keep short sail." Winston calmly dismissed his objections. "That means standing rigging only. No tops'ls or royals."

"Aye, and she'll handle like a gaff-sailed lugger."

"Just for the approach. While we land the men. We'll keep her rigged like always for the voyage over." He maneuvered the whipstaff to start bringing the stern about, sending a groan through the hull. "She seems to work well enough so far. We need to know exactly how many points off the wind we can take her. I'd guess about five, maybe six, but we've got to find out now."

He turned back to Katherine and caught her eyes. They held something—what was it? Almost an invitation? But that's not why she's here, he told himself. This woman's got a purpose in mind, all right. Except it's not you. Whatever it is, though, the looks of her'd almost make you wonder if she's

110

quite so set on marrying some stiff royalist as she thinks she is?

Don't be a fool. The last thing you need to be thinking about now is a woman. Given the news, there's apt to be big trouble ahead here, and soon. You've got to be gone.

"So perhaps you'd care to tell me . . . Katherine, to what I owe the pleasure of this afternoon's visit. I'd venture you've probably seen the western coast of this island a few hundred times before, entirely without my aid."

"I was wondering if you'd heard what's happened in London?" She held on to the shrouds, the spiderweb of ropes that secured the mast, and braced herself against the roll of the ship as the *Defiance* eased broadside to the sun. Along the curving shoreline a string of Dutch merchantmen were riding at anchor, all three-masted *fluyts*, their fore and main masts steeped far apart to allow room for a capacious hatch. In the five weeks that had passed since the *Zeelander* put in with the first cargo of Africans, four more slavers had arrived. They were anchored across the bay now, their round sterns glistening against the water as the afternoon light caught the gilding on their high, narrow after-structure. Riding in the midst of them was the *Rotterdam,* just put in from London. The sight of that small Dutch merchantman had brought back her fear. It also renewed her resolve.

"You mean about King Charles? I heard, probably before you did." He was watching her tanned face, and secretly admiring her courage. She seemed to be taking the situation calmly. "I was working down here yesterday when the *Rotterdam* put in."

"Then I'd like your version. What exactly did you hear?"

"Probably what everybody else heard. They brought word England's new 'Rump' Parliament, that mob of bloodthirsty Puritans installed by Cromwell's army, has locked King Charles in the Tower, with full intentions to chop off his head. They also delivered the story that Parliament has declared Barbados a nest of rebels, since your Assembly has never recognized the Commonwealth. Virginia and Bermuda also made that select list of outcasts." He glanced toward the bow, then tested the steering lever. "So, Miss Katherine Bedford, I'd say the Americas are about to see those stormy times we talked about once. Only it's a gale out of England, not here." He turned and yelled forward, "John, reef the foresail as we double the Point. Then prepare to take her hard about to starboard."

She watched as he shoved the steering lever to port, flipping the rudder to maneuver around the reefs at the edge of the bay, then reached for his pewter tankard, its sides dark with grease. And she tried to stifle her renewed disgust with him, his obvious unconcern, ·as she watched him drink. Maybe it really was all a game to him. Maybe nothing could make him care a damn after all. In the silence that followed, the creaks of the weathered planking along the deck grew louder, more plaintive.

"Given some of that may be true, Captain, what do you think will happen now?"

"Just call me Hugh. I presume I can enjoy my fair share of Barbados' democracy. While it lasts." He shrugged. "Since you asked, I'll tell you. I think it means the end of everything we know about the Americas. Breathe the air of independence while you still can. Maybe you didn't hear the other story going around the harbor here. The Dutchmen are claiming that after Parliament gets around to beheading the king, it plans to take over all the patents granted by the Crown. It's supposedly considering a new law called a 'Navigation Act,' which is going to decree that only English bottoms can trade with the American settlements. No Hollanders. That means the end of free trade. There's even talk in London that a fleet of warships may head this way to enforce it."

"I've heard that too. It sounds like nothing more than a Thames rumor."

"Did you know that right now all the Dutchmen here are lading as fast as they can, hoping they can put to sea before they're blockaded, or sunk, by a score of armed English men-of-war?''

"Nobody in the Assembly thinks Cromwell would go that far.''

"Well, the Dutchmen do. Whatever else you might say, a Hollander's about the last man I'd call a fool. I can tell you Carlisle Bay is a convocation of nervous Netherlanders right now.'' He squinted against the sun. "And I'll pass along something else, Katherine. They're not the only ones. I'd just as soon be at sea myself, with my men.''

She examined him, her eyes ironic. "So I take it while you're not afraid to stand up to the Council, men with pistols practically at your head, you're still worried about some navy halfway around the world.''

"The difference is that the Council owed *me* money.'' He smiled wanly. "With England, it's more like the other way around.''

"That's not the real reason, is it?''

"All right, how's this? For all we know, their navy may *not* be halfway around the world anymore.'' He glanced at the sun, then checked the sail again. "It's no state secret I'm not Mother England's favorite son. The less I see of the English navy, the happier I'll be.''

"What'll you do if a fleet arrives while you're still here?''

"I'll worry about it then.'' He turned back. "A better question might be what does Barbados plan to do if a fleet arrives to blockade you and force you into line.'' His voice grew sober. "I'd say this island faces a difficult choice. If Parliament goes ahead and does away with the king, the way some of its hotheads reportedly want to, then there'll no longer be any legal protection for you at all. Word of this new sugar project has already gotten back to London, you can be sure. I'd suspect the Puritans who've taken over Parliament want the American colonies because they'd like a piece of Barbados' sudden new fortune for themselves. New taxes for Commons and new trade for English shippers. Now that

113

you're about to be rich here, your years of being ignored are over." He lifted the tankard and took another drink of sack. "So what are you going to do? Submit? Or declare war on Parliament and fight the English navy?"

"If everybody here pulls together, we can resist them."

"With what?" He turned and pointed toward the small stone fortress atop Lookout Point. The hill stood rocky and remote above the blue Caribbean. "Not with *that* breastwork, you won't. I doubt a single gun up there's ever been set and fired. What's more, I'd be surprised if there're more than a dozen trained gunners on the whole of the island, since the royalist refugees here were mostly officers back home. The way things stand now, you don't have a chance."

"Then we'll have to *learn* to fight, won't we?" She tried to catch his eye. "I suppose you know something about gunnery."

"Gunners are most effective when they've got some ordnance to use." He glanced back, then thumbed toward the Point. "What's in place up there?"

"I think there're about a dozen cannon. And there're maybe that many more at the Jamestown breastwork. So the leeward coast is protected. There's also a breastwork at Oistins Bay, on the south." She paused, studying his profile against the sun. An image rose up unbidden of him commanding a battery of guns, her at his side. It was preposterous yet exhilarating. "Those are the places an invasion would come, aren't they?"

"They're the only sections of shoreline where the surf's light enough for a troop ship to put in."

"Then we've got a line of defense. Don't you think it's enough?"

"No." He spoke quietly. "You don't have the heavy ordnance to stop a landing. All you can hope to do without more guns is just try and slow it down a bit."

"But assuming that's true, where would we get more cannon? Especially now?" This was the moment she'd been

114

dreading. Of course their ordnance was inadequate. She already knew everything he'd been saying. There was only one place to get more guns. They both realized where.

"Well, you've got a problem, Katherine." He smiled lightly, just to let her know he was on to her scheme, then looked away, toward the shoreline. On their right now the island was a mantle of deep, seemingly eternal green reaching down almost to the water's edge, and beyond that, up the rise of the first hill, were dull-colored scatterings of plantation houses. The *Defiance* was making way smoothly now, northward, holding just a few hundred yards off the white, sandy shore. "You know, I'm always struck by what a puny little place Barbados is." He pointed toward a small cluster of clapboard houses half hidden among the palms along the shore. "If you put to sea, like we are now, you can practically see the whole island, north to south."

She glanced at the palm-lined coast, then back. "What are you trying to say?"

"That gathering of shacks we're passing over there is the grand city of Jamestown." He seemed to ignore the question as he thumbed to starboard. "Which I seem to recall is the location of that famous tree everybody here likes to brag about so much."

Jamestown was where stood the massive oak into whose bark had been carved the inscription "James, King of E.," and the date 1625. That was the year an English captain named John Powell accidentally put in at an empty, forested Caribbean island and decided to claim it for his king.

"That tree proclaims this island belongs to the king of England. Well, no more. The king's finished. So tell me, who does it belong to now?"

"I'll tell you who it doesn't belong to. Cromwell and the English Parliament." She watched the passing shoreline, and tried to imagine what it would be like if her dream came true. If Barbados could make the stand that would change the Americas permanently.

When she'd awakened this morning, birds singing and the island sun streaming through the jalousies, she'd suddenly been struck with a grand thought, a revolutionary idea. She had ignored the servants' pleas that she wait for breakfast and ordered Coral saddled immediately. Then she'd headed inland, through the moss-floored forests whose towering ironwood and oak trees still defied the settlers' axes. Amidst the vines and orchids she'd convinced herself the idea was right.

What if all the English in the New World united? Declared their independence?

During her lifetime there had been a vast migration to the Americas, two out of every hundred in England. She had never seen the settlement in "New England," the one at Plymouth on the Massachusetts Bay, but she knew it was an outpost of Puritans who claimed the Anglican Church smacked too much of "popery." The New Englanders had always hated King Charles for his supposed Catholic sympathies, so there was no chance they'd do anything except applaud the fanatics in England who had toppled the monarchy.

But the settlements around the Chesapeake were different. Virginia was founded because of profit, not prayer books. Its planters had formed their own Assembly in 1621, the first in the Americas, and they were a spirited breed who would not give in easily to domination by England's new dictatorship. There was also a settlement on Bermuda, several thousand planters who had their own Assembly too; and word had just come they had voted to banish all Puritans from the island, in retaliation against Cromwell.

Hugh Winston, who thought he knew everything, didn't know that Bermuda had already sent a secret envoy to Dalby Bedford proposing Barbados join with them and form an alliance with Virginia and the other islands of the Caribbees to resist the English Parliament. Bermuda wanted the American colonies to stand firm for the restoration of the monarchy.

The Barbados Assembly appeared to be leaning in that direction too, though they still hoped they could somehow avoid a confrontation.

But that was wrong, she'd realized this morning. So very wrong. Don't they see what we really should do? This is our chance. We should simply declare the richest settlements in the Americas—Virginia, Barbados, St. Christopher, Nevis, Bermuda—independent of England. A new nation.

It was an idea she'd not yet dared suggest to Dalby Bedford, who would likely consider it close to sedition. And she certainly couldn't tell a royalist like Anthony. He'd only fight for the monarchy. But why, she asked herself, do we need some faraway king here in the Americas? We could, we should, be our own masters.

First, however, we've got to show Cromwell and his illegal Parliament that they can't intimidate the American settlements. If Barbados can stand up to them, then maybe the idea of independence will have a chance.

"I came today to ask if you'd help us stand and fight. If we have to." She listened to her own voice and knew it was strong and firm.

He stood silent for a moment, staring at her. Then he spoke, almost a whisper above the wind. "Who exactly is it wants me to help fight England? The Assembly?"

"No. I do."

"That's what I thought." He shook his head in disbelief, or was it dismay, and turned to check the whipstaff. When he glanced back, his eyes were skeptical. "I'll wager nobody knows you came down here. Am I correct?"

"I didn't exactly make an announcement about it."

"And that low-cut bodice and pretty smile? Is that just part of your negotiations?"

"I thought it mightn't hurt." She looked him squarely in the eye.

"God Almighty. What you'd do for this place! I pity Cromwell and his Roundheads." He sobered. "I don't mind telling

117

you I'm glad at least one person here realizes this island can't defend itself as things stand now. You'd damned sure better start trying to do something." He examined her, puzzled. "But why come to me?"

She knew the answer. Hugh Winston was the only person she knew who hated England enough to declare independence. He already had. "You seem to know a lot about guns and gunnery." She moved closer and noticed absently that he smelled strongly of seawater, leather, and sweat. "Did I hear you say you had an idea where we could get more cannon, to help strengthen our breastworks?"

"So we're back to business. I might have expected." He rubbed petulantly at his scar. "No, I didn't say, though we both know where you might. From those Dutchmen in the harbor. Every merchantman in Carlisle Bay has guns. You could offer to buy them. Or just take them. But whatever you do, don't dally too long. One sighting of English sail and they'll put to sea like those flying fish around the island."

"How about the cannon on the *Defiance*? How many do you have?"

"I have a few." He laughed, then reflected with pride on his first-class gun deck. Twenty-two demi-culverin, nine-pounders and all brass so they wouldn't overheat. He'd trained his gunners personally, every man, and he'd shot his way out of more than one harbor over the past five years. His ordnance could be run out in a matter of minutes, primed and ready. "Naturally you're welcome to them. All you'll have to do is kill me first."

"I hope it doesn't come to that."

"So do I." He studied the position of the waning sun for a moment, then yelled forward for the men to hoist the staysail. Next he gestured toward Mewes. "John, take the whipstaff a while and tell me what you think of the feel of her. I'd guess the best we can do is six points off the wind, the way I said."

"Aye." Mewes hadn't understood what all the talk had

been about, but he hoped the captain was getting the best of the doxy. "I can tell you right now this new rigging of yours makes a handy little frigate work like a damn'd five-hundred-ton galleon."

"Just try taking her about." He glanced at the shoreline. They were coming in sight of Speightstown, the settlement at the north tip of the island. "Let's see if we can tack around back south and make it into the bay."

"But would you at least help us if we were blockaded?" She realized she was praying he would say yes.

"Katherine, what's this island ever done for *me?* Besides, right now I've got all I can manage just trying to get the hell out of here. I can't afford to get caught up in your little quarrel with the Commonwealth." He looked at her. "Every time I've done an errand for Barbados, it's always come back to plague me."

"So you don't care what happens here." She felt her disappointment surge. It had all been for nothing, and damned to him. "I suppose I had a somewhat higher opinion of you, Captain Winston. I see I was wrong."

"I've got my own plan for the Caribbean. And that means a lot more to me than who rules Barbados and its slaves."

"Then I'm sorry I bothered asking at all."

"I've got a suggestion for you though." Winston's voice suddenly flooded with anger. "Why don't you ask your gentleman fiancé, Anthony Walrond, to help? From what I hear, he was the royalist hero of the Civil War."

"He doesn't have a gun deck full of cannon." She wanted to spit in Winston's smug face.

"But he's got you, Katherine, doesn't he?" He felt an unwanted pang at the realization. He was beginning to like this woman more than he wanted to. She had brass. "Though as long as you're here anyway, why don't we at least toast the sunset? And the free Americas that're about to vanish into history." He abruptly kissed her on the cheek, watched as she flushed in anger, then turned and yelled to

119

a seaman just entering the companionway aft, "Fetch up another flask of sack."

Benjamin Briggs stood in the open doorway of the curing-house, listening to the "sweee" call of the long-tailed fly-catchers as they flitted through the groves of macaw palms. The long silence of dusk was settling over the sugarworks as the indentures and the slaves trudged wearily toward their thatched huts for the evening dish of *loblolly* mush. Down the hill, toward the shore, vagrant bats had begun to dart through the shadows.

In the west the setting sun had become a fiery disk at the edge of the sea's far horizon. He watched with interest as a single sail cut across the sun's lower rim. It was Hugh Winston's *Defiance*, rigged in a curious new mode. He studied it a moment, puzzling, then turned back to examine the darkening interior of the curing house.

Long racks, holding wooden cones of curing sugar, extended the length of one wall. He thought about the cones for a time, watching the slow drip of molasses into the tray beneath and wondering if it mightn't pay to start making them from clay, which would be cheaper and easier to shape. Though the Africans seemed to understand working clay—they'd been using it for their huts—he knew that only whites could be allowed to make the cones. The skilled trades on Barbados must always be forbidden to blacks, whose tasks had to be forever kept repetitive, mind-numbing. The Africans could never be allowed to perfect a craft. It could well lead to economic leverage and, potentially, resistance to slavery and the end of cheap labor.

He glanced back toward the darkening horizon, but now Winston's frigate had passed from view, behind the trees. Winston was no better than a thieving rogue, bred for gallows-bait, but you had to admire him a trifle nonetheless. He was one of the few men around who truly understood the need for risk here in the Americas. The man who never chanced what he had gained in order to realize more would never prosper. In the Americas a natural aristocracy was rising up, one not of birth but of boldness.

Boldness would be called for tonight, but he was ready. He had done what had to be done all his life.

The first time was when he was thirty-one, a tobacco importer in Bristol with an auburn-haired wife named Mary and two blue-eyed daughters, a man pleased with himself and with life. Then one chance-filled afternoon he had discovered, in a quick succession of surprise and confession, that Mary had a lover. The matter of another man would not have vexed him unduly, but the fact that her gallant was his own business partner did.

The next day he sold his share of the firm, settled with his creditors, and hired a coach for London. He had never seen Bristol again. Or Mary and his daughters.

In London there was talk that a syndicate of investors led by Sir William Courteen was recruiting a band of pioneers to try and establish a new settlement on an empty island in the Caribbees, for which they had just received a proprietary patent from the king. Though Benjamin Briggs had never heard of Barbados, he joined the expedition. He had no family connections, no position, and only a few hundred pounds. But he had the boldness to go where no Englishman had ever ventured.

Eighty of them arrived in the spring of 1627, on the *William and John,* with scarcely any tools, only to discover that the entire island was a rain forest, thick and overgrown. Nor had anyone expected the harsh sunshine, day in and day out. They all would have starved from inexperience had not the Dutch helped them procure a band of Arawak Indians from Surinam, who brought along seeds to grow plantains and corn, and cassava root for bread. The Indians also taught the cultivation of cotton and tobacco, cash crops. Perhaps just as importantly, they showed the new adventurers from London

121

how to make a suspended bed they called a *hammock*, in order to sleep up above the island's biting ants, and how to use smoky fires to drive off the swarms of mosquitoes that appeared each night. Yet, help notwithstanding, many of those first English settlers died from exposure and disease by the end of the year. Benjamin Briggs was one of the survivors. Later, he had vowed never to forget those years, and never to taste defeat.

The sun was almost gone now, throwing its last, long shadows through the open thatchwork of the curinghouse walls, laying a pattern against the hard earthen floor. He looked down at his calloused hands, the speckle of light and shade against the weathered skin, and thought of all the labors he had set them to.

The first three years those hands had wielded an axe, clearing land, and then they had shaped themselves to the handle of a hoe, as he and his five new indentures set about planting indigo. And those hands had stayed penniless when his indigo crops were washed away two years running by the autumn storms the Carib Indians called *huracán*. Next he had set them to cotton. In five years he had recouped the losses from the indigo and acquired more land, but he was still at the edge of starvation, in a cabin of split logs almost a decade after coming out to the Caribbees.

He looked again at his hands, thinking how they had borrowed heavily from lenders in London, the money just enough to finance a switch from cotton to tobacco. It fared a trifle better, but still scarcely recovered its costs.

Though he had managed to accumulate more and more acres of island land over the years, from neighbors less prudent, he now had only a moderate fortune to show for all his labor. He'd actually considered giving up on the Americas and returning to London, to resume the import trade. But always he remembered his vow, so instead he borrowed again, this time from the Dutchmen, and risked it all one last time. On sugar.

He scraped a layer from the top of one of the molds and rubbed the tan granules between his fingers, telling himself that now, at last, his hands had something to show for the two long decades of callouses, blisters, emptiness.

He tasted the rich sweetness on a horned thumb and its savor was that of the Americas. The New World where every man started as an equal.

Now a new spirit had swept England. The king was dethroned, the hereditary House of Lords abolished. The people had risen up . . . and, though you'd never have expected it, new risk had risen up with them. The American settlements were suddenly flooded with the men England had repudiated. Banished aristocrats like the Walronds, who'd bought their way into Barbados and who would doubtless like nothing better than to reforge the chains of class privilege in the New World.

Most ironic of all, these men had at their disposal the new democratic institutions of the Americas. They would clamor in the Assembly of Barbados for the island to reject the governance of the English Parliament, hoping thereby to hasten its downfall and lead to the restoration of the monarchy. Worse, the Assembly, that reed in the winds of rhetoric, would doubtless acquiesce.

Regardless of what you thought of Cromwell, to resist Parliament now would be to swim against the tide. And to invite war. The needful business of consolidating the small tracts on Barbados and setting the island wholesale to sugar would be disrupted and forestalled, perhaps forever.

Why had it come down to this, he asked himself again. Now, of all times. When the fruits of long labor seemed almost in hand. When you could finally taste the comforts of life—a proper house, rich food, a woman to ease the nights.

He had never considered taking another wife. Once had been enough. But he had always arranged to have a comely Irish girl about the house, to save the trouble and expense of visiting Bridgetown for an evening.

A prudent man bought an indentured wench with the same careful eye he'd acquire a breeding mare. A lusty-looking one might cost a few shillings more, but it was money well invested, your one compensation for all the misery.

The first was years ago, when he bought a red-headed one straight off a ship from London, not guessing till he got her home that he'd been swindled; she had a sure case of the pox, the French disease. Her previous career, it then came out, included Bridewell Prison and the taverns of Turnbull Street. He sent her straight to the fields and three months later carefully bought another, this one Irish and seventeen. She had served out her time, five years, and then gone to work at a tavern in Bridgetown. He had never seen her since, and didn't care to, but after that he always kept one about, sending her on to the fields and buying a replacement when he wearied of her.

That was before the voyage down to Pernambuco. Brazil had been an education, in more ways than one. You had to grant the Papists knew a thing or so about the good life. They had bred up a sensuous Latin creation: the *mulata*. He tried one at a tavern, and immediately decided the time had come to acquire the best. He had worked hard, he told himself; he had earned it.

There was no such thing as a *mulata* indenture in Pernambuco, so he'd paid the extra cost for a slave. And he was still cursing himself for his poor judgment. Haughtiness in a servant was nothing new. In the past he'd learned you could easily thrash it out of them, even the Irish ones. This *mulata*, though, somehow had the idea she was gifted by God to a special station, complete with high-born Latin airs. The plan to be finally rid of her was already in motion.

She had come from Pernambuco with the first cane, and she would be sold in Bridgetown with the first sugar. He already had a prospective buyer, with an opening offer of eighty pounds.

He'd even hinted to Hugh Winston that she could be taken

as part payment for the sight drafts, but Winston had refused the bait. It was men and provisions, he insisted, nothing else.

Winston. May God damn his eyes. . . .

Footsteps sounded along the gravel pathway and he turned to examine the line of planters approaching through the dusk, all wearing dark hats and colorless doublets. As he watched them puffing up the rise of the hill, he found himself calculating how much of the arable land on the island was now controlled by himself and these eleven other members of the Council. Tom Lancaster owned twelve hundred acres of the rolling acres in St. George's parish; Nicholas Whittington had over a thousand of the best land in Christ's Church parish; Edward Bayes, who had ridden down from his new plantation house on the northern tip of the island, owned over nine hundred acres; John Tynes had amassed a third of the arable coastal land on the eastern, windward side of the island. The holdings of the others were smaller, but together they easily owned the major share of the good cane land on Barbados. What they needed now was the rest.

"Your servant, sir." The planters nodded in chorus as they filed into the darkened curinghouse. Every man had ridden alone, and Briggs had ordered his own servants to keep clear of the curinghouse for the evening.

"God in heaven, this much already." Bayes emitted a low whistle and rubbed his jowls as he surveyed the long rows of sugar molds. "You've got a fortune in this very room, sir. If this all turns out to be sugar, and not just pots of molasses like before."

"It'll be white sugar or I'll answer for it, and it'll be fine as any Portugal could make." Briggs walked to the corner of the room, returning with two flasks of kill-devil and a tray of tankards. "The question now, gentlemen, is whether we'll ever see it sold."

"I don't follow you, sir." Whittington reached for a brown flask and began pouring himself a tankard. "As soon as we've all got a batch cured, we'll market it to the Dutchmen. Or we'll ship it to London ourselves.''

"I suppose you've heard the rumor working now amongst the Dutchmen? That there might be an embargo?''

"Aye, but it's no more than a rumor. There'll be no embargo, I promise you. It'd be too costly.''

"It's not just a rumor. There was a letter from my London broker in the mail packet that came yesterday on the *Rotterdam*. He saw fit to include this.'' Briggs produced a thin roll of paper. "It's a copy he had made of the Act prepared in the Council of State, ready to be sent straight to Commons for a vote.'' He passed the paper to Whittington, who unscrolled it and squinted through the half-light. Briggs paused a moment, then continued, "The Act would embargo all shipping into and out of Barbados till our Assembly has moved to recognize the Commonwealth. Cromwell was so sure it'd be passed he was already pulling together a fleet of warships to send out and enforce it. Word has't the fleet will be headed by the *Rainbowe*, which was the king's flagship before Cromwell took it. Fifty guns.''

A disbelieving silence enveloped the darkened room.

"And you say this Act was set to pass in Parliament?'' Whittington looked up and recovered his voice.

"It'd already been reported from the Council of State. And the letter was four weeks old. More'n likely it's already law. The *Rainbowe* could well be sailing at the head of a fleet right now as we talk.''

"If Cromwell does that, we're as good as on our knees.'' Tynes rubbed his neck and took a sip from his tankard. "What do you propose we can do?''

"As I see it, there're but two choices.'' Briggs motioned for the men to sit on a row of empty kegs he had provided. "The first is to lie back and do nothing, in which case the royalists will probably see to it that the Assembly here votes to defy Commons and declare for Charles II.''

126

"Which means we'll be at war with England, God help us." Lancaster removed his hat to wipe his dusty brow.

"Aye. A war, incidentally, which would *force* Cromwell to send the army to subdue the island, if he hasn't already. He'd probably post troops to try and invade us, like some people are saying. Which means the Assembly would doubtless call up every able-bodied man on the island to fight. All the militia, *and* the indentures. Letting the cane rot in the fields, if it's not burned to cinders by then."

"Good Jesus." Whittington's face seemed increasingly haggard in the waning light. "That could well set us back years."

"Aye, and who knows what would happen with the indentures and the slaves? Who'll be able to watch over them? If we have to put the island on a war footing, it could endanger the lives of every free man here. God knows we're outnumbered by all the Irish Papists and the Africans."

"Aye, the more indentures and slaves you've got, the more precarious your situation." Lancaster's glazed eyes passed down the row of sugar molds as he thought about the feeble security of his own clapboard house. He also remembered ruefully that he owned only three usable muskets.

"Well, gentlemen, our other choice is to face up to the situation and come to terms with Parliament. It's a bitter draught, I'll grant you, but it'll save us from anarchy, and maybe an uprising."

"The Assembly'll never declare for the Commonwealth. The royalist sympathizers hold a majority." Whittington's face darkened. "Which means there's nothing to be done save ready for war."

"There's still a hope. We can do something about the Assembly." Briggs turned to Tynes, a small, tanned planter with hard eyes. "How many men do you have in your regiment?"

"There're thirty officers, and maybe two hundred men."

"How long to raise them?"

"Raise them, sir?" He looked at Briggs, uncomprehending. "To what purpose? They're militia, to defend us against attack by the Spaniards."

"It's not the Spaniards we've to worry about now. I think we can agree there's a clear and present danger nearer to hand." Briggs looked around him. "I say the standing Assembly of Barbados no longer represents the best interests of this island. For any number of reasons."

"Is there a limit on their term?" Lancaster looked at him questioningly. "I don't remember the law."

"We're not adjudicating law now, gentlemen. We're discussing the future of the island. We're facing war. But beyond that, it's time we talked about running Barbados the way it should be, along economic principles. There'll be prosperity, you can count on it, but only if we've got a free hand to make some changes." He took a drink, then set down his tankard.

"What do you mean?" Lancaster looked at him.

"Well sir, the main problem now is that we've got an Assembly here that's sympathetic to the small freeholders. Not surprisingly, since thanks to Dalby Bedford every man here with five acres can vote. Our good governor saw to that when he drew up the voting parishes. Five acres. They're not the kind who should be in charge of governing this settlement now. I know it and so does every man in this room."

"All the same, they were elected."

"That was before sugar. Think about it. These small freeholders on the Assembly don't understand this island wasn't settled just so we'd have a batch of five-acre gardens. God's blood, I cleared a thousand acres myself. I figured that someday I'd know why I was doing it. Well, now I do."

"What are you driving at?" Bayes squinted past the rows of sugar cones.

"Well, examine the situation. This island could be the finest sugar plantation in the world. The Dutchmen already claim it's better than Brazil. But the land here's got to be assembled and put to efficient use. If we can consolidate the holdings of these small freeholders, we can make this island the richest spot on earth. The Assembly doesn't understand that. They'd go to war rather than try and make some prosperity here.''

"What are you proposing we do about it?" Lancaster interjected warily.

"What if we took action, in the interests of the island?" Briggs lowered his voice. "We can't let the Assembly vote against the Commonwealth and call down the navy on our heads. They've got to be stopped."

"But how do we manage it?" Tynes' voice was uneasy.

"We take preventive action." He looked around the room. "Gentlemen, I say it'd be to the benefit of all the free Englishmen on Barbados if we took the governor under our protection for the time being, which would serve to close down the Assembly while we try and talk sense with Parliament."

"We'd be taking the law into our own hands." Tynes shifted uncomfortably.

"It's a question of whose law you mean. According to the thinking of the English Parliament, this Assembly has no legal standing anyway, since they've yet to recognize the rule of Commons. We'd just be implementing what's already been decided."

"I grant you this island would be wise not to antagonize Cromwell and Parliament just now." Whittington searched the faces around him. "And if the Assembly won't take a prudent course, then . . ."

"What we're talking about here amounts to overturning the sitting governor, and closing down the Assembly." Lancaster's voice came through the gloom. "We've not the actual authority, even if Parliament has . . ."

"We've got something more, sir." Briggs met his troubled gaze. "An obligation. To protect the future of the island."

What we need now, he told himself, is responsible leadership. If the Council can deliver up the island, the *quid pro quo* from Cromwell will have to be acting authority to govern

Barbados. Parliament has no brief for the Assembly here, which fits nicely with the need to be done with it anyway.

The irony of it! Only if Barbados surrenders do we have a chance to realize some prosperity. If we stand and fight, we're sure to lose eventually, and then none of us will have any say in what comes after.

And in the long run it'll be best for every man here, rich *and* poor. When there's wealth—as there's sure to be if we can start evicting these freeholders and convert the island over to efficient sugar plantations—everybody benefits. The wealth will trickle down, like the molasses out of these sugar cones, even to the undeserving. It's the way things have to be in the Americas if we're ever to make a go of it.

But one step at a time. First we square the matter of Bedford and the Assembly.

"But have we got the men?" Lancaster settled his tankard on a keg and looked up hesitantly.

"With the militia we already have under our command, I'd say we've got sympathetic officers, since they're all men with sizable sugar acreage. On the other hand, it'd probably not be wise to try calling up any of the small freeholders and freemen. So to get the numbers we'll be wanting, I'd say we'll just have to use our indentures as the need arises."

"You've named a difficulty there." Whittington took a deep breath. "Remember the transfer over to Winston takes place day after tomorrow. That's going to leave every man here short. After that I'll have no more than half a dozen Christians on my plantation. All the rest are Africans."

"Aye, he'll have the pick of my indentures as well," Lancaster added, his voice troubled.

"He'll just have to wait." Briggs emptied his tankard and reached for the flask. "We'll postpone the transfer till this thing's settled. And let Winston try to do about it what he will."

Chapter Six

A light breeze stirred the bedroom's jalousie shutters, sending strands of the midnight moon dancing across the curves of her naked, almond skin. As always when she slept she was back in Pernambuco, in the whitewashed room of long ago, perfumed with frangipani, with moonlight and soft shadows that pirouetted against the clay walls.

. . . Slowly, silently, the moon at the window darkens, as a shadow blossoms through the airless space, and in her dream the form becomes the ancient *babalawo* of Pernambuco, hovering above her. Then something passes across her face, a reverent caress, and there is softness and scent in its touch, like a linen kerchief that hints of wild berries. The taste of its honeyed sweetness enters the dream, and she finds herself drifting deeper into sleep as his arms encircle her, drawing her up against him with soft Yoruba words.

Her body seems to float, the dream deepening, its world of light and shadow absorbing her, beckoning, the softness of the bed gliding away.

Now she feels the touch of her soft cotton shift against her breasts and senses the hands that lower it about her. Soon she is buoyed upward, toward the waiting moon, past the jalousies at the window, noiselessly across the rooftop. . . .

She awoke as the man carrying her in his arms dropped abruptly to the yard of the compound. She looked to see the face, and for an instant she thought it truly was the old priest in Brazil . . . the same three clan marks, the same burning eyes. Then she realized the face was younger, that of another man, one she knew from more recent dreams. She struggled to escape, but the drugged cloth came again, its pungent, cloying sweetness sending her thoughts drifting back toward the void of the dream.

. . . Now the wall of the compound floats past, vaulted by the figure who holds her draped in his arms. His Yoruba words are telling her she has the beauty of Oshun, beloved wife of Shango. That tonight they will live among the Orisa, the powerful gods that dwell in the forest and the sky. For a moment the cool night air purges away the sweetness of the drug, the potion this *babalawo* had used to numb her senses, and she is aware of the hard flex of his muscle against her body. Without thinking she clings to him, her fear and confusion mingled with the ancient comfort of his warmth, till her mind merges once more with the dark. . . .

Atiba pointed down toward the wide sea that lay before them, a sparkling expanse spreading out from the shoreline at the bottom of the hill, faintly tinged with moonlight. "I brought you here tonight to make you understand something. In Ife we say: 'The darkness of night is deeper than the shadow of the forest.' Do you understand the chains on your heart can be stronger than the chains on your body?"

He turned back to look at Serina, his gaze lingering over the sparkling highlights the moon now sprinkled in her hair. He found himself suddenly remembering a Yoruba woman he had loved once, not one of his wives, but a tall woman who served the royal compound at Ife. He had met with her secretly, after his wives were killed in the wars, and he still thought of her often. Something in the elegant face of this *mulata* brought back those memories even more strongly. She too had been strong-willed, like this one. Was this woman also sacred to Shango, as that one had been . . . ?

"You only become a slave when you *give up your people.*" His voice grew gentle, almost a whisper. "What is your Yoruba name?"

"I'm not Yoruba." She spoke quickly and curtly, forcing the words past her anger as she huddled for warmth, legs drawn up, arms encircling her knees. Then she reached to pull her shift tighter about her and tried to clear her thoughts. The path on which he'd carried her, through forests and fields, was a blurred memory. Only slowly had she realized they were on a hillside now, overlooking the sea. He was beside her, wearing only a blue shirt and loincloth, his profile outlined in the moonlight.

"Don't say that. The first thing you must know is who you are. Unless you understand that, you will always be a slave."

"I know who I am. I'm *mulata.* Português. I'm not African." She glanced down at the grass beside her bare feet and suddenly wished her skin were whiter. I'm the color of dead leaves, she thought shamefully, of the barren earth. Then she gripped the hem of her shift and summoned back her pride. "I'm not a *preto.* Why would I have an African name?"

She felt her anger rising up once more, purging her feelings of helplessness. To be stolen from her bed by this ignorant *preto,* brought to some desolate spot with nothing but the distant sound of the sea. That he would dare to steal her away, a highborn *mulata.* She did not consort with blacks. She was almost . . . white.

The wind laced suddenly through her hair, splaying it across her cheeks, and she realized the night air was perfumed now, almost as the cloth had been, a wild fragrance that seemed to dispel a portion of her anger, her humiliation. For a moment she found herself thinking of the forbidden things possible in the night, those hidden hours when the rules of day can be sacrificed to need. And she became aware of the warmth of his body next to hers as he crouched, waiting, motionless as the trees at the bottom of the hill.

If she were his captive, then nothing he did to her would be of her own willing. How could she prevent him? Yet he made no move to take her. Why was he waiting?

"But to have a Yoruba name means to possess something the *branco* can never own." He caressed her again with his glance. Even though she was pale, he had wanted her from the first moment he saw her. And he had recognized the same want in her eyes, only held in check by her pride.

Why was she so proud, he wondered. If anything, she should feel shame, that her skin was so wan and pale. In Ife the women in the compounds would laugh at her, saying the moons would come and go and she would only wet her feet, barren. No man would take some frail albino to share his mat.

Even more—for all her fine Inglês clothes and her soft bed she was ten times more slave than he would ever be. How to make her understand that?

"You only become a slave when you give up the ways of your people. Even if your father was a *branco*, you were born of a Yoruba woman. You still can be Yoruba. And then you will be something, have something." The powerful hands that had carried her to this remote hilltop were now toying idly with the grass. "You are not the property of a *branco* unless you consent to be. To be a slave you must first submit, give him your spirit. If you refuse, if you remember your own people, he can never truly enslave you. He will have only your body, the work of your hands. The day you understand that, you are human again."

"You are wrong." She straightened. "Here in the Americas you are whatever the *branco* says. You will never be a man unless he says you are." She noticed a tiny race in her heartbeat and told herself again she did not want to feel desire for this *preto*, now or ever. "Do you want to know why? Because your skin is black. And to the Inglês black is the

134

color of evil. They have books of learning that say the Christian God made Africans black because they are born of evil; they are less than human. They say your blackness outside comes from your darkness within." She looked away, shamed once more by the shade of her own skin, her unmistakable kinship with this *preto* next to her. Then she continued, bitterly repeating the things she'd heard that the Puritan divines were now saying in the island's parish churches. "The Inglês claim Africans are not men but savages, something between man and beast. And because of that, their priests declare it is the will of their God that you be slaves. . . ."

She had intended to goad him more, to pour out the abusive scorn she had so often endured herself, but the softness of the Yoruba words against her tongue sounded more musical than she had wanted. He was quietly smiling as she continued. "And now I order you to take me back before Master Briggs discovers I'm gone."

"The sun is many hours away. So for a while yet you won't have to see how black I am." He laughed and a pale glimmer of moonlight played across the three clan marks on his cheek. "I thought you had more understanding than is expected of a woman. Perhaps I was wrong. We say 'The thread follows the needle; it does not make its own way.' For you the Português, and now this *branco* Briggs, have been the needle; you merely the thread." He grasped her shoulder and pulled her around. "Why do you let some *branco* tell you who you are? I say *they* are the savages. They are not my color; they are sickly pale. They don't worship my gods; they pray to some cruel God who has no power over the earth. Their language is ugly and harsh; mine is melodic, rich with verses and ancient wisdom." He smiled again at the irony of it. "But tonight you have told me something very important about the mind of these Inglês. You have explained why they want so much to make me submit. If they think we are evil, then they must also think us powerful."

Suddenly he leaped to his feet and joyously whirled in a

circle, entoning a deep, eerie chant toward the stars. It was like a song of triumph.

She sat watching till he finished, then listened to the medley of frightened night birds from the dark down the hill. How could this *preto* understand so well her own secret shame, see so clearly the lies she told herself in order to live?

Abruptly he reached down and slipped his hands under her arms, lifting her up to him. "The first thing I want to do tonight is give you back a Yoruba name. A name that has meaning." He paused. "What was your mother called?"

"Her name was Dara."

"Our word for 'beautiful.' " He studied her angular face gravely. "It would suit you as well, for truly you are beautiful too. If you took that name, it would always remind you that your mother was a woman of our people."

She found herself wishing she had the strength to push his warm body away, to shout out to him one final time that he was a *preto,* that his father was a *preto* and her own a *branco,* that she had no desire to so much as touch him. . . . But suddenly she was ashamed to say the word "white," and that shame brought a wave of anger. At him, at herself. All her life she had been proud to be *mulata.* What right did this illiterate *preto* have to make her feel ashamed now? "And what are you? You are a *preto* slave. Who brings me to a hilltop in the dark of night and brags about freedom. Tomorrow you will be a slave again, just like yesterday."

"What am I?" Angrily he gripped her arms and pulled her face next to his. The fierceness of his eyes again recalled the old *babalawo* in Brazil; he had had the same pride in himself, his people. "I am more than the Inglês here are. Ask of them, and you will discover half once were criminals, or men with no lands of their own, no lineage. In my veins there is royal blood, a line hundreds of generations old. My own father was nearest the throne of the ruling Oba in Ife. He was a *babalawo*, as I am, but he was also a warrior. Before he was betrayed in battle, he was the second most powerful man in Ife. That's who I am, my father's son.''

''What happened? Was he killed?'' Impulsively she took his hand and was surprised by its warmth.

''He disappeared one day. Many markets later I learned he was betrayed by some of our own people. Because he was too powerful in Ife. He was captured and taken down to the sea, sold to the Português. I was young then. I had only known twelve rainy seasons. But I was not too young to hunt down the traitors who made him slave. They all died by my sword.'' He clenched his fist, then slowly it relaxed. ''But enough. Tonight I want just one thing. To teach you that you still can be free. That you can be Yoruba again.''

''Why do you want so much to change me?''

''Because, Dara''—his eyes were locked on hers—''I would have you be my wife. Here. I will not buy you with a bride price; instead I will kill the man who owns you.''

She felt a surge of confusion, entwined with want. But again her disdain of everything *preto* caught in her breast. Why, she wondered, was she even bothering to listen?

''After you make me 'Yoruba,' I will still be a slave to the Inglês.''

''Only for a few more days.'' His face hardened, a tenseness that spread upward through his high cheeks and into his eyes. ''Wait another moon and you will see my warriors seize this island away from them.''

''I'll not be one of your Yoruba wives.'' She drew back and clasped her arms close to her breasts, listening to the night, alive now with the sounds of whistling frogs and crickets.

''Rather than be wife to a Yoruba, you would be whore to an Inglês.'' He spat out the words. ''Which means to be nothing.''

''But if you take this island, you can have as many wives as you like. Just as you surely have now in Ife.'' She drew

137

away, still not trusting the pounding in her chest. "What does one more mean to you?"

"Both my wives in Ife are dead." His hand reached and stroked her hair. "They were killed by the Fulani, years ago. I never chose more, though many families offered me their young women."

"Now you want war again. And death. Here."

"I raised my sword against my enemies in Yorubaland. I will fight against them here. No Yoruba will ever bow to others, black *or* white." He gently touched her cheek and smoothed her pale skin with his warm fingers. "You can stand with us when we rise up against the Inglês."

His touch tingled unexpectedly, like a bridge to some faraway time she dreamed about and still belonged to. For an instant she almost gave in to the impulse to circle her arms around him, pull him next to her.

He stroked her cheek again, lovingly, before continuing. "Perhaps if I kill all the Inglês chiefs, then you will believe you are free. That your name is Dara, and not what some Português once decided to call you." He looked at her again and his eyes had softened now. "Will you help me?"

She watched as the moonlight glistened against the ebony of his skin. This *preto* slave was opening his life to her, something no other man had ever done. The *branco* despised his blackness even more than they did hers, but he bore their contempt with pride, with strength, more strength than she had ever before sensed in a man.

And he needed her. Someone finally needed her. She saw it in his eyes, a need he was still too proud to fully admit, a hunger for her to be with him, to share the days ahead when . . .

Yes

. . . when she would stand with him to destroy the *branco*.

"Together." Softly she reached up and circled her arms around his broad neck. Suddenly his blackness was exquisite

138

and beautiful. "Tonight I will be wife to you. Will you hold me now?"

The wind whipped her long black hair across his shoulder, and before she could think she found herself raising her lips to his. He tasted of the forest, of a lost world across the sea she had never known. His scent was sharp, and male.

She felt his thumb brush across her cheek and sensed the wetness of her own tears. What had brought this strange welling to her eyes, here on this desolate hillside. Was it part of love? Was that what she felt now, this equal giving and accepting of each other?

She shoved back his open shirt, to pass her hands across the hard muscles of his chest. Scars were there, deep, the signs of the warrior he once had been. Then she slipped the rough cotton over his back, feeling the open cuts of the lashes, the marks of the slave he was now. Suddenly she realized he wore them as proudly as sword cuts from battle. They were the emblem of his manhood, his defiance of the Inglês, just as his cheek marks were the insignia of his clan. They were proof to all that his spirit still lived.

She felt his hands touch her shift, and she reached gently to stop him.

Over the years in Brazil so many men had used her. She had been given to any white visitor at the plantation who wanted her: first it was Portuguese traders, ship captains, even priests. Then conquering Hollanders, officers of the Dutch forces who had taken Brazil. A hundred men, all born in Europe, all unbathed and rank, all white. She had sensed their *branco* contempt for her with anger and shame. To this black Yoruba, this strong, proud man of Africa, she would give herself freely and with love.

She met his gaze, then in a single motion pulled the shift over her head and tossed it away, shaking out the dark hair that fell across her shoulders. As she stood naked before him in the moonlight, the wind against her body seemed like a foretaste of the freedom, the love, he had promised.

He studied her for a moment, the shadows of her firm breasts casting dark ellipses downward across her body. She was *dara*.

Slowly he grasped her waist and lifted her next to him. As she entwined her legs about his waist, he buried his face against her and together they laughed for joy.

Later she recalled the touch of his body, the soft grass, the sounds of the night in her ears as she cried out in completeness. The first she had ever known. And at last, a perfect quiet had seemed to enfold them as she held him in her arms, his strength tame as a child's.

In the mists of dawn he brought her back, through the forest, serenaded by its invisible choir of egrets and whistling frogs. He carried her home across the rooftop, to her bed, to a world no longer real.

"Damn me, sir, I suppose you've heard the talk. I'll tell you I fear for the worst." Johan Ruyters wiped his mouth with a calloused hand and shoved his tankard across the table, motioning for a refill. The Great Cabin of the *Defiance* was a mosaic of flickering shadows, lighted only by the swaying candle-lantern over the large oak table. "It could well be the end of Dutch trade in all the English settlements, from here to Virginia."

"I suppose there's a chance. Who can say?" Winston reached for the flask of sack and passed it over. He was exhausted, but his mind was taut with anticipation. Almost ready, he told himself; you'll be gone before the island explodes. There's only one last thing you need: a seasoned pilot for Jamaica Bay. "One of the stories I hear is that if Barbados doesn't swear allegiance to Parliament, there may be a blockade."

"Aye, but that can't last long. And frankly speaking, it matters little to me who governs this damned island, Parliament or its own Assembly." He waved his hand, then his look darkened. "No, it's this word about some kind of Navigation Act that troubles me."

"You mean the story that Parliament's thinking of passing an Act restricting trade in all the American settlements to English bottoms?"

"Aye, and let's all pray it's not true. But we hear the damned London merchants are pushing for it. We've sowed, and now they'd be the ones to reap."

"What do you think you'll do?"

"Do, sir? I'd say there's little we *can* do. The Low Countries don't want war with England. Though that's what it all may lead to if London tries stopping free trade." He glanced around the timbered cabin: there was a sternchaser cannon lashed to blocks just inside the large windows aft and a locked rack of muskets and pistols secured forward. Why had Winston invited him aboard tonight? They had despised each other from the first. "The better part of our trade in the New World now's with Virginia and Bermuda, along with Barbados and St. Christopher down here in the Caribbees. It'll ruin every captain I know if we're barred from ports in the English settlements."

"Well, the way things look now, you'd probably be wise just to weigh anchor and make for open sea, before there's any trouble here. Assuming your sight drafts are all in order."

"Aye, they're signed. But now I'm wondering if I'll ever see them settled." He leaned back in his chair and ran his fingers through his thinning gray hair. "I've finished scrubbing down the *Zeelander* and started lading in some cotton. This was going to be my best run yet. God damn Cromwell and his army. As long as the Civil War was going on, nobody in London took much notice of the Americas."

"True enough. You Hollanders got rich, since there was scarcely any English shipping. But in a way it'll be your own fault if Barbados has to knuckle under now to England and English merchants."

"I don't follow you, sir." Ruyters regarded him questioningly.

"It'd be a lot easier for them to stand and fight if they didn't have these new slaves you sold them."

"That's a most peculiar idea, sir." He frowned. "How do you see that?"

Winston rose and strolled aft to the stern windows, studying the leaded glass for a moment before unlatching one frame and swinging it out. A gust of cool air washed across his face. "You Hollanders have sold them several thousand Africans who'd probably just as soon see the island turned back to a forest. So they'll be facing the English navy offshore, with a bunch of African warriors at their backs. I don't see how they can man both fronts."

"That's a curious bit of speculation, sir. Which I'm not sure I'd be ready to grant you. But it scarcely matters now." Ruyters stared down at the table. "So what do you think's likely to happen?"

"My guess is the Assembly'll not surrender the island to Cromwell without a fight. There's too much royalist sentiment there." He looked back at Ruyters. "If there's a blockade, or if Cromwell tries to land English forces, I'd wager they'll call up the militia and shoot back."

"But they've nothing to fight with. Scarcely any ordnance worth the name."

"That's what I'm counting on." Winston's eyes sobered.

"What do you mean, sir?"

"It's the poor man that remembers best who once lent him a shilling. I figure that anybody who helps them now will be remembered here in the days to come, regardless of how this turns out."

"Why in the name of hell would you bother helping them? No man with his wits about him wants to get caught in this, not if he's looking to his own interests."

"I'll look to my interests as I see fit." Winston glanced back. "And you can do the same."

"Aye, to be sure. I intend to. But what would you be doing getting mixed up in this trouble? There'll be powder and shot spent before it's over, sir, or I'm not a Christian."

"I figure there's today. And then there's tomorrow, when this island's going to be a sugar factory. And they'll need shippers. They won't forget who stood by them. If I pitch in a bit now—maybe help them fortify the Point, for instance—I'll have first call. I'm thinking of buying another bottom, just for sugar." He looked at Ruyters and laughed. "Why should all the new sugar profits go to you damned Butterboxes?"

"Well, sir, you're not under my command anymore. I can't stop you from trying." The Dutchman cleared his throat noisily. "But they'd not forget so soon who's stood by them through all the years. Ask any planter here and he'll tell you we've kept this island, and all the rest of the English settlements, from starving for the last twenty years." He took a swallow from his tankard, then settled it down thoughtfully. "Though mind you, we needed them too. England had the spare people to settle the Americas, which the Low Countries never had, but we've had the bottoms to ship them what they need. It's been a perfect partnership." He looked back at Winston. "What exactly do you think you can do, I mean this business about fortifying the Point?"

"Just a little arrangement I'm making with some members of the Assembly."

"I'm asking you as one gentleman to another, sir. Plain as that."

Winston paused a few moments, then walked back from the window. The lantern light played across his lined face. "As a gentleman, then. Between us I'm thinking I'll off-load some of the ordnance on the *Defiance* and move it up to the Point. I've got twice the cannon on board that they've got in place there. I figure I might also spare them a few budge-barrels of powder and some round shot if they need it."

"I suppose I see your thinking." Ruyters frowned and

drank again. "But it's a fool's errand, for all that. Even if they *could* manage to put up a fight, how long can they last? They're isolated."

"Who can say? But I hear there's talk in the Assembly about trying to form an alliance of all the American settlements. They figure Virginia and Bermuda might join with them. Everybody would, except maybe the Puritans up in New England, who doubtless can be counted on to side with the hotheads in Parliament."

"And I say the devil take those New Englanders. They've started shipping produce in their own bottoms, shutting us out. I've seen their flags carrying lumber to the Canaries and Madeira; they're even sending fish to Portugal and Spain now. When a few years past we were all but keeping them alive. Ten years ago they even made Dutch coin legal tender in Massachusetts, since we handled the better part of their trade. But now I say the hell with them." His face turned hopeful. "But if there was an alliance of the other English settlements, I'll wager there'd be a chance they might manage to stand up to Cromwell for a while. Or at least hold out for terms, like you say. They need our shipping as much as we need them."

"I've heard talk Bermuda may be in favor of it. Nobody knows about Virginia." Winston drank from his tankard. "But for now, the need's right here. At least that's what I'm counting on. If I can help them hold out, they'll remember who stood by them. Anyway, I've got nothing to lose, except maybe a few culverin."

Ruyters eyed him in silence for a moment. The rhythmic creaking of the boards sounded through the smoky gloom of the cabin. Finally he spoke. "Let's be plain. What are they paying you?"

"I told you." Winston reached for the flask. "I've spoken to Bedford, and I'm planning a deal for sugar contracts. I'll take it out in trade later."

Ruyters slammed down his own tankard. "God's wounds, they could just as well have talked to some of us! I'll warrant

144

the Dutch bottoms here've got enough ordnance to fortify both of the breastworks along the west coast." He looked up. "There're a good dozen merchantmen anchored in the bay right now. And we've all got some ordnance. I've even got a fine set of brass nine-pounders they could borrow."

"I'd as soon keep this an English matter for now. There's no need for you Dutchmen to get involved." Winston emptied the flask into his tankard. "The way I see it, I can fortify the breastwork up on the Point with what I've got on board. It'll help them hold off Cromwell's fleet for a while, maybe soften the terms." He turned and tossed the bottle out the open stern window. "Which is just enough to get me signatures on some contracts. Then I take back the guns and Cromwell can have the place."

"What the pox, it's a free trade matter, sir. We've all got a stake in it." Ruyters' look darkened. He thought of the profits he had enjoyed over the years trading with the English settlements. He'd sold household wares, cloth, and liquor to colonists in Virginia and the Caribbees, and he'd shipped back to Europe with furs and tobacco from North America, cotton and dye woods from the Caribbean. Like all Dutch *fluyts,* his ship was specially built to be lightly manned, enabling him to consistently undercut English shippers. Then too, he and the other Dutch traders made a science of stowage and took better care of their cargos. They could always sell cheaper, give longer credits, and offer lower freight rates than any English trader could. But now that they had slaves to swap for sugar, there would finally be some real profits. "I can't speak for the other men here, but it'd be no trouble for me to lend them a few guns too. . . . And I'd be more than willing to take payment in sugar contracts. Maybe you could mention it privately to Bedford. It'd have to be unofficial, if they're going to be using Dutch guns against the English navy."

"I'm not sure why I'd want to do that."

"As a gentleman, sir. We both have a stake in keeping

free trade. Maybe you could just drop a word to Bedford and ask him to bring it up with the Assembly. Tell him we might mislay a few culverin, if he could arrange to have some contracts drawn up.''

"What's in it for me?"

"We'll strike an arrangement, sir. Word of honor.'' Ruyters look brightened. "To be settled later. When I can return the favor.''

"Maybe you can do something for me now . . . *if* I agree."

"You can name it, sir."

"I've been thinking I could use a good bosun's mate. How about letting me have that crippled Spaniard on the *Zeelander* if you've still got him? What's his name . . . the one who had a limp after that fall from the yardarm when we were tacking in to Nevis?"

"You don't mean Vargas?"

"Armando Vargas, that's the one."

Ruyters squinted through the dim light. "He's one of the handiest lads aloft I've got, bad leg or no. A first-rate yardman."

"Well, I think I'd like to take him on."

"I didn't know you were short-handed, sir."

"That's my bargain." Winston walked back to the window. "Let me have him and I'll see what I can do about talking to Bedford."

"I suppose you remember he used to be a navigator of sorts for the Spaniards. For that matter, I'll wager he knows as much as any man you're likely to come across about their shipping in the Windward Passage and their fortifications over there on the Main." Ruyters' eyes narrowed. "Damn my soul, what the devil are you planning?"

"I can always use a good man." He laughed. "Those are my terms."

"You're a lying rogue, I'll stake my life." He shoved back his chair. "But I still like the bargain, for it all. You've got a man. Have Bedford raise our matter with the Assembly."

"I'll see what I can do. Only it's just between us for now, till we see how many guns they need."

"It goes without saying." Ruyters rose and extended his hand. "So we'll shake on it. A bargain sealed." He bowed. "Your servant, sir."

Winston pushed open the cabin door and followed him down the companionway to the waist of the ship. Ruyters' shallop was moored alongside, its lantern casting a shimmering light across the waves. The oarsmen bustled to station when they saw him emerge. He bowed again, then swung heavily down the rope ladder.

Winston stood pensively by the railing, inhaling the moist evening air and watching as the shallop's lantern slowly faded into the midnight. Finally he turned and strolled up the companionway to the quarterdeck.

Miss Katherine Bedford should be pleased, he told himself. In any case, better they borrow Dutch guns than mine. Not that the extra ordnance will make much difference if Cromwell posts a fleet of warships with trained gunners. With these planters manning their cannon, the fleet will make short work of the island.

He started back for the cabin, then paused to watch the moonlight breaking over the crests and listen to the rhythmic pound of light surf along the shore. He looked back at the island and asked himself if Katherine's was a cause worth helping. Not if the Americas end up the province of a few rich slaveholders—which on Barbados has got to be sure as the sunrise. So just hold your own course, and let this island get whatever it deserves.

He glanced over the ship and reflected again on his preparations, for the hundredth time. It wouldn't be easy, but the plan was coming together. The sight drafts were still safely locked away in the Great Cabin, ready for delivery day after tomorrow, when the transfer of the indentures became official. And the work of outfitting the ship for transport of men was all but finished. The gun deck had been cleared, with the spare budge barrels of powder and the auxiliary round shot moved to the hold, permitting sleeping hammocks to be lashed up for the new men. Stores of salt fish, cheese, and biscuit had been assembled in a warehouse facing Carlisle Bay; and two hundred half pikes had been forged, fitted with staffs, and secured in the fo'c'sle, together with all of Anthony Walrond's new flintlock muskets.

Everything was ready. And now he finally had a pilot. Armando Vargas had made Jamaica harbor a dozen times back when he sailed with the Spaniards; he always liked to brag about it. Once he'd even described in detail the lookout post on a hilltop somewhere west of Jamaica Bay. If they could slip some men past those sentries on the hill, the fortress and town would fall before the Spaniards' militia even suspected they were around.

Then maybe he would take out time to answer the letter that'd just come from England.

He turned and nodded to several of the men as he moved slowly back down the companionway and into the comforting quiet of the cabin. He'd go up to Joan's tavern after a while, share a last tankard, and listen to that laugh of hers as he spun out the story of Ruyters and the guns. But now he wanted solitude. He'd always believed he thought best, worked best, alone.

He closed the large oak door of the Great Cabin, then walked to the windows aft and studied the wide sea. The Caribbean was home now, the only home left. If there was any question of that before, there wasn't anymore, not after the letter.

He stood a moment longer, then felt for the small key he always kept in his left breeches pocket. Beneath a board at the side of the cabin was a movable panel, and behind it a heavy door, double secured. The key slipped easily into the metal locks, and he listened for the two soft clicks.

Inside were the sight bills, just visible in the flickering light of the lantern, and next to them was a stack of shipping invoices. Finally there was the letter, its outside smeared with grease and the red wax of its seal cracked and half missing. He slipped it out and unfolded it along the creases, feeling his anger well up as he settled to read it one more time.

Sir (I shall never again have the pleasure to address you as my obedient son), after many years of my thinking you perished, there has late come word you are abroad in the Caribbees, a matter long known to certain others but until this day Shielded from me, for reasons I now fully Comprehend. The Reputation I find you have acquired brings me no little pain, being that (so I am now advis'd) of a Smuggler and Brigand.

He paused to glance out the stern window once again, remembering how the letter had arrived in the mail packet just delivered by the *Rotterdam*. It was dated two months past, and it had been deposited at Joan's tavern along with several others intended for seamen known to make port in Barbados.

Though I had these many long years thought you dead by the hands of the Spaniard, yet I prayed unceasing to God it should not be so. Now, upon hearing News of what you have become, I am constrained to question God's will. In that you have brought Ignominy to my name, and to the name of those other two sons of mine, both Dutiful, I can find no room for solace, nor can they.

He found his mind going back to memories of William and James, both older. He'd never cared much for either of them, and they'd returned his sentiment in full measure. William was the first—heavyset and slow of wit, with a noticeable weakness for sherry. Since the eldest son inherited everything, he had by now doubtless taken charge of the two thousand acres that was Winston Manor, becoming a country squire who lived off rents from his tenants. And what of James, that nervous image of Lord Harold Winston and no less ambitious and unyielding? Probably by now he was a rich barrister, the profession he'd announced for himself sometime about age ten. Or maybe he'd stood for Parliament, there to uphold the now-ended cause of King Charles. . . .

That a son of mine should become celebrated in the Americas for his contempt of Law brings me distress beyond the telling of it. Though I reared you with utmost care and patience, I oft had cause to ponder if you should ever come to any good end, being always of dissolute and unruly inclination. Now I find your Profession has been to defraud the English crown, to which you should be on your knees in Reverence, and to injure the cause of honest Merchants, who are the lifeblood of this Christian nation. I am told your name has even reached the ears of His Majesty, causing him no small Dismay, and adding to his distresses at a time when the very throne of England is in peril from those who would, as you, set personal gain above loyalty and obedience. . . .

He stopped, not wanting to read more, and crumpled the letter.

That was the end of England. Why would he want to go back? Ever? If there'd once been a possibility, now it was gone. The time had come to plant roots in the New World. So what better place than Jamaica? And damned to England. He turned again to the stern windows, feeling the end of all the unease that had come and gone over the years. This was it.

But after Jamaica, what? He was all alone.

A white cloud floated past the moon, with a shape like the beakhead of a ship. For a moment it was a gargoyle, and then it was the head of a white horse. . . .

150

He had turned back, still holding the paper, when he noticed the sound of distant pops, fragile explosions, from the direction of the Point. He walked, puzzling, back to the safe and was closing the door, the key already in the lock, when he suddenly stopped.

The Assembly Room was somewhere near Lookout Point, just across the bay. It was too much of a coincidence.

With a silent curse he reached in and felt until his hand closed around the leather packet of sight bills, the ones he would exchange for the indentures. Under them were the other papers he would need, and he took those too. Then he quickly locked the cabinet and rose to make his way out to the companionway. As he passed the table, he reached for his pistols, checking the prime and shoving them into his belt as he moved out into the evening air.

He moved aft to the quartergallery railing to listen again. Now there could be no mistaking. Up the hill, behind Lookout Point, there were flashes of light in the dark. Musket fire.

"What do you suppose it could be, Cap'n?" John Mewes appeared at the head of the companionway.

"Just pray it's not what I think it is. Or we may need some powder and shot ourselves." He glanced back toward the hill. "Sound general muster. Every man on deck."

"Aye." Mewes turned and headed for the quarterdeck.

Even as the bell was still sounding, seamen began to appear through the open hatch, some half dressed and groggy. Others were mumbling that their dice game had been interrupted. Winston met them on the main deck, and slowly they formed a ragged column facing him. Now there was more gunfire from the hill, unmistakable.

"I'm going to issue muskets." He walked along the line, checking each seaman personally. Every other man seemed to be tipsy. "To every man here that's sober. We're going ashore, and you'll be under my command."

"Beggin' yor pardon, Cap'n, what's all that commotion up

there apt to be?'' A grizzled seaman peered toward the sounds as he finished securing the string supporting his breeches.

''It might just be the inauguration of a new Civil War, Hawkins.'' Winston's voice sounded down the deck. ''So look lively. We collect on our sight bills. Tonight.''

Chapter Seven

The jagged peninsula known as Lookout Point projected off the southwestern tip of Barbados, separating the windy Atlantic on the south from the calm of the leeward coast on the west. At its farthest tip, situated on a stone cliff that rose some hundred feet above the entrance to Carlisle Bay, were the breastwork and gun emplacements. Intended for harbor defense only, its few projecting cannon all pointed out toward the channel leading into the bay, past the line of coral reefs that sheltered the harbor on its southern side.

From the deck of the *Defiance*, at anchor near the river mouth and across the bay from the peninsula, the gunfire seemed to be coming from the direction of the new Assembly Room, a thatched-roof stone building up the hill beyond the breastwork. Constructed under the authority of Governor Dalby Bedford, it housed the General Assembly of Barbados, which consisted of two representatives elected from each of the eleven parishes on the island. All free men in possession of five acres or more could vote, ballots being cast at the parish churches.

While Winston unlocked the gun racks in the fo'c'sle and began issuing the muskets and the bandoliers of powder and shot, John Mewes ordered the two longboats lashed amidships readied and launched. The seamen lined up single file at the doorway of the fo'c'sle to receive their muskets, then swung

153

down the rope ladders and into the boats. Winston took his place in one and gave command of the other to John Mewes.

As the men strained against the oars and headed across the bay, he studied the row of cannon projecting out over the moon-lit sea from the top of the breastwork. They've never been used, he thought wryly, except maybe for ceremonial salutes. That's what they call harbor defenses! It's a mercy of God the island's so far windward from the Main that the Spaniards've never troubled to burn the place out.

He sat on the prow of the longboat, collecting his thoughts while he tasted the air and the scent of the sea. The whitecaps of the bay slipped past in the moonlight as they steered to lee-ward of the line of Dutch merchantmen anchored near the shore. He then noticed a bob of lanterns on the southeast horizon and realized it was an arriving merchantman, with a heading that would bring it directly into the harbor. He watched the lights awhile, marveling at the Dutch trading zeal that would cause a captain to steer past the reefs into the harbor in the hours after midnight. He congratulated himself he'd long ago given up trying to compete head-on with the Hollanders. They practically owned the English settlements in the Americas. Scarce wonder Cromwell's first order of business was to be rid of them.

The sound of the tide lapping against the beach as the two longboats neared the shore beneath the breastwork brought his attention back. When they scraped into the shallows, he dropped off the prow and waded through the knee-high surf that chased up the sand in wave after wave. Ahead the beach glistened white, till it gave way to the rocks at the base of the Point.

John Mewes puffed along close at his heels, and after him came the first mate, Dick Hawkins, unshaven but alert, musket at the ready. Close behind strode tall Edwin Spurre, master's mate, a musket in each hand, followed by the rest. In all, some twenty of Winston's men had crossed the bay with him. He ordered the longboats beached, then called the men together and motioned for quiet.

"Are all muskets primed?"

154

"Aye." Spurre stepped forward, holding his two muskets up as though for inspection. "An' every man's got an extra bandolier of powder an' shot. We're ready for whatever the whoresons try." He glanced up the rise, puzzled, still not understanding why the captain had assembled them. But Hugh Winston liked having his orders obeyed.

"Good." Winston walked down the line. "Spread out along the shore and wait. I'm going up to see what the shooting's about. Just stand ready till you hear from me. But if you see me fire a pistol shot, you be up that hill like Jack-be-nimble. Is that clear?"

"You mean us against all that bleedin' lot up there?" John Mewes squinted toward the dark rise. "There's apt to be half their militia up there, Cap'n, from the sound of it."

"Did I hear you question an order, John? You know ship's rules. They go for officers too." He turned to the other men. "Should we call a vote right here?"

"God's life." Mewes pushed forward, remembering Winston's formula for discipline on the *Defiance*. He didn't even own a cat-o'-nine-tails, the lash used by most ship captains for punishment. He never touched an offender. He always just put trial and punishment to a show of hands by the men—whose favorite entertainment was keelhauling any seaman who disobeyed Captain's orders, lashing a line to his waist and ducking him under the hull till he was half drowned. "I wasn't doin' no questioning. Not for a minute. I must've just been mumbling in my sleep."

"Then try and stay awake. I'm going up there now, alone. But if I need you, you'd better be there, John. With the men. That's an order."

"Aye." Mewes performed what passed for a salute, then cocked his musket with a flourish.

Winston loosened the pistols in his belt, checked the packet containing the sight bills and the other papers he had brought, then headed directly up the rise. The approach to Lookout Point was deserted, but up the hill, behind a new stack of logs, he could see the shadowy outline of a crowd. The barricade, no more than fifty yards from the Assembly Room, was in the final stages of construction, as men with torches dragged logs forward. Others, militia officers, were stationed behind the logs with muskets and were returning pistol fire from the half-open doorway of the Assembly Room.

Above the din he could hear the occasional shouts of Benjamin Briggs, who appeared to be in charge. Together with him were the members of the Council and officers from their regiments. The command of the militia was restricted to major landholders: a field officer had to own at least a hundred acres, a captain fifty, a lieutenant twenty-five, and even an ensign had to have fifteen.

On the barricade were straw-hatted indentures belonging to members of the Council, armed only with pikes since the planters did not trust them with muskets. Winston recognized among them many whom he had agreed to take.

The firing was sputtering to a lull as he approached. Then Briggs spotted him and yelled out. "You'd best be gone, sir. Before someone in the Assembly Room gets a mind to put a round of pistol shot in your breeches."

"I'm not part of your little war."

"That you're decidedly not, sir. So we'll not be requiring your services here tonight."

"What's the difficulty?" Winston was still walking directly toward them.

"It's a matter of the safety of Barbados. I've said it doesn't concern you."

"Those indentures concern me. I don't want them shot."

"Tell that to the Assembly, sir. We came here tonight offering to take Dalby Bedford under our care, peacefully. To protect him from elements on the island who're set to disown Parliament. But some of the hotheads in there mistook our peaceful purpose and opened fire on us."

"Maybe they think they can 'protect' him better than you can." Another round of fire sounded from the doorway of the

Assembly Room and thudded into the log barricade. When two of the planters cursed and fired back, the door was abruptly slammed shut.

"It's the Assembly that's usurped rightful rule here, sir, as tonight should amply show. When they no longer represent the true interests of Barbados." Briggs glared at him. "We're restoring proper authority to this island, long overdue."

"You and the Council can restore whatever you like. I'm just here to take care of my indentures, before you manage to have some of them killed."

"They're not yours yet, sir. The situation's changed. We're not letting them go whilst the island's unsettled."

"The only unsettling thing I see here are all those muskets." He reached into the pocket of his jerkin and lifted out the leather packet containing the sight drafts. "So we're going to make that transfer, right now."

"Well, I'm damned if you'll have a single man. This is not the time agreed." Briggs looked around at the other members of the Council. Behind them the crowd of indentures had stopped work to listen.

"The sight bills are payable on demand. We've settled the terms, and I'm officially calling them in." Winston passed over the packet. "You've got plenty of witnesses. Here're the sight bills. As of now, the indentures are mine." He pulled a sheaf of papers from the other pocket of his jerkin. "You're welcome to look over the drafts while I start checking off the men."

Briggs seized the leather packet and flung it to the ground. Then he lifted his musket. "These indentures are still under our authority. Until we say so, no man's going to take them. Not even . . ."

A series of musket shots erupted from the window of the Assembly Room, causing Briggs and the other planters to duck down behind the log barricade. Winston remained standing as he called out the first name on the sheet.

"Timothy Farrell."

The red-faced Irishman climbed around Briggs and moved

forward, his face puzzled. He remained behind the pile of logs as he hunkered down, still holding his half-pike.

"That's my name, Yor Worship. But Master Briggs . . .

"Farrell, here's the indenture contract we drew up for your transfer." Winston held out the first paper from the sheaf. "I've marked it paid and had it stamped. Come and get it and you're free to go."

"What's this, Yor Worship?" He gingerly reached up for the paper and stared at it in the torchlight, uncomprehending. "I heard you was like to be buying out my contract. By my reckoning there's two more year left on it."

"I did just buy it. It's there in your hand. You're a free man."

Farrell sat staring at the paper, examining the stamped wax seal and attempting to decipher the writing. A sudden silence enveloped the crowd, punctuated by another round of musket fire from the Assembly Room. After it died away, Winston continued, "Now Farrell, if you'd care to be part of an expedition of mine that'll be leaving Barbados in a few days' time, that's your privilege. Starting tonight, your pay'll be five shillings a week."

"Beggin' Yor Worship's pardon, I reckon I'm not understandin' what you've said. You've bought this contract? An' you've already marked it paid?"

"With those sight bills." He pointed to the packet on the ground beside Briggs.

Farrell glanced at the leather bundle skeptically. Then he looked back at Winston. "An' now you're sayin' I'm free?"

"It's stamped on that contract. Have somebody read it if you care to."

"An' I can serve Yor Worship for wage if I like?" His voice began to rise.

"Five shillings a week for now. Maybe more later, if you . . ."

"Holy Mother Mary an' all the Saints! I'm free!" He crumpled the paper into his pocket, then leaped up as he flung his straw hat into the air. "Free! I ne'er thought I'd stay breathin' long enough to hear the word.'' He glanced quickly at the Assembly Room, then dismissed the danger as he began to dance beside the logs.

> "At the dirty end o' Dirty Lane,
> Liv'd a dirty cobbler, Dick Maclane . . .''

"That man still belongs to me.'' Briggs half cocked his musket as he rose.

Farrell whirled and brandished his half-pike at the planter. "You can fry in hell, you pox-rotted bastard. I've lived on your corn mush an' water for three years, till I'm scarce able to stand. An' sweated sunup to sundown in your blazin' fields, hoein' your damn'd tobacco, and now your God-cursed cane. With not a farthing o' me own to show for it, or a change o' breeches. But His Worship says he's paid me out. An' his paper says I'm free. That means free as you are, by God. I'll be puttin' this pike in your belly—by God I will—or any man here, who says another word against His Worship. I'll serve him as long as I'm standin', or pray God to strike me dead.'' He gave another whoop. "Good Jesus, who's got a thirst! I'm *free!*''

"Jim Carroll.'' Winston's voice continued mechanically, sounding above the din that swept through the indentures.

"Present an' most humbly at Yor Worship's service.'' A second man elbowed his way forward through the cluster of Briggs' indentures, shoving several others out of his path.

"Here's your contract, Carroll. It's been stamped paid and you're free to go. Or you can serve under me if you choose. You've heard the terms.''

"I'd serve you for a ha'penny a year, Yor Worship.'' He seized the paper and gave a Gaelic cheer, a tear lining down one cheek. "I've naught to show for four years in the fields but aches an' an empty belly. I'll die right here under your command before I'd serve another minute under that whoreson.''

"God damn you, Winston.'' Briggs full-cocked his musket with an ominous click. "If you think I'll . . .''

Carroll whirled and thrust his pike into Briggs' face. "It's free I am, by God. An' it's me you'll be killin' before you harm a hair o' His Worship, if I don't gut you first."

Briggs backed away from the pike, still clutching his musket. The other members of the Council had formed a circle and cocked their guns.

"You don't own these damned indentures yet," Nicholas Whittington shouted. "We've not agreed to a transfer now."

"You've got your sight drafts. Those were the terms. If you want these men to stay, tell it to them." He checked the sheaf of papers and yelled out the next name: "Tom Darcy." As a haggard man in a shabby straw hat pushed forward, Winston turned back to the huddle that was the Council. "You're welcome to offer them a wage and see if they'd want to stay on. Since their contracts are all stamped paid, I don't have any say in it anymore."

"Well, I have a say in it, sir." Whittington lifted his musket. "I plan to have an end to this knavery right now, before it gets out of hand. One more word from you, and it'll be your . . ."

Winston looked up and yelled to the crowd of indentures. "I gather you've heard who's on the list. If those men'll come up, you can have your papers. Your contracts are paid, and you're free to go. Any man who chooses to serve under me can join me here now."

Whittington was knocked sprawling by the surge of the crowd, as straw hats were flung into the air. A milling mob of indentures waving half-pikes pressed forward.

Papers from the sheaf in Winston's hand were passed eagerly through the ranks. The Council and the officers of their militia had drawn together for protection, still grasping their muskets.

In the confusion no one noticed the shaft of light from the doorway of the Assembly Room that cut across the open space separating it from the barricade. One by one the members of the Assembly gingerly emerged to watch. Leading them was Anthony Walrond, wearing a brocade doublet and holding a long flintlock pistol, puzzlement in his face.

Briggs finally saw them and whirled to cover the Assembly-men with his musket. "We say deliver up Bedford or there'll be hell to pay, I swear it!"

"Put down that musket, you whoreson." Farrell gave a yell and threw himself across the barrel of the gun, seizing the muzzle and shoving it in to the dirt. There was a loud report as it discharged, exploding at the breech and spewing burning powder into the night.

"Christ Almighty." Walrond moved out into the night and several men from the Assembly trailed after him, dressed in plain doublets and carrying pistols. "What the devil's this about?"

"Nothing that concerns you." Winston dropped a hand to one of the guns in his belt. "I'd advise you all to go back inside till I'm finished."

"We were just concluding a meeting of the Assembly, sir." Walrond examined Winston icily, then glanced toward the men of the Council. "When these rogues tried to commandeer the room, claiming they'd come to seize the governor, to 'protect' him. I take it you're part of this conspiracy."

"I'm here to protect my interests. Which gives me as much right as you have to be here. I don't recall that you're elected to this body."

"I'm here tonight in an advisory capacity, Captain, not that it's any of your concern." Walrond glanced back at the others, all warily holding pistols. "To offer my views regarding the situation in England." As he spoke Dalby Bedford emerged from the crowd. Walking behind him was Katherine.

Winston turned to watch, thinking she was even more beautiful than he had realized before. Her face was radiant, self-assured as she moved through the dim torchlight in a glistening skirt and full sleeves. She smiled and pushed toward him.

"Captain Winston, are you to be thanked for all this confusion?"

"Only a part of it, Miss Bedford. I merely stopped by to

161

enquire about my indentures, since I got the idea some of your Assemblymen were shooting at them."

Anthony Walrond stared at Katherine. "May I take it you know this man? It does you no credit, madam, I warrant you." Then he turned and moved down the path, directly toward Briggs and the members of the Council. "And I can tell all of *you* this night is far from finished. There'll be an accounting here, sirs, you may depend on it. Laws have been violated."

"You, sir, should know that best of all." Briggs stepped forward and dropped his hand to the pistol still in his belt. "Since you and this pack of royalist agitators that calls itself an Assembly would unlawfully steer this island to ruin. The Council of Barbados holds that this body deserves to be dissolved forthwith, and new elections held, to represent the interests of the island against those who'd lead us into a fool's war with the Commonwealth of England."

"You, sir, speak now in the very same voice as the rebels there. I presume you'd have this island bow to the criminals in Parliament who're now threatening to behead our lawful king."

"Gentlemen, please." Dalby Bedford moved between them and raised his hand. "I won't stand for this wrangling. We all have to try to settle our differences like Englishmen. I, for one, would have no objection to inviting the Council to sit with us in the Assembly, have a joint session, and try to reason out what's the wisest course now."

"I see no reason this body need share a table with a crowd of rebels who'll not bend a knee to the rightful sovereign of England." Walrond turned back to the members of the Assembly. "I say you should this very night draw up a loyalty oath for Barbados. Any man who refuses to swear fealty to His Majesty should be deported back to England, to join the traitors who would unlawfully destroy the monarchy."

"No!" Katherine abruptly pushed in front of him. "This island stayed neutral all through the Civil War. We never took a part, either for king or Parliament. Why should we take sides now, with the war over and finished?"

162

Walrond looked down at her, startled. "Because the time has come to stand and be counted, Katherine. Why do you suppose? The rebels may have seized England for now, but that's no reason we in the Americas have to turn our back on the king."

"But there's another choice." She drew a deep breath. Winston saw determination in her eyes as she turned to face the men of the Assembly. "Think about it. We never belonged to England; we belonged to the Crown. But the monarchy's been abolished and the king's patents invalidated. I say we should join with the other English settlements and declare the Americas a new nation. Barbados should lead the way and declare our own independence."

"That's the damnedest idea I've ever heard." Briggs moved forward, shaking away the indentures who still crowded around him menacingly. "If we did that, there'd be war for sure. We've got to stay English, or Cromwell'll send the army to burn us out." He turned to Walrond. "Rebel or no, Cromwell represents the might of England. We'd be fools to try to stand against him. Either for king or for some fool dream of independence." He looked back at Katherine. "Where'd you get such an idea, girl? It'd be the end of our hopes for prosperity if we tried going to war with England. There'd be no room to negotiate."

"You, sir, have no say in this. You're apt to be on trial for treason before the week's out." Walrond waved his pistol at Briggs, then turned back to Katherine. "What are you talking about? England is beholden to her king, madam, much the way, I might remind you, a wife is to her husband. Or don't you yet understand that? It's our place to revere and serve the monarchy."

"As far as I'm concerned, the king's only a man. And so's a husband, sir."

"A wife takes an oath in marriage, madam, to obey her husband. You'd best remember that." He turned and motioned the members of the Assembly to gather around him as he stepped over to a large log and mounted it. "On the subject of obedience, I say again an oath of loyalty to His Majesty King Charles

163

should be voted in the Barbados Assembly this very morning. We need to know where this island stands.'' He stared back at Dalby Bedford. "Much as a husband would do well to know what he can expect when he takes a wife.''

"You've got no authority to call a vote by the Assembly,'' Briggs sputtered. "You're not elected to it.'' He looked at Walrond, then at Bedford. "This, by God, was the very thing we came here tonight to head off.''

"You, sir, have no authority to interfere in the lawful processes of this body.'' Walrond turned back to the Assembly members, now huddled in conference.

Winston looked at Katherine and found himself admiring her idealism—and her brass, openly defying the man she was supposed to marry. She wanted independence for the Americas, he now realized, while all Anthony Walrond wanted was to turn Barbados into a government in exile for the king, maybe to someday restore his fortune in England. She was an independent woman herself too, make no mistaking. Sir Anthony Walrond was going to have himself a handful in the future, with the Commonwealth *and* with her.

Come to think of it, though, independence wasn't all that bad an idea. Why the hell not? Damned to England.

"I think there've been enough high-handed attempts to take over this island for one night.'' He moved to confront Walrond.

"You have your brass, Captain, to even show your face here.'' He inspected Winston with his good eye. "When you pillaged a ship of mine off Nevis Island, broadcloth and muskets, no more than two years past.''

"Now that you've brought it up, what I did was save the lives of some fifty men who were about to drown for want of a seaworthy longboat. Since you saved so much money on equipage, I figured you could afford to compensate me for my pains.''

"It was theft, sir, by any law.''

"Then the law be hanged.''

"Hardly a surprising sentiment, coming from you.'' Walrond shifted his pistol toward Winston's direction. "You should be on Tortuga, with the other rogues of your own stripe, rather than here on Barbados amongst honest men. Your profession, Captain, has trained you best for the end of a rope."

"What's yours trained you for?" He stood unmoving. "Get yourself elected to the Assembly, then make your speeches. I'm tired of hearing about your king. In truth, I never had a very high opinion of him myself."

"Back off, sirrah. I warn you now." Walrond pointed his long pistol. "You're speaking your impertinences to an officer of the king's army. I've dealt with a few thieves and smugglers in years past, and I just may decide to mete out some more long-overdue justice here and now."

Dalby Bedford cleared his throat and stepped between them. "Gentlemen, I think there's been more heat here tonight than need be, all around. It could be well if we cooled off a day or so. I trust the Assembly would second my motion for adjournment of this session, till we've had time to reflect on what's the best course for us. This is scarcely a light matter. We could be heading into war with England."

"A prospect that does not deter certain of us from acting on principle, sir." Walrond's voice welled up again. "I demand this Assembly take a vote right now on . . ."

"You'll vote on nothing, by God," Briggs yelled, then drew his own pistol. Suddenly a fistfight erupted between two members of the Assembly, one for and the other opposing the monarchy. Then others joined in. In the excitement, several pistols were discharged in the fray.

Good God, Winston thought, Barbados' famous Assembly has been reduced to this. He noticed absently that the first gray coloring of dawn was already beginning to appear in the east. It'd been a long night. What'll happen when day finally comes and news of all this reaches the rest of the island? Where will it end. . . .

"Belay there! Cool down your ordnance!" Above the shouts and bedlam, a voice sounded from the direction of the shore.

Winston turned to see the light of a swinging sea lantern

165

approaching up the rise. He recognized the ragged outline of Johan Ruyters, still in the clothes he had worn earlier that night, puffing up the hill.

Ruyters topped the rise and surveyed the confusion. His presence seemed to immediately dampen the melee, as several Assemblymen paused in embarrassment to stare. The Dutchman walked directly up to Dalby Bedford and tipped his wide-brimmed hat. "Your servant, sir." Then he gazed around. "Your most obedient servant, gentlemen, one and all." He nodded to the crowd before turning back to address Bedford. "Though it's never been my practice to intrude in your solemn English convocations, I thought it would be well for you to hear what I just learned." He drew a deep breath and settled his lantern onto the grass. "The *Kostverloren*, bound from Amsterdam, has just dropped anchor in the bay, and Captain Liebergen called us all together in a rare sweat. He says when dark caught him last evening he was no more than three leagues ahead of an English fleet."

"Great God help us." Walrond sucked in his breath.

"Aye, that was my thinking as well." Ruyters glanced back. "If I had to guess, I'd say your English Parliament's sent the navy, gentlemen. So we may all have to be giving God a hand if we're not to have the harbor taken by daylight. For once a rumor's proved all too true."

"God's life, how many were sailing?" Bedford whirled to squint toward the dim horizon.

"His maintopman thinks he may've counted some fifteen sail. Half of them looked to be merchantmen, but the rest were clearly men-of-war, maybe thirty guns apiece. We're all readying to weigh anchor and hoist sail at first light, but it's apt to be too late now. I'd say with the guns they've got, and the canvas, they'll have the harbor in a bottle by daybreak."

"I don't believe you." Walrond gazed skeptically toward the east.

"As you will, sir." Ruyters smiled. "But if you'd be pleased

166

to send a man up to the top of the hill, right over there, I'd wager he just might be able to spy their tops'ls for himself.''

Winston felt the life suddenly flow out of him. It was the end of his plans. With the harbor blockaded, he'd never be able to sail with the indentures. He might never sail at all.

"God Almighty, you don't have to send anybody." Bedford was pointing toward the horizon. "Don't you see it?"

Just beneath the gray cloudbank was an unmistakable string of flickering pinpoints, mast lights. The crowd gathered to stare in dismay. Finally Bedford's voice came, hard and determined. "We've got to meet them. The question is, what're their damned intentions?"

Ruyters picked up his lantern and extinguished it. "By my thinking the first thing you'd best do is man those guns down there on the Point, and then make your enquiries. You can't let them into the bay. We've got shipping there, sir. And a fortune in cargo. There'll be hell to pay, I promise you, if I lose so much as a florin in goods."

Bedford gazed down the hill, toward the gun emplacements at the ocean cliff. "Aye, but we don't yet know why the fleet's come. We've only had rumors."

"At least one of those rumors was based on fact, sir." Briggs had moved beside them. "I have it on authority, from my broker in London, that an Act was reported from the Council of State four weeks past to embargo our shipping till the Assembly votes recognition of the Commonwealth. He even sent me a copy. And this fleet was already being pulled together at the time. I don't know how many men-o'-war they've sent, but I heard the flagship was to be the *Rainbowe*. Fifty guns." He looked back at the Assembly. "And the surest way to put an end to our prosperity now would be to resist."

He was rudely shouted down by several Assemblymen, royalists cursing the Commonwealth. The air came alive with calls for defiance.

"Well, we're going to find out what they're about before we do anything, one way or the other." Bedford looked around him. "We've got guns down there in the breastwork. I'd say we can at least keep them out of the bay for now."

"Not without gunners, you won't." Ruyters' voice was somber. "Who've you got here? Show me a man who's ever handled a linstock, and I'll give you leave to hang me. And I'll not be lending you my lads, though I'd dearly love to. It'd be a clear act of war."

Winston was staring down at the shore, toward his own waiting seamen. If the English navy entered Carlisle Bay, the first vessel they'd confiscate would be the *Defiance*.

"God help me." He paused a moment longer, then walked to the edge of the hill and drew a pistol. The shot echoed through the morning silence.

The report brought a chorus of yells from the shore. Suddenly a band of seamen were charging up the hill, muskets at the ready, led by John Mewes. Winston waited till they topped the rise, then he gestured them forward. "All gunnery mates report to duty at the breastwork down there at the Point, on the double." He pointed toward the row of rusty cannon overlooking the bay. "Master Gunner Tom Canninge's in charge."

Several of the men gave a loose salute and turned to hurry down the hill. Winston watched them go, then looked back at Bedford. "How much powder do you have?"

"Powder? I'm not sure anybody knows. We'll have to check the magazine over there." Bedford gestured toward a low building situated well behind the breastwork, surrounded by its own stone fortification. "I'd say there's likely a dozen barrels or so."

Winston glanced at Mewes. "Go check it, John. See if it's usable."

"Aye." Mewes passed his musket to one of the French seamen and was gone.

"And that rusty pile of round shot I see down there by the breastwork? Is that the best you've got?"

"That's all we have on the Point. There's more shot at Jamestown and over at Oistins."

"No time." He motioned to Ruyters. "Remember our agreement last night?"

"Aye, and I suppose there's no choice. I couldn't make open sea in time now anyway." The Dutchman's eyes were rueful. "I'll have some round shot sent up first, and then start offloading my nine-pound demi-culverin."

"All we need now is enough shot to make them think we've got a decent battery up here. We can bring up more ordnance later."

"May I remind you," Bedford interjected, "we're not planning to start an all-out war. We just need time to try and talk reason with Parliament, to try and keep what we've got here."

Winston noticed Briggs and several members of the Council had convened in solemn conference. If an attack comes, he found himself wondering, which of them will be the first to side with Parliament's forces and betray the island?

"There's twenty budge-barrels, Cap'n." Mewes was returning. "I gave it a taste an' I'll wager it's dry and usable."

Winston nodded, then motioned toward Edwin Spurre. "Have the men here carry five barrels on down to the Point, so the gunnery mates can start priming the culverin. Be sure they check all the touch holes for rust."

"Aye." Spurre signaled four of the seamen to follow him as he started off toward the powder magazine. Suddenly he was surrounded and halted by a group of Irish indentures.

Timothy Farrell approached Winston and bowed. "So please Yor Worship, we'd like to be doin' any carryin' you need here. An' we'd like to be the ones meetin' them on the beaches."

"You don't have to involve yourself, Farrell. I'd say you've got little enough here to risk your life for."

"Aye, Yor Worship, that's as it may be. But are we to understand that fleet out there's been sent by that whoreson archfiend Oliver Cromwell?"

"That's what we think now."

"Then beggin' Yor Worship's pardon, we'd like to be the men

169

to gut every scum on board. Has Yor Worship heard what he did at Drogheda?''

"I heard he sent the army.''

"Aye. When Ireland refused to bow to his Parliament, he claimed we were Papists who had no rights. He led his Puritan troops to Irish soil, Yor Worship, and laid siege to our garrison-city of Drogheda. Then he let his soldiers slaughter our people. Three thousand men, women, and children. An' for it, he was praised from the Puritan pulpits in England." Farrell paused to collect himself. "My cousin died there, Yor Worship, wi' his Meggie. An' one of Cromwell's brave Puritan soldiers used their little daughter as a shield when he helped storm an' burn the church, so they could murder the priests. Maybe that heretic bastard thinks we've not heard about it here." He bowed again. "We don't know enough about primin' and firin' cannon, but wi' Yor Worship's leave, we'd like to be the ones carryin' all the powder and shot for you.''

"Permission granted." Winston thumbed them in the direction of Spurre.

The armada of sails was clearly visible on the horizon now, and rapidly swelling. As the first streaks of dawn showed across the waters, English colors could be seen on the flagship. It was dark brown and massive, with wide cream-colored sails. Now it had put on extra canvas, pulling away from the fleet, bearing down on the harbor.

Winston studied the man-of-war, marveling at its majesty and size. How ironic, he thought. England's never sent a decent warship against the Spaniards in the New World, even after they burned out helpless settlements. But now they send the pick of the navy, against their own people.

"Damned to them, that *is* the *Rainbowe*." Bedford squinted at the ship. "She's a first-rank man-of-war, fifty guns. She was King Charles' royal ship of war. She'll transport a good two hundred infantry.''

Winston felt his stomach tighten. Could it be there'd be more than a blockade? Had Parliament really sent the English army to invade the island?

"I'm going down to the breastwork." He glanced quickly at Katherine, then turned and began to make his way toward the gun emplacements. Edwin Spurre and the indentures were moving slowly through the early half-light, carrying kegs of powder.

"I think we can manage with these guns, Cap'n." Canninge was standing by the first cannon, his long hair matted against the sweat on his forehead. "I've cleaned out the touch holes and checked the charge delivered by the powder ladle we found. They're eighteen-pounders, culverin, and there's some shot here that ought to serve."

"Then prime and load them. On the double."

"Aye."

Using a long-handled ladle, he and the men began to shove precisely measured charges of powder, twenty pounds, into the muzzle of each cannon. The indentures were heaving round shot onto their shoulders and stacking piles beside the guns.

Winston watched the approaching sail, wondering how and why it had suddenly all come to this. Was he about to be the first man in the Americas to fire a shot declaring war against England? He looked around to see Dalby Bedford standing behind him, with Katherine at his side.

"You know what it means if we open fire on the *Rainbowe?* I'd guess it's Cromwell's flagship now."

"I do indeed. It'd be war. I pray it'll not come to that. I'd like to try and talk with them first, if we can keep them out of the bay." The governor's face was grim. "Try once across her bow. Just a warning. Maybe she'll strike sail and let us know her business."

"Care to hold one last vote in the Assembly about this, before we fire the first shot? Something tells me it's not likely to be the last."

"We've just talked. There's no need for a vote. No man here, royalist or no, is going to stand by and just hand over this place.

171

We'll negotiate, but we'll not throw up our hands and surrender. There's too much at stake.''

Winston nodded and turned to Canninge. ''They're pulling close to range. When you're ready, lay a round across her bow. Then hold for orders.''

''Aye.'' Canninge smiled and pointed toward a small gun at the end of the row, its dark brass glistening in the early light. ''I'll use that little six-pounder. We'll save the eighteen-pounders for the work to come.

''Have you got range yet?''

''Give me a minute to set her, and I'll wager I can lay a round shot two hundred yards in front of the bow.'' He turned and barked an order. Seamen hauled the tackles, rolling the gun into position. Then they levered the breech slightly upward to lower the muzzle, jamming a wooden wedge between the gun and the wooden truck to set it in position.

Winston took a deep breath, then glanced back at Bedford. ''This may be the most damn foolhardy thing that's ever been done.''

Bedford's voice was grave. ''It's on my authority.''

He turned back to Canninge. ''Fire when ready.''

The words were swallowed in the roar as the gunner touched a piece of burning matchrope to the cannon's firing hole. Dark smoke boiled up from the muzzle, acrid in the fresh morning air. Moments later a plume erupted off the bow of the English man-of-war.

Almost as though the ship had been waiting, it veered suddenly to port. Winston realized the guns had already been run out. They'd been prepared. Puffs of black smoke blossomed out of the upper gun deck, and moments later a line of plumes shot up along the surf just below the Point.

''They fired when they dipped into a swell.'' Canninge laughed. ''English gunnery still disappoints me.''

A fearful hush dropped over the crowd, and Winston stood listening as the sound of the guns echoed over the Point. ''They probably don't suspect we've got any trained gunners up here

.this morning. Otherwise they'd never have opened fire when they're right under our ordnance." He glanced at Bedford. "You've got their reply. What's yours?"

"I suppose there's only one answer." The governor looked back and surveyed the waiting members of the Assembly. Several men removed their hats and began to confer together. Moments later they looked up and nodded. He turned back. "What can you do to her?"

"Is that authority to fire?"

"Full authority."

"Then get everybody back up the hill. Now." He watched as Bedford gave the order and the crowd began to quickly melt away. The Irish indentures waited behind Winston, refusing to move. He gestured a few of the men forward, to help set the guns, then turned back to Canninge.

"Is there range?"

"Aye, just give me a minute to set the rest of these culverin."

Winston heard a rustle of skirts by his side and knew Katherine was standing next to him. He reached out and caught her arm. "You've got a war now, Katherine, whether you wanted it or not. It'll be the first time a settlement in the Americas has ever fired on an English ship. I guess that's the price you're going to have to pay for staying your own master. But I doubt you'll manage it."

"We just might." She reached and touched the hand on her arm. Then she turned and looked out to sea. "We have to try."

Winston glanced toward the guns. Canninge and the men had finished turning them on the *Rainbowe*, using long wooden handspikes. Now they were adjusting the wooden wedge at the breech of each gun to set the altitude. "How does it look?"

"I know these eighteen-pounders, Cap'n, like I was born to one. At this range I could line-of-sight these whoresons any place you like."

"How about just under the lower gun deck? At the water line? The first round better count."

173

"Aye, that's what I've set them for." He grinned and reached for a burning linstock. "I didn't figure we was up here to send a salute."

Book Two
REVOLUTION

Chapter Eight

The Declaration

We find these Acts of the English Parliament to oppose the freedom, safety, and well-being of this island. We, the present inhabitants of Barbados, with great danger to our persons, and with great charge and trouble, have settled this island in its condition and inhabited the same, and shall we therefore be subjected to the will and command of those that stay at home? Shall we be bound to the government and lordship of a Parliament in which we have no Representatives or persons chosen by us?

It is alleged that the inhabitants of this island have, by cunning and force, usurped a power and formed an independent Government. In truth the Government now used among us is the same that hath always been ratified, and doth everyway agree with the first settlement and Government in this place.

Futhermore, by the above said Act all foreign nations are forbidden to hold any correspondency or traffick with the inhabitants of this island; although all the inhabitants know very well how greatly we have been obliged to the Dutch for our subsistence, and how difficult it would have been for us, without their assistance, ever to have inhabited these places in the Americas, or to have brought them into order. We are still daily aware what necessary comfort they bring us, and that they do sell their commodities a great deal cheaper than our own nation will do. But this comfort would be taken from us by those whose Will would be a Law unto us. However, we declare that we will never be so unthankful to the Netherlanders for their former help and assistance as to deny or forbid them, or any other nation, the freedom of our harbors, and the protection of our Laws, by which they may continue, if they please, all freedom of commerce with us.

Therefore, we declare that whereas we would not be wanting to use all honest means for obtaining a continuance of commerce, trade, and good correspondence with our country, so we will not alienate ourselves from those old heroic virtues of true Englishmen, to prostitute our freedom and privileges, to which we are born, to the will and opinion of anyone; we can not think that there are any amongst us who are so simple, or so unworthily minded, that they would not rather choose a noble death, than forsake their liberties.

The General Assembly of Barbados

Sir Edmond Calvert studied the long scrolled document in the light of the swinging ship's lantern, stroking his goatee as he read and reread the bold ink script.

"Liberty" or "death."

A memorable choice of words, though one he never recalled hearing before. Would the actions of these planters be as heroic as their rhetoric?

Or could the part about a "noble death" be an oblique reference to King Charles' bravery before the executioner's axe? It had impressed all England. But how could they have heard? The king had only just been beheaded, and word could scarcely have yet reached the Barbados Assembly.

One thing was clear, however: Barbados' Assembly had rebelled against the Commonwealth. It had rejected the authority of Parliament and chosen to defy the Navigation Act passed by that body to assert England's economic control of its settlements in the New World.

Wearily he settled the paper onto the table and leaned back in his sea chair, passing his eyes around the timbered cabin and letting his gaze linger on a long painting of Oliver Cromwell hanging near the door. The visage had the intensity of a Puritan zealot, with pasty cheeks, heavy-lidded eyes, and the short, ragged hair that had earned him and all his followers the sobriquet of "Roundhead." He had finally executed the king. England belonged to Cromwell and his Puritan Parliament now, every square inch.

Calvert glanced back at the *Declaration*, now lying next to his sheathed sword and its wide shoulder strap. England might belong to Parliament, he told himself, but the Americas clearly didn't. The tone of the document revealed a stripe of independence, of courage he could not help admiring.

And now, to appease Cromwell, I've got to bludgeon them into submission. May God help me.

The admiral of the fleet was a short stocky Lincolnshire man, who wore the obligatory ensemble of England's new Puritan leadership: black doublet with wide white collar and cuffs. A trim line of gray hair circled his bald pate, and his face was dominated by a heavy nose too large for his sagging cheeks. In the dull light of the lantern his thin goatee and moustache looked like a growth of pale foliage against his sallow skin.

His father, George Calvert, had once held office in the Court of King Charles, and for that reason he had himself, many years past, received a knighthood from the monarch. But Edmond Calvert had gone to sea early, had risen through merit, and had never supported the king. In fact, he was one of the few captains who kept his ship loyal to Parliament when the navy defected to the side of Charles during the war. In recognition of that, he had been given charge of transporting Cromwell's army to Ireland, to suppress the rebellion there, and he bore the unmistakably resigned air of a man weary of wars and fighting.

The voyage out had been hard, for him as well as for the men, and already he longed to have its business over and done, to settle down to a table covered not with contentious proclamations but spilling over with rabbit pies, blood puddings, honeyed ham. Alas, it would not soon be. Not from the sound of the island's *Declaration*.

He lowered the wick of the lantern, darkening the shadows across the center table of the Great Cabin, and carefully rolled the document back into a scroll. Then he rose and moved toward the shattered windows of the stern to catch a last look at the island before it was mantled in the quick tropical night.

As he strode across the wide flooring-planks of the cabin, he carefully avoided the remaining shards of glass, mingled with gilded splinters, that lay strewn near the windows. Since all able-bodied seamen were still needed to man the pumps and patch the hull along the waterline, he had prudently postponed the repairs of his own quarters. As he looked about the cabin, he reminded himself how lucky he was to have been on the quarterdeck, away from the flying splinters, when the shelling began.

The first volley from the Point had scored five direct hits along the portside. One English seaman had been killed outright, and eleven others wounded, some gravely. With time only for one answering round, he had exposed the *Rainbowe*'s stern to a second volley from the breastwork on the Point while bringing her about and making for open sea. That had slammed into the ship's gilded poop, destroying the ornate quartergallery just aft of the Great Cabin, together with all the leaded glass windows.

The island was considerably better prepared than he had

been led to believe. Lord Cromwell, he found himself thinking, will not be pleased when he learns of the wanton damage Barbados' rebels have wreaked on the finest frigate in the English navy.

Through the ragged opening he could look out unobstructed onto the rising swells of the Caribbean. A storm was brewing out to sea, to add to the political storm already underway on the island. High, dark thunderheads had risen up in the south, and already spatters of heavy tropical rain ricocheted off the shattered railing of the quartergallery. The very air seemed to almost drip with wetness. He inhaled deeply and asked himself again why he had agreed to come out to the Americas. He might just as easily have retired his command and stayed home. He had earned the rest.

Edmond Calvert had served the Puritan side in the war faithfully for a decade, and over the past five years he had been at the forefront of the fighting. In reward he had been granted the command of the boldest English military campaign in history.

Oliver Cromwell was nothing if not audacious. Having executed the king, he had now conceived a grand assault on Spain's lands in the New World. The plan was still secret, code named *Western Design:* its purpose, nothing less than the seizure of Spain's richest holdings. Barbados, with its new sugar wealth, would someday be merely a small part of England's new empire in the Americas, envisioned by Cromwell as reaching from Massachusetts to Mexico to Brazil.

But first, there was the small matter of bringing the existing settlements in the Americas back into step.

He had never been sure he had the stomach for the task. Now, after realizing the difficulties that lay ahead in subduing this one small island, he questioned whether he wanted any part of it.

He swabbed his brow, clammy in the sweltering heat, and wondered if all the islands of the Caribbees were like this.

Doubtless as bad or worse, he told himself in dismay. He had seen and experienced Barbados only for a day, but already he had concluded it was a place of fierce sun and half-tamed forest, hot and miserable, its very air almost a smoky green. There was little sign among the thatched-roof shacks along the shore of its reputed great wealth. Could it be the stories at home were gross exaggerations? Or deliberate lies? It scarcely mattered now. Barbados had to be reclaimed. There was no option.

On his left lay the green hills of the island, all but obscured in sudden sheets of rain; on his right the line of English warships he had ordered positioned about the perimeter of Carlisle Bay, cannons run out and primed. He had stationed them there, in readiness, at mid-morning. Then, the siege set, he had summoned his vice admiral and the other commanders to a council on board the *Rainbowe*.

They had dined on the last remaining capons and drawn up the terms of surrender, to be sent ashore by longboat. The island was imprisoned and isolated. Its capitulation, they told each other, was merely a matter of time.

Except that time would work against the fleet too, he reminded himself. Half those aboard were landsmen, a thrown-together infantry assembled by Cromwell, and the spaces below decks were already fetid, packed with men too sick and scurvy-ravished to stir. Every day more bodies were consigned to the sea. If the island could not be made to surrender in a fortnight, two at most, he might have few men left with the strength to fight.

The *Declaration* told him he could forget his dream of an easy surrender. Yet he didn't have the men and arms for a frontal assault. He knew it and he wondered how long it would take the islanders to suspect it as well. He had brought a force of some eight hundred men, but now half of them were sick and useless, while the island had a free population of over twenty thousand and a militia said to be nearly seven thousand. Worst of all, they appeared to have first-rate gunners manning their shore emplacements.

Barbados could not be recovered by strength of arms; it could only be frightened, or lured, back into the hands of England.

A knock sounded on the cabin door and he gruffly called permission to enter. Moments later the shadow moving toward him became James Powlett, the young vice admiral of the fleet.

"Your servant, sir." Powlett removed his hat and brushed at its white plume as he strode gingerly through the cabin, picking his way around the glass. He was tall, clean shaven, with hard blue eyes that never quite concealed his ambition. From the start he had made it no secret he judged Edmond Calvert too indecisive for the job at hand. "Has the reply come yet? I heard the rebels sent out a longboat with a packet."

"Aye, they've replied. But I warrant the tune'll not be to your liking." Calvert gestured toward the *Declaration* on the table as he studied Powlett, concerned how long he could restrain the vice admiral's hot blood with cool reason. "They've chosen to defy the rule of Parliament. And they've denounced the Navigation Acts, claiming they refuse to halt their trade with the Dutchmen."

"Then we've no course but to show them how royalist rebels are treated."

"Is that what you'd have us do?" The admiral turned back to the window and stared at the rain-swept bay. "And how many men do you think we could set ashore now? Three hundred? Four? That's all we'd be able to muster who're still strong enough to lift a musket or a pike. Whilst the island's militia lies in wait for us—God knows how many thousand—men used to this miserable heat and likely plump as partridges."

"Whatever we can muster, I'll warrant it'll be enough. They're raw planters, not soldiers." Powlett glanced at the

Declaration, and decided to read it later. There were two kinds of men in the world, he often asserted: those who dallied and discussed, and those who acted. "We should ready an operation for tomorrow morning and have done with letters and declarations. All we need do is stage a diversion here in the harbor, then set men ashore up the coast at Jamestown."

Calvert tugged at his wisp of a goatee and wondered momentarily how he could most diplomatically advise Powlett he was a hotheaded fool. Then he decided to dispense with diplomacy. "Those 'raw planters,' as you'd have them, managed to hole this flagship five times from their battery up there on the Point. So what makes you think they couldn't just as readily turn back an invasion? And if they did, what then, sir?" He watched Powlett's face harden, but he continued. "I can imagine no quicker way to jeopardize what little advantage we might have. And that advantage, sir, is they still don't know how weak we really are. We've got to conserve our strength, and try to organize our support on the island. We need to make contact with any here who'd support Parliament, and have them join with us when we land."

The question now, he thought ruefully, is how much support we actually have.

Sir Edmond Calvert, never having been convinced that beheading the lawful sovereign of England would be prudent, had opposed it from the start. Events appeared to have shown him right. Alive, King Charles had been reviled the length of the land for his arrogance and his Papist sympathies; dead, you'd think him a sovereign the equal of Elizabeth, given the way people suddenly began eulogizing him, that very same day. His execution had made him a martyr. And if royalist sentiment was swelling in England, in the wake of his death, how much more might there be here in the Americas—now flooded with refugees loyal to the monarchy.

He watched his second-in-command slowly redden with anger as he continued, "I tell you we can only reclaim this island if it's divided. Our job now, sir, is to reason first, and only then resort to arms. We have to make them see their interests lie with the future England can provide.''

''Well, sir, if you'd choose that tack, then you can set it to the test quick enough. What about those men who've been swimming out to the ships all day, offering to be part of the invasion? I'd call that support.''

''Aye, it gave me hope at first. Then I talked with some of them, and learned they're mostly indentured servants. They claimed a rumor's going round the island that we're here to set them free. For all they care, we could as well be Spaniards.'' Calvert sighed. ''I asked some of them about defenses on the island, and learned nothing I didn't already know. So I sent them back ashore, one and all. What we need now are fresh provisions, not more mouths to feed.''

That's the biggest question, he told himself again. Who'll be starved out first: a blockaded island or a fleet of ships with scarcely enough victuals to last out another fortnight?

He turned back to the table, reached for the *Declaration*, and shoved it toward Powlett. ''I think you'd do well to peruse this, sir. There's a tone of defiance here that's unsettling. I don't know if it's genuine, or a bluff. It's the unknowns that trouble me now, the damned uncertainties.''

Those uncertainties, he found himself thinking, went far beyond Barbados. According to the first steps of Cromwell's plan, after this centerpiece of the Caribbees had been subdued, part of the fleet was to continue on to any other of the settlements that remained defiant. But Cromwell's advisors felt that would probably not be necessary: after Barbados acknowledged the Commonwealth, the rest of the colonies were expected to follow suit. Then the Western Design could be set into motion, with Calvert's shipboard infantry augmented by fighting men from the island.

The trouble with Cromwell's scheme, he now realized, was that it worked both ways. If Barbados succeeded in defying England's new government, then Virginia, Bermuda, the other

185

islands of the Caribbees, all might also disown the Commonwealth. There even was talk they might try attaching themselves to Holland. It would be the end of English taxes and trade anywhere in the Americas except for that scrawny settlement of fanatic Puritans up in "New England." There would surely be no hope for the Western Design to succeed, and Edmond Calvert would be remembered as the man who lost England's richest lands.

While Powlett studied the *Declaration,* skepticism growing on his face, Calvert turned back to the window and stared at the rainswept harbor, where a line of Dutch merchant *fluyts* bobbed at anchor.

Good God. *That's* the answer. Maybe we can't land infantry, but we most assuredly can go in and take those damned Dutchmen and their cargo. They're bound to have provisions aboard. It's our best hope for keeping up the blockade. And taking them will serve another purpose, too. It'll send the Commonwealth's message loud and clear to all Holland's merchants: that trade in English settlements is for England.

"There's presumption here, sir, that begs for a reply." The vice admiral tossed the *Declaration* back onto the table. "I still say the fittest answer is with powder and shot. There's been enough paper sent ashore already."

"I'm still in command, Mr. Powlett, whether you choose to approve or no. There'll be no more ordnance used till we're sure there's no other way." He walked back to the table and slumped wearily into his chair. Already waiting in front of him were paper and an inkwell. What, he asked himself, would he write? How could he describe the bright new future that awaited a full partnership between England and these American settlers?

The colonies in the Caribbees and along the Atlantic seaboard were merely England's first foothold in the New World. Someday they would be part of a vast empire stretching the length of the Americas. The holdings of Spain would fall soon, and after that England would likely declare war against

Holland and take over Dutch holdings as well. There was already talk of that in London. The future was rich and wide, and English.

I just have to make them see the future. A future of partnership, not defiance; one that'll bring wealth to England and prosperity to her colonies. They have to be made to understand that this *Declaration* is the first and last that'll ever be penned in the Americas.

He turned and dismissed Powlett with a stiff nod. Then he listened a moment longer to the drumbeat of tropical rain on the deck above. It sounded wild now, uncontrollable, just like the spirits of nature he sensed lurking above the brooding land mass off his portside bow. Would this dark, lush island of the Caribbees harken to reason? Or would it foolishly choose to destroy itself with war?

He sighed in frustration, inked his quill, and leaned forward to write.

The Assembly Room was crowded to capacity, its dense, humid air rank with sweating bodies. Above the roar of wind and rain against the shutters, arguments sounded the length of the long oak table. Seated down one side and around the end were the twenty-two members of the Assembly; across from them were the twelve members of the Council. At the back of the room milled others who had been invited. Winston was there, along with Anthony Walrond and Katherine.

Dalby Bedford was standing by the window, holding open the shutters and squinting through the rain-swept dusk as he studied the mast lights of the warships encircling the harbor. He wiped the rain and sweat from his face with a large handkerchief, then turned and walked back to his chair at the head of the table.

"Enough, gentlemen. We've all heard it already." He waved his hand for quiet. "Let me try and sum up. Our *Declaration* has been delivered, which means we've formally

187

rejected all their terms as they now stand. The question before us tonight is whether we try and see if there's room for negotiation, or whether we refuse a compromise and finish preparing to meet an invasion.''

Katherine listened to the words and sensed his uneasiness. She knew what his real worries were: how long would it be before the awkward peace between the Council and the Assembly fell apart in squabbling? What terms could the admiral of the fleet offer that would split the island, giving enough of the planters an advantage that they would betray the rest? Who would be the first to waver?

The opening terms sent ashore by Edmond Calvert had sent a shock wave across Barbados—its standing Assembly and Council were both to be dissolved immediately. In future, England's New World settlements would be governed through Parliament. A powerless new Council would be appointed from London, and the Assembly, equally impotent, would eventually be filled by new elections scheduled at the pleasure of Commons. Added to that were the new "Navigation Acts," bringing high English prices and shipping fees. The suddenly ripening plum of the Americas would be plucked.

The terms, signed by the admiral, had been ferried ashore by longboat and delivered directly to Dalby Bedford at the compound. Members of Council and the Assembly had already been gathering in the Assembly Room by then, anxious to hear the conditions read.

Katherine remembered the worry on the governor's face as he had finished dressing to go down and read the fleet's ultimatum.''The first thing I have to do is get them to agree on something, anything. If they start quarreling again, we're good as lost.''

"Then try to avoid the question of recognizing Parliament." She'd watched him search for his plumed hat and rose to fetch it from the corner stand by the door. "I suspect most of the Council would be tempted to give in and do that, on the idea it might postpone a fight and give them time to finish this year's sugar while they appeal to Parliament to soften the terms.''

"Aye. The sugar's all they care about. That's why I think we best go at it backwards." He'd reached for his cane and tested it thoughtfully against the wide boards of the floor. "I think I'll start by raising that business in the Navigation Acts about not letting the Dutchmen trade. Not a man in the room'll agree to that, not even the Council. I'll have them vote to reject those, then see if that'll bring us enough unity to proceed to the next step."

Just as he had predicted, the Council and the Assembly had voted unanimously to defy the new Navigation Acts. They could never endure an English stranglehold on island commerce, regardless of the other consequences.

They had immediately drafted their own reply to the admiral's terms, a *Declaration* denouncing them and refusing to comply, and sent it back to the fleet. The question left unresolved, to await this evening's session, was whether they should agree to negotiate with Parliament at all. . . .

"I say there's nothing to negotiate." Benjamin Briggs rose to his feet and faced the candle-lit room. "If we agreed to talk, it'd be the same as recognizing Parliament."

"Are you saying the Council's decided to oppose recognition?" Bedford examined him in surprise. Perhaps the business about dissolving the Council had finally made an impression after all.

"Unalterably, sir. We've talked it over, and we're beginning to think this idea of independence that came up a while back could have some merit." Briggs gazed around the room. "I'll grant I was of a different mind before we heard the terms. But now I say we stand firm. If we bow to the rule of Parliament, where we've got no representation, we'll never be rid of these Navigation Acts. And that's the end of free trade, free markets. We'd as well be slaves ourselves." He pushed back his black hat, revealing a leathery brow fur-

189

rowed by the strain. "I'll wager Virginia will stand with us when their time comes. But the fleet's been sent here first, so for now we'll have to carry the burden of resistance ourselves, and so be it. Speaking for the Council, you know we've already ordered our militia out. They're to stay mustered till this thing's finished. We'd have the rest of the island's militia called up now, those men controlled by the Assembly, and have them on the beaches by daybreak."

Dalby Bedford looked down the line of faces and knew he had gained the first step. The Council was with him. But now, he wondered suddenly, what about the Assembly?

As an interim measure, eight hundred men had already been posted along the western and southern shorelines, militia from the regiments commanded by the members of the Council. The small freeholders had not yet mustered. Many of the men with five-acre plots were already voicing reservations about entering an all-out war with England, especially when its main purpose seemed to be preserving free markets for the big plantation owners' sugar.

"I think it's time we talked about cavalry." Nicholas Whittington joined in, wiping his beard as he lifted his voice above the din of wind and rain. "I'd say there's apt to be at least four hundred horses on the island that we could pull together." He glared pointedly across the table at the Assemblymen, brown-faced men in tattered waistcoats. "That means every horse, in every parish. We have to make a show of force if we're to negotiate from strength. I propose we make an accounting, parish by parish. Any man with a nag who fails to bring it up for muster should be hanged for treason."

As she watched the members of the Assembly start to mumble uneasily, Katherine realized that a horse represented a sizable investment for most small freeholders. How much use would they be anyway, she found herself wondering. The horses on the island were mostly for pulling plows. And the "cavalry" riding them would be farmers with rusty pikes.

As the arguing in the room continued, she found herself

thinking about Hugh Winston. The sight of him firing down on the English navy through the mists of dawn had erased all her previous contempt. Never before had she seen a man so resolute. She remembered again the way he had taken her arm, there at the last. Why had he done it?

She turned to study him, his lined face still smeared with oily traces of powder smoke, and told herself they were a matched pair. She had determination too. He'd soon realize that, even if he didn't now.

At the moment he was deep in a private conference with Johan Ruyters, who had asked to be present to speak for Dutch trading interests. The two of them had worked together all day, through the sultry heat that always preceded a storm. Winston and his men had helped heave the heavy Dutch guns onto makeshift barges and ferry them ashore, to be moved up the coast with ox-drawn wagons. Now he looked bone tired. She could almost feel the ache he must have in his back.

As she stood studying Winston, her thoughts wandered again to Anthony. He had worked all day too, riding along the shore and reviewing the militia deployed to defend key points along the coast.

What was this sudden ambivalence she felt toward him? He was tall, like Winston, and altogether quite handsome. More handsome by half than Hugh Winston, come to that. No, it was something about Winston's manner that excited her more than Anthony did. He was . . . yes, he was dangerous.

She laughed to realize she could find that appealing. It violated all the common sense she'd so carefully cultivated over the years. Again she found herself wondering what he'd be like as a lover. . . .

"And, sir, what then? After we've offered up our horses and our muskets and servants for your militia?" One of the members of the Assembly suddenly rose and faced the Council. It was John Russell, a tall, rawboned freeholder who held fifteen acres on the north side. "Who's to protect our wives and families after that?" He paused nervously to clear his throat and peered down the table. "To be frank, gentlemen, we're beginning to grow fearful of all these Africans that certain of you've bought and settled here now. With every white man on the island mustered and on the coast, together with all our horses and our muskets, we'll not have any way to defend our own if these new slaves decide to stage a revolt. And don't say it can't happen. Remember that rising amongst the indentures two years ago. Though we promptly hanged a dozen of the instigators and brought an end to it, we've taught no such lesson to these blacks. If they were to start something, say in the hills up in mid-island, we'd be hard pressed to stop them from slaughtering who they wished with those cane knives they use." He received supportive nods from several other Assemblymen. "We'd be leaving ourselves defenseless if we mustered every able-bodied man and horse down onto the shore."

"If that's all that's troubling you, then you can ease your minds." Briggs pushed back his hat and smiled. "All the blacks've been confined to quarters, to the man, for the duration. Besides, they're scattered over the island, so there's no way they can organize anything. There's no call for alarm, I give you my solemn word. They're unarmed now and docile as lambs."

"But what about those cane knives we see them carrying in the fields?"

"Those have all been collected. The Africans've got no weapons. There's nothing they can do save beat on drums, which seems to keep them occupied more and more lately, anyhow." He looked around the room, pleased to see that the reassuring tone in his voice was having the desired effect. "I think we'd best put our heads to more pressing matters, such as the condition of the breastworks here and along the coasts." He turned toward Winston. "You've not had much to say tonight, sir, concerning today's work. I, for one, would welcome a word on the condition of our ordnance."

All eyes at the table shifted to Winston, now standing by the window and holding a shutter pried open to watch as the winds and rain bent the tops of the tall palms outside. Slowly he turned, his lanky form seeming to lengthen, and surveyed the room. His eyes told Katherine he was worried; she'd begun to know his moods.

"The ordnance lent by the Dutchmen is in place now." He thumbed at Ruyters. "For which I'd say a round of thanks is overdue."

"Hear, hear." The planters voices chorused, and Ruyters nodded his acknowledgement. Then he whispered something quickly to Winston and disappeared out the door, into the rain. The seaman waited, watching him go, then continued, "You've got gunners—some my men and some yours—assigned now at the Point, as well as at Jamestown and over at Oistins Bay. I figure there's nowhere else they can try a landing in force . . . though they always might try slipping a few men ashore with longboats somewhere along the coast. That's why you've got to keep the militia out and ready."

"But if they do try landing in some spot where we've got no cannon, what then, sir?" Briggs' voice projected above the howl of the storm.

"You've got ordnance in all the locations where they can safely put in with a frigate. Any other spot would mean a slow, dangerous approach. But if they try it, your militia should be able to meet them at the water's edge and turn them back. That is, if you can keep your men mustered." He straightened his pistols and pulled his cloak about him. "Now if it's all the same, I think I'll leave you to your deliberations. I've finished what it was I'd offered to do."

"One moment, Captain, if you please." Anthony Walrond stepped in front of him as the crowd began to part. "I think you've done considerably more than you proposed. Unless it included basely betraying the island."

Winston stopped and looked at him. "I'm tired enough to let that pass."

"Are you indeed, sir?" Walrond turned toward the table. "We haven't yet thanked Captain Winston for his other service, that being whilst he was making a show of helping deploy the Dutchmen's ordnance, he ordered a good fifty of his new men, those Irish indentures he's taken, to swim out to the ships of the fleet and offer their services to the Roundheads." He turned to the room. "It was base treachery. And reason enough for a hempen collar . . . if more was required."

"You, sir, can go straight to hell." Winston turned and started pushing through the planters, angrily proceeding toward the door.

Katherine stared at him, disbelieving. Before he could reach the exit, she elbowed her way through the crowd and confronted him. "Is what he said true?"

He pushed back his hair and looked down at her. "It's really not your concern, Miss Bedford."

"Then you've much to explain, if not to me, to the men in this room."

"I didn't come down here tonight to start explaining." He gestured toward the door. "If you want to hear about it, then why not call in some of the men who swam out to the ships. They're back now and they're outside in the rain, or were. I'm sure they'll be pleased to confess the full details. I have no intention of responding to Master Walrond's inquisition."

"Then we most certainly will call them in." She pushed her way briskly to the doorway. Outside a crowd of indentures stood huddled in the sheets of rain. Timothy Farrell, who had appointed himself leader, was by the door waiting for Winston. The planters watched as Katherine motioned him in.

He stepped uncertainly through the doorway, bowing, and then he removed his straw hat deferentially. "Can I be of service to Yor Ladyship?"

194

"You can explain yourself, sir." She seized his arm and escorted him to the head of the table. "Is it true Captain Winston ordered you and those men out there to swim out to the ships and offer to consort with their forces?"

"We wasn't offerin' to consort, beggin' Yor Ladyship's pardon. Not at all. That's not our inclination, as I'm a Christian." Farrell grinned. "No, by the Holy Virgin, what we did was offer to help them." He glanced toward Winston, puzzling. "An' whilst they were mullin' that over, we got a good look below decks. An' like I reported to His Worship, I'd say they've not got provision left to last more'n a fortnight. An' a good half the men sailin' with them are so rotted with scurvy they'd be pressed to carry a half-pike across this room. Aye, between decks they're all cursin' the admiral an' sayin' he's brought 'em out here to starve in the middle o' this plagued, sun-cooked wilderness."

She turned slowly toward Winston. "You sent these men out as spies?"

"Who else were we going to send?" He started again toward the door.

"Well, you could have told us, sir."

"So some of the Puritan sympathizers on this island could have swum out after them and seen to it that my men were shot, or hanged from a yardarm. Pox on it."

"But this changes everything," Briggs interjected, his face flooding with pleasure. "This man's saying the fleet's not got the force to try a landing."

"You only believe half of what you hear." Winston paused to look around the room. "Even if it's true, it probably just means they'll have to attack sooner. Before their supplies get lower and they lose even more men." He pushed on toward the door. "Desperate men do desperate things. There'll be an attempt on the island, you can count on it. And you'll fight best if you're desperate too." Suddenly he stopped again and glanced back at Briggs. "By the way, I don't know exactly who your speech on the docile slaves was intended to

195

fool. Your Africans just may have some plans afoot. I doubt they care overmuch who wins this war, you or Cromwell. So look to it and good night.'' He turned and gestured for Farrell to follow as he walked out into the blowing night rain.

Katherine watched him leave, recoiling once more against his insolence. Or maybe admiring him for it. She moved quickly through the milling crowd to the side of Dalby Bedford, bent over and whispered something to him, then turned and slipped out the door.

The burst of rain struck her in the face, and the wind blew her hair across her eyes. Winston had already started off down the hill, the crowd of indentures trailing after. Like puppy dogs, she found herself thinking. He certainly has a way with his men. She caught up her long skirts and pushed through the crowd, their straw hats and shoes now bedraggled by the downpour.

''Captain, I suppose we owe you an apology, and I've come to offer it.'' She finally reached his side. ''No one else thought of having some men swim out to spy on the fleet.''

''Katherine, no one else in there has thought of a lot of things. They're too busy arguing about who can spare a draft horse.''

''What do you mean?'' She looked up. ''Thought of what?''

''First, they should be off-loading what's left of the food and supplies on those Dutch merchantmen blockaded in the bay. Ruyters agreed just now to put his men on it tonight, but I'm afraid it's too late.'' He stared through the rain, toward the bay. ''Something tells me the fleet's likely to move in tomorrow and commandeer whatever ships they can get their hands on. It's exactly what any good commander would do.'' He continued bitterly. ''There're enough supplies on those merchantmen, flour and dried corn, to feed the island for weeks. Particularly on the ships that made port the last few days and haven't finished unlading. Believe me, you're going to need it, unless you expect to start living on sugarcane and horsemeat. But this island's too busy fighting with itself right now to listen to anybody.'' He turned and headed on through the cluster of indentures. ''I'm going down to try and off-load my own supplies tonight, before it's too late.''

She seized her skirts and pushed after him. ''Well, I still want to thank you . . . Hugh. For what you've done for us.''

He met her gaze, smiled through the rain, and raised his hand to stop her. ''Wait a minute. Before you go any further—and maybe say something foolish—you'd better know I'm not doing it for your little island of Barbados.''

''But you're helping us fight to stay a free state. If we can stand up to the fleet, then we can secure home rule, the first in the Americas. After us, maybe Virginia will do the same. Who knows, then some of the other settlements will probably . . .''

''A free state?'' He seemed to snort. ''Free for who? These greedy planters? Nobody else here'll be free.'' He pulled his cloak tighter about him. ''Just so you'll understand, let me assure you I'm not fighting to help make Barbados anything. I'm just trying to make sure I keep my frigate. Besides, Barbados'll never be 'free,' to use that word you seem to like so much. The most that'll ever happen here is it'll change masters. Look around you. It's going to be a settlement of slaves and slaveholders forever, owned and squeezed by a Council, or a Parliament, or a king, or a somebody. From now on.''

''You're wrong.'' Why did he try so hard to be infuriating? ''Home rule here is just a start. Someday there'll be no more indentures, and who knows, maybe one day they'll even decide to let the slaves be free.'' She wanted to grab him and shake him, he was so shortsighted. ''You just refuse to try and understand. Isn't there *anything* you care about?''

''I care about living life my own way. It may not sound like much of a cause, but it's taken me long enough to get around to it. I've given up thinking that one day I'll go back home and work for the honor of the Winston name, or settle down and grow fat on some sugar plantation in the Caribbees.'' He turned on her, almost shouting against the storm. ''Let me tell *you* something. I'm through living by somebody else's rules. Right now I just want to get out. Out to a place I'll make for myself. So if getting there means I first have to fight alongside the likes of Briggs and Walrond to escape Barbados, then that's what it'll be. And when I fight, make no mistake, I don't plan to lose.''

''That's quite a speech. How long have you been practicing it?'' She seized his arm. ''And the point, I take it, is that you like to run away from difficulties?''

''That's exactly right, and I wish you'd be good enough to have a brief word with the admiral of the fleet out there about it.'' He was smiling again, his face almost impish in the rain. ''Tell him there's a well-known American smuggler who'd be pleased to sail out of here if he'd just open up the blockade for an hour or so.''

''Well, why not ask him yourself? He might be relieved, if only to be rid of you and your gunners.'' She waited till a roll of thunder died away. ''And after you've sailed away? What then?''

''I plan to make my own way. Just as I said. I'm heading west by northwest, to maybe turn around a few things here in the Caribbean. But right now I've got more pressing matters, namely keeping my provisions, and those of the Dutchmen, out of the hands of the fleet.'' He turned and continued toward the shore, a dim expanse of sand shrouded in dark and rain. ''So you'd best go on back to the Assembly Room, Katherine, unless you plan to gather up those petticoats and lend me a hand.''

''Perhaps I just will.'' She caught up with him, matching his stride.

''What?''

''Since you think I'm so useless, you might be surprised to know I can carry tubs of Hollander cheese as well as you can.'' She was holding her skirts out of the mud. ''Why shouldn't I? We both want the same thing, to starve the Roundheads. We just want it for different reasons.''

"It's no place for a woman down here.''

"You said that to me once before. When we were going out to Briggs' sugarworks. Frankly I'm a little weary of hearing it, so why don't you find another excuse to try telling me what to do.''

He stopped and looked down again. Waves of rain battered against the creases in his face. "All right, Katherine. Or Katy, as I've heard your father call you. If you want to help, then come on. But you've got to get into some breeches if you don't want to drown.'' His dour expression melted into a smile. "I'll try and find you a pair on the *Defiance*. It'll be a long night's work.''

"You can tell everyone I'm one of your seamen. Or one of the indentures.''

He looked down at her bodice and exploded with laughter. "I don't think anybody's apt to mistake you for one of them. But hadn't you best tell somebody where you'll be?''

"What I do is my own business.'' She looked past him, toward the shore.

"So be it.'' A long fork of lightning burst across the sky, illuminating the shoreline ahead of them.

The muddy road was leveling out now as they neared the bay. The ruts, which ran like tiny rapids down the hill, had become placid streams, curving their way seaward. Ahead, the mast lanterns of the Dutch merchantmen swayed arcs through the dark, and the silhouettes of Dutch seamen milled along the shore, their voices muffled, ghostlike in the rain. Then she noticed the squat form of Johan Ruyters trudging toward them.

"Pox on it, we can't unlade in this squall. And in the dark besides. There's doubtless a storm brewing out there, maybe even a *huracán*, from the looks of the swell.'' He paused to nod at Katherine. "Your servant, madam.'' Then he turned

199

back at Winston. "There's little we can do now, on my honor."

"Well, I'll tell you one thing you can do, if you've got the brass."

"And what might that be, sir?"

"Just run all the ships aground here along the shore. That way they can't be taken, and then we can unlade after the storm runs its course."

"Aye, that's a possibility I'd considered. In truth I'm thinking I might give it a try. The *Zeelander*'s been aground before. Her keel's fine oak, for all the barnacles." His voice was heavy with rue. "But I've asked around, and most of the other men don't want to run the risk."

"Well, you're right about the squall. From the looks of the sea, I'd agree we can't work in this weather. So maybe I'll just go ahead and run the *Defiance* aground." He studied the ship, now rolling in the swell and straining at her anchor lines. "There'll never be a better time, with the bay up the way it is now."

"God's blood, it's a quandary." Ruyters turned and peered toward the horizon. The mast lights of the fleet were all but lost in the sheets of rain. "I wish I knew what those bastards are thinking right now. But it's odds they'll try to move in and pilfer our provisions as soon as the sea lets up. Moreover, we'd be fools to try using any ordnance on them, bottled in the way we are. They've got us trapped, since they surely know the battery up there on the Point won't open fire on the bay while we're in it." He whirled on Winston. "You wouldn't, would you?"

"And risk putting a round through the side of these ships here? Not a chance!"

"Aye, they'll reason that out by tomorrow, no doubt. So grounding these frigates may be the only way we can keep them out of English hands. Damn it all, I'd best go ahead and bring her up, before the seas get any worse." He bowed

200

toward Katherine. "Your most obedient, madam. If you'll be good enough to grant me leave . . ."

"Now don't try anything foolish." Winston was eyeing him.

"What are you suggesting?"

"Don't go thinking you'll make a run for it in the storm. You'll never steer past the reefs."

"Aye. I've given that passing thought as well. If I had a bit more ballast, I'd be tempted." He spat into the rain, then looked back. "And I'd take odds you've considered the same."

"But I've not got the ballast either. Or that Spaniard of yours we agreed on. Don't forget our bargain."

"My word's always been my bond, sir, though I wonder if there'll ever be any sugar to ship. For that matter, you may be lucky ever to see open seas again yourself. Just like the rest of us." Ruyters sighed. "Aye, every Christian here tonight's wishing he'd never heard of Barbados." He nodded farewell and turned to wade toward a waiting longboat. In moments he had disappeared into the rain.

"Well, Miss Katy Bedford, unless the rest of the Dutchmen have the foresight Ruyters has, those merchantmen out there and all their provisions will be in the fleet's hands by sundown tomorrow." He reached for her arm. "But not the *Defiance*. Come on and I'll get you a set of dry clothes. And maybe a tankard of sack to warm you up. We're about to go on a very short and very rough voyage."

She watched as he walked to where the indentures were waiting. He seemed to be ordering them to find shelter and return in the morning. Timothy Farrell spoke something in return. Winston paused a moment, shrugged and rummaged his pockets, then handed him a few coins. The Irishmen all saluted before heading off toward the cluster of taverns over next to the bridge.

"Come on." He came trudging back. "The longboat's moored down here, if it hasn't been washed out to sea yet."

"Where're your men?"

"My gunnery mates are at the batteries, and the rest of the lads are assigned to the militia. I ordered John and a few of the boys to stay on board to keep an eye on her, but the rest are gone." His face seemed drawn. "Have no fear. In this sea it'll be no trick to ground her. Once we weigh the anchor, the swell should do the rest."

As he led her into the water, the surf splashing against her shins, she reflected that the salt would ruin her taffeta petticoats, then decided she didn't care. The thrill of the night and the sea were worth it.

Directly ahead of them a small longboat bobbed in the water. "Grab your skirts, and I'll hoist you in."

She had barely managed to seize the sides of her dress before a wave washed over them both. She was still sputtering, salt in her mouth, as he swept her up into his arms and settled her over the side. She gasped as the boat dipped crazily in the swell, pounded by the sheets of rain.

He traced the mooring line back to the post at the shore where it had been tied and quickly loosened it. Then he shoved the boat out to sea and rolled over the side, as easily as though he were dropping into a hammock.

The winds lashed rain against them as he strained at the oars, but slowly they made way toward the dark bulk of the *Defiance*. He rowed into the leeward side and in moments John Mewes was there, reaching for the line to draw them alongside. He examined Katherine with a puzzled expression as he gazed down at them.

" 'Tis quite a night, m'lady, by my life." He reached to take her hand as Winston hoisted her up. "Welcome aboard. No time for Godfearin' folk to be at sea in a longboat, that I'll warrant."

"That it's not, John." Winston grasped a deadeye and drew himself over the side. "Call the lads to station. After I take Miss Bedford back to the cabin and find a dry change of clothes for her, we're going to weigh anchor and try beaching the ship."

"Aye." Mewes beamed as he squinted through the rain. "In truth, I've been thinkin' the same myself. The fornicatin' Roundheads'll be in the bay and aimin' to take prizes soon as the weather breaks." He headed toward the quarterdeck. "But they'll never get this beauty, God is my witness."

"Try hoisting the spritsail, John, and see if you can bring the bow about." He took Katherine's hand as he helped her duck under the shrouds. "This way, Katy."

"What do you have for me to wear?" She steadied herself against a railing as the slippery deck heaved in the waves, but Winston urged her forward. He was still gripping her hand as he led her into the companionway, a dark hallway beneath the quarterdeck illuminated by a single lantern swaying in the gusts of wind.

"We don't regularly sail with women in the crew." His words were almost lost in a clap of thunder as he shoved open the door of the Great Cabin. "What would you say to some of my breeches and a doublet?"

"What would *you* say to it?"

He laughed and swept the dripping hair out of his eyes as he ushered her in. "I'd say I prefer seeing women in dresses. But we'll both have to make do." He walked to his locker, seeming not to notice the roll of the ship, and flipped open the lid. "Take your pick while I go topside." He gestured toward the sideboard. "And there's port and some tankards in there."

"How'll I loosen my bodice?"

"Send for your maid, as always." There was a scream of wind down the companionway as he wrenched open the door, then slammed it again behind him. She was still grasping the table, trying to steady herself against the roll of the ship, when she heard muffled shouts from the decks above and then the rattle of a chain.

She reached back and began to work at the knot in the long

laces that secured her bodice. English fashions, which she found absurd in sweltering Barbados, required all women of condition to wear this heavy corset, which laced all the way up the back, over their shift.

This morning it had been two layers of whitest linen, with strips of whalebone sewn between and dainty puffed sleeves attached, but now it was soaked with salt water and brown from the sand and flotsam of the bay. She tugged and wriggled until it was loose enough to draw over her head.

She drew a breath of relief as her breasts came free beneath her shift, and then she wadded the bodice into a soggy bundle and discarded it onto the floor of the cabin. Her wet shift still clung to her and she looked down for a moment, taking pleasure in the full curve of her body. Next she began unpinning her skirt at the spot where it had been looped up stylishly to display her petticoat.

The ship rolled again and the lid of the locker dropped shut. As the floor tilted back to an even keel, she quickly stepped out of the soaking dress and petticoats, letting them collapse onto the planking in a dripping heap. In the light of the swinging lamp the once-blue taffeta looked a muddy gray.

The ship suddenly pitched backward, followed by a low groan that sounded through the timbers as it shuddered to a dead stop. The floor of the cabin lay at a tilt, sloping down toward the stern.

She stepped to the locker and pried the lid back open. Inside were several changes of canvas breeches, as well as a fine striped silk pair. She laughed as she pulled them out to inspect them in the flickering light. What would he say if I were to put these on, she wondered? They're doubtless part of his vain pride.

Without hesitating she shook out the legs and drew them on under her wet shift. There was no mirror, but as she tied the waiststring she felt their sensuous snugness about her thighs. The legs were short, intended to fit into hose or boots, and they revealed her fine turn of ankle. Next she lifted out a velvet doublet, blue and embroidered, with gold buttons down the front. She admired it a moment, mildly surprised that he would own such a fine garment, then laid it on the table while she pulled her dripping shift over her head.

The rush of air against her skin made her suddenly aware how hot and sultry the cabin really was. Impulsively she walked back to the windows aft and unlatched them. Outside the sea churned and pounded against the stern, while dark rain still beat against the quartergallery. She took a deep breath as she felt the cooling breeze wash over her clammy face and breasts. She was wondering how her hair must look when she heard a voice.

"You forgot your port."

She gasped quietly as she turned. Hugh Winston was standing beside her, holding out a tankard. "Well, do you care to take it?" He smiled and glanced down at her breasts.

"My, but that was no time at all." She reached for the tankard, then looked back toward the table where her wet shift lay.

"Grounding a ship's no trick. You just weigh the anchor and pray she comes about. Getting her afloat again's the difficulty." He leaned against the window frame and lifted his tankard. "So here's to freedom again someday, Katy. Mine, yours."

She started to drink, then remembered herself and turned toward the table to retrieve her shift.

"I don't expect you'll be needing that."

She continued purposefully across the cabin. "Well, sir, *I* didn't expect . . ."

"Oh, don't start now being a coquette. I like you too much the way you are." A stroke of lightning split down the sky behind him. He drank again, then set down his tankard and was moving toward her.

"I'm not sure I know what you mean."

"Take it as a compliment. I despise intriguing women." He seemed to look through her. "Though you do always manage to get whatever you're after, one way or other, going about it your own way." A clap of thunder sounded through the open stern windows. "I'd also wager you've had your share of experience in certain personal matters. For which I suppose there's your royalist gallant to thank."

"That's scarcely your concern, is it? You've no claim over me." She settled her tankard on the table, reached for his velvet doublet—at least it was dry—and started draping it over her bare shoulders. "Nor am I sure I relish bluntness as much as you appear to."

"It's my fashion. I've been out in the Caribbees too long, dodging musket balls, to bother with a lot of fancy court chatter."

"There's bluntness, and there's good breeding. I trust you at least haven't forgotten the difference."

"I suppose you think you can enlighten me."

"Well, since I'm wearing your breeches, which appear meant for a gentleman, perhaps it'd not be amiss to teach you how to address a lady." She stepped next to him, her eyes mischievous. "Try repeating after me. 'Yours is a comely shape, Madam, on my life, that delights my very heart. And your fine visage might shame a cherubim.' " She suppressed a smile at his dumbfounded look, then continued. " 'Those eyes fire my thoughts with promised sweetness, and those lips are like petals of the rose . . .' "

"God's blood!" He caught her open doublet and drew her toward him. "If it's a fop you'd have me be, I suppose the rest could probably go something like '. . . begging to be kissed. They seem fine and soft. Are they kind as well?' " He slipped his arms about her and pulled her against his wet jerkin.

After the first shock, she realized he tasted of salt and gunpowder. As a sudden gust of rain from the window extinguished the sea lamp, she felt herself being slowly lowered against the heavy oak table in the center of the cabin.

Now his mouth had moved to her breasts, as he half-kissed,

half-bit her nipples—whether in desire or merely to tease she could not tell. Finally she reached and drew his face up to hers.

"I'm not in love with you, Captain Winston. Never expect that. I could never give any man that power over me." She laughed at his startled eyes. "But I wouldn't mind if you wanted me."

"Katy, I've wanted you for a fortnight." He drew back and looked at her. "I had half a mind not to let you away from this ship the last time you were here. This time I don't plan to make the same mistake. Except I don't like seeing you in my own silk breeches."

"I think they fit me very nicely."

"Maybe it's time I showed you what I think." He abruptly drew her up and seized the string at her waist. In a single motion, he pulled it open and slipped away the striped legs. Then he admired her a moment as he drew his hands appreciatively down her long legs. "Now I'd like to show you how one man who's forgot his London manners pays court to a woman."

He pulled her to him and kissed her once more. Then without a word he slipped his arms under her and cradled her against him. He carried her across the cabin to the window, and gently seated her on its sill. Now the lightning flashed again, shining against the scar on his cheek.

He lifted her legs and twined them around his shoulders, bringing her against his mouth. A glow of sensation blossomed somewhere within her as he began to tease her gently with his tongue. She tightened her thighs around him, astonished at the swell of pleasure.

The cabin was dissolving, leaving nothing but a great, consuming sensation that was engulfing her, readying to flood her body. As she arched expectantly against him, he suddenly paused.

"Don't stop now . . ." She gazed at him, her vision blurred.

He smiled as he drew back. "If you want lovemaking from me, you'll have to think of somebody besides yourself. I want you to be with me, Katy Bedford. Not ahead."

He rose up and slipped away his jerkin. Then his rough, wet breeches. He toyed with her sex, bringing her wide in readiness, then he entered her quickly and forcefully.

She heard a gasp, and realized it was her own voice. It was as though she had suddenly discovered some missing part of herself. For an instant nothing else in the world existed. She clasped her legs about his waist and moved against him, returning his own intensity.

Now the sensation was coming once more, and she clung to him as she wrenched against his thighs. All at once he shoved against her powerfully, then again, and she found herself wanting to thrust her body into his, merge with him, as he lunged against her one last time. Then the lightning flared and the cabin seemed to melt into white.

After a moment of quiet, he wordlessly took her in his arms. For the first time she noticed the rain and the salt spray from the window washing over them.

"God knows the last thing I need now is a woman to think about." He smiled and kissed her. "I'd probably be wise to pitch you out to sea this minute, while I still have enough sense to do it. But I don't think I will."

"I wouldn't let you anyway. I'm not going to let you so much as move. You can just stay precisely where you are." She gripped him tighter and pulled his lips down to hers. "If anything, I should have done with *you,* here and now."

"Then come on. We'll go outside together." He lifted her through the open stern window, onto the quartergallery. The skies were an open flood.

She looked at him and reached to gently caress his scarred cheek. "What was that you were doing—at the first? I never knew men did such things." Her hand traveled across his chest, downward. "Do . . . do women ever do that too?"

He laughed. "It's not entirely unheard of in this day and age."

"Then you must show me how. I'll wager no Puritan wife does it."

"I didn't know you were a Puritan. You certainly don't make love like one."

"I'm not. I want to be as far from them as I can be." Her lips began to move down his chest.

"Then come away with me." He smoothed her wet hair. "To Jamaica."

"Jamaica?" She looked up at him in dismay. "My God, what are you saying? The Spaniards . . ."

"I'll manage the Spaniards." He reached down and kissed her again.

"You know, after this morning, up on the Point, I'd almost believe you." She paused and looked out at the line of warships on the horizon, dull shadows in the rain. "But nobody's going to leave here for a long time now."

"I will. And the English navy's not going to stop me." He slipped his arms around her and drew her against him. "Why not forget you're supposed to wed Anthony Walrond and come along? We're alike, you and me."

"Hugh, you know I can't leave." She slid a leg over him and pressed her thigh against his. "But at least I've got you here tonight. I think I already fancy this. So let's not squander all our fine time with a lot of talk."

Chapter Nine

"I've changed my mind. I'll not be part of it." Serina pulled at his arm and realized she was shouting to make herself heard above the torrent around them. In the west the lightning flared again. "Take me back. Now."

Directly ahead the wide thatched roof of the mill house loomed out of the darkness. Atiba seemed not to hear as he circled his arm about her waist and urged her forward. A sheet of rain off the building's eaves masked the doorway, and he drew her against him to cover her head as they passed through. Inside, the packed earthen floor was sheltered and dry.

The warmth of the room caused her misgivings to ebb momentarily; the close darkness was like a protective cloak, shielding them from the storm. Still, the thought of what lay ahead filled her with dread. The Jesuit teachers years ago in Brazil had warned you could lose your soul by joining in pagan African rituals. Though she didn't believe in the Jesuits' religion, she still feared their warning. She had never been part of a true Yoruba ceremony for the gods; she had only heard them described, and that so long ago she had forgotten almost everything.

When Atiba appeared at her window, a dark figure in the storm, and told her she must come with him, she had at first refused outright. In reply he had laughed lightly, kissed her, then whispered it was essential that she be present. He did not say why; instead he went on to declare that tonight was the perfect time. No cane was being crushed; the mill house was empty, the oxen in their stalls, the entire plantation staff ordered to quarters. Benjamin Briggs and the other *branco* masters were assembled in Bridgetown, holding a council of war against the Inglês ships that had appeared in the bay at sunrise.

When finally she'd relented and agreed to come, he had insisted she put on a white shift—the whitest she had—saying in a voice she scarcely recognized that tonight she must take special care with everything. Tonight she must be Yoruba.

"Surely you're not afraid of lightning and thunder?" He finally spoke as he gestured for her to sit, the false lightness still in his tone. "Don't be. It could be a sign from Shango, that he is with us. Tonight the heavens belong to him." He turned and pointed toward the mill. "Just as in this room, near this powerful iron machine of the *branco*, the earth is sacred to Ogun. That's why he will come tonight if we prepare a place for him."

She looked blankly at the mill. Although the rollers were brass, the rest of the heavy framework was indeed iron, the metal consecrated to Ogun. She remembered Atiba telling her that when a Yoruba swore an oath in the great palace of the Oba in Ife, he placed his hand not on a Bible but on a huge piece of iron, shaped like a tear and weighing over three hundred pounds. The very existence of Yorubaland was ensured by iron. Ogun's metal made possible swords, tipped arrows, muskets. If no iron were readily at hand, a Yoruba would swear by the earth itself, from whence came ore.

"I wish you would leave your Yoruba gods in Africa, where they belong." How, she asked herself, could she have succumbed so readily to his *preto* delusions? She realized now that the Yoruba were still too few, too powerless to revolt.

She wanted to tell him to forget his gods, his fool's dream of rebellion and freedom.

He glanced back at her and laughed. "But our gods, our Orisa, are already here, because our people are here." He looked away, his eyes hidden in the dark, and waited for a roll of thunder to die away. The wind dropped suddenly, for an instant, and there was silence except for the drumbeat of rain. "Our gods live inside us, passed down from generation to generation. We inherit the spirit of our fathers, just as we take on their strength, their appearance. Whether we are free or slave, they will never abandon us." He touched her hand gently. "Tonight, at last, perhaps you will begin to understand."

She stared at him, relieved that the darkness hid the disbelief in her eyes. She had never seen any god, anywhere, nor had anyone else. His gods were not going to make him, or her, any less a slave to the *branco*. She wanted to grab his broad shoulders and shake sense into him. Tonight was the first, maybe the last, time that Briggs Hall would be theirs alone. Why had he brought her here instead, for some bizarre ceremony? Finally her frustration spilled out. "What if I told you I don't truly believe in your Ogun and your Shango and all the rest? Any more than I believe in the Christian God and all His saints?"

He lifted her face up. "But what if you experienced them yourself? Could you still deny they exist?"

"The Christians claim their God created everything in the world." Again the anger flooding over her, like the rain outside. She wanted to taunt him. "If that's true, maybe He created your gods too."

"The Christian God is nothing. Where is He? Where does He show Himself? Our Orisa create the world anew every day, rework it, change it, right before our eyes. That's how we know they are alive." His gaze softened. "You'll believe in our gods before tonight is over, I promise you."

"How can you be so sure?"

"Because one of them is already living inside you. I know the signs." He stood back and examined her. "I think you are consecrated to a certain god very much like you, which is as it should be."

He reached down and picked up a cloth sack he had brought. As the lightning continued to flare through the open doorway, he began to extract several long white candles. Finally he selected one and held it up, then with an angry grunt pointed to the black rings painted around it at one-inch intervals.

"Do you recognize this? It's what the *branco* call a 'bidding candle.' Did you know they used candles like this on the ship? They sold a man each time the candle burned down to one of these rings. I wanted Ogun to see this tonight."

He struck a flint against a tinderbox, then lit the candle, shielding it from the wind till the wick was fully ablaze. Next he turned and stationed it on the floor near the base of the mill, where it would be protected from the gale.

She watched the tip flicker in the wind, throwing a pattern of light and shadow across his long cheek, highlighting the three small parallel scars. His eyes glistened in concentration as he dropped to his knees and retrieved a small bag from his waistband. He opened it, dipped in his hand, and brought out a fistful of white powder; then he moved to a smooth place on the floor and began to dribble the powder out of his fist, creating a series of curved patterns on the ground.

"What are you doing?"

"I'm preparing the symbol of Ogun."

"Will drawings in the dirt lure your god?"

He did not look up, merely continued to lay down the lines of white powder, letting a stream slip from his closed fist. "Take care what you say. I am consecrating this earth to Ogun. A Yoruba god will not be mocked. I have seen hunters return from an entire season in the forest empty-handed because they scorned to make offerings."

"I don't understand. The Christians say their God is in the

213

sky. Where are these gods of Africa supposed to be?'' She was trying vainly to recall the stories her mother Dara and the old *babalawo* of Pernambuco had told. But there was so much, especially the part about Africa, that she had willed herself to forget. ''First you claim they are already inside you, and then you say they must come here from somewhere.''

''Both things are true. The Orisa are in some ways like ordinary men and women.'' He paused and looked up. ''Just as we are different, each of them is also. Shango desires justice—though wrongs must be fairly punished, he is humane. Ogun cares nothing for fairness. He demands vengeance.''

''How do you know what these gods are supposed to want? You don't have any sacred books like the Christians. . . .''

''Perhaps the Christians need their books. We don't. Our gods are not something we study, they're what we are.''

''Then why call them gods?''

''Because they are a part of us we cannot reach except *through* them. They dwell deep inside our selves, in the spirit that all the Yoruba peoples share.'' He looked down and continued to lay out the drawing as he spoke. ''But I can't describe it, because it lies in a part of the mind that has no words.'' He reached to take more of the white powder from the bag and shifted to a new position as he continued to fashion the diagram, which seemed to be the outline of some kind of bush. ''You see, except for Olorun, the sky god, all our Orisa once dwelt on earth, but instead of dying they became the communal memory of our people. When we call forth one of the gods, we reach into this shared consciousness where they wait. If a god comes forth, he may for a time take over the body of one of us as his temporary habitation.'' He paused and looked up. ''That's why I wanted you here tonight. To show you what it means to be Yoruba.'' He straightened and critically surveyed the drawing. His eyes revealed his satisfaction.

On the ground was a complex rendering of an African cotton tree, the representing-image of Ogun. Its trunk was flanked on each side by the outline of an elephant tusk, another symbol of the Yoruba god. He circled it for a moment, appraising it, then went to the cache of sacred utensils he had hidden behind the mill that afternoon and took up a stack of palm fronds. Carefully he laid a row along each side of the diagram.

"That's finished now. Next I'll make the symbol for Shango. It's simpler." He knelt and quickly began to lay down the outline of a double-headed axe, still using the white powder from the bag. The lines were steady, flawless. She loved the lithe, deft intensity of his body as he drew his sacred signs—nothing like the grudging *branco* artists who had decorated the cathedral in Pernambuco with Catholic saints, all the while half-drunk on Portuguese wine.

"Where did you learn all these figures?"

He smiled. "I've had much practice, but I was first taught by my father, years ago in Ife."

The drawing was already done. He examined it a moment, approved it, and laid aside the bag of white powder. She picked it up and took a pinch to her lips. It had the tangy bitterness of cassava flour.

"Now I'll prepare a candle for Shango." He rummaged through the pile. "But in a way it's for you too, so I'll find a pure white one, not a bidding candle."

"What do you mean, 'for me too'?"

He seemed not to hear as he lit the taper and placed it beside the symbol. Next he extracted a white kerchief from his waistband and turned to her. "I've brought something for you. A gift. Here, let me tie it." He paused to caress her, his fingertips against her cinnamon skin, then he lovingly pulled the kerchief around her head. He lifted up her long hair, still wet from the rain, and carefully coiled it under the white cloth. Finally he knotted it on top, African style. "To-

215

night you may discover you truly are a Yoruba woman, so it is well that you look like one.''

Abruptly, above the patter of rain, came the sound of footfalls in the mud outside. She glanced around and through the dark saw the silhouettes of the Yoruba men from the slave quarters. The first three carried long bundles swathed in heavy brown wraps to protect them from the rain.

They entered single file and nodded in silence to Atiba before gathering around the diagrams on the floor to bow in reverence. After a moment, the men carrying the bundles moved to a clear space beside the mill and began to unwrap them. As the covering fell away, the fresh goatskin tops of three new drums sparkled white in the candlelight.

She watched the drummers settle into position, each nestling an instrument beneath his left arm, a curved wooden mallet in his right hand. From somewhere in her past there rose up an identical scene, years ago in Brazil, when all the Yoruba, men and women, had gathered to dance. Then as now there were three hourglass-shaped instruments, all held horizontally under the drummer's arm as they were played. The largest, the *iya ilu*, was almost three feet long and was held up by a wide shoulder strap, just as this one was tonight. The other two, the *bata* and the *go-go*, were progressively smaller, and neither was heavy enough to require a supporting strap.

The man holding the *iya ilu* tonight was Obewole, his weathered coffee face rendered darker still by the contrast of a short grey beard. His muscles were conditioned by decades of swinging a long iron sword; in the fields he could wield a cane machete as powerfully as any young warrior. He shifted the shoulder strap one last time, then held out the mallet in readiness and looked toward Atiba for a signal to begin.

When Atiba gave a nod, a powerful drum roll sounded above the roar of the gale. Then Obewole began to talk with the drum, a deep-toned invocation to the ceremonial high gods of the Yoruba pantheon, Eleggua and Olorun.

216

"Omi tutu a Eleggua, omi tutu a mi ileis, Olorun modu-pue . . ."

As the drum spoke directly to the gods, the line of men passed by Atiba and he sprinkled each with liquor from a calabash, flinging droplets from his fingertips like shooting stars in the candlelight. Each man saluted him, their *babalawo,* by dropping their heads to the ground in front of him while balanced on their fists, then swinging their bodies right and left, touching each side to the floor in the traditional Yoruba obeisance. The office of *babalawo* embodied all the struggles, the triumphs, the pride of their race.

When the last man had paid tribute, all three drums suddenly exploded with a powerful rhythm that poured out into the night and the storm. Obewole's mallet resounded against the skin of the large *iya ilu,* producing a deep, measured cadence—three strokes, then rest, repeated again and again hypnotically—almost as though he were knocking on the portals of the unseen. Next to him the men holding the two smaller drums interjected syncopated clicks between the *iya ilu*'s throaty booms. The medley of tempos they blended together was driving, insistent.

As the sound swelled in intensity, the men began to circle the drawing for Ogun, ponderously shuffling from one foot to the other in time with the beat. It was more than a walk, less than a dance.

Atiba began to clang together two pieces of iron he had brought, their ring a call to Ogun. The men trudged past him, single file, the soles of their feet never leaving the earth. Using this ritual walk, they seemed to be reaching out for some mighty heart of nature, through the force of their collective strength. They had come tonight as individuals; now they were being melded into a single organic whole by the beat of the *iya ilu,* their spirits unified.

Some of them nodded to Obewole as they passed, a homage to his mastery, but he no longer appeared to see them. Instead he gazed into the distance, his face a mask, and methodically pounded the taut goatskin with ever increasing intensity.

"Ogun cyuba bai ye baye tonu . . ." Suddenly a chant rose up through the dense air, led by the young warrior Derin, who had devoted his life to Ogun. His cropped hair emphasized the strong line of his cheeks and his long, powerful neck. As he moved, now raising one shoulder then the other in time with the drums, his body began to glisten with sweat in the humid night air.

All the while, Atiba stood beside the mill, still keeping time with the pieces of iron. He nodded in silent approval as the men in the line began to revolve, their bare feet now slapping against the packed earth, arms working as though they held a bellows. This was the ritual call for Ogun, warrior and iron worker. As they whirled past the design on the floor, each man bent low, chanting, imploring Ogun to appear. While the sound soared around them, the dance went on and on, and the atmosphere of the mill house became tense with expectation.

Suddenly Derin spun away, separating himself from the line, his eyes acquiring a faraway, vacant gaze. As he passed by the musicians, the drumming swelled perceptibly, and Serina sensed a presence rising up in the room, intense and fearsome. Without warning, the clanging of iron stopped and she felt a powerful hand seize hers.

"Ogun is almost here." Atiba was pointing toward Derin, his voice a hoarse whisper. "Can you sense his spirit emerging? Soon he may try to mount Derin."

She studied the dancers, puzzling. "What do you mean, 'mount' him?"

"The Orisa can mount our mind and body, almost like a rider mounts a horse. Ogun wants to displace Derin's spirit and become the force that rules him. But Derin's self must first leave before Ogun can enter, since it's not possible to be both man and god at once. His own spirit is trying to resist, to ward off the god. Sometimes it can be terrifying

218

to watch." He studied the men a few moments in silence. "Yes, Derin's body will be the one honored tonight. He's the youngest and strongest here; it's only natural that Ogun would choose him. Don't be surprised now by what you see. And Dara"—his voice grew stern—"you must not try to help him, no matter what may happen."

At that instant the young warrior's left leg seemed to freeze to the ground, and he pitched forward, forfeiting his centering and balance. He began to tremble convulsively, his eyes terror-stricken and unfocused, his body reeling from a progression of unseen blows against the back of his neck. He was still trying to sustain the ritual cadence as he pitched backward against the mill.

Now the drums grew louder, more forceful, and his entire body seemed to flinch with each stroke of Obewole's mallet. His eyes rolled back into his head, showing only a crescent of each pupil, while his arms flailed as though trying to push away some invisible net that had encircled his shoulders. He staggered across the floor, a long gash in his shoulder where the teeth of the mill had ripped the flesh, and began to emit barking cries, almost screams, as he struggled to regain his balance.

"You've got to stop it!" She started pulling herself to her feet. But before she could rise, Atiba seized her wrist and silently forced her down. None of the other men appeared to take notice of Derin's convulsions. Several were, in fact, themselves now beginning to stumble and lose their balance. But they all continued the solemn dance, as though determined to resist the force wanting to seize their bodies.

At that moment the measured booms of the large *iya ilu* drum switched to a rapid, syncopated beat, a knowing trick by Obewole intended to throw the dancers off their centering. The sudden shift in drumming caused Derin to lose the last of his control. He staggered toward the drummers, shouted something blindly, then stiffened and revolved to face Atiba.

His eyes were vacant but his sweat-drenched body had assumed a mystical calm. He stood silent for a moment, glared fiercely about the mill house, then reached for the long iron machete Atiba was holding out for him.

"*Obi meye lori emo ofe . . .*" He was intoning in a deep, powerful voice, declaring he would now reveal who he was.

"*Ogun!*"

He abruptly brandished the machete about his head and with a leap landed astride the diagram Atiba had traced in the dirt.

The other men hovered back to watch as he launched a violent dance, slashing the air with the blade while intoning a singsong chant in a voice that seemed to emanate from another world. The drums were silent now, as all present knelt to him, even those older and more senior. Derin the man was no longer present; his body belonged to the god, and his absent eyes burned with a fierceness and determination Serina had never before seen.

She gripped Atiba's hand, feeling her fingers tremble. Now, more than ever, she was terrified. The pounding of rain on the roof seemed almost to beckon her out, into the night, away from all this. But then she began to understand that the men around her were no longer slaves, in the mill room of a plantation in the English Caribbees; they were Yoruba warriors, invoking the gods of their dark land.

Now Derin was finishing the ritual chant that proclaimed him the earthly manifestation of Ogun. The words had scarcely died away when Atiba stepped forward and demanded he speak to the men, offer them guidance for the days ahead. When Derin merely stood staring at him with his distant eyes, Atiba grabbed him and shook him.

Finally, above the sound of wind and rain, Derin began to shout a series of curt phrases. His voice came so rapidly, and with such unearthly force, Serina found she could not follow.

"What is he saying?" She gripped Atiba's hand tighter.

"Ogun demands we must right the wrongs that have been set upon us. That we must use our swords to regain our freedom and our pride. He declares tonight that his anger is fierce, like the burning sun that sucks dry the milk of the coconut, and he will stand with us in the name of vengeance. That victory will be ours, but only if we are willing to fight to the death, as worthy warriors. . . ."

Atiba stopped to listen as Derin continued to intone in a deep chilling voice. When he had concluded his declaration, he abruptly turned and approached Serina. He stood before her for a moment, then reached out with his left hand and seized her shoulder, tearing her white shift. She gasped at the tingle in her arm, realizing his fingers were cold and hard as iron. His eyes seemed those of a being who saw beyond the visible, into some other world. She wanted to pull away, but his gaze held her transfixed.

"Send this one back where she belongs, to the compounds of your wives. Yoruba warriors do not hold council with women. She . . . will lead you . . . to . . ." The voice seemed to be receding back into Derin's body now, to be calling from some faraway place.

Suddenly he leaped backward, circled the machete about his head, and with a powerful stroke thrust it into the earth, buried halfway to the hilt. He stared down for a moment in confusion, as though incredulous at what he had just done, then tremulously touched the dark wooden handle. Finally he seized his face in his hands, staggered backward, and collapsed.

Atiba sprang to catch him as he sprawled across the remains of the trampled palm fronds. Several other men came forward, their eyes anxious.

"Ogun has honored us tonight with his presence." He looked about the dark room, and all the men nodded in silent agreement.

At that moment a long trunk of lightning illuminated the open doorway, followed by a crack of thunder that shook the pole supporting the thatched roof. Serina felt a chill sweep against her forehead.

221

"That is the voice of Shango. He too demands to be heard. We must continue." Atiba turned to Serina. "Even though it displeases Ogun, your presence here tonight is essential. You were once consecrated to Shango. Perhaps you were never told. But you are Yoruba. Your lineage is sacred to him."

"How do you know?" She felt the chill in the room deepening.

"Shango animates your spirit. As a *babalawo* I can tell. It must have been divined the day you were born and sanctified by a ceremony to Olorun, the high god. There are signs, but I must not reveal to you what they are."

"No! I won't have any part of this. It's pagan, terrifying." She wrapped her arms about her, shivering from the cold. "I only came here to please you. I'll watch. But that's all."

Atiba motioned to the drummers. "But Shango will not be denied. You have nothing to fear. Most of his fire tonight is being spent in the skies." The drums began again, their cadence subtly changed from before. The lightning flashed once more, closer now, as he urged her toward the dancers.

"We must know the will of Shango, but we are all men of Ogun. Shango would never come and mount one of us. He will only come to you, his consecrated."

As the line of men encircled her and pushed her forward, into the crowd of half-naked bodies sweating in the candlelight, Atiba's face disappeared in the tumult of heaving chests and arms. She tried to yell back to him, to tell him she would never comply, but her voice was lost in the drumming and the roar of the rain.

She was moving now with the line of men. Before she realized what she was doing, she had caught the hem of her swaying white shift and begun to swing it from side to side in time with the booms of the *iya ilu* drum. It was a dance figure she remembered from some lost age, a joyous time long ago. She would dance for her love of Atiba, but not for his gods.

Now the rhythm of the drums grew more dizzying, as

though pulling her forward. It was increasingly hard to think; only through the dance could she keep control, stay centered on her own self. Only by this arcing of her body, as the movement of her hips flowed into her swaying torso, could she . . .

Suddenly she saw herself, in Pernambuco, being urged gently forward by her Yoruba mother as the slaves drummed in the cool evening air. It was Sunday, and all the *preto* had gathered to dance, the black women in ornate Portuguese frocks of bright primary colors and the men in tight-fitting trousers. The drums were sounding and the plantation air was scented by a spray of white blossoms that drifted down from the spreading tree. The *senhor de engenho* was there, the white master, clapping and leering and calling something to Dara about her *mulata* daughter's new frock. He was watching her now, waiting. Soon, very soon, he would take her.

Lightning flashed again, and she felt its warmth against her icy skin. She wanted to laugh, to cry, to stay in that world of faraway whose warmth beckoned. But now she felt her own will beginning to ebb. Something was happening. . . .

"No! Please, no!" She forced her long fingernails into her palm, and the pain seemed to restore some of the awareness she had felt slipping from her. Desperately she tore herself away from the dance and seized the center post of the mill, gasping for air and digging her nails into the wood until she felt one snap. Then she pulled away the African kerchief and threw back her head, swirling her hair about her face till it caught in her mouth. All at once she was thirsty, hungry, yearning for a dark presence that hovered over her body like a lover.

Again the blossoms of Pernambuco drifted down, tiny points of fire as they settled against her face, and she began to hum a simple Portuguese song she had known as a child. It was spring in Brazil, and as she looked up she saw the face of the old Yoruba *babalawo*.

"Dara, come." He was reaching toward her, beckoning

her away from the Portuguese master, saying something about Shango she did not understand, and the sight of his sad eyes and high black cheeks filled her with love. But now there was a youthfulness in his face, as though he were here and powerful and young. Her old *babalawo* had come back: there was the same glistening black skin, the same three face-marks cut down his cheek, the powerful eyes she had somehow forgotten over the years.

She gasped as he pulled her back into the circle of dancers.

He was Atiba. His clan-marks were Atiba's. And so was his voice . . .

Lightning illuminated the doorway and its whiteness washed over her, bleaching away the mill, the moving bodies, the face of Atiba. As she stumbled back among the dancers, her mind seemed to be thinning, turning to pale mist, merging with the rain.

"Boguo yguoro ache semilenu Shango . . ." The men were moving beside her now, intoning their singsong chant. She suddenly recalled the long-forgotten Yoruba verses and wanted to join in, but the words floated away. She was no longer part of the men in the room; she was distant, observing from some other world. Instead of the sweating bodies, there was the fragrance of frangipani and the faces of *preto* slaves on the Pernambuco plantation as they gathered around at the moment of her birth to praise her light skin. Dara's warm, nourishing breast was against her lips, and the world was bright and new.

She gasped for breath, but the air was wet, oppressive. Its heaviness was descending over her, then her left leg seemed to catch in a vise, as though it belonged to the deep earth. She wrenched her body to look down, and felt a crack of thunder pound against her back. The world was drifting up through her, drowning her in white. . . .

. . . She is floating, borne by the drums, while a weight has settled against her back, a stifling weariness that insists the dance must stop. Yet some power propels her on, swirls about her, forces her forward. She senses the touch of wet skin as she falls against one of the dancers, but no hands reach out to help. Only the drums keep her alive. But they too are fading, leaving her, as the world starts to move in slow motion. A white void has replaced her mind. Her breath comes in short bursts, her heart pounds, her hands and feet are like ice. She is ready now to leave, to surrender, to be taken. Then a voice comes, a voice only she can hear, whose Yoruba words say her mind can rest. That her body is no longer to struggle. She holds her eyes open, but she no longer sees. A powerful whiteness has settled against her forehead. . . .

"Okunrin t'o lagbara!" A hard voice cut through the room, silencing the drums. *"Shango!"*

The Yoruba men fell forward to touch the feet of the tall *mulata* who towered over them, demanding worship. Her eyes glowed white, illuminating the darkness of the room; her arm stretched out toward Atiba as she called for her scepter.

He hesitated a moment, as though stunned that she was no longer Dara, then rose to hand her a large stone that had been chipped into the form of a double-headed axe. He had fashioned it himself, in anticipation of just this moment. As he offered the sacred implement, her left hand shot out and seized his throat. She grabbed the axe head with her right hand and examined it critically. Then she roughly cast him aside, against the mill. While the men watched, she raised the stone axe above her head and began to speak.

"Opolopo ise l'o wa ti enikan ko le da se afi bi o ba ir oluranlowo. . . ."

The voice of Shango was telling them that the Yoruba must join with the other men of Africa if they would not all die as slaves. Otherwise they and their children and their children's children for twenty generations would be as cattle to the *branco*. Even so, he would not yet countenance the spilling of innocent blood. Not until Yoruba blood had been spilled.

They must not kill those among the *branco* who had done them no hurt. Only those who would deny their manhood.

Suddenly she turned and glared directly at Atiba. The voice grew even harsher.

"Atiba, son of Balogun, *bi owo eni ko te eku ida a ki ibere iku ti o pa baba eni!*"

It was the ancient call to arms of Ife: "No man who has not grasped his sword can avenge the death of his father." But Atiba sensed there was a deeper, more personal message. The voice had now become that of Balogun himself, clearly, unmistakably. He felt his heart surge with shame.

Her last words were still ringing when a sphere of lightning slid down the centerpole of the roof and exploded against the iron mill. Rings of fire danced across the rollers and dense dark smoke billowed in the room. Atiba had already sprung to catch her as she slumped forward, sending her stone axe clattering across the packed floor.

"*Olorun ayuba bai ye baye tonu . . .*" Through the smoke he quickly began to intone a solemn acknowledgement to the Yoruba high god. Then he lifted her into his arms and pressed his cheek against hers as he led the men out.

She was only dimly aware of a whisper against her ear. "You are truly a woman of the Yoruba, and tonight you have brought us Shango's power. With him to help us, we will one day soon plant our yams where the *branco*'s compounds stand."

As they started down the pathway, single file, the lightning had gone. Now there was only the gentle spatter of Caribbean rain against their sweating faces as they merged with the night.

Chapter Ten

As the bell on the *Rainbowe* struck the beginning of the first watch, Edmond Calvert stood on the quarterdeck studying the thin cup of crescent moon that hung suspended in the west. In another hour it would be gone and the dense tropical dark would descend. The time had arrived to commence the operation.

He reflected grimly on how it had come to this. The ultimate responsibility, he knew, must be laid at the door of a greedy Parliament. Before the monarchy was abolished, the American settlements had been the personal domain of the king, and they had suffered little interference from Commons. Scarce wonder Parliament's execution of Charles was received with so much trepidation and anger here—yesterday he'd heard that in Virginia the Assembly had just voted to hang anyone heard defending the recent "traitorous proceedings" in England. What these Americans feared, naturally enough, was that Parliament would move to try and take them over. They were right. And the richest prize of all was not Virginia, not Massachusetts, but the sugar island of Barbados. Why else had he been sent here first?

How could Oliver Cromwell have so misjudged these colonists? He thought all they needed was intimidation, and expected the fleet to manage that handily. What he'd failed to understand was the strong streak of independence that had developed here over the years, especially in Barbados. Instead of acting sensibly, the islanders had met the fleet with a cannon barrage and a *Declaration* stating that they would fight to the death for their liberty. What was worse, they had steadfastly refused to budge.

Even so, he had tried every means possible to negotiate a surrender. He'd started a propaganda campaign, sending ashore letters and posters warning that resistance was foolhardy, that they needed the protection of England. But Dalby Bedford's reply was to demand that the island be allowed to continue governing itself by its own elected Assembly, when everyone knew Parliament would never agree. Yet for a fortnight they had continued their fruitless exchange of letters, cajolery, threats—neither side willing to relent.

What else, he asked himself, was left to do now? Add to that, invasion fever was becoming rife in the fleet. This morning he had hung out the Flag of Council, summoning the captains of all the ships aboard the *Rainbowe* for a final parlay, and over a luncheon table groaning with meat and drink from the fourteen captured Dutch merchant *fluyts,* the men had done little else save brag of victory. Finally, his last hope of avoiding bloodshed gone, he had reluctantly issued orders. It had come to this—England and her most populous American colony were going to war.

He then spent the afternoon watch on the quarterdeck, alone, pensively studying the flying fish that glided across the surface of the tranquil blue Caribbean. Hardest to repress was his own anguish at the prospect of sending English infantry against a settlement in the Americas. These New World venturers were not rebel Papist Irishmen, against whom Cromwell might well be justified in dispatching his army. They were fellow Protestants.

As he turned and ordered the anchor weighed, he experienced yet another disquieting reflection—unless there was some weakness in the island he did not yet know, it could *win*.

"Are we ready to issue muskets now, and bandoliers of powder and shot?" Vice Admiral James Powlett was coming up the companionway with a purposeful stride.

He heard Powlett's question and decided to pass the decision on issuing of arms to the invasion commander, Colonel Richard Morris, now waiting beside him wearing breastplate and helmet.

Deep wrinkles from fifty years of life were set in Morris' brow, and the descending dark did not entirely obscure the worry in his blue eyes or the occasional nervous twitch in his Dutch-style goatee. A seasoned army officer, he had chafed for days waiting to take his men ashore. On board the ships, he and his infantry were under naval command. On land, he would be in total charge. His impatience could not have been greater.

During the forenoon watch he had personally visited each of the troop ships and picked some two hundred of the fittest infantry for the invasion. He had organized them into attack squadrons, appointed field commanders, and held a briefing for the officers. Then the men had been transferred in equal numbers to the *Rainbowe*, the *Marston Moor*, and the *Gloucester*, where the captains had immediately ordered them down to the already-crowded gun decks to await nightfall.

"We'll issue no arms till it's closer to time." Morris squinted at Powlett through the waning moonlight. "I'll not have some recruit light a matchcord in the dark down there between decks and maybe set off a powder keg. Though I'd scarcely fault any man who did, considering the conditions you've placed my infantry under."

"In truth, sir, I think we're all a trifle weary of hearing your complaints about how the navy has been required to garrison your men." Powlett scowled. "May I remind you that while you've seen fit to occupy yourself grumbling, the navy has arranged to replenish our water and provisions,

229

courtesy of all the Butterboxes who were anchored in the bay. In fact, I only just this afternoon finished inventorying the last Dutch *fluyt* and securing her hatches.''

Powlett paused to watch as the *Rainbowe* began to come about, her bow turning north. She would lead the way along the coast, the other two warships following astern and steering by a single lantern hanging from her maintopmast. Their destination was the small bay off the settlement at Jamestown, up the coast from Carlisle Bay.

''What this navy has done, sir,'' Morris' voice was rising, ''is to seize and pilfer the merchantmen of a nation England has not declared war on.''

''We don't need Letters of Marque to clear our American settlements of these Dutchmen,'' Powlett continued. ''They've grown so insolent and presumptuous they're not to be suffered more. If we don't put a stop to them, they'll soon make claim to all the Americas, so that no nation can trade here but themselves. Besides, it's thanks to these interloping Hollanders that we've now got fresh water and meat enough to last for weeks.''

''Aye, so I'm told, though my men have yet to see a sliver of this Dutch meat we hear about.''

''There's been time needed to inventory, sir. I've had the beef we took cut into quarter pieces and pickled and put aboard the provision ships. And the pork and mutton cut into half pieces and salted. We've got enough in hand now to sit and watch this island starve, if it comes to that.''

Morris chewed on his lip and thought bitterly of the noonday Council of War called aboard the *Rainbowe*. All the fleet captains had gorged themselves on fresh pork and fat mutton, washing it down with fine brandy and sack—all taken from the captain's larder of the *Kostverloren*. ''The treatment of my men on this voyage has been nothing short of a crime.'' He continued angrily, ''It cries to heaven, I swear it.''

The infantrymen had been confined to the hold for the entire trip, on dungeonlike gun decks illuminated by only a few dim candles. Since naval vessels required a far larger crew than merchant ships, owing to the men needed for the gun crews, there was actually less space for extra personnel than an ordinary merchantman would have afforded. A frigate the size of the *Rainbowe* already had two watches of approximately thirty men each, together with twenty-five or more specialists—carpenters, cooks, gunnery mates. How, Morris wondered, could they expect anything save sickness and misery on a ship when they took aboard an additional hundred or two hundred landsmen sure to be seasick for the whole of the voyage? Need anyone be surprised when his soldiers were soon lying in their own vomit, surrounded by sloshing buckets of excrement and too sick to make their way to the head up by the bowsprit, where the seamen squatted to relieve themselves. Scarce wonder more men died every day.

"What's your latest estimate of their strength here on this side of the island?" Morris turned back to Powlett, trying to ignore the stench that wafted up out of the scuttles. "Assuming the intelligence you've been getting is worth anything."

"I can do without your tone, sir," the vice admiral snapped. "We have it on authority that the rebels have managed to raise some six thousand foot and four hundred horse. But their militia's strung out the length of the coast. Any place we make a landing—unless it's bungled—we should have the advantage of surprise *and* numbers. All you have to do is storm the breastwork and spike their ordnance. It should be a passing easy night's work."

"Nothing's easy. The trick'll be to land the men before they can alert the entire island." Morris turned back to Calvert. "I'll need flintlocks for the first wave, not matchlocks, if we're to have the benefit of surprise. And I've got a feeling we'll need every advantage we can muster."

"We can manage that easily enough. I'd guess we've got nearly two hundred flintlocks. And about six hundred matchlocks. So I can issue every man you have a musket and pike, and a bandolier with twelve rounds of powder and shot. As well as six yards of matchcord for the matchlocks."

"So what you're saying is, we've got mostly matchlocks?" Morris' voice was grim.

"That's all their militia'll have, depend on it."

That was doubtless true, Morris told himself. It would be an oldstyle war, but plenty deadly, for it all.

From the time some two centuries earlier when the musket came into general use, the most common means for firing had been to ignite a small amount of powder in an external container, the "powder pan," which then directed a flash through a tiny hole in the side of the barrel, igniting the powder of the main charge. The powder pan of a matchlock was set off using a burning "matchcord," a powder-impregnated length of cotton twine kept lit in readiness for firing the gun. The technique differed very little from the way a cannon was fired. A smoldering end of the matchcord was attached to the hammer or "cock" of the gun, which shoved it into the powder pan whenever the trigger was pulled. An infantryman using a matchlock musket carried several yards of matchcord, prudently burning at both ends. Matchlocks were cheap and simple and the mainstay of regular infantry throughout Europe.

There was, however, an improved type of firing mechanism recently come into use, called the flintlock, much preferred by sportsmen and anyone wealthy enough to afford it. The flintlock musket ignited the powder in the external pan by striking flint against steel when the trigger was pulled, and it was a concealable weapon which could also be used in rainy weather, since it did not require a burning cord. A flintlock cost three or four times as much as a matchlock and required almost constant maintenance by a skilled gunsmith. Morris suspected that whereas a few of the rich royalist exiles on Barbados might own flintlocks, most of the poorer planters probably had nothing more than cheap matchlocks.

"We'd also be advised to off-load some provisions once

we get ashore, in case we get pinned down.'' Morris looked coldly at Powlett. ''I'm thinking a few quarters of that pickled beef you took from the Dutchmen wouldn't be amiss.''

''In time, sir. For now I can let you have twenty hogsheads of water, and I'll set ashore some salt pork from our regular stores.''

''What if I offered to trade all that for just a few kegs of brandy?'' Morris appealed to Calvert. ''I warrant the men'd sooner have it.''

Calvert glanced at Powlett, knowing the vice admiral had hinted at their noonday Council he preferred keeping all the Dutch brandy for the navy's men. ''I'd say we can spare you a couple of kegs. It should be enough for a day or two's supply. But I'll not send it ashore till the breastwork is fully secured. . . .''

Now the *Rainbowe* was entering the outer perimeter of the small bay at Jamestown, and the admiral excused himself to begin giving orders for reefing the mainsail. Through the dark they could see the outline of the torch-lit breastwork, a low brick fortress outlined against the palms.

It's all but certain to be bristling with ordnance, Morris thought. And what if their militia's waiting for us somewhere in those damned trees? How many men will I lose before daylight?

He inhaled the humid night air, then turned to Powlett. ''We should start bringing the men up on deck. We've got to launch the longboats as soon as we drop anchor. Before the militia in the breastwork has time to summon reinforcements.''

Powlett nodded and passed the order to the quartermaster. ''Then I'll unlock the fo'c'sle, so we can begin issuing muskets and bandoliers.''

The infantrymen emerged from the hold in companies, each led by an officer. The general mismatch of body armor, the ''breast'' and ''back,'' bespoke what a ragtag army it was. Also, the helmets, or ''pots,'' for those fortunate enough to

233

have one, were a mixture of all the age had produced: some with flat brims, some that curled upward front and back. Some were too large for their wearers, others too small. Doublets too were a rainbow of colors, many with old-fashioned ruffs—taken from dead or captured royalists during the Civil War—and the rest plain and patched with rough country cloth.

The night perfume of the tropical shore and the sea was obliterated by the stench of the emerging soldiers. Their faces were smeared with soot from the beams of the gun decks where they had been quartered, and they smelled strongly of sweat and the rankness of the hold. As they set grimly to work readying their weapons, a row of longboats along midships was unlashed and quietly lowered over the side. The two other warships, which had anchored astern of the *Rainbowe,* also began launching their invasion craft. Kegs of water, salt pork, and black powder were assembled on deck and readied to be landed after the first wave of the assault.

The guns of the warships were already primed and run out, set to provide artillery support if necessary when the longboats neared the beach. But with luck the breastwork could be overrun and its gun emplacements seized before the militia had a chance to set and fire its ordnance. Once the Jamestown fortress was disabled, there would be a permanent breach in the island's defenses, a chink not easily repaired.

The longboats had all been lowered now, and they bobbed in a line along the port side of the *Rainbowe.* Next, rope ladders were dropped and the infantrymen ordered to form ranks at the gunwales. Those assigned to lead the attack, all armed with flintlocks, were ordered over the side first. They dropped down the dangling ladders one by one, grumbling to mask their fear. The second wave, men with matchlocks, were being issued lighted matchcord, which they now stood coiling about their waists as they waited to disembark.

Edmond Calvert watched silently from the quarterdeck, heartsick. With them went his last hope for negotiation. Now it was a state of war, England against her own settlements in the New World.

"Katy, all I'm trying to say is you'll jeopardize your chances for a proper marriage if this goes on much more. I only hope you have some idea of what you're about." Dalby Bedford leaned back in his chair and studied the head of his cane, troubled by his conflicting emotions. The night sounds from the compound outside, crickets and whistling frogs, filtered in through the closed jalousies.

He loved his daughter more than life itself. What's more, he had vowed long ago never to treat her as a child. And now . . . now that she no longer *was* a child, what to do? It was too late to dictate to her; the time for that was years ago. She was a woman now—she was no longer his little girl. She was no longer *his*.

They'd always been best of friends. In the evenings they'd often meet in the forecourt of the compound, where, after she was old enough to understand such things, they would laugh over the latest gossip from London: what pompous Lord had been cuckolded, whose mistress had caused a scene at court. He had never thought to warn her that, as a woman, she might someday have desires of her own.

But now, he was still her father, still worried over her, still wanted the right thing for her . . . and she was throwing away her best chance to secure a fine marriage—all for the company of a man whose rough manner he could not help but despise, however much he might respect his courage and talent.

Hugh Winston was the antithesis of everything Dalby Bedford stood for: he was impulsive, contemptuous of law and order. How could Katy be attracted to him, be so imprudent? Had she learned nothing in all their years together?

Dalby Bedford found himself puzzled, disturbed, and—yes, he had to admit it—a trifle jealous.

"Katy, you know I've never tried to interfere in what you choose to do, but in truth I must tell you I'm troubled about this Winston. Your carousing about with a smuggler is hardly demeanor fitting our position here. I fear it's already been cause for talk."

She set down the leather bridle she was mending and lifted her eyes, sensing his discomfort. "You'd suppose there were more important things for the island to talk about, especially now."

"What happens to you *is* important to me; I should hope it's important to you as well, young woman."

She straightened her skirt, and the edge of her crinoline petticoat glistened in the candlelight. "Hugh's a 'smuggler' when I'm out with him, but he's 'Captain Winston' when the militia needs a batch of raw ten-acre freeholders drilled in how to form ranks and prime a musket. I thought it was 'Captain Winston,' and not a 'smuggler' who's been working night and day helping keep trained gunners manning all the breastworks along the coast."

"There's no arguing with you, Katy. I gave that up long ago. I'm just telling you to mind yourself." He swabbed his brow against the heat of early evening and rose to open the jalousies. A light breeze whispered through the room and fluttered the curtains. "I'll grant you he's been a help to us, for all his want of breeding. But what do you know about him? No man who lives the way he does can be thought a gentleman. You've been out riding with him half a dozen times, once all the way over to the breastwork at Oistins. In fact, you must have passed right by the Walrond plantation. It's not gone unnoticed, you can be sure."

He settled back into his chair with a sigh and laid aside his cane. These last few days he had realized more than ever how much he depended on Katherine. "Anthony Walrond's a man of the world, but you can't push him too far. I'm just telling you to try and be discreet. In faith, my greater worry is that . . . that I'd sooner you were here with me more now.

Between us, I think the fleet's going to try and invade soon. If not tonight, then tomorrow or the day after for certain. Talk has run its course. And if we've got to fight the English army on our own beaches, God help us.''

He could sense the unity on the island dissolving. Many of the smaller planters were growing fearful, and morale in the militia was visibly deteriorating. Half the men would just as soon have done with the constant alerts and dwindling supplies. There was scarcely any meat to be had now, and flour was increasingly being hoarded and rationed. Cassava bread was finding its way onto the tables of English planters who a fortnight earlier would have deemed it fit only for indentures—while the indentures themselves, God knows, were being fed even less than usual. Without the steady delivery of provisions by the Dutch shippers, there probably would be starvation on Barbados inside a month. And with all the new Africans on the island, many militiamen were reluctant to leave their own homes unprotected. Little wonder so many of the smaller freeholders were openly talking about surrender.

''Katy, I hate to ask this, but I do wish you'd stay here in the compound from now on. It's sure to be safer than riding about the island, no matter who you're with.''

''I thought I was of age. And therefore free to come and go as I wish.''

''Aye, that you are. You're twenty-three and twice as stubborn as your mother ever was. I just don't want to lose you too, the way I lost her.'' He looked at her, his eyes warm with concern. ''Sometimes you seem so much like her. Only I think she truly loved Bermuda. Which I'll warrant you never really did.''

''It always seemed so tame.'' She knew how much he cherished those few years of happiness, before his long stretch of widowerhood in Barbados. ''There's a wildness and a mystery about this island I never felt there.''

''Aye, you were of your own opinion, even then. But still

I've always been regretful I agreed to take this post." He paused and his look darkened. "Especially considering what happened on the trip down. If only I'd taken your mother below decks when the firing began, she'd still be with us."

"But she wanted to see the canoes." She picked up the bridle again. "I did too."

"Well, you've been a comfort to a dull old man—no, don't try and deny it—more than any father has a right to expect, I suppose. You became a woman that day your mother died, no question of it." The sparkle returned to his eyes. "You'd never do anything I told you after that. May God curse you with a daughter of your own someday, Katy Bedford. Then you'll know what it's like."

At that moment she wanted nothing so much as to slip her arms around his neck and tell him she would be his dutiful daughter forever. But she was no longer sure it was true.

"Now admit it to me, Katy. This is no time for pretense. You're smitten with this Winston, aren't you? I can see the change in you." He watched as she busied herself with the bridle, trying not to look surprised. "I realize you're a woman now. I suppose I can understand how a man like him might appeal to you. And I guess there's nothing wrong with having a bit of a dalliance. God knows it's fashionable in London these days. But your Winston's a curious fellow, and there're doubtless a lot of things about him neither of us knows." He looked at her. "I'm sure your mother wouldn't have approved, any more than I do."

"What does she have to do with this?" She knew he always invoked her mother's alleged old-fashioned views any time he couldn't think of a better argument.

"Perhaps you're right. What you do now is on my head, not hers." He paused, not wanting to meet her eyes. "I'll grant you I might have sowed a few wild oats myself, when I was your age. And I can't say I've entirely regretted it. The fact is, as I get older that's one of the few things from my early years I remember at all. After a while, all other memories fade." His voice drifted away. "And now, the way things have come to pass, these days may be the last either of us has left to . . ." He raised his hand suddenly, as though to silence himself. From down the hill came the faint crack of a musket, then another and another. Three shots.

They both waited, listening in the dim candlelight as the night sounds of crickets and frogs resumed once more. Finally he spoke.

"Well, there it is."

She rose and walked over behind his chair. She hesitated for a moment, then slipped her arms around his neck and nuzzled her cheek against his. There were so many things she'd wanted to say to him over the years. Now suddenly it was almost too late, and still she couldn't find the words. She wanted to hold him now, but something still stopped her.

Silently he touched her hand, then reached for his cane and stood. "I've ordered the carriage horses kept harnessed, in case." He was already halfway to the door. "I suppose I'd best go down to the Point first, just to be sure."

"I want to go with you." She grabbed the bridle and ran after him. To let him get away, with so much still unsaid. . . .

"No, you'll stay here, and for once that's an order." He took her hand and squeezed it. "I didn't tell you that five members of the Assembly have already called for surrender. Five out of twenty-two. I wonder how many more'll be ready to join them after tonight. If the Assembly votes to give in, Katy, you know it'll probably mean a trial in London for me." He kissed her on the cheek. "You'll have to look out for yourself then, and that'll be time aplenty to go chasing around the island in the dark." He drew back. "In the meantime, you'd best decide what you plan to do about this Winston fellow if that happens. Don't go losing your heart to him. He's a rogue who'll not do the right thing by you. Or any woman. Mark it. A father still can see a few things. He's already got one woman, that ship of his, and a seaman like that never has room for anyone else."

She had to concede that, in truth, there was something to what he said. Up till now she'd been managing to keep things in balance. But was she starting to let desire overrule that better judgment? For the hundredth time she warned herself to keep her head.

"In the first place I don't wish to marry Hugh Winston. So it's just as well, isn't it, that he's got his ship. I see all too well what he is. I'm going to marry Anthony, and try and make the best of things." Her eyes hardened. "And secondly, we're not going to lose. You just have to delay the Assembly from voting a surrender. Hugh thinks the militia can drive them back."

"Aye, we may hold out for a time. We've got trained gunners for every breastwork on the west and south coasts. But how long before some of the militia starts defecting? Then what can we do? With guns at our backs as well . . ." He exhaled pensively. "By the way, on the subject of Winston, I've noticed something a trifle incongruous about that man. He appears to know a lot more about cannon and fortifications than a seaman reasonably ought, probably as much or more even than Anthony Walrond. Has he ever said where he learned it?"

"He never talks much about his past." She had found herself increasingly puzzled, and not a little infuriated, by Winston's secretiveness. Probably the only woman he ever confided in was Joan Fuller. "But sometimes I get the idea he may have learned a lot of what he knows from a Frenchman. Now and then he slips and uses a French name for something. I'd almost guess he helped a band of Frenchmen set up defenses somewhere in the Caribbean once."

Dalby Bedford quietly sucked in his breath and tried to mask his dismay. The only "band of Frenchmen" to fit that description would be the little settlement of planters on the French side of St. Christopher, or the Cow-Killers on Tortuga. And Hugh Winston hardly looked like a planter.

"Well, maybe it's just as well we don't know, Katy." He

reached for his hat. "Now mind yourself, and make sure all the servants have muskets. Don't open the door to anyone." He pecked her quickly on the cheek. "Just be glad your friend Winston's frigate is aground. His 'other woman' is beached for now; try and keep her that way."

Suddenly James, their stooping, white-haired Irish servant pushed through the doorway from the paneled entry foyer. The night breeze set the candles flickering. "Excellency!" He bowed nervously. "Pardon me, Excellency. There's a . . . gentleman to see you. He just rode into the compound all in a sweat. Claims he's come up from Mistress Fuller's place."

The Assembly had voted to place Hugh Winston in command of the gunnery crews for the cannon emplacements at the four major breastworks along the coast: Lookout Point, Bridgetown, and Jamestown on the west; and Oistins Bay, on the south. In line with that responsibility, he had taken the front room of Joan's tavern and converted it into a meeting place for his gunnery officers. Several of Joan's rickety pine tables had been lashed together to form a desk; from that makeshift post he assigned the daily watches for each of the breastworks and monitored supplies. He also maintained close communication with the commanders of the field militia, both infantry and cavalry, who were drawn from the ranking planters and royalist officers in each parish. The militia itself had individual field command posts in each of the parish churches.

The tavern was a comfortable rendezvous place for the men assigned to the guns, mostly seamen or former seamen who had gained their experience with heavy ordnance on a gun deck. Joan's familiar clapboard establishment enjoyed a commanding view of the harbor, and, unlike the parish churches, offered the finest food and grog remaining on the island. Joan presided over the accommodations, making sure necessary amenities were always at hand. She also kept a close eye on the loyalties of those who gathered.

Tonight, however, the tavern was all but empty save for Winston, his quartermaster John Mewes and his master's mate Edwin Spurre, since all gunnery mates were on alert and at their posts at the various breastworks along the coast. The three of them were waiting for the signal, horses saddled and ready.

The night was clear and humid, and a light breeze had just sprung up in the south. Winston leaned against the doorjamb, half in and half out, exhausted from a day-long ride reviewing gun emplacements along the shore. John Mewes was stationed outside on the porch, tankard in hand, keeping an eye on the sentry post atop Lookout Point. A system of lantern signals had been arranged to alert the Bridgetown command post to any change in the disposition of the fleet.

"I've got a feelin' about tonight, Cap'n. Word from up on the Point at midday was they were holdin' a big meetin' aboard the *Rainbowe*. An' then she got underway and made about a league out to sea, along with the troop ships." Mewes took a nervous puff from the long stem of his white clay pipe. "I'd say it's odds they're planning a little surprise for us tonight. More'n likely somewhere along the west coast."

"I've got the same feeling, John." He strolled across the narrow porch and stared up the hill, toward the sentry post stationed at the north end of the Point. "What was the latest signal?"

"Same as usual. Five flashes on the quarter hour, meanin' no sightings." Mewes reached to tap his pipe against the heavy beam at the corner of the building. "I told tonight's watch to report anything that moved. But they'll be hard pressed to see much beyond the bay here."

"Then you stay lively too. And try not to get too thirsty." Winston lifted a flintlock musket he had brought ashore from the *Defiance* and tested the lock by the light of a candle lantern. Next he started polishing the barrel with a cloth he had borrowed from Joan. "I've got an idea they may try and land up at Jamestown, or maybe even farther north."

"Then hadn't we best advise the militia commanders to double the security on the breastwork up that way?"

"I spoke with Walrond, up at Jamestown, late this afternoon. We both figure that's the most likely location. He's already ordered up reinforcements for tonight." He drew a musket patch from his pocket and began to clean the sooty powder pan of the musket.

"I didn't see any militia moving out from around here."

"Nobody was to move till dark. We don't want the fleet's Puritan spies here to know we're ready. We'd lose our chance to catch their infantry in a noose."

"Betwixt you an' me, I'd just as soon they *never* got around to landing infantry." Mewes shifted up his trousers. "A man could well get his balls shot off amidst all that musket fire."

Winston pulled back the hammer of the musket, checking its tension. "Sometimes I wonder why the hell I keep you on, John. I'd wager most of Joan's girls have more spirit for a fight."

"Aye, I'd sooner do my battlin' on a feather mattress, I'll own it. So the better question is why I stay on under *your* command."

"Could be the fine caliber of men you're privileged to ship with."

"Aye, that crew of gallows-bait are a rare species of gentility, as I'm a Christian." He started to laugh, then it died in his throat. "God's wounds, was that a signal up at the point?"

"Looked to be." Winston flipped over the musket and examined the barrel. Then he selected a "charge holder"—a tiny metal flask—from among the twelve strung from the bandolier draped over his shoulder and began pouring its black powder into the muzzle. "Three longs and a short. That means a mast lantern putting in at Jamestown, right?" He fitted a patch over the ramrod and began to tamp in the powder. "Probably the *Rainbowe.*"

"Aye, that's the signal." Mewes shoved the pipe into his pocket. "Want me to fetch the muskets?"

"Tell Joan to give you those two leaning in the corner, at the back. I just got through priming them."

Mewes vaulted the steps leading to the open tavern door. Seconds later, Joan appeared, holding the two flintlocks.

"What is it, darlin'?" Her eyes were bloodshot with fatigue. "Are we finally due for some company?"

"Right on schedule. The surf's been down all day. I figured they'd try it tonight." He finished tapping the ball down the muzzle of the musket, then placed the gun carefully on the step. "I guess that means I win our wager."

"God's blood, I never thought it'd come to this. I was sure they'd never have the brass to try it." She passed him the muskets. "So we'll be going to war after all. I'd wager you another shilling you'll not hold them off, darlin', save there'd be no way to collect if I won."

"All wagers are off now. This one's too hard to call." He handed one of the flintlocks to John Mewes, then cocked the other and aimed it into the dark night air. "Ready, John?"

"Aye." Mewes cocked the musket and aimed it at the sliver of moon on the western horizon. "Tell me again. The signal for Jamestown's one shot, a count of five, another shot, a count of ten, and then the third?"

"That's it."

"Fire when ready."

Winston squeezed the trigger and the powder pan flashed in the dark. Five seconds later Mewes discharged the second musket, then after ten seconds Winston fired the third, the one he had just loaded.

"All right, John. Get the horses."

"Aye." Mewes disappeared around the side of the tavern, headed for the makeshift stable located at the rear.

Approximately a minute later the signal of three musket shots was repeated by militiamen in the field command post at Black Rock, on the road to Jamestown. Shortly after there again came a faint repetition of the pattern of shots, farther north. The prearranged signal was moving quickly up the coast.

Mewes emerged from the dark leading two speckled mares. He patted one on the side of her face, muttered an endearment, then passed the reins to Winston. "I'm ready to ride."

"All right, John, I'll see you at Jamestown. Put Spurre in charge here and go up to the governor's compound to tell Bedford. If he's not there, then try the Assembly Room. If they're meeting tonight, tell them to adjourn and get every man up to Jamestown, on the double. We may need them all."

Mewes bellowed instructions through the doorway. Then he seized the saddle horn of the smaller horse and pulled himself up. "Aye. I'll be up there myself soon as I can manage, depend on it."

Joan stood beside Winston, watching as he vanished into the dark. "Well now, that's most curious." She cocked back her head and her eyes snapped in the lantern light. "I'm surprised you'd not take the opportunity to go up to His Excellency's compound yourself. Seein' you're so well acquainted with the family these days."

"All in the line of duty."

"Duty my arse, you whoremaster. But you'll get what you deserve from that one, on my honor. She thinks she's royalty itself." She held the reins while he mounted. "Don't say I didn't give you a friendly warning."

"I'm warned." He vaulted into the saddle as Edwin Spurre emerged through the doorway to assume lookout duty. "Edwin, prime and ready the muskets. In case they try to attack on two fronts. Do you know the signals?"

"Aye, Cap'n."

Joan handed up the reins. "Godspeed. You know if you let those Puritan hypocrites take over the island, there'll be a lot of wives thinkin' they can finally close me down. Just because they've got nothing better to fret about."

"We'll win." He looked at Joan a moment and reached out to take her hand. Tonight he felt almost like he was defending the only home he had left. Now he had no ship, and Jamaica seemed farther away than ever.

He leaned over in the saddle and kissed her. She ran her arms around his neck, then drew back and pinched his cheek. "Show those Roundhead bastards a thing or two about how to shoot, love. I'm counting on you, though damned if I know why."

"Just keep the grog under lock and key till I get back." He waved lightly, then reined the mare toward the road north.

As the horse clattered across the loose boards of the bridge, he glanced over his shoulder, up the hill toward the compound. What'll happen to Bedford and Katy, he wondered to himself, if we can't hold off the attack? It'll be the Tower and a trial for him, not a doubt. Probably charged with leading a rebellion. And what about her . . . ?

More riders were joining him now, militiamen who had been waiting for the signal. The distance to Jamestown was several miles, and they were all riding hard. None spoke, other than a simple greeting, each man thinking of the stakes. No one wanted to contemplate what would happen should they lose.

We'll win, he kept telling himself as he spurred his mare. By God, we have to.

Chapter Eleven

Jeremy Walrond slid his hand down the long steel barrel of the flintlock, letting his fingers play across the Latin motto engraved along the top, *Ante ferit quam flamma micet.* "It strikes before the flash is seen."

The piece had been given to him on his twelfth birthday by his brother Anthony, and it was superb—crafted in Holland, with a fine Flemish lock and carved ivory insets of hunting scenes in the stock. With it he had once, in a stroke of rare luck, brought down a partridge in flight. Now through a dismaying and improbable chain of events he must turn this work of artistry against a fellow human being.

It was true he had been part of the royalist cause in the Civil War, a clerk helping direct the transport of supplies, but he had never been near enough to the lines to fire a musket. Or to have a musket fired at him. The thought of battle brought a moistness to his palms and a dull, hollow ache in his gut.

While the men around him in the trench—all now under his command—reinforced their courage with a large onion-flask of homemade kill-devil, he gazed over the newly mounded earth and out to sea, ashamed at his relief there was as yet no flash of lantern, no telltale red dots of burning matchcord.

The only moving lights were the darting trails of fireflies, those strange night creatures that so terrified newcomers to the Caribbees. In a few more moments the last of the moon, now a thin lantern, would drop beneath the western horizon, causing the coast and the sea to be swallowed in blackness. After that happened, he told himself, he might see nothing more, hear nothing more, till the first musket ball slammed home.

War, he meditated, was man's greatest folly. Excused in the name of abstractions like "liberty" and "country" and "dignity." But what dignity was there for those who died with a musket ball in their chest? No beast of the earth willfully killed its own kind. Only man, who then styled himself the noblest of God's creatures.

He loosened his hot lace collar, hoping to catch some of the on-again, off-again breeze that had risen in the south and now swept the pungent smell of Bridgetown's harbor up along the coast. Aside from the rattle of militiamen's bandoliers and occasional bursts of gallows laughter, the only sounds were night noises—the clack of foraging land crabs, the chirps and whistles of crickets and toads, the distant batter of surf and spray against the sand. Inland, the green hills of Barbados towered in dark silence.

He looked out to sea once more and realized the surf was beginning to rise, as wave after frothy wave chased up the crystalline sand of the shore, now bleached pale in the last waning moonlight. The ships were out there, he knew, waiting. He could almost feel their presence.

Both the trench and the breastwork were back away from the shore—back where the sand merged with brown clay and the first groves of palms, heralds of the hardwood thickets farther upland. Through the palms he could barely discern the silhouettes of the gunners as they loitered alongside the heavy ordnance, holding lighted linstocks. Fifteen cannon were there tonight, ranging in gauge from nine to eighteen-pound shot, shielded on the sea side by a head-high masonry wall cut with battlements for the guns.

Though the original Jamestown gun emplacement had been built two decades earlier, as a precaution against Spanish attack, that threat had faded over the years, and gradually the planters of Barbados had grown complacent. They had permitted the fort to slowly decay, its guns to clog with rust from the salt air.

How ironic, he thought, that now an English attack, not Spanish, had finally occasioned its first repairs. Over the past fortnight the old cannon had been cleaned of rust and primed; and new Dutch guns, all brass, had been hauled up by oxcart from Carlisle Bay and set in place. Now six of these, small demi-culverin, had just been removed from the breastwork and hauled to safety inland at first word of the invasion.

He heard the murmur of approaching voices and looked up to see two shadowy figures moving along the dirt parapet that protected the trench. One was tall and strode with a purposeful elegance; the other lumbered.

"It'll be a cursed dark night once we've lost the moon, and that's when they're apt to start launching the longboats. Damn Winston if he's not in place by then. Are his men over where they're supposed to be?" The hard voice of Benjamin Briggs drifted down. The silhouette that was Anthony Walrond merely nodded silently in reply.

Jeremy rose and began climbing up the parapet, his bandolier rattling. Anthony turned at the noise, recognized him, and motioned him forward.

"Are your men ready?"

"Yes, sir."

Anthony studied him thoughtfully a moment. "Watch yourself tonight, lad." He paused, then looked away. "Do remember to take care."

"That I will." Jeremy broke the silence between them. "But I'm not afraid, truly." He patted his bandolier for emphasis, causing the charge holders to clank one against the other. He knew he owed his assignment of the rank of ensign—which normally required holdings of at least fifteen acres—and the leadership of a squad solely to the influence of his older brother, who commanded the vital Jamestown defenses by unanimous consent of the Assembly.

Jeremy's militiamen—eight in number—were all small freeholders with rusty matchlocks and no battle experience. He had been too ashamed to tell Anthony he didn't desire the honor of being an officer. It was time to prove he was a Walrond.

"Jeremy, we all know fear, but we learn to rise above it. You'll make me proud tonight, I'll lay odds." He reached and adjusted the buckle of the shoulder strap holding Jeremy's sword. "Now have your men light their matchcord and ready the prime on their muskets."

Jeremy gave his brother a stiff salute and passed the order into the trench. A burning taper was handed slowly down the line of men, and each touched it to the tip of his matchcord, then threaded the glowing fuse through the serpentine cock of his musket. He secretly rejoiced he had a new-style flintlock; at least there would be no lighted matchcord to betray his own whereabouts in the dark. He stood for a moment watching his men prepare, then glanced back at the squat outline of Benjamin Briggs. What, he wondered, was *he* doing here tonight?

Briggs was gazing down at the parapet now, critically scuffing his boots against the soft earth. "This trench of yours will do damned little to protect these lads from cannon fire if somebody in the fleet takes a mind to shell the breastwork. I pray to God it was worth the time and trouble."

A crew of indentures, as well as many of Winston's new men, had worked around-the-clock for three days digging the trench. The idea had come from Anthony Walrond.

"I'm betting on an invasion, not an artillery duel." Anthony nodded toward Jeremy one last time, a light farewell, then turned back to Briggs. "An open shelling with their big ordnance would be foolhardy; right now it's too dark to try and fire on our emplacements. Add to that, we have word the commander in charge of the army is a Roundhead rogue named Dick Morris. I know him all too well. He doesn't believe in a lot of cannon fire, when a few men can achieve what he wants. He'll just try to land enough men to overrun and disable our guns.''

"Well and all, may Almighty God damn our luck that it's come down to this. The last thing we need is war with England. But if it's fight we must, then I say give them our all. And don't let them catch us short.'' Briggs gazed past Jeremy, down the trench. "Do all these men have enough matchrope, powder, and shot?''

Anthony felt himself nearing his limit of tolerance for civilians. All the planter had found to do since arriving was denigrate their readiness. "We've managed to get bandoliers, and 'the twelve apostles,' for all the men''—he deliberately used the irreverent battlefield nickname for the dozen chargeholders of musket powder on a standard bandolier—"and there's plenty of matchcord, with what we got from the Dutchmen before they were seized.'' He tightened his eyepatch and surveyed the line of ragged planters and indentures marshalled down the trench, trying to envision them under attack. The picture was discouraging, at the very least.

How many here have ever taken musket fire, he wondered. This bunker will likely be overrun by the first wave of Morris' infantry. God curse Cromwell for sending him. He's tenacious as an English bulldog. And crafty as a fox. He'll land the pick of his troops, and the minute they open fire, it's odds this line of farmers will panic and run for those green hills. We've got superiority of numbers, but it doesn't mean a thing. What we need, and don't have, is nerve, experience, and most of all, the will to fight. I'll wager not one man in ten here tonight has all three.

"I'd like to know, sir, what's your true opinion of the plan that's been worked out.'' Briggs turned to Walrond, hating the man's arrogance and his royalist politics, yet respecting his military experience. He had led a royalist attack at the battle of Marsten Moor that was still remembered as one of the most daring maneuvers of the Civil War. "Do you think we can catch their landing force in a bind, the way we're hoping?"

Anthony moved away from the edge of the trench. "Taken all for all, it's about the best we can do. If it succeeds, well and good, but if it fails, we're apt to end up . . ."

Jeremy tried to hear the rest, but Anthony's voice faded into the dark as he and Briggs moved on down the parapet.

The night was closing in again. Having drained their flask of kill-devil, the militiamen were grumbling nervously as they waited in a line down the trench, backs to the newly turned earth. Again the sounds of the dark swelled up around them—the chirps and whistles, the monotonous pendulum of surf in the distance.

War. Was it mainly waiting?

Maybe there would *be* no landing. How preposterous all this would seem then. Tomorrow he would wake in his feather-bed, dreaming he was back in England, laughing at the absurdity of it all. Sense would prevail. The fleet would hoist sail. . . .

A volley of musket fire exploded from the direction of the breastwork.

Shouts. Then clustered points of light, the tips of burning matchcord on the infantry's muskets, suddenly appeared along the shore.

The first attackers had crept up behind the cannon and fired into the gunners with flintlocks, so there would be no smoldering ignition match on their muskets to betray them. Those in the second wave had somehow masked their lighted matchcord until their longboats pulled into the surf. Now, after the surprise attack on the gun emplacement, they were splashing ashore, holding their muskets high.

Jeremy watched as the flickering red dots spread out along

the shore in disciplined rows. For a moment he had the impression Jamestown was being attacked by strings of fireflies that had emerged from the deep Caribbean sea.

"Prepare to fire." He heard a voice giving the order, and was vaguely astonished to realize it was his own.

The trench sounded with the clicks of powder pans being opened and hammers being readied.

"Take aim." That was the phrase; he had started practicing it five days before, when he was assigned the command. But now, what next? Aim where? The fireflies were inching up the shore in deadly rows. There looked to be hundreds. They would spew lead shot the moment the militia's trench was revealed.

He knew that the order to fire the first round must come from Anthony. Why was he waiting? The Roundhead infantry must be no more than fifty yards down the shore. He felt his palm grow moist against the ivory of the stock, and for a moment he thought he smelled an acrid stench of fear down the trench.

More muskets blazed from the rear of the brick fortress, followed by screams and shouts of surrender. In the jumble of musket fire and lanterns he could tell that the Jamestown breastwork had been circled and seized: its gunners overwhelmed, its cannon still directed impotently out toward the dark sea. Only two culverin had been fired. He watched heartsick as the invading infantrymen, breastplates shining in the lantern light, swarmed over the guns.

The militia manning the cannons had been sacrificed. Deliberately. To draw in the rest of the invading force. He felt his anger welling up. In war the men who actually fought counted for nothing.

Where was the rest of the militia? Were they waiting at the right perimeter, as they were supposed to be?

He knew that the plan all along had been to let the guns be seized. But now that it had happened, he felt a demoralizing pang of loss and defeat. Why should the gunners be exposed to a musket attack? Surely there was some other way. . . .

"Give fire!"

He heard Anthony's command and felt his heart jump. The infantry was practically in pistol range. This was going to be near to murder. The trigger felt cold against his finger as he sighted into the dark, directly toward one of the approaching tips of fire.

The gun flashed and kicked upward. The parapet was suddenly bathed in light as the long line of muskets around him discharged. He gasped for breath as the air in the trench turned to smoke—burning charcoal and saltpeter. The points of light danced in chaos, and then he heard screams.

The man next to him, a grizzled, frightened freeholder, had clambered up the loose dirt of the parapet to gain a better view of the fighting at the breastwork. Jeremy realized that this man, too, had never witnessed a battle before.

Then came a row of flashes from where the red dots had been, like the long string of exploding rockets fired over the Thames on St. George's Day. The freeholder beside him suddenly groaned and pitched backward, his smoking matchlock plowing into the soft dirt of the parapet as he sprawled downward into the trench. Then another man, farther down, screamed and doubled over his gun.

"Half-cock your muskets, disengage your match," Jeremy heard himself shouting. "Prepare to recharge."

Anthony had coached him that one of the primary duties of a field officer was to call out orders for priming and loading, since men in battle often forgot crucial steps. With a live matchcord attached to the hammer, it was all too easy to set off a musket while you were ramming in the charge.

"Prime your pan." He tried to bellow above the din as he began pouring priming powder from a flask on his bandolier into the flintlock's powder pan. "Close your pan. Prepare to scour."

As he and the men quickly cleaned the barrels of their

muskets, then began to ram in more powder and shot, he kept glancing toward the approaching infantry. They too had paused to reload. He could see the outlines of the men now, and hear the shouts of officers.

Which men were officers?

At the end of one row of infantrymen stood a tall man in a silver helmet who seemed to be issuing the commands for reloading. He must be one, Jeremy realized. He's faster at reloading than the others. He's almost ready.

That man, tall and comely, would make a passing good companion to share a hunt, afield and stalking grouse on a dew-laden morning. If we were both back in England now . . .

Except . . . he's here to kill me.

"You!" He shouted a challenge as he climbed up the parapet, readying his flintlock. There were shouts from the militiamen behind him, warning him to come down, but he did not hear, did not want to hear.

The officer in the silver helmet looked up and spotted the outline of the brash youth standing atop the parapet, brandishing a musket. He knew.

Jeremy watched as the man drew up his musket and took aim. He waited a moment in fascination, savoring what it was like to face death, then drew up his own flintlock and sighted the man's chest down the barrel.

There was a flash of light and a whistle past his ear, the sound of a hurried horsefly.

Then he squeezed the trigger.

The Roundhead officer opened his mouth noiselessly and seemed to wilt backward. He fumbled for his musket as it clattered against a jagged lump of coral beside him, then sprawled onto the sand, still as death, his helmet circling in drunken arcs down the slope toward the surf.

"Sir, mind you take cover!"

In the flush sweeping over him, he scarcely felt the hands tugging at his boots. He was still gripping his flintlock, knuckles white, as the other militiamen dragged him back into the trench.

He lay panting, at once dazed and exhilarated, astonished at the sensations of his own mind and body. The most curious thing of all was his marvelous new awareness of being alive; he was adrift in a new realm of the spirit, untroubled by the cacophony of musket discharges from all sides.

"We're turnin' the whoresons back." There were more shouts now, even some cheers. Finally the din of battle cut through his reverie.

"Prepare to reload." He was shouting again, almost more to himself than to the others, trying to be heard above the crack of musket fire that sounded down the length of the shoreline. Everywhere there were flashes, yells, screams. The air in the trench was rancid and opaque with black smoke.

As he began reloading his musket he suddenly felt a new closeness, almost a mystical union, with the ragged planters around him. They were a fraternity of men, standing together, defending their land. Why had Anthony never told him that war could be like this? Could teach you brotherhood as well as hate?

He was priming his powder pan again, trying to control the shake of his hands as he tilted the powder flask, when he looked up to see that more red tips were emerging from the darkness of the sea. Another wave of Roundhead infantry had landed in longboats.

There was no longer any purpose in calling out a loading sequence. Some men were priming now, some ramming in powder and shot, some threading their matchcord into the hammer, some firing again. All the discipline he had been taught so carefully by Anthony was irrelevant.

Most frightening of all, while the first wave of infantry had dropped back to reload, a fresh line of musketmen was advancing toward the parapet, guns primed and ready.

"Fire and fall back. In orderly fashion."

It was the voice of Anthony. The call to abandon the trench

meant that all the Roundhead infantry had landed. Now they were to be drawn inland with a feigned retreat.

The plan worked out was to resist strongly until all the infantry were ashore, to damage them as much as possible using the protection of the parapet, and then to fall back into the trees, luring them away from their longboats. When their lines were thinned, Hugh Winston would lead a cavalry charge that would drive a wedge along the shore, between the infantry and the sea, cutting off their escape. Next the longboats would be driven off, and the invading infantry slowly surrounded. They would be harassed by irregular fire and, with luck, soon lose heart. Cut off from their escape route, the demoralized invaders would have no choice but to surrender. Then, so the strategy went, Commander Morris and the admiral of the fleet would seek to negotiate.

Jeremy fired blindly into the dark, then reached down for his pike. As he touched it, his eyes met those of the dying freeholder lying beside him. Blood now streamed from a gash in the man's tattered jerkin, while a red rivulet flowed in pulses from the corner of his mouth. The sight flooded him with anger.

"No!" He heard himself yelling as he groped down his bandolier for another charge-holder. "No retreat." He turned to the startled men around him. "Reload. I say no retreat!"

"But that's the orders, Yor Worship." A bearded militiaman had already begun to scramble up the back side of the trench.

"Devil take the orders. Look." He seized the militiaman's jerkin and yanked him back, then pointed to the dying freeholder at their feet.

"Aye, that's Roland Jenkins, may God rest his soul. I'm like to be the one tellin' his wife." The freeholder gave a quick glance. "But there's nothin' to be done, Yor Worship. Orders are to retreat."

"And I say damn the orders." He was yelling to all the men now. "There are men here, wounded and dying. I'm staying with them. What kind of soldiers are we, to leave these men to die? It's wrong. There're higher orders to be obeyed. I say no.''

''An' we'll all end up like this poor sod, Yor Worship. There's no helpin' a man who's gone to meet his God.'' The man threw his musket onto the fresh dirt at the bottom of the trench and turned to begin clambering to safety. ''For my own part, I can do just as well not greetin' the Almighty for a few years more.''

Jeremy seized his pike and marched down the trench. ''I'll gut any man who tries to run. I'm in command here and I say we stand and fight. Now reload.''

The men stared at him in disbelief.

''Do it, I say.'' He brandished the pike once more for emphasis, then flung it down and seized a charge-holder on his bandolier. Without so much as a glance at the other men, he began pouring the grainy black powder into the barrel of his musket.

The world was suddenly a white, deafening roar.

Later he remembered mainly the flash, how as the smoke seared his eyes he recalled his own negligence, that he had forgotten to scour the barrel. It was a fool's mistake, a child's mistake. He was still wiping his eyes, seared and powder-burned, when he felt the musket being ripped from his hands. As he groped to seize it back, rough hands shoved him sprawling against the soft dirt of the trench. His face plowed into the earth, which still smelled fresh, musky and ripe, full of budding life.

''We've got another one, sor.'' A brash voice sounded near his ear. ''A right coxcomb, this rebel.''

''Damn you.'' Jeremy struck out, only half aware of the cluster of infantrymen surrounding him.

''Just hold yourself, lad.'' There were shouts as several of the wounded militiamen were disarmed. He tried to struggle, but more hands brusquely wrestled him down. ''This one's not taken any shot. He's lively as a colt. Let's have some of that rope.''

He felt his arms being pulled behind him and a rough cord lashed around his wrists. There were sounds of a brief conference, then a voice came, kindly, almost at his ear.

"This is a first-class fowling piece you're carrying. I'll wager you've brought down many a plump woodcock with it, haven't you lad?" A pause, then again the gentle voice. "What's your name, son?"

"Damned to you. What's *your* name?" There was a sickening hollowness in his gut again. The fear, and now hatred—for them, and for himself.

"It's better, for the time, if I ask the questions and you answer them." The voice emanated from a man wearing a silver helmet and sporting a short goatee. "Why didn't you run, like the rest of the rebels?" He laughed lightly as he moved closer. Jeremy felt a palm cup beneath his chin and felt his head being twisted upward. "By my word, I think your musket misfired. Your face is black as a Moor's. I'll warrant you'd have run too, if you could have seen the way. Could it be you're naught but a coward too, lad, like all the rest?"

The speaker turned to a young, blue-eyed man standing nearby. "Well, sir, who'd have reckoned it'd be this easy? You can tell Admiral Calvert this island's as good as his for the taking. This militia of theirs is nothing but a batch of scared planters, who scatter like rabbits the minute they hear a gunshot. And a few young gallants like this one, who scarcely know how to prime a musket. There's no reason to fall back and hold this position. We'd as well just go on after them, chase them back to Bridgetown, and have done with it.''

Jeremy felt a flush of victory. They had fallen into the trap. They thought Barbados wouldn't fight! In minutes they'd be surrounded by the militia and begging to surrender. As soon as the counterattack began, he would . . .

"I think we'd best take this one back to the ship, to find out who he is and if he knows anything." It was the man standing next to the goateed commander. "It's a damned bother to have prisoners to feed, but I'll warrant this engagement's got three days at most to go before they all throw down their arms and sue for peace."

"Damn your smug eyes." Jeremy reached down and seized his pike, which had been lying unnoticed against the side of the trench. He turned and faced the commander. "You'll never even get back to your ship. Men died here tonight and they didn't die in vain, by all that's holy."

"What say, lad? Pray, who's to stop us?" The commander glanced at the pike, seeming to ignore it. He waved back several infantrymen who had quickly leveled their muskets at Jeremy. "Your bold militia here has taken to its heels, one and all. A bloody lot of royalist cowards."

"There're braver men on Barbados than you know. You'll not take me, or any prisoners, back to the ship. You'll see Bridgetown soon enough, all right, at the point of a gun."

"Perhaps that's so, lad, but not at the point of a pike. Now put it away. This little engagement's over." The man with the goatee was studying him with admiration. "You're a brave one, lad. Too brave, by my life, or too foolish. . . ."

"You don't suppose there's something behind this lad's bluster." The other man turned to the commander. "Could it be their militia might've run on purpose? To thin out our lines for a counterattack?"

The shouting had died down now, as strings of captured militiamen were being assembled and placed under guard. Some were joking with their captors, clearly relieved to be out of the battle. Jeremy suspected several had deliberately surrendered—small freeholders who didn't care a damn whether Cromwell's fleet took the island or not. As he watched them with contempt, he felt ashamed to be one of them. Suddenly the horror of it all swept over him and he flung down the pike in disgust.

"Now that's a good lad." The commander nodded, then turned to the other man. "Vice Admiral Powlett, for once you may be right. In truth, I was beginning to wonder the same thing. This could all have been too easy by half."

"With your permission, sor, I'll put the young gallant here in with the rest of the rebels." One of the infantrymen had seized Jeremy's arms.

"No, leave him here a minute." The commander was pointing toward Jeremy. "The lad's no planter. He doubtless knows more of what's going on than these others do. Something he said just now troubles me."

"Should I bring up the men and start to move in, sir?" A captain of the infantry appeared out of the smoky haze that now enveloped the shoreline.

"Hold a while and keep your lines together. It's too quiet." Jeremy looked up and saw the goatee next to his face. "Now tell me, lad. There's been enough killing here for one night, as I'm a Christian. Is there going to have to be more? If you don't tell me, it'll be on your head, I swear it."

"This night is on *your* head, sir, and the Roundhead rebels who've stolen the Crown of England. And now would try to steal Barbados too."

The man waved the words aside. "Lad, I'm too old for that. Let your royalist rhetoric lie dead, where it deserves to be. My name is Morris, and if you know anything, you'll know I've seen my time fighting your royalists in the damned Civil War. But that's over, thank God, and I have no wish to start it up again. Now give me your name."

"My name is for men I respect."

"A sprightly answer, lad, on my honor. There's spark about you."

"The name on this musket looks to be Walrond, sor, if I make it out right." One of the infantrymen was handing the flintlock to Morris.

"Walrond?" Morris reached for the gun and examined it closely, running his hand along the stock and studying the

261

name etched on the lock. "A fine royalist name. By chance any kin to Sir Anthony Walrond?"

"My brother, and he's . . ."

"Your brother! You don't mean it." Morris' goatee twitched with surprise as he moved next to Jeremy and studied his face. "God is my witness, it's scarcely a name you need blush to give out. England never bred a braver, finer soldier, royalist or no. Is he your commander here tonight? You couldn't have one better."

"I have never heard my brother speak well of *you*, sir."

"Anthony Walrond? Speak well of a man who'd rid England of his precious king?" Morris laughed. "He'd sooner have God strike him dead. He's never had a good word to say for a Puritan in his life. But he's a worthy gentleman, for it all, and an honorable soldier in the field." He turned to an officer standing nearby. "Essex, regroup the men. I think we'd best just hold this breastwork for now. It could well be Anthony Walrond's in command of this militia. If he is, you can wager he'd not countenance a retreat unless he planned to counterattack. I know his *modus operandi*. And his pride."

"Aye sir. As you will." The captain turned and shouted, "Men, fall back and regroup! Form lines at the breastwork and reload."

"Now if you like, Master Walrond, I still can order all these men to march off into the dark and let your militia ambush and kill half of them—likely losing a hundred of their own in the trade. Would you really have me do it? Is this damned little island worth that much blood, over and above what's already been spilt here tonight?"

Jeremy gazed down at the line of dead militiamen, bodies torn by musket balls. Beyond them the Roundhead infantry was collecting its own dead, among them the man he himself had killed. Now it all seemed so pointless.

A blaze of musket fire flared from a position just north of the breastwork, and a phalanx of whooping and yelling militiamen opened a charge down the north side of the beach.

Jeremy watched Morris' eyes click. The kindly man was suddenly gone. With an oath, he yelled for the prisoners to be hurried to the longboats, and the devil take the wounded.

The infantry at the breastwork was returning the fire of the attacking militia, but they were now badly outnumbered. Jeremy made out what could have been the tall form of Anthony, wielding a musket as he urged the militia forward. Then he was passed by a wall of men on horseback. The cavalry. The lead horse, a bay gelding, was ridden by a tall man holding a pistol in each hand.

The infantry holding the breastwork began retreating down the south steps, on the side opposite the attackers. Jeremy could make out Morris now, ordering his men to make for the longboats.

"Get along with you, rebel." A pike punched him in the back and he was shoved in with the other prisoners. Now they were being hurried, stumbling and confused, in the direction of the water.

Part of the Barbados militia had already swarmed over the abandoned breastwork, while others were riding along the shore, muskets blazing, hurrying to seal off the escape route to the longboats. They intercepted the retreating infantry midway down the beach, and the gunfire gave way to the sound of steel against steel, as empty muskets were discarded in favor of pikes and swords.

Jeremy felt the warm surf splash his legs, and he looked up to see the outline of the waiting boats. He and the rest of the prisoners were on the far south side of the breastwork, away from the fighting, forgotten now. He was a prisoner of war.

Directly ahead, two longboats were being towed in through the surf—wide, hulking forms in the dim light, with sails furled and rows of oarsmen midships. As he watched them approach, he suddenly remembered his lost flintlock, a gift from Anthony, and the thought of its loss completed his mortification.

"Get in or be damned to you." Several infantrymen were splashing through the surf behind him now, half-pikes raised, urging on malingerers with the blades. Jeremy felt the hard gunwale of the longboat slam against his shoulder, then hands reaching down for him and grabbing his arms. He was yanked up, wet and shivering in the freshening wind, then shoved sprawling onto the boards.

"One move, any of you, and there'll be a pike in your guts." An infantryman began tying the prisoners' hands.

As Jeremy felt the rough cords against his wrists, he looked up and glanced over the side. The retreating infantry had drawn itself into a protective circle, knee-deep in the surf, yelling for its longboats to be brought in closer. At the perimeter of the circle two scrawny soldiers struggled to keep their footing in the pounding surf. They both seemed weak, almost staggering, and when a large wave slammed against their backs, they toppled headlong into the spray. The Barbados militiamen were there, pulling them up and dragging them back through the surf to the beach.

So, there'll be prisoners on both sides, he realized with relief. Now there'll be hostages onshore too.

The battle seemed to be thinning now. No one wanted to fight waist deep in the dark churning sea. The Barbados militiamen were slowing in their chase, turning back to congratulate themselves that the invasion had been repelled. Finally, as the longboats rowed closer and the infantrymen began pulling themselves aboard, the militia halted, content to end the rout by hurling curses above the roar of the surf.

"At least we spiked most of the cannon, and damn the rebels." Two officers were talking in the bow of the boat. Jeremy realized that both sides were planning to claim victory. Were there any wars ever "lost," he wondered.

"Though we've bloody little else to show for a night's work," an oarsman in a dark woolen cap mumbled under his breath, "save this fine new collection of bellies to fill." The man suddenly reached and ripped off a piece of Jeremy's lace collar. "This coxcomb'll learn soon enough what 'tis like to live on salt pork and slimy water, same as the rest of us." He flung the lace back in Jeremy's direction. "No fancy meat pies and brandied puddings for you, lad. A seaman's fare will soon take the fat out of those cheeks. I'll warrant it'll do you good, young rebel."

Ahead, the proud bow of the *Rainbowe* loomed above them in the dark, lanterns dangling from its masts. Seamen in the longboat tossed a grapple over the bulwark of the mother ship and then a rope ladder was dropped. Jeremy felt his hands being untied. Next he was urged up the ladder, shoved onto the deck, and immediately surrounded by jeering seamen, shirtless and wearing black stocking caps.

"This is the one, sir." Powlett was standing over him pointing. Next to him stood Admiral Edmond Calvert.

"I certainly can see he's a man of breeding, just as you said." Calvert studied Jeremy's ornate doublet in the flickering lantern light.

"Aye." Powlett's voice suddenly rose. " 'Twould seem he's the brother of Sir Anthony Walrond. I say we strip him and put him to work carrying slops out of the gun deck, as an example to all royalists."

"Not for a minute, sir. Not so long as I'm in command of this fleet." Calvert seemed to bellow at Powlett, almost too loudly.

A seaman was roughly yanking Jeremy to his feet, and Calvert turned on him. "You, there. Release that young gentleman, unless you'd like a timely taste of the cat on your back." He then approached and bowed ceremoniously. "Admiral Edmond Calvert, sir, your most obedient servant."

Jeremy stared in confusion and disbelief as the admiral continued, "Walrond, is it not?"

"Jeremy Walrond, and . . ."

"I'm honored." He turned and signaled to his quartermaster. "Have brandy sent to my cabin. Perhaps Master Jeremy Walrond would care to share a cup with us."

The seamen parted, doffing their caps to the admiral as he escorted Jeremy up the companionway toward the Great Cabin. "I can scarcely tell you, Master Walrond, how grateful I am to have the privilege of speaking face to face with a man of breeding from this island." He reached to steady Jeremy as he lost his footing in a roll of the ship. Then he smiled and gestured him ahead, down the lantern-lit walkway toward the stern. "First thing, we'll try and locate some dry breeches for you and a brandy to drive off the chill." He was still smiling as he shoved open a heavy wooden door. The Great Cabin was empty save for Colonel Richard Morris, now seated at the center table and rubbing the dirt off Jeremy's flintlock musket. Morris laid it carefully across the table in front of him when he saw them enter. Calvert smiled toward him, then continued, "I understand, Master Walrond, you've already made the acquaintance of our infantry commander."

Morris rose and nodded as Calvert gestured Jeremy toward an ornately carved oak chair. "After we've all made ourselves comfortable, Master Walrond, I hope you and I and Captain Morris here can become better acquainted. We've got much to talk over tonight." He flashed a quick look at Morris as he smiled. "Mind you, strictly as gentlemen."

Chapter Twelve

Katherine was relieved when she finally spotted him standing among the gunners, his face and leather jerkin covered in a dark veneer of grime. If anyone would know the truth behind the rumor spreading over the island, that Jeremy Walrond had been killed, surely Hugh would. She watched for a time, collecting her composure after the ride up from Bridgetown, then tied her mare to the trunk of a bullet-scarred palm and began working her way down the sandy slope toward the breastwork.

The mid-afternoon sun seared the Jamestown emplacement with the full heat of the day, and most of the gunners and militiamen were now shirtless and complaining about the need for rest. As she neared the stone steps leading up to the guns, the air rang with the sounds of hammering, iron against iron, and she realized Winston and the men were still working to extract the spikes from the touch holes of the large English culverin.

He looked out to study the three English warships offshore, barely visible through the smoke that mantled the bay, then turned to Thomas Canninge, his master gunner. "I think we've still got range, Tom. Try another round as soon as you're set and see if you can't hole them one last time."

Canninge and his gunners were struggling to set one of the

Dutch demi-culverin, hammering a wooden wedge out from under the breech in order to elevate the muzzle. "Aye, looks like they've started coming about, but I think we might still give the whoresons one more taste."

All the large cannon in the breastwork had been disabled by the invading Roundheads; their infantry had overrun the guns long enough to drive a large iron nail deep into each gun's touch hole, the small opening in the breech through which the powder was ignited. The facility would have been defenseless had not six of the Dutch demi-culverin been hauled out of the fort and hidden in a palm grove up the hill just prior to the attack.

As soon as the invasion was repelled and the breastwork cleared, Winston had summoned teams of horses to bring the small Dutch cannon back. His gunners had opened fire on the fleet at the first light of dawn, catching the three English frigates which were still anchored within range and preparing for a long, leisurely shelling of the Jamestown settlement. An artillery duel commenced as the warships immediately returned the fire, but when Winston's gunners honed their targeting, they had prudently hoisted anchor and retired to the edge of range. Now, while the militiamen worked with hammers and drills to finish removing the spikes from the large culverin, the battle had become mostly noise and smoke.

"Katy, God's life!" He finally noticed her as she emerged at the top of the steps. His startled look quickly melted into a smile. "This is a surprise."

"Hugh, I came to find out . . ."

"Everything's fine. We've got two of the spiked guns almost cleared, and if we can keep fire cover with these Dutch demi's, we should have all of them back in operation by nightfall." He walked over to where she stood. "So move on back out of range. It'll not be much longer. I think they've decided to give up on the shelling. Tom's already holed the *Rainbowe* twice with these little nine-pounders. Probably didn't do much harm, but at least the Roundheads know we're here."

He glanced up as a puff of smoke rose from the gun deck of the warship nearest the shore, the *Marsten Moor.*

"Round of fire!"

Before he finished the warning, the men had already dropped their hammers and were plunging behind a pile of sandbags. Winston's hard grip sent her sprawling with him behind the mound of earth-brown sacks. He rolled across her, then covered her face with his sweaty jerkin.

"This is how we brave fighting men stay alive . . ."

An eighteen-pound shot slammed against the base of the breastwork, shaking the brick foundation beneath them. After a few anxious moments, the men clambered nervously over the bags to resume work. She was still brushing the dirt from her riding habit when Winston suddenly whirled on her, his eyes fierce.

"Now you listen to me, Katy. You can't stay down here. It's still too damned dangerous. If you want to get killed, there're lots of better ways."

His back was toward the sea when the second burst of black smoke erupted from the gun deck of the *Marsten Moor.* "Hugh!" Without thinking she reached for him. Together they rolled twice across the soft earth, into the safety of the shielding bags. As they lay next to the militiamen and gunners, a round of cannon fire clipped the side of a battlement next to where they had been standing and hurtled a deadly spray of brick fragments into the sandbags. Several shards of brick ripped into the cloth and showered them with white grains.

He seemed embarrassed now as he slipped his arm under her and quietly hoisted her to her feet. Around them the militiamen were again returning to work on the disabled cannon. "I don't know whether to thank you, Katy, or order you clapped in the brig for coming here in the first place. But either way, you can't stay. So kindly wait up the hill till . . ."

269

The sound of a forceful hammer stroke followed by a clear ring produced a cheer from the group of men who had been diligently hammering on one of the spiked cannon.

"Got her cleared, Yor Worship," one of the militiamen yelled toward Winston. "Fit as the day she was cast."

He abruptly turned and headed through the crowd to inspect the breech of the gun. After scrutinizing the reopened touch hole, he motioned toward a waiting gunner. "Ladle in about five pounds of powder and see how she fires."

Tom Canninge called from the other end of the breastwork, "I've got the altitude about set on this little nine-pounder, Cap'n. It's the best of the lot."

"Then see if you can't put a round through her portside gun deck." His voice was increasingly strained.

"Good as done." Canninge ordered the demi-culverin shifted a few degrees to the left, then motioned for a linstock and lightly applied the burning end to the touch hole.

The gun roared and kicked backward in a cloud of dense, oily smoke. While the men squinted against the sun to watch, a large hole splintered open along the portside bow of the *Marsten Moor,* just above the waterline. Moments later a mate in the maintop began to unfurl tops'ls, and after that the mainsail dropped in preparation to make for open sea.

"Let's give her a sendoff, masters." Winston led the cheers, and Katherine realized he was deliberately trying to boost morale. Next he yelled down the sweating line of men. "Hear me, now. Our good master Canninge has just earned us all a tot of kill-devil. By chance I think a keg may have arrived this morning, on a cart that found its way up from Bridgetown. We should take a look up by that large tree on the left." He paused and waited for the hoorahs to subside. "Under my command, the men always drink first, then officers." He waved a dismissal. "As you will, masters."

As the gunners and militiamen threw down their tools and began to bustle in the direction of the liquor, he turned to Katherine and his voice dropped. "Now that we're both still alive, maybe we can talk. Why don't we try and find some shade ourselves?"

"You seem exhausted." As she looked at him, realizing that even his brown eyes seemed pale, she found herself almost reluctant to raise the matter of Jeremy. Maybe he had enough to worry about.

"Bone-tired is more the word. But we've got the fleet out of range for a while. Now we just have to worry about what they'll think to try next."

Hearing the open concern in his voice, she wrapped a consoling arm about his waist as they walked down the stone steps of the abandoned breastwork. "But the invasion failed. This round is won, isn't it?"

"If you can call that massacre last night 'winning,' then I suppose you could say so." He heaved a weary sigh. "Planters make poor soldiers, Katy. As best I can tell, we lost eighteen men killed outright. And a lot more were wounded. Some of them will doubtless die too, given this heat. So all we did was drive the Roundheads back to sea for a while, but at a terrible cost." He looked down. "They took some prisoners. Two longboats full. Probably about thirty men, though we don't really know yet who's captured, or missing . . . or just gone off to hide."

"Well, that's not so many."

"True enough. We managed to take a few prisoners ourselves, maybe half a dozen or so. . . . I guess maybe you didn't hear. Jeremy Walrond has disappeared. We think he was taken prisoner."

"Thank God. Then he's not dead." She stopped still. "But . . . captured? Poor Jeremy. He'd probably sooner have been killed. He was so proud."

"Anthony's proud too, and he's taking it very hard. When we heard Jeremy was missing, I offered to take the command here, to let him go back to Bridgetown and see if he was with the wounded. Then somebody suggested that Jeremy proba-

271

bly had surrendered, and Anthony threatened to kill the man. It was plain he needed some rest."

She stood silent for a moment, then looked away sadly. "What do you think will happen now?"

Winston followed her gaze, out toward the horizon. "Maybe everybody will try to negotiate some more. It's getting complicated all of a sudden, with prisoners now part of it. Unfortunately we didn't manage to take any officers, just infantry—most of them so weak from scurvy the fleet's probably just as glad to have them gone, before they died anyway."

"What'll happen to Jeremy? You don't suppose they'd hang him."

"I doubt that." He waved his hand. "So far it's a civilized war. But they may ask a price to send him back if they find out he's Anthony's brother. It's very bad."

"What do you suppose we can do?"

"Not much I can think of. Maybe they'll just try to wait us out a bit." He reached down and lightly brushed some of the dirt and sand from her hair. Then he wiped his brow, glanced at the sun, and urged her on, toward the grove of trees. "I'd guess it's a matter now of who can hold out longest." He slipped his arm about her waist and glanced down. "And how're *you* holding up, Katy?"

"I suppose I'm fine." She leaned against him, trying to ignore the heat and the stares of some of the men. Finally she gave a mirthless laugh. "No, do you want the truth? I'm more worried than ever. Isn't it odd? Just when we seem to be standing firm." She looked up at his smoke-smeared cheeks. "Can we go hide? Away from here? I think *your* morale could do with a boost too."

"You're looking at a somewhat disoriented breastwork commander. Make that 'acting commander.' But Anthony's supposed to be back around now to relieve me. Whenever he gets here, we can ride back over to Bridgetown, if I can manage to locate a horse." He helped her down beneath the shade of a spreading manchineel tree, kicking away several of the poisonous apples that lay rotting around the trunk. Then he flopped down beside her. "This is one of the hardest things I've ever tried, Katy, holding defenses together when half the men truly don't care a damn whether we win or lose. But it's the only thing I know to do. Tell me if you can think of anything better."

"Is that all you've thought about lately, Hugh?" She ran a hand along his thigh.

"It's all I care to think about for the time being."

She pulled back sharply. "Well, commander, please don't think I have nothing else to occupy my mind with except you. But that doesn't mean I've just forgotten you entirely."

"I haven't forgotten you either, Katy. God's life!" He picked up a twig and tapped it against one of the poison apples. "Tell me, what does the governor of Barbados think about his only daughter keeping company with the likes of me?"

"I do what I choose." She pressed against him. "Anyway, it's not what he says that troubles me. It's what I say to myself. I've always been able to control my feelings. But, somehow, not with you. And I hate myself for it. I truly do."

"I'm probably a poor choice for the object of your feelings."

She laughed and squeezed his hand. "God help me, as if I didn't already know that. Who'd ever have thought I'd be going about half in love with a man like you."

"I thought you once said you weren't interested in falling in love." He kissed her lightly. "Probably a safe idea. I don't know how many of us are going to live through this."

Before she could respond, he rose on one elbow and pointed toward a pair of horses approaching from the south. "It looks like we may get back to Bridgetown after all. I think that's Briggs, and he's brought Anthony with him. It's odds they both distrust me only slightly more than they hate each other, but it's enough to make them allies for a while.

Well, they're welcome to have back this command any time they want it."

"Then we can ride in together?"

"I don't think Anthony's going to like that idea, but it's your affair. God knows I know better than to try and give you advice."

She laughed. "Then you're starting to understand me better than I thought."

"Let me just have a word with Anthony about the condition of the ordnance. And make some gunnery assignments." He began to pull himself up. "Then maybe we'll retire down to the *Defiance* for a while. I've missed her." He stooped and kissed the top of her head as he rose to his feet. "And I've missed you, too. Truly."

Anthony Walrond reined in his dun mare and stared dumbly toward the shore as he and Briggs emerged from the trees. The night before it had been a melee of muskets, commands, screams; now it was a smoky landscape strewn with lost helmets and bandoliers, and stained with dark splotches where men had fallen. In its peacefulness it made the battle seem scarcely more than a violent dream, a lost episode that existed only in man's flawed memory, not in time.

Battles, he reflected, were always a matter of chance. You plan strategies for days, devise elaborate tactics, try to guess what you would do if you were the foe. But in the end little of it really matters. A man panics, or a horse stumbles, or your musket fails to fire, and suddenly nothing happens the way you thought. It becomes a contest of bravery, luck, happenstance. Whether you win or lose, it's likely as not for reasons you never envisioned.

In a way, last night's episode was no different. Dick Morris and his Roundheads lost more men than they should have. Since they only expected militia at the breastwork, the parapet caught them by surprise. Also, they seemed deceived at first by the feigned retreat, the bird limping and flopping away from her nest to lure the fox.

Except this time the fox suddenly grew wise. The limping bird somehow bungled its part, caused the fox to smell a trap. Which left no recourse but to launch a bloody counterattack directly on the breastwork.

Jeremy. They claimed he was surrounded and taken while reloading his musket. Holding his position. But why? He knew the orders. He disobeyed.

He disobeyed.

Anthony was still gripping the reins, his knuckles white, when Briggs broke the silence. "As usual, it's a good thing I rode over to check. Where're the men? Is that them drinking in the shade, whilst the breastwork is left unattended?" He drew his horse alongside Anthony's and squinted against the sun. "Winston has a peculiar idea of discipline, by my life."

"These men are not a gang of your African cane cutters. He's got enough sense to know he can't work them all day in the sun. I'll wager full half of them would just as soon not be here at all."

"Now you're beginning to sound like him." Briggs spotted the tall seaman walking up the shore and reined around. "And in truth, sir, I'm starting to question whether either of you should be kept in charge of this breastwork."

"Well, after last night, I propose you could just as well put a scullery wench in command here at Jamestown, for all the difference it would make." Walrond was studying the breastwork as they neared the shore. "There's not likely to be another attempt at a landing along here. It'd be too costly and Morris knows it. No commander in the English army would be that foolhardy. Doubtless he thought he'd managed to spike all our ordnance, and he just planned to sit back and shell the settlement here all day today. It looks as if they took a few rounds of shot this morning, but the shelling seems over. I'd guess Winston's lads managed to hold their own."

"Aye, God be praised for the Dutchmen and their demi-culverin." Briggs touched his black hat toward the approaching figure. "Your servant, Captain. How goes it?"

"Our gunners put some shot into the *Rainbowe* and the *Marsten Moor* before they weighed anchor and made way out to sea. I'd venture the better part of the ordnance here should be serviceable again by nightfall." He nodded to Walrond. "Any news of the prisoners?"

"This morning all the field commanders brought in reports." The royalist's voice was matter-of-fact. "As best we can tell, twenty-nine of our men were taken out to the *Rainbowe* last night."

"And Jeremy *was* among their number, the way somebody said? There was no mistake about that?"

"It appears likely." He looked away, to cover his embarrassment, and spotted Katherine walking toward them up the beach. He adjusted his eyepatch in anger and glanced back sharply at Winston. Could it be the rumors were all too true? If so, then damn him. Damn *her*. "I trust Miss Bedford has already been informed?"

"A few minutes ago."

"Well, sir, I fancy her dismay did not go uncomforted." He swung down the saddle. "I can assume duties here now, and relieve you, sir. She has to be taken home. This is scarcely the place for a woman."

"You're welcome to have it. I just need to make a few gunnery assignments of my own men. But I'd advise you to let the lads cool off a bit before starting them working again." He turned to hold the reins of Briggs' horse as the planter began dismounting. "One other thing. Before I go, I'd like a word with you, Master Briggs. Considering what's happened, I'd like it if you'd convey a message from me to the Council."

"Speak your mind, sir." Briggs eased himself out of the saddle and dropped down. His heavy boots settled into the loose sand.

"I lost three seamen last night, good men, when we

charged the breastwork. They'll be buried tomorrow with all the others killed.''

"It was a hard night for us all, sir.''

"Don't try my patience, Master Briggs. I'm not in the mood.'' He paused to wait as Katherine joined the circle.

"Katherine, your servant.'' Anthony coldly doffed his hat in greeting. "Here to review the militia?''

"I came to find out about Jeremy.''

"I'm still hoping there must be some mistake.'' He abruptly turned away.

"Well, now that I know, I suppose I'll go back.'' She looked at him, elegant and cool even now, and told herself she should be more embarrassed than she felt, having him see her here with Hugh. What was he really thinking?

"Katy, wait. I'm glad you're here.'' Winston motioned her forward, ignoring Anthony's pained look. "Perhaps it'd be well for you to hear this too. Maybe you can convey what I want to say to the Assembly, for whatever good it may do.'' He turned back. "I want to tell you all that I've concluded this militia is untrained, undisciplined, and, what's worse, uninterested in getting shot all to hell defending Barbados. I hear them asking each other why they're fighting at all.''

"We're holding them off nicely, sir,'' Briggs interjected. "I'm proud of . . .''

"Hear me. I tell you we were just lucky last night. Morris' men might well have held the breastwork if they hadn't panicked. The next time 'round we may not be as fortunate.'' He fixed Briggs squarely. "What you and the Council have to decide is whether you're willing to do what's necessary to win.''

"We're doing everything we can.''

"It's not enough. Next time, Morris will doubtless try and land every man he has. When he does, I wonder if this militia will even bother to meet them.''

"I don't agree with you there, sir.'' Briggs was frowning.

"But then I suppose you figure you've got some idea nobody else has thought of yet."

"Do you want to hear it?"

"*I'd* like to hear it." Anthony Walrond had finished hobbling his mare and stepped next to them.

"All right. First, I say prune out the small freeholders, send any of them home who want to go." He turned to Walrond. "Then get rid of any of the royalists who don't have battle experience. They want to give orders, but they don't know what they're about. The rest of the men don't like it." He paused carefully. "I don't like it either."

"You're presumptuous, sir, if I may say." Anthony glared.

"You may say what you please. But if you don't do something about morale, this war's as good as over."

"It most *certainly* will be, if we dismiss most of the militia, which is what it would mean if we did what you just said."

"I didn't say you don't need a militia. You just need men in it who're ready to stand and fight."

Briggs examined him quizzically. "But if we dismissed all these half-hearted freeholders, there'd be scarcely any free men left on the island to take their place."

"That's right. You'd have to *make* some free men." He gestured toward the hills inland. "Do you realize there're hundreds of firstclass fighting men here now, men with battle experience who could massacre Morris' forces if given a chance? And, more to the point, if you gave them something to fight for."

"Who do you mean?"

"You know who. These new Africans. They've got battle experience, I can tell just by looking at them. I don't know how many of them have ever handled a musket, but I'd wager a lot of them can shoot. Make them part of your militia, and Morris' infantrymen'll never know what hit them."

"I'm damned if we'll arm these savages and let them loose

278

on the island. Next thing, they'd try and take over. It'd be the end of slavery. Which means the end of sugar."

"Doesn't have to be. Let them work for wage and start treating them like men. Then, instead of worrying about having them at your back, you'd have them holding your defenses."

"That's about the damnedest idea I've ever come across." Briggs spat into the sand.

"Then you've got a choice. You can have slavery, or you can win independence. Either you get them to help, or you end up a slave to the Commonwealth yourself." He glanced at Katherine, then back at Briggs as he continued. "And the same goes for your indentures. How in hell do you expect this island to hold out against England when half the men here would just as soon see you lose? But give the slaves, and the indentures, a stake in this, and you'll have a good ten or fifteen thousand fighting men here. Morris has maybe three, four hundred. He'll never take Barbados. I want you to tell that to the Council."

"I'll be party to no such undertaking." Briggs squinted through the sunshine.

"Then give my regards to the admiral when you sit down to sign the surrender. I give you a week at most." He turned and touched Katherine's arm. "Katy, if you'd like me to see you home, then wait over there by that shade tree while I make gunnery assignments."

Atiba moved noiselessly along the wet sand of the shore, crouched low, the wind in his face, just as he had once stalked a wounded leopard in the forest three days north of Ife. This part of the harbor was almost deserted now; only two frigates remained, and they were both lodged in the sand, immobile. One was the great, stinking ship that had brought him to this forlorn place. He hated it, had vowed never to be on it again. Furthermore, tonight its decks were crowded with drinking, singing *branco*. The other one would have to supply what he needed—the one belonging to the tall Inglês *branco* with the mark on his cheek.

He secured the stolen machete in his waistwrap and waded into the water. When the first salty wave curved over him, he leaned into it with his shoulder and began to swim—out away from the shore, circling around to approach the ship from the side facing the sea.

As he swam, he thought again of what he must do. It was not a mission of his choosing. He had finally agreed to come because there was no other way to placate the elders. Until last night he had not realized how much they feared the arms of the *branco*. . . .

"We must be like the bulrush, not like brittle grass," Tahajo, the oldest and hence presumed the wisest, had declared. "A bulrush mat will bend. A grass mat breaks to pieces. Do not be brittle grass, Atiba, be like the bulrush. Do what we ask of you."

"Tahajo's wisdom is known throughout Ife." Obewole, the strongest of them all, had next conceded his own fear. "Remember it's said you cannot go to war with only a stick in your hand; you must carry a crossbow."

Atiba had intended the meeting in his hut to be their final council of war. Last evening was carefully chosen, auspicious. It was the fourth night of the new moon on the island of Barbados. In Ife it would have been the fourth day of a new month, and also the last day of the week—a cycle of four days dedicated to major gods of the Yoruba pantheon: Shango, Obatala, Orunmila, and Ogun. The appearance of the new moon was important and signified much. By telling the beginning of the month, it scheduled which days would be market days, which were sacred, what god was responsible for the birth of a child.

They had waited quietly in his thatched hut as twilight

settled across the fields of cane. Swallows twittered among the tall palms, and the half-light was spotted with darting bats. The heat of the long day still immersed the hillside. On the far western horizon, where the sea disappeared into the Caribbean mist, three of the great ships of the Inglês fleet had begun preparing their sails. They too seemed to be waiting for the appearance of the new Yoruba moon.

He began with a review of their weapons. There would be difficulties. Since the cane knives had been removed from the slave quarters on most of the plantations and secured in the great house, it would be necessary to break in and take them back, which meant the advantage of surprise would be lost. For spears, they would have to try and seize some of the pikes the *branco* now had in readiness to protect the island from the fleet. Again that meant bloodshed.

Also, their numbers were still uncertain. All the Yoruba had agreed to rise up, and final preparations had been coordinated across the island using the *iya ilu* drum. But the other men of Africa? What of them? The Ibo nursed historic hatreds toward the Yoruba, and their response to the plan for rebellion had been to shift on their feet, spit on the ground, and agree to nothing. There were also Ashanti and Mandingo. These he trusted even less than the Ibo. Command would be difficult: there were too many languages, too many loyalties, too many ancient grievances.

The men in the hut finally concluded that only the Yoruba could be relied upon. When the day of war comes, you only trust your own blood, your own gods.

After the moon had disappeared, he'd cast the cowries, praying Ogun would presage the defeat of the *branco*. The men required an omen.

And an omen there had been. At that exact moment the silence of the night was rent by sounds of gunfire rising up from the western shore, faint staccato pops through the trees. They were as drumbeats that carried no words, yet their message was unmistakable. Ogun, the god of war, had spoken—

not through the pattern in the cowries on a tray, but with his own voice.

Fear suddenly gripped the men in the hut. What was Ogun's purpose in answering the cowries this way? Thus their council of war had dissolved in meaningless talk and confusion. Finally the misgivings of the elders emerged.

There must be, they said, no rising against the *branco* unless success was assured. The elder Tahajo recalled the famous proverb: *Aki ida owo le ohun ti ako le igbe*—"A man should not attempt to raise up something he cannot lift." The other men had nodded gravely, taking his mouthing of this commonplace to demonstrate great sagacity.

Then young Derin, in a flagrant breach of etiquette amongst a council of elders, had dared to cite an opposing parable: *Bi eya ba di ekun, eran ni ikpa dze*—"When the wild cat becomes a leopard, it can devour great beasts." We must become brave like the leopard, he urged. When the *branco* see our boldness they will quake with fear as we go to war against them.

Tahajo had listened tolerantly, then countered again: *Alakatanpo oju ko le ita eran pa*—"He who has only his eyebrow for a crossbow can never kill an animal."

So it had continued long into the night. Atiba had no choice but to wait until the elders decided. Finally they agreed that Ogun would have them go to war only if they had weapons to match those of the *branco*. That was the message in the gunfire that had erupted the moment the cowries were cast. Atiba must assure them he could find muskets, or there would be no rebellion. . . .

He stroked silently on through the surf. Now the dark outline of the *branco*'s ship loomed above him, still, deserted. Soon he would find what he had come to learn.

He grasped a salt-encrusted rope ladder which dangled

from the side and pulled out of the water. He did not bother using the rungs; instead he lifted himself directly up.

His feet were noiseless as he dropped onto the deck. A quick reconnaissance revealed only one sentry, a fat *branco* snoring loudly in a chair on the high deck at the back of the ship. He slipped up the companionway, gripping each weathered board with his toes, and stood over the man, wondering if he should kill him, lest he waken suddenly and sound an alarm.

Then he remembered the words of Shango that night in the mill house. It would be a bad omen to spill innocent blood before the rebellion even began. Shango had declared he would only countenance the killing of men who threatened harm. Also, lying beside the man was an empty flask, which surely had contained the strong wine made from cane. This snoring *branco* would not soon awaken.

He turned and inched his way back down the companionway. The only sounds now were the gentle splash of surf against the side of the ship and the distant chirp of crickets from the shore. He moved stealthily along the creaking boards until he reached the locked door at the front of the ship, the place where the *branco* captains stored their weapons.

He tried to still his heart, feeling it begin to race with anticipation. If there were weapons here, muskets or pikes, they would be easy to seize when the moment came to rise up. There would be no need to storm the plantation houses for guns and spears, and their plans could proceed in total secrecy till the moment the *branco* slaveholders were surprised and cut down.

He recalled the rumor that the *branco* who owned this ship had bought and freed two hundred white slaves, and then had given some of them weapons to fight the warriors of the Inglês fleet. Surely he had more muskets and pikes than any of the *branco* planters. How many would be left?

He slipped the machete from his waistband and wedged it silently under a hinge on the heavy wooden door. The wood was old and the nails pulled easily. When the three hinges had been removed, he laid the machete on the deck and lifted the door around.

The interior of the fo'c'sle was dark, but he dared not try to make a light. The risk was too great that he might set off any gunpowder stored here. Instead he felt his way forward.

The space was crowded with racks, and in them were rows of new pikes and half-pikes, hundreds. Then his hand touched a row of long steel cylinders.

Musket barrels.

Ogun had answered their prayers.

This ship had an arsenal that would equip an entire army, a cache that would ensure their victory. The second week following, seven days hence, the time sacred to Ogun, he would bring the men and they would overwhelm the ship, seize the weapons. . . .

He had turned to grope his way back to the deck when he first saw the two silhouettes against the dim light of the doorway. A tall man was there, blocking his exit, and next to him was the outline of a *branco* woman.

"John, what in the name of hell are you doing in the fo'c'sle?" The voice sounded tired and annoyed. "Is this how you stand watch?"

"Hugh, take care." It was the voice of the *branco* woman he remembered from the first night in the boiling house.

He froze against a wall and reached for his machete.

It was missing. Like a fool he'd left it outside.

Quietly he lifted one of the pikes from the rack and inched slowly toward the figures in the doorway.

Through the dark came a shout from the other end of the deck. The sleeping *branco* had awakened. "God's wounds, Cap'n. I'm watching this ship like a hawk over a henhouse. There's no need to be carryin' on." The man laughed. "Lest you upset the lady."

"John, is that you?" The tall man's voice quickened. "Then, by Jesus, who's . . ."

Atiba lunged toward the doorway, his pike aimed at the tall shadow.

The man had already feinted back against the shrouds. He carried no sword, but a pistol had appeared in his right hand, as though by magic. With the other he shoved the *branco* woman back against the shrouds, out of reach. The pike missed him, tangled in a knot of lines dangling from the mast, and was lost.

Then the glint of his machete caught Atiba's notice and he dropped toward the darkness of the deck. He rolled twice, bringing himself within reach of its wooden handle. He was on his feet, swinging for the man, when he heard the crack of the pistol and felt a tremor in his wrist.

The tip of the machete blade sang into the night, but the stump was still left, and still deadly. Now the fight would be at close quarters. He told himself he welcomed that—and sprang for the dark silhouette.

He was thrusting the blade upward, toward the tall man's neck, when he heard an unexpected click from the pistol barrel, followed by a hard voice. It was a threat that needed no translation.

"*No,* by God. Or I'll blow your bloody head off."

The hot muzzle of the pistol was against his cheek.

But his blade was against the man's throat.

"*Meu Deus.* Briggs' Yoruba." The man quickly switched to Portuguese. "*Felicitacao,* senhor. You're every bit as fast as I'd thought. Shall we call it a draw?"

It was the *branco,* the one who had freed his slaves. The last man on the island he wished to kill. Shango would be incensed.

"I think one of us must die." He held the broken blade hard against the flesh, and he could almost feel the pulse of blood just beneath the skin.

"It's both of us, or neither, by Jesus. Think about that."

"Your pistol had only one bullet. It is gone."

"Take a look and you'll see there're two barrels." The tall man had not wavered.

"Shall I just blow the thievin' bastard to hell, Cap'n?" It was the voice of the man who had been asleep. From the corner of his eye Atiba could see him standing by the foremast. There was the click of a flintlock being cocked.

"No, John. He's like to slit my throat in the bargain with what's left of his god-cursed machete." The words were in English. Then the man switched back to Portuguese. "A trade, senhor. A life for a life."

"In Ife we say we cannot dwell in a house together without speaking to one another. But if you betray me, you will answer for it to all my clan. Remember that." The broken machete slowly pulled away, then dropped to the deck.

"Hold the musket on him, John. I don't know whether to trust these Africans." Again Portuguese. "Life for life. Agreed." He lowered the pistol, then slipped it into his belt. With an easy motion he pulled down a lantern hanging from the shrouds and struck a flint to it. A warm glow illuminated the open door of the fo'c'sle, and the tanned face of the *branco* woman. "Now, Atiba the Yoruba, you be gone and I'll forget you were ever here. Briggs would likely have you whipped into raw meat for his dogs if he ever found out about this." The *branco* was looking into his eyes. "But you probably already know that. I salute your courage, senhor. Truth is, I once thought about having you help me."

"Help you?" He studied the *branco*'s face. "For what purpose?"

"If you weren't too stubborn to take orders, I'd planned to train you into a first-class fighting man. Maybe make you second-in-command for a little war of my own. Against the Spaniards." The man was outlined in the pale light. "I'd hoped we might fight together, instead of against each other."

"That is a strange idea for a *branco*." He was studying the scar on the tall man's cheek. "But then you have the mark on your cheek like the clan sign of a Yoruba. Perhaps the

286

place you got it taught you something of brotherhood as well.''

''It was a long time past, though maybe it did at that. I do know I'm still a brother to any man I like. You were once in that category, senhor, till you came on my ship trying to knife me. Now you'd best tell me what you're doing here.''

''I wanted to see your ship.''

''Well, you've seen it. You also tore off some hinges.''

''I will replace them for you.'' He smiled. ''Wrapping a razor preserves its sharpness.''

The man seemed momentarily startled; then a look of realization spread through his eyes. Finally he turned and spoke in English to the fat *branco* holding the musket. ''John, fetch a hammer and some fresh nails from below decks. You know where ship's carpenter keeps them.''

''What're you saying, Cap'n?'' The fat *branco* had not moved. ''You'd have me go aft? An' the musket I'm holdin' on the bastard? Who's to handle that whilst I'm gone?''

''I'll take it.'' The *branco* woman stepped forward.

''Give it to her.''

''You'd best keep a close eye, Cap'n.'' The fat man hesitated. ''I think this one'd be a near match for you. . . .''

''Just fetch the hammer, John.''

''Aye.'' He reluctantly passed the musket and began backing slowly toward the hatch leading to the lower deck.

Atiba watched him disappear into the dark, then turned back to Winston. ''You do not own slaves, senhor. Yet you do nothing about those on this island who do.''

''What goes on here is not my affair. Other men can do what they like.''

''In Ife we say, 'He who claps hands for the fool to dance is no better than the fool.' '' He glanced back at the arsenal stored in the dark room behind him. ''If you do nothing to right a wrong, then are you not an accomplice?''

The man suddenly seemed to understand everything. Without a word he walked over and shoved the door against the

287

open fo'c'sle. "Let me give you some wisdom from this side of the wide ocean, my friend. I think all the drumming I've been hearing, and now this, means you're planning some kind of revolt. I'm not going to help you, and I'm damned if you're going to use any of my muskets." He reached up and adjusted the lantern. "I've done everything I can to end slavery. Nobody on this island listens to me. So whatever you do is up to you."

"But without weapons, we have no chance of winning our freedom."

"You've got no chance in any case. But if you steal some of these muskets of mine, you'll just manage to kill a lot of people before you have to surrender and be hanged." He watched the fat man emerge from the hatch. "I'd hate to see you hanged, Atiba the Yoruba."

"What's the savage got to say for himself, Cap'n?" The man was carrying a hammer. "Was he plannin' to make off with a few o' those new flintlocks we got up at Nevis?"

"I think he was just exploring, John." The words were in English now. "Help him put the door back and show him how to fix the hinges."

"As you will, Cap'n. But keep an eye on him, will you? He's like to kill the both of us if he takes a mind."

"Katy, keep him covered."

"God, but he's frightening. What were you two talking about?"

"We'd best go into that later." He glanced at Mewes. "John, give him the hammer."

The fat *branco* reluctantly surrendered the tool, then warily reached to hold the hinges in place. There was a succession of quick, powerful strokes, and the door was aligned and swinging better than before.

"Now go on back to Briggs' plantation. And pray to whatever gods you have that he doesn't find out you were gone tonight." He picked up the broken machete and passed it over. "Take this. You're going to need it."

288

"You know we will need more than this." Atiba reached for the handle, turned the broken blade in the light, then slipped it into his waistband.

"That's right. What you need is to learn how to wait. This island is about to be brought to its knees by the new government of England. In a way, it's thanks to you. When the government on this island falls, something may happen about slavery, though I'm not sure what." He took down the lantern from the shrouds. "But if you start killing whites now, I can assure you you're not apt to live very long, no matter who rules."

"I will not continue to live as a slave."

"I can understand that. But you won't be using my flint-locks whilst getting yourself killed." He held the lantern above the rope ladder and gestured for Atiba to climb down into the shallow surf. "Never, ever try stealing muskets from my ship. Mark it well."

Atiba threw one leg over the gunwale and grasped a dead-eye to steady himself. "I think you will help us when the time comes. You speak like a Yoruba." He slipped over the side with a splash, and vanished into the dark.

"God's blood, Cap'n, but that's a scary one." Mewes stared after him nervously. "I got the feelin' he seemed to know you."

"I've seen him a time or two before." He retrieved the musket from Katherine and handed it back to Mewes. Then he doused the lantern. "Come on, Katy. Let's have a brandy."

"I could use two."

As they entered the companionway leading aft to the Great Cabin he called back, "By the way, John, it'd be just as well not to mention to anybody that he was here. Can I depend on you?"

"Aye, as you will."

He slipped his arm about Katherine's waist and pushed open the door of the cabin. It was musty and hot.

"I've got a feeling that African thinks he's coming back for the muskets, Katy, but I'll not have it."

"What'll you do?" She reached back and began to loosen the knot on her bodice, sensing a tiny pounding in her chest.

"I plan to see to it he gets a surprise instead." He lit the lamp, then pulled off his sweaty jerkin and tossed it into the corner. "Enough. Let's have a taste of you." He circled his arms around her and pulled her next to him. As he kissed her, he reached back and started unlacing her bodice. Then he whispered in her ear.

"Welcome back aboard."

Chapter Thirteen

With every step Jeremy took, the wooded trail leading inland from Oistins Bay felt more perilous, more alien. Why did the rows of stumps, once so familiar, no longer seem right? Why had he forgotten the spots in the path where the puddles never dried between rains, only congealed to turgid glue? He had ridden it horseback many a time, but now as he trudged up the slope, his boots still wet from the surf, he found he could remember almost nothing at all. This dark tangle of palms and bramble could scarcely be the direction home.

But the way home it was. The upland plantation of Anthony Walrond was a wooded, hundred and eighty acre tract that lay one mile inland from the settlement around Oistins Bay—itself a haphazard collection of clapboard taverns and hewn-log tobacco sheds on the southern, windward side of the island. The small harbor at Oistins was host to an occasional Dutch frigate or a small merchant vessel from Virginia or New England, but there was not enough tobacco or cotton to justify a major landing. It was, however, the ideal place to run a small shallop ashore from a ship of the fleet.

He reached a familiar arch of palms and turned right, starting the long climb along the weed-clogged path between the trees that led up to the house. As he gripped his flintlock and listened to the warbling of night birds and the menacing clatter of land crabs, he reflected sadly that he was the only man on Barbados who knew precisely what lay in store. He had received a full briefing from the admiral of the fleet aboard the *Rainbowe*. What would Anthony do when he heard?

He tried to sort out once more what had happened, beginning with that evening, now only two days past, when Admiral Calvert had passed him the first tankard. . . .

"If I may presume to say, it's a genuine honor to share a cup with you, Master Walrond." Calvert's dark eyes had seemed to burn with determination as he eased back into his sea chair and absently adjusted his long white cuffs. He'd been wearing a black doublet with wide white epaulettes and a pristine bib collar, all fairly crackling with starch. "And to finally have a word with a man of breeding from this infernal settlement."

Jeremy remembered taking a gingerly sip of the brandy, hoping perhaps it might somehow ease the pain of his humiliation. Still ringing in his ears were the screams of dying men, the volleys of musket fire, the curses of the Roundhead infantry in the longboat. But the liquor only served to sharpen his horrifying memory of the man he had killed less than an hour before, his finger on the trigger of the ornate flintlock now resting so innocently on the oak table between them.

"The question we all have to ask ourselves is how long this damnable state of affairs can be allowed to go on. Englishmen killing their own kind." Calvert had posed the question more to the air than to the others in the room. Colonel Morris, his face still smeared with powder smoke, had shifted his glance back and forth between them and said nothing. He clearly was impatient at being summoned to the Great Cabin when there were wounded to attend. Why, Jeremy had found himself wondering, was Morris present at all? Where was the brash vice admiral, the man who had wanted him imprisoned below decks? What was the hidden threat behind Calvert's too-cordial smiles? But the admiral betrayed nothing as he continued. "The Civil War is over, may Almighty God forgive us for it, and I say it's past time we started healing the wounds."

Jeremy had listened as the silence once more settled around them. For the first time he'd become aware of the creaking of the boards as the *Rainbowe* groaned at anchor. After so much death, he'd found himself thinking, you begin to notice the quietness more. Your senses are honed. Could it be even creatures of the field are the same; does the lowly hare feel life more exquisitely when, hounds baying on its scent, it hovers quivering in the grass?

He wondered what he would do if the musket on the table were primed and in his hands. Would he raise it up and destroy this man who had come to conquer the last safe place on earth left for him? As he tried to still the painful throb in his temples, Calvert continued.

"I'm a plain-speaking seaman, Master Walrond, nothing more. Though my father served in your late king's court, watching his Catholic queen prance amongst her half-dressed Jezebels, I never had any part of it. But I've seen dead men enough whose spilled blood is on that king's head, for all his curls and silks."

Calvert had suddenly seemed to remember himself and rose to pour a tankard for Morris. He took another sip from his own, then turned back. "And there's apt to be more killing now, here in the Americas, before this affair's finished. But to what purpose, sirrah? I ask you. We both know the island can't hold out forever. We've got her bottled now with this blockade, and the bottle's corked. What's more, I know for a fact you're all but out of meat and bread, whilst we've made free with all the victuals these interloping Hollanders in Carlisle Bay kindly had waiting to supply us. So my men'll be feasting on capon and port whilst your planters are starving, with nothing in the larder save tobacco and cane. You've never troubled to grow enough edibles here, since you could always buy from these Hollanders, and now it's going to be your downfall.'' Calvert's eyes had flashed grimly in the lantern light. When Morris had stirred, as though to speak, he'd silenced the commander with a brisk wave of his hand, then continued.

''But we're not planning just to wait and watch, that I can promise you. Colonel Morris here will tell you he's not going to sleep easy till this island is his. At the break of day he'll commence his first shelling, right here at Jamestown where he's spiked the ordnance. You'll see that spot, breastwork and the rest, turned to rubble by nightfall tomorrow. No, Colonel Morris is not of my mind; he's not a country angler who'd sit and wait for his line to bob. He's a man who'll wade in and take his perch with both hands.'' Calvert had sighed and risen to open the windows at the stern. Cool air washed over them, bringing with it the moans of wounded men from the deck above. Jeremy noted the windows had been severely damaged by cannon fire and temporarily repaired with wood rather than leaded glass. Calvert listened glumly for a moment, then shoved the windows closed and turned back. ''But what's the point of it, Master Walrond, by all that's holy?''

''You'll never take Barbados, blockade or no.'' Jeremy had tried to meet the glare in Calvert's eyes. ''We'll never surrender to Cromwell and this rabble army.''

''Ah, but take you we will, sir, or I'm not a Christian. The only question is when.'' He had paused to frown. ''And how? Am I to be forced to humble this place till there's nothing left, to shell her ports, burn her crops? I daresay you're not fully aware what's in store for this island. But it's time somebody heard, and listened. I came here with peace in mind, praying your governor and Assembly would have the sense to recognize the Commonwealth. If I was met with defiance, my orders were to bring Barbados to its knees, man and boy. To see every pocket of resistance ferreted out. More than that, you'd best know I'll not be staying here forever. There'll

294

be others to follow, and that young stalwart you met out on decks, my vice admiral, may well claim the only way to keep the island cooperative is to install a permanent garrison. Believe me when I tell you he'd as soon hang a royalist as bag a partridge. Think on that, what it's apt to be like here if you force me to give him free rein."

Jeremy had felt Calvert's eyes bore into him. "But, Master Walrond, I think Barbados, the Americas, deserve better." He glanced toward Morris. "And I'll warrant our commander here feels much the same. Neither of us wants fire and sword for this place. Nor, I feel safe in thinking, does anyone on this island. But someone here has got to understand our purpose and harken to reason, or it's going to be damnation for your settlement and for the rest of the Americas."

"Then that's what it'll be, if you think you've got the means to attempt it." Jeremy had pulled himself upright in the chair. "But you try landing on this island again and we'll meet you on the beaches with twice the men you've got, just like tonight."

"But why be so foolhardy, lad? I'll grant there're those on this island who have no brief for the Commonwealth, well and good, but know this—all we need from the Americas is cooperation, plain as that; we don't ask servitude." He lowered his voice. "In God's name, sir, this island need merely put an end to its rebellious talk, agree to recognize Parliament, and we can dispense with any more bloodletting."

Then Calvert had proceeded to outline a new offer. Its terms were more generous—he'd hammered home time and again—than anyone on the island had any cause to expect. The point he had emphasized most strongly was that Jeremy Walrond stood at the watershed of history. On one side was war, starvation, ignominy; on the other, moderation. And a new future . . .

* * *

Ahead the log gables of the Walrond plantation house rose out of the darkness. On his left, through the trees, were the thatched lean-to's of the indentures. A scattering of smoky fires told him some of the servants or their women were still about, frying corn mush for supper. The indentures' few remaining turkeys and pigs were penned now and the pathway was mostly quiet. The only sounds came from clouds of stinging gnats, those pernicious merrywings whose bite could raise a welt for a whole day, their tiny bugles sending a chorus through the dark. In the evening stillness the faint stench of rotting corn husks wafted from a pile in which pigs rooted behind the indentures' quarters, while the more pungent odor of human wastes emanated from the small vegetable patches farther back.

He heard occasional voices in the dark, curses from the men and the Irish singsong of women, but no one in the indenture compound saw or heard him pass. Ahead the half-shuttered windows of the plantation house glimmered with the light of candles. It meant, he realized with relief, that Anthony was home, that he'd lit the pewter candelabra hanging over their pine dining table.

He stopped for a moment to think and to catch his breath, then moved on past the front portico, toward the servants' entrance at the rear of the house. There was good reason not to announce his arrival publicly. What he had to say was for Anthony, and Anthony alone.

As he passed one of the windows he could just make out a figure seated at the table, tankard in hand. The man wore a white kerchief around his neck and a doublet of brown silk, puffed at the shoulders. His dark brown hat rested next to him on the table, its white plume glistening in the dull light.

As he pushed on, he noticed that the chimney of the log cookroom in back of the house gave off no smoke, meaning Anthony's servants had already been dismissed for the night.

Good. The time could not have been better.

Ahead now, just at the corner, was the back doorway. It

296

was ajar and unlatched; as usual the help had been careless as they crept away with meat scraps from Anthony's table to season their own bland meal.

He paused at the first step and tried to think how he would begin. For no reason at all he found himself staring up at the stars. The heavens in the Caribbees always reminded him of one dusk, many years ago, when he had first seen London from afar—a jewel box of tiny sparklers hinting of riches, intrigues, delicious secrets. What waited there amidst those London lights, he had pondered, those thousands of flickering candles and cab lanterns? Was it as joyful as it seemed? Or was misery there too, as deep and irreducible as his own?

That answer never came. But now this canopy of stars above the Caribbees mantled a place of strife and despair wrenching as man could devise.

He gently pushed open the split-log door and slipped through. The back hallway was narrow and unlighted, but its walls were shadowed from the blaze of distant candles. He remembered that Anthony always lit extra tapers when he was morose, as though the burning wicks might somehow rekindle his own spirit.

As he moved through the rough-hewn archway leading into the main room, he saw the seated figure draw back with a start and reach for the pistol lying on the table.

"By God, what . . ."

Suddenly the chair was kicked away, and the man was rushing forward with open arms. "Jeremy! God's life, it's you! Where in heaven's name have you been?" Anthony wrapped him in his arms. "We heard you'd been taken by Morris and the Roundheads." He drew back and gazed in disbelief and joy. "Are you well, lad? Were you wounded?"

"I've been with Admiral Calvert on the *Rainbowe*." He heard his own voice, and its sound almost made him start.

"You've been . . . ?" Anthony's eyes narrowed slightly. "Then you managed to escape! Did you commandeer a longboat? For the love of God, lad, what happened?"

What happened?

He almost laughed at the question. Would that any man ever knew, he found himself thinking. What ever "happens" . . . save that life flows on, of its own will, and drags you with it willy-nilly?

Without a word he carefully settled his flintlock in the corner, next to the rack that held Anthony's own guns—three matchlocks and two flintlocks—and slumped into a vacant chair by the table. "I've a thirst." He glanced distractedly about the room, barely remembering it. For the past two days—now it seemed like an entire age—life had been a ship. "Is there brandy?"

"Aye, there's a flask in the sideboard, as always." Anthony examined him curiously. Jeremy rarely drank anything stronger than Madeira wine. "What is it, lad? For God's sake let's have it. All of it."

With a tankard in his hand, Jeremy discovered that the first part of the story fairly tumbled forth—the Roundhead captain he had killed, the anger, the dismay, the loose discipline of the men in the trench. He even managed to confess straight out the circumstances of his capture, that he had ignored the call to retreat, only to have his musket misfire. Finally he reached the part where he first met Admiral Calvert. Then the tale seemed to die within him.

"Well, lad, what happened next? You say Morris knew who you were?"

"Aye, and he spoke of you." Jeremy looked at his brother. "With considerable respect, to tell it truthfully."

"A Roundhead schemer, that's Dick Morris, who'd not speak the truth even if he knew how." Anthony leaned forward and examined his tankard. "But I'm beginning to grow fearful he may have the last say in this matter, truth or no." He looked up. "What did you see of their forces, lad? Can they mount another landing?"

"They can. They will. They've got the Dutch provisions,

and Calvert claims they could hold out for weeks. But he says he'll not wait. He plans to invade."

"Aye, I'd feared as much. If he does, I say God help us. This damned militia is plagued with more desertions every day. These freeholders seem to think they've done all they need, after Jamestown. They're saying let somebody else fight the next time, when there isn't anybody else. We're having trouble keeping enough men called up just to man the breast-works." He scratched at his eyepatch distractedly. "I suppose we can still meet them if they try another assault, but it'll be a pitched battle, as God is my witness."

Jeremy drank off the tankard, rose, and walked shakily to the sideboard. The onion-flask of brandy was still over half full. He wished he could down it all, then and there. "I heard their plans from Admiral Calvert." He finished pouring and set down the bottle. After a deep drink he moved back to his chair, without meeting Anthony's gaze. "I would all the Assembly and Council could have heard what he said."

"What did that Roundhead criminal do? Threaten you, and then send you home in hopes you'd somehow cozen me?" Anthony looked up. "Jeremy, that man's a base traitor to his king. His father was in Charles' court, and Edmond Calvert was knighted for no more cause than being George Calvert's son. Then when Prince Rupert and the navy declared their support for the king, he took his ship and defected to Parliament. . . ."

"It wasn't a threat."

Suddenly the words came again. Out poured Calvert's story of Cromwell's plans for the island if it defied him. The Assembly and Council would be dismissed and Powlett set up as governor. A garrison would be installed. Moreover, Powlett might well see fit to reward loyal Puritan islanders with the estates of recalcitrant royalists. Anthony Walrond stood to lose all his acres, again.

The elder Walrond listened thoughtfully till the story was finished. Then he slowly drained his tankard. "It's the final humiliation. Cromwell, may God damn him, can't rest content merely to strike off the head of his Most Royal Majesty. Now he must needs reduce all that king's loyal subjects to nothing.''

"But it needn't be." Jeremy put down his tankard. His hands quivered, as though to match the flicker of the candles.

"There's something you haven't told me yet, isn't there, lad? You haven't said why they set you ashore. You didn't escape, did you?" Anthony studied him with sudden dismay. "I'll wager you were sent back. Why was it?"

"Aye. The reason is this." He rose and reached into the pocket of his doublet. The letter was still there, waiting, its wax seal warm against his shirt. "It's for you."

He found himself wishing it had been lost, though he believed with all his heart the message meant salvation. It was a gift of God. Yet something about it now seemed the work of the devil.

"What is it, Jeremy?" Anthony stared at the envelope. "Some kind of threat to try and frighten me too?" He looked up and bristled. "They can spare their ink and paper."

"Admiral Calvert asked me to deliver this. He and Captain Morris said that whilst you were their staunchest foe, they also knew you for a gentleman. They said you were the only man on the island they felt they could trust. That you alone could prevent this place being brought to ruin by Cromwell—which would probably mean fighting all over the Americas for years, when they just want to settle this and be gone.''

"Are they asking me to be a traitor to the island?"

"They've made an offer, a private offer. They said the Assembly can't be made to reason, that it'd sooner bring ruination to the island than agree to a compromise.''

"This is damned knavery. To presume I'd be party to disloyalty.''

"But think on't." Jeremy drank again and felt his boldness renewed. "Why should you sacrifice yourself helping the greedy Puritans on this island? The Council scorns to listen to you, and you've still not been elected to the Assembly. I'd say you've received naught but contempt, from the day you arrived.'' His voice rose. "Make no mistake on it, there'll be a new regime here after the island surrenders, which it'll have to eventually. Right now, Calvert and Morris just want to keep Barbados out of the hands of this man Powlett.''

Anthony turned the envelope in his hand. "So what does this cursed letter of Calvert's say?''

"Merely that you're a reasonable man, that you're surely sensible of the ruin a total war would mean. And that he's got terms to offer you that are truly in the best interest of Barbados, if only you'd give them ear.''

"I suppose he made you privy to these most generous terms.'' Anthony tossed the letter onto the rough pine boards in front of him.

"If you'd use your influence to work for peace, and convince your Windward Regiment here in this parish to cooperate, he'll take steps to thwart the designs of Powlett. If the island laid down its arms, then there'd be no garrison of troops. He'll guarantee it. And there'd be amnesty for all the planters.''

"It's more damn'd Roundhead lies. That's not the voice of Cromwell. That's the voice of an admiral who fears he can't take this place by force. So he'd try doing it by deceit.'' Anthony's face reddened. "Does the man have the cheek to think I've no scruples whatsoever?''

"But he's promised more. He'd form a new Council and make you its head. He and you'd appoint the others together. Of course they'd needs be men of moderate stripe, who'd stood for peace. But you could both work together to ensure the treaty was kept. Powlett might still have to serve as governor for a time, but he'd not be able to do anything without the approval of your new Council.''

"It's all a deception, lad.'' Anthony sighed wistfully. "Would it were true. You're young, and I fear to say still a bit gullible. These are promises made in the moonlight and shrugged away at sunrise.''

"I'm old enough to know there's been enough killing." Jeremy choked back a lump of guilt that rose in his chest. "But the letter's not addressed to me. It's to you. What harm in reading it? Morris would like to arrange a meeting, unarmed, to discuss its terms."

"A meeting!" Anthony seemed to spit out the words.

"Aye, here along the coast at Oistins. He's to come ashore by longboat tomorrow night, alone, to hear what you have to say." Jeremy took another drink of brandy and its fire burned through him. "There's no harm in that, for sure. It could be the beginning of peace."

"Lad, talk sense. They'll not hold to these conditions you've described. Once the island is disarmed, it'll be the end for every free man here."

"He said he'd give you all the terms in writing, signed." Jeremy noticed his tankard was dry. He wanted to rise for more brandy, but the room swirled about him. "It's our chance, don't you see. If Barbados goes down fighting, there'll be no terms. No concessions. Just more needless deaths. If you don't hear them out, it'll be on our heads."

"I'll not do it."

"But what's the Council ever done for you? For that matter, what has Bedford done?"

Anthony stared into the empty tankard in his hand and his voice grew bitter. "He's let Katherine take up company with the criminal who robbed our ship at Nevis, whilst we're at this very time negotiating a marriage portion. And made me a laughing stock in the bargain, if you must know." He looked up. "In truth, that's the most Dalby Bedford's done for me as of late."

Jeremy felt his face grow flush with embarrassment. "Then I say you owe it to decency to hear what Morris has to offer tomorrow night. Otherwise there'll just be more killing. Next it'll be starvation too. Please. I entreat you to think on it."

Anthony picked up the letter and turned it in his hand.

"Liberty or death." His voice was strangely subdued. "That's what the Assembly claimed they wanted. But it turns out that was just talk. They don't even want liberty enough to stand and fight for it, that's all too clear now."

He pushed open the wax seal with his thumb and unfolded the paper. Jeremy watched his face as he began to read.

My Lord, I send this to you as one who is master of a great deal of reason, and truly sensible of the ruin of the island if it should longer be obstinate. Only after appeal to your Lordship could I satisfy mine own conscience that I had done my duty in avoiding what I can the shedding of blood and the ruin of this island; for although I may by some be looked upon as an Enemy, yet really I do you office of a Friend in urging your Lordship and those engaged with you to judge of the Necessity of your Lordship's and their giving their due obedience to the State of England or else to suffer yourselves to be swallowed up in the destruction which a little time must inevitably bring upon you, which I cannot suppose rational men would wish.

My Lord, may it please you to know that I am not ignorant of the Interests of this Island, and very well know the impossibility of its subsistence without the Patronage of England. It is clear to me that God will own us in our attempts against this island (as He hath hitherto done), and yet to show you that I would endeavour what I can to avoid the shedding of blood and the loss of estates, I have thought fit to send this to your Lordship, to offer you such reasonable conditions as may be honourable for the State to give. . . .

Anthony studied the terms carefully; they were just as described by Jeremy. Calvert was offering a leniency most uncharacteristic of Cromwell. The island would be beholden to Parliament, to be sure, but it would not be humiliated.

Moreover, he suddenly thought, when Charles II moved to restore the monarchy, this island's strength and arms would be intact, ready to help throw off the yoke of Cromwell's oppression. With a surge of pleasure he realized this could well be a strategic retreat, in the finest military sense. If Calvert were willing to honor these generous terms, the fight could still be won another day. Particularly if Anthony Walrond controlled the new Council of Barbados.

Chapter Fourteen

"I've always called it 'Little Island,' since nobody's ever troubled giving it a name." She reined in her mare and directed Winston's gaze toward the atoll that lay a few hundred yards off the coast. The waters along the shore shimmered a perfect blue in the bright midday sun. "At low tide, like now, you can wade a horse right through the shallows."

"Does anybody ever come out here?" He drew in his gelding and stared across the narrow waterway. The island was a curious anomaly; there was a high rocky peak at its center, the lookout Katherine had described, and yet the shores were light sand and verdant with palms. Little Island was less than a quarter mile across and shaped like an egg, almost as though God had seen fit to set down a tiny replica of Barbados here off its southern shore. Looking west you could see the forested coast of the mother island, while to the east there was the road leading to Oistins and the Atlantic beyond.

"Never. I've ridden out here maybe a dozen times, but there's never been a soul."

He turned and surveyed the coast. "What else is around this place?"

"Nothing much, really. . . . Just the Walrond plantation, up the coast, inland a mile or so, about halfway between here and Oistins."

"Good Christ! I'm beginning to understand it all." He laughed wistfully. "I'll wager you've probably come out here with that gallant of yours." Then he looked at her, his eyes sardonic. "Didn't he get his fancy silk breeches wet riding across the shallows?"

"Hugh, not another word. Try to understand." She turned and studied him. These occasional flares of jealousy; did he mean them? She wasn't sure. Maybe it was all just a game to him, playing at being in love. But then, she asked herself, what was *she* doing? Perhaps wanting to have everything, a lover *and* a husband. But why couldn't you? Besides, Hugh would be gone soon. Better to enjoy being in love with him while she could. "I mean that. And Anthony must never learn we came here."

He was silent for a moment, letting the metrical splash of the surf mark the time. Somehow she'd managed to get away with her little game so far. Anthony Walrond was too busy rallying his royalists to take much notice of anything else. Or maybe he was willing just to turn his blind eye to it all.

"Katy, tell me something. How, exactly, am I supposed to fit into all this? You think you can have an *amour* with me and then wed a rich royalist when I'm gone? I suppose you figure he'll be governor here someday himself, so you won't even have to move out of the compound."

"Hugh, I'm in love with you. There, I said it. But I'm going to marry Anthony. It's the sensible thing for me to do. Love needn't have anything to do with that." She urged her horse forward as a white egret swooped past, then turned back brightly. "Let's ride on over. The island's truly a lovely spot, whether you decide to use it or not."

He stared after her in amazement. Maybe she was right. Maybe life was just being sensible, taking whatever you could. But that was also a game two could play. So back to business. The island.

Time was growing short, and he knew there was no longer any means to finish lading the stores on the *Defiance* without everyone in Bridgetown suspecting something was afoot. The frigate was aground directly in front of the main tobacco sheds, in full view of every tavern around the harbor. But there was still a way to assemble what was needed—using an old trick he had learned years ago. You pull together your stores in some secluded haven, to be picked up the night you make your break.

It had been a week since the invasion at Jamestown, and now what seemed to be a battle of nerves was underway. What else could it be? A new set of terms had been sent ashore by the commander of the fleet, terms the Assembly had revised and sent back, only to have them rejected. After that, there had been quiet. Was Barbados being left to starve quietly in the sun?

Or, he'd begun to wonder, was something else afoot? Maybe even a betrayal? Could it be some Puritan sympathizers in the Assembly were trying to negotiate a surrender behind Bedford's back? Even Katherine was worried; and the governor had taken the unprecedented step of arming his servants. A turn for the worse seemed all too likely, given the condition of the island's morale. But she'd insisted they not talk about it today.

She touched Coral lightly across the rump with her crop, and the mare stepped eagerly into the crystalline blue water of the shallows, happy to escape the horseflies nipping at its shanks. Winston spurred his mount and splashed after her. Ahead of them, Little Island stood like a tropical mirage in the sea.

"You're right about one thing. I'm damned if this place isn't close to paradise. There's not a lovelier spot in the Caribbees." The bottom was mostly gravel, with only an occasional rivulet of sand. "See over there? It looks to be a school of angelfish." He was pointing off to the left, toward an iridescent mass of turquoise and yellow that shimmered just beneath the surface. "I had no idea there was any place like this along here. Tell me, are you sure there's enough draft on the windward side for me to put in and lade?''

''When we reach those rocks up ahead, we can tie the horses and walk the shore. Then I suppose you can decide for yourself, Captain.''

She watched as the glimmer of fish darted forward. To be free like that! Able to go anywhere, do anything. ''I remember one place where the bottom seems to drop almost straight down. You could probably anchor there.''

''Good thing we came early.'' He glanced up to the sky, then at her. She detected a smile. ''This may take a while.''

What was he thinking? Did he feel the freedom of this place too? She loved being here alone with him, just the two of them. What a proper scandal it would make if anybody found out. ''Maybe the real reason I told you about this spot was to lure you out here. And then keep you here all to myself.''

He started to laugh, then stopped. ''I'd probably be an easy captive, betwixt your designs and the guns of the English navy.''

''Oh, for God's sake don't be so dreary and melancholy. I'm sure you'll be gone from Barbados soon enough, never fear. If that's what you want.'' She sensed she had pressed him too hard. ''But maybe you'll remember me once in a while, after you've sailed off to get yourself killed by the Spaniards.''

''Well, I'm not done with Barbados yet, I can promise you that.''

What did he mean? She wished he'd continue, but then his horse stumbled against a rock and he glanced down, distracted. When he looked up again, they were already nearing the shallows of the island.

''If I can get a good cart and a couple of draft horses, I'll wager I can bring the other stores I'll need out here with no trouble at all. It's mainly hogsheads of water we're short now, and maybe a few more barrels of salt pork.'' His gelding emerged from the water, threw back its head and snorted, then broke into a prance along the sandy beach. "No more than two days' work, the way I figure it. I'll have a few of the indentures give my boys a hand."

Her mare had already trotted ahead, into the shade of a tall palm whose trunk emerged from behind a rocky embankment. She slipped from the saddle and glanced back at Winston. He was still staring down the shoreline in delight.

"If you'd care to tether your frolicking horse, Captain, we can walk around to the other side."

"Why don't we swim it?" He pulled his mount alongside hers and dropped onto the sand, his eyes suddenly sparkling. While the horse nuzzled curiously at the salty wetness on its legs, he collected the reins and kneeled down to begin hobbling it. "Can you make it that far?"

"Have you gone mad from the heat!" They were alone, miles from anything. He was all hers now, no gunnery mates, no seamen. To swim! What a sensible . . . no, romantic idea.

He laughed and began to tie a leather thong to her mare's forelegs. "Katy, you should know better than to try being coy with me. I'll wager you can swim like a fish. You probably learned for no other reason than it's not ladylike." He finished with the mare and rose up, facing her. His face was like fine leather against the blue of the sky. "Besides, I think I'd like seeing you out of that bodice."

"Remember, you're not on your quarterdeck today, so I needn't harken to your every wish." She slipped her hands beneath his jerkin and ran them slowly across the muscles on his sides. The feel of him reminded her of their first night together. As she ran her fingers upward, toward his shoulders, his lips came down to hers.

"You might get used to it if you tried it once." His voice was almost a whisper. As he kissed her he wrapped her in his arms and deftly pulled the knot at the base of her bodice. "So get yourself out of this thing and let's try the water." He wiggled the laces open and slipped it over her head. She wore nothing beneath, and her breasts emerged milky-white in the sunshine. He paused to examine her, then continued, "Why stand about in this heat when there's a cool lagoon waiting?"

He stepped away, slipped off his jerkin, and tossed it across his saddle. He was reaching down to unbuckle his boots when she stopped him. She dropped to her knees, slipped her hands around his waist, and nuzzled her face against his thighs. Then she released him and bent down. "Let me unbuckle your boots."

"What?"

"I enjoy doing things for you sometimes."

He seemed startled; she'd suspected he wouldn't like it. But he didn't pull away. "Come on then." He quickly stepped out of the boots. As she laid them against the trunk of the palm, she noticed they were still smeared with powder residue from that day at the Jamestown breastwork. "We're going to see how far around this island we can swim. Pretend that's an official order from the quarterdeck." He pulled his pistols from his waist and secured them on his saddle. Then he unbuckled his belt and glanced at her. "I don't know about you, but I don't plan to try it in my breeches." He solemnly began slipping off his canvas riding trousers.

She watched for a moment, then reached for the waist of her skirt.

She found herself half wishing he couldn't see her like this, plain and in the sunlight. She liked her body, but would he? Would he notice that her legs were a trifle too slim? Or that her stomach wasn't as round as it should be?

Now he was leading the way down the incline toward the lagoon. The white sand was a warm, textured cushion against their bare feet as they waded into the placid waters. Around the island, on the windward side, the waves crashed against the shore, but here the lagoon remained serene. As she noticed the brisk wind against her skin, she suddenly didn't care *what* he thought. She felt like the most beautiful woman alive.

310

When she was younger, she could ride and shoot as well as any lad on the island; then one day she awoke to find herself cloaked in a prison of curves and bulges, with a litany in her ears about all the things she wasn't supposed to be seen doing anymore. It infuriated her. Why did men have things so much easier?

Like Winston. He moved the same way he handled his flintlock pistols, with a thoughtless poise. As he walked now, his shoulders were slightly forward and his broad back seemed to balance his stride. But, even more, she loved the hard rhythm of his haunches, trim and rippled with muscles. She stopped to watch as he splashed into the shallows.

God forgive me, she thought. how I do adore him. What I'd most like right now is just to enfold him, to capture him in my arms. And never let . . .

Good God, what am I saying?

The water was deliciously cool, and it deepened quickly. Before she knew, she felt the rhythm of the waves against her thighs.

"Katy, the time has come." He turned back and admired her for a second, then thumped a spray of water across her breasts. "Let's see if you really can swim." Abruptly he leaned forward, dipped one shoulder, and stroked powerfully. The curves of his body blended with the ripples as he effortlessly glided across the surface. A startled triggerfish darted past, orange in the sun. He stroked again, then yelled over his shoulder, "I'm still not sure I can always believe everything you say."

"Nor I you, Hugh. Though truly you say little enough." She leaned into the water, fresh and clean against her face. She gave a kick and another stroke and she was beside him. The sea around them seemed a world apart from the bondage of convention. He was right for wanting to swim. "So today, to repay me for showing you this spot, I want you to tell me everything, all the things you've been holding back."

"Unlike you, who's held nothing back? Like this island and what it means to you?"

She just ignored him, the best way to handle Hugh when he was like this, and stroked again, staying even, the taste of salt on her lips. The white sands of the shoreline were gliding past now, and behind them the palms nodded lazily in the sun. Then she rolled over and kicked, drifting through the blue. He rolled over too and reached to take her hand. They slid across the surface together as one body.

She was lost in the quiet and calm, almost dreaming, when she saw his face rise up. "How far can you see from those rocks up there?" He was pointing toward the craggy rise in the center of the island. "I'd like to go up after a while and have a look."

"You want to know everything about this place. All at once. Is that the only thing you care about?"

"Not quite." He pulled next to her. "I'll grant you've proved you can swim. And damned well." He smiled wryly. "It's doubtless a good thing to know how to do. We may all be needing to swim out of here soon, God help us."

"Not a word, remember your promise." Her eyes flashed as she flung a handful of water. Then she looked past him, at the white sand and the line of green palms. "Let's go ashore for a while. That spot up there, at the trees—it's too beautiful to pass."

The afternoon sun had begun to slant from the west as they waded out onto the sparkling sand, his arm circled around her waist. The breeze urged a sprightly nip against their skin. "Hugh, I love you. Truly." She leaned against him to feel his warmth. "I don't know what I should do."

He was subdued and quiet as they stepped around a gleaming pile of shells. Then he stopped and quietly enfolded her in his arms. "It's only fair to tell you I've never before felt about a woman the way I feel about you." He kissed her softly. "The troubling part is, I ought to know better."

He turned and led her on in silence, till they reached the

shade of a low palm. She dropped down onto the grass and watched him settle beside her. A large conch shell lay nearby, like a petrified flower. She picked it up and held it toward the sun, admiring its iridescent colors, then tossed it back onto the grass and looked at him. "I meant it when I said I wanted you to tell me everything."

He glanced up and traced his fingertips across the gentle curve at the tops of her white breasts. "Are you sure you want to hear it?"

"Yes, I do." She thought she detected a softness in his eyes, almost a yielding.

He leaned back in the grass. "I guess you think there's a lot to tell, yet somehow it all adds up to nothing. To lying here under a palm, on an empty island, with a price on my head in England and little to show for all the years." He looked out to sea and shaded his eyes as he studied a sail at the horizon. "It seems I'm something different to everybody. So which story do you want to hear?"

"Why not try the real one?" She pushed him onto his back and raised on her elbow to study his face. It was certainly older than its years. "Why won't you ever tell me about what happened when you first came out here? What was it about that time that troubles you so much?"

"It's not a pretty tale. Before I came, I never even thought much about the New World." He smiled at the irony of it now. "It all started when I was apprenticed and shipped out to the Caribbean for not being royalist enough."

"Where to?"

"Well . . ." He paused automatically, then decided to continue. "In truth it was Tortuga. Back when the Providence Company had a settlement on the island."

"But wasn't that burned out by the Spaniards? We all heard about it. I thought everybody there was killed. How did you survive?"

"As it happens, I'd been sort of banished by then. Since I didn't get along too well with the Puritans there, they'd sent

313

me over to the north side of Hispaniola, to hunt. Probably saved my life. That's where I was when the Spaniards came.''

"On Hispaniola?'' She stared at him. "Do you mean to say you were once one of . . .''

"The Cow-Killers.'' It was said slowly and casually. He waited to see how she would respond, but there was only a brief glimmer of surprise in her eyes.

"Then what some people say is true. I'd never believed it till now.'' She laughed. "I suppose I should be shocked, but I'm not.''

He smiled guardedly. "Well, in those days they only hunted cattle. Until toward the last.'' He paused a moment, then looked at her sharply. "But, yes, that's who I was with. However, Katy, don't credit quite everything you may hear about me from the Walronds.''

"But you left them. At least that tells me something about you.'' She held his hand lightly against her lips. The callouses along the palm were still soft from the water. "Why did you finally decide to go?''

He pulled her next to him and kissed her on the mouth, twice. Then he ran his fingers down her body, across her smooth waist, till he reached the mound of light chestnut hair at her thighs. "I've never told anyone, Katy. I'm not even sure I want to tell you now.'' He continued with his fingertips, on down her skin.

"Why won't you tell me?'' She passed her hand across his chest. Beneath the bronze she could feel the faint pumping of his heart. "I want to know all about you, to have all that to think about when you're gone. We're so much alike, in so many ways. I feel I have a right to know even the smallest little things about you.''

"I tried to shoot one of them. One of the Cow-Killers.'' He turned and ripped off a blade of grass, then crumpled it in his hand and looked away.

"Well, I'm sure that's not the first time such a thing has happened. I expect you had good reason. After all . . .''

"The difference was who I tried to kill." He rolled over and stared up at the vacant sky. It was deep blue, flawless.

"What do you mean? Who was it?"

"You probably wouldn't know." He glanced at her. "Ever hear of a man who goes by the name of Jacques le Basque?"

"Good God." She glanced at him in astonishment. "Isn't he the one who's been pillaging and killing Spaniards in the Windward Passage for years now? In Bridgetown they say the Spaniards call him the most bloodthirsty man in the Caribbean. I'm surprised he let you get away with it."

"I didn't escape entirely unscathed." Winston laughed. "You see, he was leader of the Cow-Killers back then. I suppose he still is."

"So what happened?"

"One foggy morning we had a small falling out and I tried a pistol on him. It misfired." He pushed back her hair and kissed her on the cheek. "Did you know, Katy, that the sun somehow changes the color of your eyes? Makes them bluer?"

She grabbed his hand and pushed him back up. "You're trying to shift the topic. I know your tricks. Don't do that with me. Tell me the rest."

"What do you suppose? After I made free to kill him, he naturally returned the favor." Winston stroked the scar on his cheek. "His pistol ball came this close to taking off my head. That's when I thought it healthy to part company with him and his lads." He traced his tongue down her body and lightly probed a nipple. It blushed pink, then began to harden under his touch.

"No, you don't. Not yet. You'll make me lose track of things." She almost didn't want him to know how much she delighted in the feel of his lips. It would give him too much power over her. Could she, she wondered, ever have the same power over *him?* She had never yet kissed him all over, the way she wanted, but she was gathering courage for it. What would he do when she did?

315

She reached up and cradled his face in her hands. The tongue that had been circling her nipple drew away and slowly licked one of her fingers. She felt herself surrendering again, and quickly drew her hand back. "Talk to me some more. Tell me why you tried to kill him."

"Who?"

"The man you just said." She frowned, knowing well his way of teasing. Yes, Hugh Winston was quite a tease. In everything. "Just now. This Jacques le Basque."

"Him? Why did I try to kill him?" He pecked at her nose, and she sensed a tenseness in his mouth. "I scarcely remember. It's as though the fog that morning never really cleared from my mind. As best I recall, it had something to do with a frigate." He smiled, the lines in his face softening. Then he slipped an arm beneath her and drew her next to him. Her skin was warm from the sun. "Still, days like this make up for a lot in life. Just being here. With you. Trouble is, I worry I'm beginning to trust you. More than I probably ought."

"I think I trust you too." She turned and kissed him on the lips, testing their feel. The tenseness had vanished, as mysteriously as it had come. She kissed him again, now with his lips meeting hers, and she wanted to crush them against her own. Gone now, all the talk. He had won. He had made her forget herself once again. "I also love you, and I know you well enough by now to know for *sure* that's unwise."

She moved across him, her breasts against his chest. Would he continue to hold back, to keep something to himself, something he never seemed willing—or able—to give? Only recently had she become aware of it. As she learned to surrender to him more and more fully, she had slowly come to realize that only a part of him was there for her.

Then the quiet of the lagoon settled around them as their bodies molded together, a perfect knowing.

He pulled her against his chest, hard, as he knew she liked to be held. And she moved against him, instinctively. She felt herself wanting him, ready for that most exquisite moment of all. She slipped slowly downward, while he moved carefully to meet her. Her soft breasts were still pillowed against his chest.

She gasped lightly, a barely discernible intake of breath, and closed her eyes as she slowly received him. Her eyes flooded with delight and she rose up, till her breasts swung above him like twin bells. "This is how I want to stay. Forever." She bent back down and kissed him full on the mouth. "Say you'll never move."

"Not even like this . . . ?"

Now the feel of her and the scent of her, as she enclosed him and worked her thighs against him, fully awoke his own desire. It had begun, that need both to give and to take, and he sensed in her an intensity matching his own. So alien, yet so alike.

Gradually he became aware of a quickening of her motions against him, and he knew that, at this instant, he had momentarily ceased to exist for her; he had lost her to something deeper. She leaned closer, not to clasp him but to thrust her breasts against him, wordlessly telling him to touch the hard buds of her nipples. Then the rhythms that rippled her belly shifted downward, strong and driven. With small sounds of anticipation she again rose above him, then suddenly cried aloud and grasped his body with her hands, to draw him into her totally.

This was the moment when together they knew that nothing else mattered. As he felt himself giving way to her, he felt her gasp and again thrust against him, as though to seize and hold the ecstasy that had already begun to drift beyond them.

But it had been fleeting, ephemeral, and now they were once more merely man and woman, in each other's arms, amidst the sand and gently waving palms. Finally she reached up and took his hands from her soft breasts, her eyes resigned and bewildered. He drew her to him and kissed her gently, to comfort her for that moment now lost to time.

Then he lifted her in his arms and lay her against the soft grass, her body open to him. He wanted this woman, more than anything.

The afternoon sky was azure now, the hue of purest lapis lazuli, and its scattering of soft white clouds was mirrored in the placid waters of the lagoon. He held her cradled in his arms, half dozing, her face warm against his chest.

"Time." His voice sounded lightly against her ear.

"What, darling?"

"It's time we had a look around." He sat up and kissed her. "We've got to go back where we left the horses, and get our clothes and boots." He turned and gazed toward the dark outcrop of rocks that rose up from the center of the island. "Then I'd like to go up there, to try and get some idea what the shoreline looks like on the windward side."

"Want to swim back?" She stared up at him, then rubbed her face against his chest. As she rose she was holding his hand and almost dancing around him.

"You swim back if you like. For myself, I think I'm getting a bit old for such. What if I just walked the shore?"

"Oh, you're old, to be sure. You're ancient. But mostly in your head." She grabbed his hand. "Come on."

"Well, just part way." He rose abruptly, then reached over and hoisted her into his arms. He bounced her lightly, as though she were no more weighty than a bundle of cane, and laughed at her gasp of surprise. "What do you know! Maybe I'm not as decrepit as I thought." He turned and strode toward the shoreline, still cradling her against his chest.

"Put me down. You're just showing off."

"That's right." They were waist deep when he balanced her momentarily high above the water and gave a shove. She landed with a splash and disappeared, only to resurface sputtering. "Careful, Katy, or you'll frighten the angelfish." He ducked the handful of water she flung at him and dived head-

318

first into the sea. A moment later he emerged, stroking. "Come on then, you wanted to swim. Shall we race?"

"You'll regret it." She dived after him like a dolphin and when she finally surfaced she was already ahead. She yelled back, "Don't think I'll let you win in the name of pride."

He roared with laughter and moved alongside her. "Whose pride are we talking about, mine or yours?"

And they swam. He was always half a length behind her, yelling that he would soon pass her, but when they reached the point along the shore even with their clothes, she was still ahead.

"Now shall I carry *you* ashore, Captain?" She let her feet touch the sandy bottom and turned to watch him draw next to her. "You're most likely exhausted."

"Damn you." He stood up beside her, breathing heavily. "No seaman ever lets himself get caught in the water. Now I know why." He seized her hand and glanced at the sun. It was already halfway toward evening. "Come on, we're wasting time. I want to reconnoiter this damned island of yours before it's too dark."

She pulled him back and kissed him one last time, the waters of the lagoon still caressing them. "Hugh, this has been the loveliest day of my life. I'll remember it always." She kissed him again, and now he yielded, enfolding her in his arms. "Can we come back? Soon?"

"Maybe. If you can find time amidst all your marriage negotiations." He ran his hand over her smooth buttocks, then gave her a kiss that had the firmness of finality. "But now we go to work, Katy. Come on."

The horses watched them expectantly, snorting and pawing with impatience, while they dressed again. She finished drawing the laces of her bodice, then walked over and whispered to her mare.

"We can take the horses if you think they could use a stretch." He gazed up toward the outcrop. "I suppose they can make it."

"Coral can go anywhere you can."

"Then let her prove it." He reached down and untied the hobble on his gelding's forefeet. Then he grabbed the reins and vaulted into the saddle. "Let's ride."

The route up the island's center spine was dense with scrub foliage, but the horses pushed their way through. The afternoon was silent save for the occasional grunts of wild hogs in the underbrush. Before long they emerged into the clear sunshine again, the horses trotting eagerly up a grassy rise, with only a few large boulders to impede their climb. When they reached the base of the rocky outcropping that marked the edge of the plateau, he slipped from the saddle and tied his mount to a small green tree. "No horse can make that." He held Coral's reins as she dismounted. "Let's walk."

Behind them now the long shore of Barbados stretched into the western horizon. The south side, toward Oistins Bay, was shielded by the hill.

"This could be a good lookout post." He took her arm and helped her over the first jagged extrusion of rock. Now the path would be winding, but the way was clear, merely a steep route upward. "I'll wager you can see for ten leagues out to sea from up there at the top."

"I've always wondered what Oistins looked like from here. I never got up this far before." She ran a hand fondly down the back of his jerkin. It was old and brown and sweat-encrusted. She knew now that he had fancy clothes secreted away, but he seemed to prefer things as worn and weathered as he could find. "The harbor must be beautiful this time of the afternoon."

"If you know where to look upland, you might just see your Walrond gallant's plantation." He gestured off to the left. "Didn't you say it's over in that direction somewhere?"

She nodded silently, relieved he hadn't said anything more. They were approaching the top now, a rocky plateau atop the rough outcrop in front of them.

"Up we go, Katy." He seized a sharp protrusion and

pulled himself even. Then he reached down and took her hand. She held to his grip as he hoisted her up over the last jagged rocks.

"It's just like . . ." Her voice trailed off.

"What?" He glanced back at her.

"Oh God, Hugh! I don't believe it!" She was pointing toward the southeast, and the color had drained from her face.

He whirled and squinted into the afternoon haze.

At sea, under full sail with a heading of north by northeast, were eight English warships, tawny-brown against the blue Caribbean. Their guns were not run out. Instead their decks were crowded with steel-helmeted infantry. They were making directly for Oistins Bay.

"The breastwork! Why aren't they firing!" He instinctively reached for the handle of the pistol in the left-hand side of his belt. "I've not heard a shot. Where's Walrond's Windward Regiment? They're just letting them land!"

"Oh Hugh, how could the Windwards do this to the island? They're the staunchest royalists here. Why would they betray the rest of us?"

"We've got to get back to Bridgetown, as hard as we can ride. To pull all the militia together and try to get the men down from Jamestown."

"But I've heard no warnings." She watched the English frigates begin to shorten sail as they entered the bay. Suddenly she glanced down at his pistols. "What's the signal for Oistins?"

"You're right." He slipped the flintlock from the left side of his belt and handed it to her. "It's four shots—two together, followed by two apart. Though I doubt there's anybody around close enough to hear."

"Let's do it anyway. There's a plantation about half a mile west down the coast. Ralph Warner. He's in the Assembly."

He pulled the other pistol from his belt. "Now, after you fire the first barrel, pull that little trigger there, below the lock, and the second one revolves into place. But first check the prime.''

"That's the first thing I did." She frowned in exasperation. "I'll wager I can shoot almost as well as you can. Isn't it time now you learned to trust me?''

"Katy, after what's just happened, you're about the only person on Barbados I trust at all. Get ready.''

He raised the gun above his head and there was the sharp crack of two pistol shots in rapid succession. Then she quickly squeezed off the rest of the signal. She passed back the gun, then pointed toward the settlement at Oistins. "Look, do you see them? That must be some of the Windward Regiment, down by the breastwork. That's their regimental flag. They've probably come down to welcome the fleet.''

"Your handsome fiancé seems to have sold his soul, and his honor. The royalist bastard . . .''

He paused and caught her arm. From the west came two faint cracks of musket fire, then again. The signal.

"Let's get back to Bridgetown as fast as these horses will take us. I'm taking command of this militia, and I'm going to have Anthony Walrond's balls for breakfast.'' He was almost dragging her down the incline. "Come on. It's one thing to lose a fair fight. It's something else to be cozened and betrayed. Nobody does that to me. By Christ I swear it.''

She looked apprehensively at his eyes and saw an anger unlike any she had ever seen before. It welled up out of his very soul.

That was what *really* moved him. Honor. You kept your word. Finally she knew.

She grasped for the saddle horn as he fairly threw her atop her horse. The mare snorted in alarm at the sudden electricity in the air. A moment later Winston was in his saddle and plunging down the brushy incline.

"Hugh, let's . . . ride together. Don't . . .'' She ducked a swinging limb and then spurred Coral alongside. "Why would Anthony do it? And what about Jeremy? He'll be mortified.''

"You'd better be worrying about the Assembly. That's your father's little creation. Would they betray him?"

"Some of them were arguing for surrender. They're worried about their plantations being ruined if there's more fighting, more war."

"Well, you can tell them this. There's going to be war, all right. If I have to fight with nobody helping me but my own lads." He spurred his horse onto the grassy slope that led down to the sand. Moments later the frightened horses were splashing through the shallows. Ahead was the green shore of Barbados. "By Christ, there'll be war like they've never seen. Mark it, by sunrise tomorrow this God damned island is going to be in flames."

Chapter Fifteen

"Your servant, sir." Anthony Walrond stood in the shadow of the Oistins breastwork, his hand resting lightly on his sword. Edmond Calvert was walking slowly up the beach from the longboat, flanked by James Powlett and Richard Morris. The hour was half past three in the afternoon, exactly as agreed. There had to be enough light to get the men and supplies ashore, and then the timely descent of darkness to shield them. "Your punctuality, I trust, portends your constancy in weightier concerns."

"And yours, sir, I pray may do the same." Calvert slipped off his dark hat and lightly bowed a greeting. Then he turned and indicated the two men behind him. "You've met Vice Admiral Powlett. And I understand Colonel Morris is not entirely unknown to you."

"We've had some acquaintance in times past." Walrond nodded coldly in the direction of Morris, but did not return the commander's perfunctory smile. The old hatred, born of years of fighting in England, flowed between them.

"Then shall we to affairs?" Calvert turned back and withdrew a packet from his waistcoat. "The supplies we agreed on are ready. I've had my Chief Purser draw up a list for your inspection."

Walrond took the papers, then glanced out toward the ships.

So it's finally come to this, he thought wistfully. But, God is my witness, we truly did all any man could ask. There's no turning back now.

As he thumbed open the wax seal of the packet, he noted absently that it was dated today, Friday. Had all this really come to pass since only sundown Monday, when he had first met Powlett, received the initial set of terms from Edmond Calvert, and begun negotiations? He had tried his best to counsel reason to the Assembly, he told himself, to arrange an honorable treaty that would preserve the militia. But a handful of hotheads had clamored for hopeless defiance, and prevailed. The only way to save the island now was to force it to surrender as quickly and painlessly as possible. Victory lay in living to fight another day.

He gazed back at the ships of the fleet, and thought of the road that had brought them to this: the defection of his own regiment, once the finest fighting men in England, the royalist Windwards.

Monday at sundown he had commandeered the back room of the Dolphin Tavern, which stood hard by the shore of Oistins Bay, and met Powlett. Through the night emissaries had shuttled terms back and forth between the tavern and the *Rainbowe*, berthed offshore. By the time the flagship hoisted anchor and made way for open sea at dawn, Anthony Walrond held in his hand a document signed by Edmond Calvert; it provided for the end of the blockade, the island's right to keep its arms and rule itself in local matters, and a full amnesty for all. The price, as price there must be, was an agreement to recognize the Commonwealth and the appointment of a new governor and Council by Calvert.

Tuesday he had summoned a trusted coterie of his royalist officers to the Dolphin and set forth the terms. They had reviewed them one by one, debated each, then agreed by show of hands that none more favorable could reasonably be obtained. Healths were drunk to the eventual restoration of Charles II to the throne, and that night a longboat was dispatched to the *Rainbowe*, carrying a signed copy of the agreement.

Wednesday, as agreed, Edmond Calvert had ordered a duplicate copy of the terms forwarded to the Assembly, indicating it was his last offer. No mention was made of the secret negotiations that had produced the document. At that meeting of the Assembly Dalby Bedford had risen to declare he would not allow his own interests to be the cause of a single new death, that he would accept the terms and resign forthwith if such was the pleasure of the Assembly—which was, he said, a democratic body that must now make its own decision whether to continue fighting or to negotiate. He next moved that the document be put to a vote. It was narrowly approved by the Assembly; an honorable peace seemed within reach.

But then the fabric so carefully sewed was ripped apart. A committee was formed to draw up the statement of the Assembly's response. In an atmosphere of hot spirits and general confusion, several of the more militant members had managed to insert a new clause into the treaty: that "the legal and rightful government of this island shall remain as it is now established, by law and our own consent."

The response was then carried by voice vote and sent back to Calvert, a gauntlet flung across the admiral's face. The defiant faction in the Assembly exulted and drank toasts to the destruction of any who would have peace on the original terms.

That night Calvert had delivered a new message to Anthony Walrond, inviting him to join with the forces of the Commonwealth—a move, he said, that would surely induce the Assembly to show reason. With this invitation he had inserted an additional offer: he would endeavor to persuade Oliver Cromwell to restore the sequestrated estates in England of any royalist officer who consented to assist.

On Thursday, Anthony held another meeting of the officers of the Windward Regiment, and they voted enthusiastically to defect to the side of the fleet. After all, they reasoned, had not an honorable peace already been refused by the extremists in the Assembly? That night he so advised Edmond Calvert, demanding as conditions a supply of musket shot and fifty kegs of musket powder.

This morning just before dawn a longboat from the *Rainbowe* had returned Calvert's reply—a signed acceptance of the terms. With feelings mixed and rueful, he had ordered an English flag hoisted above the breastwork at Oistins, the agreed-upon signal to Calvert. Then, to ensure security, he ordered that no militia-man be allowed to leave Oistins till the ships of the fleet had put in and landed their infantry.

The *Rainbowe* led the eight warships that entered the bay at midafternoon. Anthony had seen Edmond Calvert mount the quarterdeck to watch as the guns in the breastwork were turned around and directed inland, part of his conditions. Then the admiral had ordered a longboat lowered and come ashore. . . .

"These supplies all have to be delivered now, before dark." Anthony was still scrutinizing the list. "Or my men'll not be in the mood to so much as lift a half-pike."

What matter, Calvert told himself. It's done. The Barbados landing is achieved. The island is ours. "You'll have the first load of powder onshore before sundown." He gestured toward the paper. "Your musket shot, and the matchcord, are on the *Marsten Moor,* but I think we can have the bulk off-loaded by then too."

"What of the rest of the powder, sir?" Walrond squinted at the list with his good eye. "That was our main requirement. Some of these regiments had little enough to start with, and I fear we'll be needing yours if there's any fighting to be done."

Good Christ. Calvert cast a dismayed look toward Morris. Had I but known how scarcely provisioned their forces were, I might well not have . . .

"Well, sir. What of the powder?" Anthony's voice grew harder. "We can choose to halt this operation right now if . . ."

"I've ordered ten kegs sent ashore. Surely that should be adequate for the moment. You'll have the rest by morning, my word of honor.'' He squinted toward the horizon. ''How much time do you think we've got to deploy the infantry?''

''Less than we'd hoped. We heard the signal for Oistins being sent up the coast about half an hour past.'' Walrond turned and followed Calvert's gaze. The sun was a fiery disc above the western horizon, an emblem of the miserable Caribbees ever reminding him of the England he had lost. ''If their militia plans to meet us, they'll likely be assembling at Bridgetown right now. It's possible they'll be able to march some of the regiments tonight. Which means they could have men and cavalry here on our perimeter well before dawn.''

''Then we've got to decide now where the best place would be to make a stand.'' Calvert turned and motioned Morris forward. The commander had been watching apprehensively as his tattered troops disembarked from the longboats and waded in through the surf. ''What say you, sir? Would you have us hold here at Oistins, or try to march along the coastal road toward Bridgetown while there's still some light?''

Morris removed his helmet and slapped at the buzzing gnats now emerging in the evening air, hoping to obscure his thoughts. Did the admiral realize, he wondered, how exposed their men were at this very moment? Why should anyone trust the loyalties of Anthony Walrond and his royalists? It could all be a trap, intended to lure his men onshore. He had managed to muster almost four hundred infantrymen from the ships, but half of those were weak and vomiting from scurvy. Already, even with just the militia he could see, his own forces were outnumbered. If Walrond's regiments turned on them now, the entire Commonwealth force would be in peril. Could they even manage to make their way back to the ships?

Caution, that's what the moment called for now, and that meant never letting the Windward Regiment, or any island militia, gain a position that would seal off their escape route.

''We'll need a garrison for these men, room for their tents.'' He glanced carefully at Walrond. ''I'm thinking it would be best for now if we kept our lads under separate command. Each of us knows his own men best.''

"As you will, sir.'' Anthony glanced back, smelling Morris' caution. It's the first mark of a good commander, he told himself, but damn him all the same. He knows as well as I we've got to merge these forces. "I propose we march the men upland for tonight, to my plantation. You can billet your officers in my tobacco sheds, and encamp the men in the fields.''

"Will it be ground we can defend?'' Morris was carefully monitoring the line of longboats bringing his men ashore. Helmets and breastplates glistened in the waning sun.

"You'll not have the sea at your back, the way you do now, should we find need for a tactical retreat.''

"Aye, but we'll have little else, either.'' Morris looked back at Calvert. "I'd have us off-load some of the ship ordnance as soon as possible. We're apt to need it to hold our position here, especially since I'll wager they'll have at least twice the cavalry mustered that these Windwards have got.''

"You'll not hold this island from the shores of Oistins Bay, sir, much as you might wish.'' Anthony felt his frustration rising. "We've got to move upland as soon as we can.''

"I'd have us camp here, for tonight.'' Morris tried to signal his disquiet to Calvert. "Those will be my orders.''

"Very well, sir,'' Walrond continued, squinting toward the Windward Regiment's cavalry, their horses prancing as they stood at attention. "And don't forget the other consideration in our agreement. The Assembly is to be given one more opportunity to accept the terms. You are obliged to draft one final communication for Bedford, beseeching him to show himself an Englishman and persuade the Assembly to let us reach an accord.''

"As you will, sir.'' Calvert turned away, biting his tongue before he said more.

Keep an even keel, he told himself. There'll be time and plenty to reduce this island, Sir Anthony Walrond with it. The work's already half done. Now to the rest. After we've brought them to heel, we'll have time enough to show them how the Commonwealth means to rule the Americas.

Time and plenty, may God help them all.

"Shango, can you hear me?" She knelt beside her mat, her voice pleading. How, she wondered, did you pray to a Yoruba god? Really pray? Was it the same as the Christian God?

But Shango was more.

He was more than just a god. He was also part of her, she knew that now. But must he always wait to be called, evoked? Must he first seize your body for his own, before he could declare his presence, work his will?

Then the hard staccato sounds came again, the drums, their Yoruba words drifting up over the rooftop from somewhere in the distance and flooding her with dread, wrenching her heart.

Tonight, they proclaimed, the island will be set to the torch. And the *branco* will be consumed in the fires.

The men of the Yoruba, on plantations the length of the island, were ready. This was the day consecrated to Ogun, the day the fields of cane would be turned to flame. Even now Atiba was dictating final orders, words that would be repeated again and again by the drums.

After the fires began, while the *branco* were still disorganized and frightened, they would attack and burn the plantation houses. No man who owned a *preto* slave would be left alive. With all the powerful *branco* slaveholders dead, the drums proclaimed, the white indentures would rise up and join with the Yoruba. Together they would seize the island.

Oh Shango, please. She gripped the sides of the thin mattress. Make him understand. No white will aid them. To the *branco* the proud Yoruba warriors are merely more *preto*, black and despised. Make him understand it will be the end of his dream. To rise up now will mean the slaughter of his people. And ensure slavery forever.

In truth, the only one she cared about was Atiba. To know

330

with perfect certainty that she would see him hanged, probably his body then quartered to frighten the others, was more than she could endure. His rebellion had no chance. What could he hope to do? Not even Ogun, the powerful god of war, could overcome the *branco*'s weapons and cunning. Or his contempt for any human with a trace of African blood.

Atiba had hinted that he and his men would somehow find muskets. But where?

This afternoon, only hours ago, she had heard another signal cross the island, the musket shots the *branco* had devised to sound an invasion alert. Following that, many groups of cavalry had ridden past, headed south. The sight of them had made her reflect sadly that Atiba and his Yoruba warriors had no horses.

Afterward she had learned from the white servants that the soldiers of the Inglês fleet had again invaded the island, this time on the southern coast. This meant that all the Barbados militiamen surely must be mobilized now. Every musket on the island would be in the hands of a white. There would be no cache of guns to steal. Moreover, after the battle—regardless of who won—the soldiers of the fleet would probably help the militiamen hunt down Atiba and his men. No *branco* wanted the island seized by African slaves.

Shango, stop them. Ogun has made them drunk for the taste of blood. But the blood on their lips will soon be their own.

Slowly, sadly, she rose. She pulled her white shift about her, then reached under the mat to retrieve the small wand she had stolen from Atiba's hut. She untied the scarf she had wrapped around it and gazed again at the freshly carved wood, the double axe. Then she held it to her breast and headed, tiptoeing, down the creaking back stair. She had no choice but to go. To the one place she knew she could find Shango.

"I say damn their letter." Benjamin Briggs watched as the mounted messenger from Oistins disappeared into the dark, down the road between the palms, still holding the white flag above his head. "I suppose they'd now have us fall back and negotiate? When we've got the men and horse ready to drive them into the sea."

"It's addressed to me, presumably a formality. Doubtless it's meant for the entire Assembly." Bedford turned the packet in his hand and moved closer to the candles on the table. "It's from Admiral Calvert."

The front room of Nicholas Whittington's plantation house was crowded with officers of the militia. There were few helmets; most of the men wore the same black hats seen in the fields. Muskets and bandoliers of powder and shot were stacked in the corner. Intermittent gusts of the night breeze washed the stifling room through the open shutters.

The afternoon's mobilization had brought together less than three thousand men, half the militia's former strength. They had marched west from Bridgetown at sunset, and now they were encamped on the Whittington plantation grounds, in fields where tobacco once had grown. The plantation was a thousand acre tract lying three miles to the southwest of Anthony Walrond's lands, near the southern coast.

"Well, we've got a quorum of the Assembly here." Colonel George Heathcott stepped forward, rubbing at his short beard. He was still stunned by Anthony Walrond's defection to the Roundheads. "We can formally entertain any last minute proposals they'd care to make."

"I trust this time the Assembly will discern treachery when they see it," Briggs interjected. "I warned you this was likely to happen. When you lose your rights, 'tis small matter whether you hand them over or give them up at the point of a musket barrel. They're gone and that's the end of it, either way."

"Aye, I'll wager there's apt to be a Walrond hand in this too, regardless who authored it. Just another of his attempts to cozen the honest men of this island." Tom Lancaster spat toward the empty fireplace. He thought ruefully of the cane he had in harvest—five hundred acres, almost half his lands, had been planted—and realized that now the fate of his future profits lay with an untrustworthy militia and the Assembly, half the voting members of which were men with fewer than a dozen acres. "He's sold the future, and liberty, of this island for forty pieces of silver."

"Or for the governorship," Heathcott interjected. "Mark it."

"Not so long as I've got breath." Briggs' complexion was deepening in the candlelight as he began wondering what the Commonwealth's men would do with his sugar. Confiscate it and ruin him in the bargain? "I say we fight to the last man, no matter what."

Dalby Bedford finished scanning the letter and looked up. "I think we should hold one last vote. There's . . ."

"What are the terms?" Briggs interrupted.

"They seem to be the same. I presume he thought we might surrender, now that they've landed." Bedford hesitated. Was independence worth the killing sure to ensue if they went to war—a war that had now become planter against planter? "But it does appear he's willing to negotiate."

"Then let's hear it." Briggs glanced about the room. "Though I'd have every man here remember that we've got no guarantees other than Calvert's word, and anything he consents to will still have to be approved by Parliament."

"If you'll allow me, sir." Bedford motioned for quiet, then lifted a candlestick from the table and held it over the parchment.

"To the right honorable etc.

"My Lord—I have formerly sent you many Invitations to persuade you to a fair compliance with that new Power which governs your Native Country, thereby preserving yourself and all the Gent. of this island from certain ruin, and this Island from that desolation which your, and their, obstinacy may bring upon it.

"Although I have now been welcomed by a considerable part of the Island, with my Commission published— that being to appoint your Governor for the State of England—yet I am still the same reasonable Man as before and hold forth the same grace and favor to you I formerly did, being resolved no change of fortune shall change my nature. Thus I invite you to accept this same Commission as the others have done—in recognition that we each now possess considerable portions of this noble Island . . .''

Briggs stepped forward. "I already see there's deceit in it. They hold Oistins, not an acre more. With the men and horse we've got . . .''

"Let me read the rest." Bedford interrupted. "There're only a few lines more." He lifted the candle closer and continued.

"Therefore I am bound in Honour as well as good nature to endeavour your preservations, to which purpose I have enclosed the Articles which the Windward Regiment have accepted. If you have any Exceptions to these Articles, let me know them by your commissioners and I shall appoint fit persons to consider them. By ratifying this Negotiation you will prevent further effusion of blood, and will preserve your Persons and Estates from ruin.

"If you doubt mine own power to grant these Articles, know I shall engage not only mine own but the Honour of the State of England which is as much as can be required by any rational man. And so I rest,

Your Servant,

Admiral Edmond Calvert''

Briggs reached for the letter. "What's his prattle about honor, by God! This island's been betrayed by the very men who speak about it most." He gazed around at the members of the Assembly. "They've already heard our 'exceptions' and their reply was to invade. I propose we settle this with arms, and then talk of honor.''

"There's a threat in that letter, for all the soothing words.''

A grizzled Assembly member spoke up, fingering his bandolier. "Calvert's saying we're in a war against the might of England, with our own people divided."

"Aye, but when you find out a dog you'd kick will bite back, you learn to stand clear of him." Briggs waved him down. He thought again of the years of profits that lay just ahead, if only English control could be circumvented. "We've but to teach Cromwell a sound lesson, and he'll let us be."

"But does this dog you speak of have enough bite to drive back a full-scale invasion?" Heathcott peered around him at the other members. The dark-beamed room grew silent as his question seemed to hang in the air. No one knew the full strength of the invading forces, now that they had been merged with the Windwards. And, more importantly, whether the Barbados militia would have the stomach to meet them.

"He's here, Yor Worships." At that moment a thin, wiry servant in a brown shirt appeared at the doorway. Behind him, in the hallway, another man had just been ushered in. He was hatless and wearing a powder-smeared jerkin. His face was drawn, but his eyes were intense.

Hugh Winston was now in full command of the Barbados militia, commissioned by unanimous vote of the Assembly.

"Your servant, Captain." Bedford nodded a greeting. "We're waiting to hear what you've managed to learn."

"My lads just got back. They say the Roundheads haven't started moving upland yet. They're still encamped along the shore at Oistins, and together with the Windwards they're probably no more than a thousand strong."

"By God, we can stop them after all." Briggs squinted through the candlelight. "What are they doing now? Preparing to march?"

"Doesn't appear so. At least not yet. They look to be waiting, while they off-load some of the heavy ordnance from the *Marsten Moor*. Their nine-pounders. The guns have already been hoisted up on deck and made ready to bring ashore."

"There you have it, gentlemen," Briggs growled. "They'd

try to lull us with talk of negotiation, whilst they prepare to turn their ships' guns against our citizens.''

Bedford's eyes narrowed and he held up the letter. "Then what shall our answer be? For my own part, I say if we want to stay our own masters, we'll have to fight."

There were grave nods among the assembled men as Bedford turned to Winston. "How does it stand with the militia?"

"I'd say we've got just about all the infantry and horse we're likely to muster. I've gone ahead and issued what's left of the powder and shot." He was still standing by the doorway. "We've got to move on out tonight and deploy around their position with whatever men, horse, and cannon we can manage, lest the weather change by morning and end our mobility." He thumbed toward the east. "There're some dark clouds moving in fast, and I don't care for the looks of them. There's some wind out of the west, too, off the ocean. Though that may slow them down a bit."

"What do you mean?" Briggs eyed him.

"It means the bay's doubtless picked up a little chop by now, so Calvert and his officers may decide to wait till dawn to off-load those heavy guns. It could give us just enough time."

"Then I take it you'd have us move out now, in the dark?" Heathcott nervously peered out the window, widening the half-open shutters.

"If we do, we've got a chance to deploy cannon on their perimeter, and then hit them at dawn while they're still unprepared. Before they have a chance to fortify their position with that ship ordnance. They'll have the bay at their back and no heavy guns to speak of, save what's in the breastwork."

"Then I formally move that we draft a reply to this letter and send it over by one of our cavalry. Lest they mistake our resolve." Bedford's voice was hard. "And then we let Captain Winston move on out with the men."

"Aye, I second the motion." Heathcott scrambled to his feet, his eyes ablaze. "Let's prepare a response right now and get on with it."

"It's done." Whittington turned to a plump Irish serving girl, who had been standing agog in the kitchen doorway watching this meeting of the Barbados Assembly in her master's parlor, and ordered quill and paper to be brought from his study.

"Gentlemen." Bedford quieted the buzz in the room. "I propose we say something along the lines of the following:

"I have read your letter and acquainted the Council and Assembly with it, and now return their resolution to you, in which they do continue with much wondering that what is rightfully theirs by law—being the governing of this island as it presently is—should be denied them."

"Aye," Briggs interjected. "And make mention of Anthony Walrond, if you please. Lest he think we're not sensible that he's sold the island for his personal gain."

"Patience, sir." Bedford gestured for quiet. "I would also add the following:

"Neither hath the Treachery of one Man so far discouraged us, nor the easiness of certain others being seduced by him so much weakened us, as that We should accept a dishonorable Peace. And for the procuring of a just Peace, none shall endeavor more than the lawful Assembly of Barbados or

Your Servant,

Governor Dalby Bedford"

"Well phrased, as I'm a Christian." Whittington gravely nodded his approval. "They can mull over it all night if they choose. But there'll be no mistaking our resolve come the morrow."

Bedford called for a show of hands. Every man in the room signified approval.

"Done." He quickly penned the letter, signed it with a flourish, and passed it to Whittington. "Have one of your servants call in the captain of the horse. We'll send this down to Oistins right now. He can have his man take along the safe-conduct pass Calvert sent with his letter."

While Whittington rang for the servants, Bedford motioned toward Winston. "Now, Captain. You've got your approval to move the militia. I propose we all move with it." He turned once more to the room. The men were already stirring, donning bandoliers and sorting out their muskets. "This meeting of the Barbados Assembly is hereby adjourned. It may be the last we ever hold, if we don't succeed tomorrow. May God preserve democracy in the Americas. Let's all say a prayer, gentlemen, as we ride."

Winston turned without a word and led the way as the group of black-hatted men moved out into the evening air. A crisp breeze had sprung up from the east, providing a cooling respite from the heat of the day. Horses neighed and pawed in the lantern light, while the night was alive with the rattle of bandoliers. He strode to a circle of men waiting by the cistern at the side of the house and called for the officers. He was passing orders to mount and ride when a buzz of confusion rose up from the direction of the Assemblymen emerging from the house. There were murmurs and pointing.

"God's life, it's peculiar." Heathcott was gazing toward the north, in the direction of the upland plantations. "I've never seen anything like it."

Winston turned to look. Across the horizon a dull glow flickered out of the dark. Before he had time to puzzle over what it might be, he heard a chorus of shouts from the servants' quarters at the rear of the house.

"Master Whittington! There's a fire in the southern sixty. In the cane!"

"Damn me!" Whittington trotted past the side of the house to look. At the base of the hill the red tongues of flame could be seen forking upward in the dark. "I was fearful something

338

just like this might happen, what with all these careless militiamen idling about.''

"The militia's not camped down there, sir." Briggs had moved alongside him to look. Suddenly his eyes went wild. "God's blood! Is that another fire we're seeing there in the north!"

Whittington watched the whip of flames a moment longer, as though disbelieving, and then his body seemed to come alive. "We've got to get some of these men down there and dig a break in the cane fields. Stop it before it reaches this house."

"I'm more worried about it reaching our heavy ordnance." Winston gazed down the road toward the militia's encampment. "We've got to get our men and gun carriages mobilized and out of here."

"I demand that some of these layabouts stay to try and save my cane." Whittington pointed toward the crowd of militiamen at the foot of the rise. "They're doubtless the one's responsible."

"That little cane fire will burn itself out soon enough." Winston raised his hand. "We've got to move these men and supplies now. We can't wait around fighting cane fires."

"Damn me. God damn me." Briggs' voice was shrill as he pushed his way through the crowd toward Winston. "I'm beginning to think that glow we see in the north might well be a blaze on some of *my* acres."

"Well, even if it is, there's not much we can do now."

"Damned if there's not." Briggs peered again at the horizon, then back at Winston. "I've got to take my men over, as quick as we can ride. Maybe we can still save it."

"You'll not have a single horse, or man." Winston raised his hand. "As soon as I brief my field commanders, we're moving on Oistins. We have to be in position, with our cannon, before dawn. If we don't attack them before they've managed to off-load the ordnance, we'll forfeit what little chance we've got."

"Are you mad, sir? We let these fires go unattended and we could well lose everything." Briggs gazed around at the Assem-

339

blymen. "There's the looks of a conspiracy in this. It's apt to be some sort of uprising, of the indentures or maybe even these damned Africans. Which means that we've got to protect our homes."

Winston watched in dismay as the assembled men began to grumble uncertainly. Several were already calling for their horses. The night took on an air of fear.

"Let me tell you this, gentlemen." Winston's voice sounded above the din. "We've got but one chance to stop the invasion, and that's to move our heavy guns and militia tonight. You have to decide whether you're going to do it."

"Damn me, sir, it's a matter of priorities." Briggs' voice was almost a shout. "If we're burned out, it'll take us years to rebuild. Reckoning with Parliament would be nothing compared with the effects of a fire, or a slave uprising. I'll wager there's some kind of island-wide rebellion afoot, like we had a few years back." He was untying the reins of his horse from the porch railing. "I'm riding home and taking my indentures." He glared at Winston. "The few I've got left. I've got a house and a sugarmill, and I intend to protect them."

"I need that horse." Winston stood unmoving. "Tonight."

"This nag belongs to me, sir." Briggs swung heavily into the saddle. "You'll get her when I'm done, not a minute before."

Several of the other militiamen were nervously mounting, having realized with alarm that their own plantation houses were unprotected. Winston whirled on Bedford. "Can't we stop this? If every man here with a house to worry about abandons us, I'll have nobody save my own men. Am I expected to fight Walrond's regiment, and the Commonwealth, all by myself?"

"I can't stop them." Bedford shook his head. "Maybe we can reassemble in the morning, assuming this rebellion matter can be contained."

"But morning's going to be too late. By then the sea may let up, and they'll have their heavy ordnance in place." Winston felt his gut tighten as he watched the cavalry and militia begin

340

to disperse into the night. "They'll slice us to ribbons with cannon fire if we try to storm their position then."

"This is not an army. It's a militia." Bedford sighed. "No man here can be ordered to fight."

"Well, you've lost it. Before you even began." He gave the governor a quick salute, then seized the reins of his gelding. The horse was still lathered from the run back from Little Island to Bridgetown. "If it's going to be every man for himself, I've got my own affairs to look to. So damned to them. And to their sugar and slaves."

"Where are you going?" Bedford stared at him gloomily.

"If this war's as good as lost—which it is—then I've got to get the *Defiance* afloat. As soon as I can." He vaulted into the saddle, and gave his horse the spur. "The Americas just swapped liberty for sugar. They can have it."

Chapter Sixteen

They had waited in the open field to watch as the moon broke above the eastern horizon, sending faint pastel shimmers through the rows of cane. The first shadow cast by the moon on this the fourth day of the Yoruba week—the day sacred to Ogun—was the signal to begin.

"May Ogun be with you, son of Balogun." Tahajo, ancient and brittle as the stalks around them, bent over and brushed Atiba's dusty feet. His voice could scarcely be heard above the chorus of crickets. "Tonight, at the first coming of dark, when I could no longer see the lines in the palm of my hand, I sacrificed a cock to Ogun, as a prayer that you succeed."

Atiba looked at him with surprise, secretly annoyed that Tahajo had performed the sacrifice without his knowledge. But the old man had the prerogatives of an elder. "What did the sacrifice foretell?"

"I could not discern, Atiba, in truth I could not. The signs were mixed. But they seemed to hold warning." Concern showed in his aged eyes. "Know that if you do not succeed, there will be no refuge for any of us. Remember what the elders of Ife once warned, when our young men called for a campaign of war against the Fulani in the north. They declared 'The locust can eat, the locust can drink, the locust can go—but where can the grasshopper hide?' We are like grasshoppers, my son, with no compounds or women to return to for shelter if we fail.''

"We will not fail." Atiba held up his new machete. Its polished iron glistened in the light of the moon. "Ogun will not turn his face from us."

"Then I pray for you, Atiba." He sighed. "You are surely like the pigeon who feeds among the hawks, fearless of death."

"Tonight, Tahajo, we are the hawks."

"A hawk has talons." The old man looked up at the moon. "What do you have?"

"We will have the claws of a leopard, of steel, before the sun returns." Atiba saluted him in traditional fashion, then turned to Obewole. The tall drummer's arms were heavy with bundles of straw, ready to be fired and hurled among the cane.

"Is everything prepared?"

"The straw is ready." Obewole glanced around at the expectant faces of the men as he stepped forward. "As we are. You alone have the flint."

Atiba called for quiet. Next he intoned an invocation, a whisper under his breath, then circled the men and cast a few drops of water from a calabash toward the four corners of the world. "We will fire this field first." He stood facing them, proud of the determination in their faces. These men, he told himself, are among the finest warriors of Ife. Tonight the *branco* will learn how a Yoruba fights for his people. "The west wind is freshening now and it will carry the flames to the other fields, those in the direction of the rising moon. Next we will fire the curing house, where the *branco* keeps the sweet salt we have made for him with our own hands. Then we will burn his mill house . . .''

Obewole cast a nervous glance at Atiba. "The mill house shelters the great machine made of the sacred iron of Ogun.

343

Is it wisdom to bring Shango's fire to that place, sacred to Ogun?''

"You know, good Obewole, that in Ife we say, 'Do not expect to find a man wearing white cloth in the compound of a palm-oil maker.' " Atiba's face was expressionless. "Ogun's spirit is not in the mill house tonight. He is here with us."

The drummer bowed in uncertain acknowledgement and turned to begin distributing the straw bundles down the line of men. The young warrior Derin was first, and he eagerly called for two. Atiba watched silently till each man had a sheaf of straw, then he intoned one last prayer. As the words died away into silence, he produced a flint and struck it against the blade of his machete. A shower of sparks flew against the bundle held by Obewole. After the brown stalks had smoldered into flame, the drummer walked slowly down the line of men and, with a bow to each, fired the rest.

Serina settled the candle carefully atop the iron frame supporting the rollers, then stood for a moment studying the flickering shadows it cast across the thatched ceiling of the mill house. From the gables above her head came the chirp of crickets, mingled with the occasional night murmurs of nesting birds.

The room exuded an eerie peacefulness; again it called to mind the sanctuary of whitewash and frangipani scent that had been her home in Pernambuco. Once before, the magic of this deserted mill house had transported her back to that place of long ago, back to gentle afternoons and soft voices and innocence. To the love of her Yoruba mother Dara, and the kindliness of an old *babalawo* so much like Atiba.

Shango's spirit had taken her home. He had come to this place that night, and he had lifted her into his being and taken her back. And here, for the first time, she had understood his awesome power. Shango. The great, terrifying god of

West Africa was now here in the Caribbees, to guard his people. One day, she told herself, even the Christians would be on their knees to him.

Carefully she unwrapped the wand—its wood carved with an African woman's fertile shape, then topped with a double-headed axe—and placed it beside the candle. Atiba had made it with his own hands, and he always kept it hidden in his hut, as part of his *babalawo*'s cache of sacred implements.

The mill had not turned since the day the great ships of the Inglês appeared in the bay, before the night of the storm. Traces of white cassava flour were still mingled with the fine dust on the floor. The place where Atiba had drawn Shango's sign was . . . she squinted in the candlelight . . . was there, near the square corner of the iron frame. Nothing remained now of the symbol save a scattering of pale powder.

But across the room, near the post by the doorway, lay the small bag of cassava flour he had used. It must, she told herself, have been knocked there during the ceremony.

Perhaps it was not empty.

Timorously she picked it up and probed inside. Some flour still remained, dry and fine as coral dust. As she drew out a handful and let it sift through her fingers, the idea came—almost as though Shango had whispered it to her in the dark.

The drawing of the double-headed axe. Shango's sign. Had it somehow summoned him that night? Beckoned him forth from the ancient consciousness of Africa, to this puny room?

She stood for a moment and tried again to breathe a prayer. What precisely had Atiba done? How had he drawn the symbol? Her legs trembling, she knelt with a handful of the white powder and carefully began laying down the first line.

It was not as straight as she had wished, nor was its width even, but the flour flowed more readily than she had thought it might. The symbol Atiba had drawn was still etched in her memory. It was simple, powerful, it almost drew itself: the crossed lines, their ends joined, formed two triangles meeting at a common point, and then down the middle the bold stroke

345

that was its handle. The drawing came into form so readily she found herself thinking that Shango must be guiding her hand, urging her on in this uncertain homage to his power.

She stood away and, taking the candle, studied the figure at her feet. The white seemed to undulate in the flickering light. She held the candle a moment longer, then reached out and placed it directly in the center of the double axe-head.

Perhaps it was a gust of wind, but the wick suddenly flared brighter, as though it now drew strength from the symbol it illuminated. The mill, the walls of the room, all glowed in its warm, quivering flame. Was it imagination or was the candle now giving off that same pale radiance she remembered from languorous afternoons long ago in Brazil—the half-light of mist and rainbows that bathed their courtyard in a gossamer sheen when an afternoon storm swept overhead.

She backed away, uneasy and disturbed, groping blindly toward the mill frame. When her touch caught the hard metal, she slipped her hand across the top till her grasp closed on the wand. The stone axe at its tip was strangely warm now, as though it had drawn heat from the iron. Or perhaps it had been from the candle.

She clasped it against her shift, feeling its warmth flow into her. First it filled her breasts with a sensation of whiteness, then it passed downward till it mingled in her thighs. It was a sensation of being fulfilled, brought to completeness, by some essence that flowed out of Shango.

She glanced back at the flickering candle. Now it washed the drawing with a glow of yellow and gold. The candle, too, seemed to be becoming part of her. She wanted to draw its fiery tip into her body, to possess it.

Sweat poured down her thighs; and in its warmth she felt the desire of Shango. As she clasped the wand ever more tightly against her breasts, she gasped, then shuddered. The white presence was entering her, taking her body for its own. She sensed a heat in her eyes, as though they might now burn through the dark.

A heaviness was growing in her legs, and she planted her feet wide apart to receive and support the burden she felt swelling in her breasts. The room was hot and cold and dark and light. She no longer saw anything save whiteness. Then she plunged the wand skyward and called out in a distant voice, deep and resonant.

"E wa nibi! SHANGO!"

The flames billowed along the edge of the field, and the crackling of the cane swelled into a roar as a carpet of red crept up the hillside. Clusters of gray rats scurried to escape, lending a chorus of high-pitched shrieks to the din. As the night breeze quickened from the west, it whipped the flames toward the dense, unharvested acres that lay beyond.

Suddenly the urgent clanging of a bell sounded from the direction of the main compound, and soon after, silhouettes appeared at the perimeter of the indentures' quarters, the circle of thatched-roof huts beside the pathway leading to the sugarworks. Figures of strawhatted women—the men were all gone away with the militia—stood out against the moonlit sky as they watched in fearful silence. Never had a fire in the fields erupted so suddenly.

Now! Atiba wanted to shout. Join us! Throw off your chains. Free yourselves!

He had not been able to enlist their help sooner, for fear a traitor among them might betray the revolt. But now, now they would see that freedom was within their grasp. He tried to call to them. To beckon them forward.

Give me the words, Mighty Ogun. Tell me the words that will make the *branco* slaves join us.

But the prayer passed unanswered. He watched in dismay as the women began, one by one, to back away, to retreat toward their huts in awe and dread.

Still, they had done nothing to try and halt the flames. So perhaps there still was hope. If they were afraid to join the

347

rebellion, neither would they raise a hand to save the wealth of their *branco* master.

Also, these were but women. Women did not fight. Women tended the compounds of warriors. When the men returned, the rebellion would begin. They would seize their chance to kill the *branco* master who enslaved them. He signaled the other Yoruba, who moved on quickly toward the curing house, where the pots of white sugar waited.

The sky had taken on a deep red glow, as the low-lying clouds racing past reflected back the ochre hue of flames from fields in the south. Across the island, the men of the Yoruba had honored their vows. They had risen up.

Atiba noticed the savor of victory in his mouth, that hardening of muscle when the foe is being driven before your sword, fleeing the field. It was a strong taste, dry and cutting, a taste he had known before. Something entered your blood at a moment like this, something more powerful, more commanding, than your own self.

As they pushed through the low shrubs leading toward the sugarworks, he raised his hand and absently touched the three clan marks down his cheek, their shallow furrows reminding him once again of his people. Tonight, he told himself, all the men of Ife would be proud.

"Atiba, son of Balogun, I must tell you my thoughts." Old Tahajo had moved forward, ahead of the others. "I do not think it is good, this thing you would have us do now."

"What do you mean?" Atiba eased his own pace slightly, as though to signify deference.

"A Yoruba may set fires in the forest, to drive out a cowardly foe. It is all part of war. But we do not fire his compounds, the compounds that shelter his women."

"The curing house where sugar is kept is not the compound of the *branco*'s women." Atiba quickened his stride again, to reassert his leadership, and to prevent the other men from hearing Tahajo's censure, however misguided. "It's a part of his fields. Together they nourish him, like palm oil and salt. Together they must be destroyed.''

"But that is not warfare, Atiba. That is vengeance.'' The old man persisted. "I have set a torch to the fields of an enemy—before you were born the Fulani once forced such a course upon us, by breaking the sacred truce during the harvest festival—but no Yoruba would deliberately burn the seed yams in his enemy's barn.''

"This barn does not hold his yams; it holds the fruits of our unjust slavery. The two are not the same.''

"Atiba, you are like that large rooster in my eldest wife's compound, who would not suffer the smaller ones to crow. My words are no more than summer wind to you.'' The old man sighed. "You would scorn the justice Shango demands. This is a fearsome thing you would have us do now.''

"Then I will bear Shango's wrath on my own head. Ogun would have us do this, and he is the god we honor tonight. It is our duty to him.'' He moved on ahead, leaving Tahajo to follow in silence. The thatched roof of the curing house was ahead in the dark, a jagged outline against the rosy sky beyond.

Without pausing he opened the door and led the way. All the men knew the room well; standing before them were long rows of wooden molds, containers they had carried there themselves, while a *branco* overseer with a whip stood by.

"These were placed here with our own hands. Those same hands will now destroy them.'' He looked up. "What better justice could there be?'' He sparked the flint off his machete, against one of the straw bundles, and watched the blaze a moment in silence. This flame, he told himself, would exact the perfect revenge.

Revenge. The word had come, unbidden. Yes, truly it was revenge. But this act was also justice. He recalled the proverb: "One day's rain makes up for many days' drought.'' Tonight one torch would make up for many weeks of whippings, starvation, humiliation.

"Mark me well." Atiba held the burning straw aloft and turned to address the men. "These pots are the last sugar you will ever see on this island. This, and the cane from which it was made, all will be gone, never to return. The forests of the Orisa will thrive here once more."

He held the flaming bundle above his head a moment longer, while he intoned a verse in praise of Ogun, and then flung it against the thatched wall behind him, where it splayed against a post and disintegrated. They all watched as the dry-reed wall smoldered in the half-darkness, then blossomed with small tongues of fire.

Quickly he led them out again, through the narrow doorway and into the cool night. The west wind whipped the palm trees now, growing ever fresher. Already the flame had scaled the reed walls of the curing house, and now it burst through the thatched roof like the opening of a lush tropical flower.

As they made ready to hurry on up the path toward the mill room, the drum of hoofbeats sounded through the night. Next came frantic shouts from the direction of the great house. It was the voice of Benjamin Briggs.

Atiba motioned them into the shadows, where they watched in dismay as a scattering of white indentures began lumbering down the hill, toting buckets of water and shovels, headed for the burning fields.

The Yoruba men all turned to Atiba, disbelieving. The male *branco* slaves had not risen up. They had come back to aid in the perpetuation of their own servitude. As Atiba watched the fire brigade, he felt his contempt rising, and his anger.

Could they not see that this was the moment?

But instead of turning their guns on their enemy, setting torch to his house, declaring themselves free—the *branco* slaves had cravenly done as Briggs commanded. They were no better than their women.

"The *branco* chief has returned to his compound. Like him, all the *branco* masters on the island must now be trembling in fear." Atiba felt his heart sink as he motioned the men forward. Finally he understood the whites. Serina had been right. Color counted for more than slavery. Now more than ever they needed the muskets from the ship. "Quickly. We must burn the mill, then go and seize the guns. There's no time to lose."

The mill house was only a short distance farther up the hill. They left the path and moved urgently through the brush and palms toward the back of the thatched building. It stood silent, waiting, a dark silhouette against the glowing horizon.

"Atiba, there is no longer time for this." Obewole moved to the front of the line and glanced nervously at the darkening skies. Heavy clouds obscured the moon, and the wind had grown sharp. "We must hurry to the ship as soon as we can and seize the *branco*'s guns. This mill house is a small matter; the guns are a heavy one. The others will be there soon, waiting for us."

"No. This must burn too. We will melt forever the chains that enslave us."

He pressed quickly up the slope toward the low thatched building. From the center of the roof the high pole projected skyward, still scorched where the lightning of Shango had touched it the night of the ceremony.

"Then hurry. The flint." Obewole held out the last bundle of straw toward Atiba as they edged under the thatched eaves. "There's no time to go in and pray here."

Atiba nodded and out of his hand a quick flash, like the pulse of a Caribbean firefly, shot through the dark.

Shango was with her, part of her. As Serina dropped to her knees, before the drawing of the axe, she no longer knew who she was, where she was. Unnoticed, the dull glow from the open doorway grew brighter, as the fires in the cane fields beyond raged.

"Shango, *nibo l'o nlo?* Shango?" She knelt mumbling, sweat soaking through her shift. The words came over and over, almost like the numbing cadence of the Christian rosary, blotting out all other sounds.

She had heard nothing—not the shouts at the main house nor the ringing of the fire bell nor the dull roar of flames in the night air. But then, finally, she did sense faint voices, in Yoruba, and she knew Shango was there. But soon those voices were lost, blurred by the distant chorus of crackling sounds that seemed to murmur back her own whispered words.

The air around her had grown dense, suffocating. Dimly, painfully she began to realize that the walls around her had turned to fire. She watched, mesmerized, as small flametips danced in circles of red and yellow and gold, then leapt and spun in pirouettes across the rafters of the heavy thatched roof.

Shango had sent her a vision. It could not be real.

Then a patch of flame plummeted onto the floor beside her, and soon chunks of burning straw were raining about her. Feebly, fear surging through her now, she attempted to rise.

Her legs refused to move. She watched the flames in terror for a moment, and then she remembered the wand, still in her outstretched hand. Without thinking, she clasped it again to her pounding breast. As the room disappeared in smoke, she called out the only word she still remembered.

"Shango!"

The collapse of the burning thatched wall behind her masked the deep, sonorous crack that sounded over the hillside.

"Damn me!" Benjamin Briggs dropped his wooden bucket and watched as the dark cloudbank hovering in the west abruptly flared. Then a boom of thunder shook the night sky. Its sound seemed to unleash a pent-up torrent, as a dense sheet of island rain slammed against the hillside around him with the force of a mallet.

The fires that blazed in the fields down the hill began to sputter into boiling clouds of steam as they were swallowed in wave after wave of the downpour. The night grew suddenly dark again, save for the crisscross of lightning in the skies.

"For once, a rain when we needed it. It'll save the sugar, by my life." He turned and yelled for the indentures to reclaim their weapons and assemble. "Try and keep your matchcord dry." He watched with satisfaction as the men, faces smeared with smoke, lined up in front of him. "We've got to round up the Africans now, and try and find out who's responsible for this. God is my witness, I may well hang a couple this very night to make an example."

"I think I saw a crowd of them headed up toward the mill house, just before the rain started in." The indenture's tanned face was emerging as the rain purged away the soot. "Like as not, they were thinkin' they'd fire that too."

"God damn them all. We lose the mill and we're ruined." He paused, then his voice came as a yell. "God's blood! The curing house! Some of you get over there quick. They might've tried to fire that as well. I've got a fortune in white sugar curing out." He looked up and pointed at two of the men, their straw hats dripping in the rain. "You, and you. Move or I'll have your hide. See there's nothing amiss."

"Aye, Yor Worship." The men whirled and were gone.

"Now, lads." Briggs turned back to the others. A half dozen men were left, all carrying ancient matchlock muskets. "Keep an eye on your matchcord, and let's spread out and collect these savages." He quickly checked the prime on his flintlock musket and cocked it. "We've got to stop them before they try to burn the main house." He stared through the rain, then headed up the hill, in the direction of the mill house. "And stay close to me. They're rampaging like a pack of wild island hogs."

Something was slapping at the smoldering straw in her hair and she felt a hand caress her face, then an arm slide beneath her. The room, the mill, all were swallowed in dark, blinding smoke; now she was aware only of the heat and the closeness of the powerful arms that lifted her off the flame-strewn floor.

Then there were other voices, faraway shouts, in the same musical language that she heard whispered against her ear. The shouts seemed to be directed at the man who held her, urging him to leave her, to come with them, to escape while there was time. Yet still he held her, his cheek close against her own.

Slowly Atiba rose, holding her body cradled against him, and pushed through the smoke. The heat was drifting away now, and she felt the gentle spatters of rain against her face as sections of the water-soaked thatched roof collapsed around them, opening the room to the sky.

The sound of distant gunfire cut through the night air as he pushed out the doorway into the dark. She felt his body stiffen, painfully, as though he had received the bullets in his own chest. But no, the firing was down the hill, somewhere along the road leading to the coast.

The cold wetness of the rain, and the warmth of the body she knew so well, awoke her as though from a dream. "You must go." She heard her own voice. Why had he bothered to save her, instead of leading his own men to safety. She was nothing now. The revolt had started; they must fight or be killed. "Hurry. Before the *branco* come."

As she struggled to regain her feet, to urge him on to safety, she found herself wanting to flee also. To be with him, in death as in life. If he were gone, what would there be to live for. . . .

"We have failed." He was caressing her with his sad eyes. "Did you hear the thunder? It was the voice of Shango." Now he looked away, and his body seemed to wither from some grief deep within. "I somehow displeased Shango. And now he has struck us down. Even Ogun is not powerful enough to overcome the god who commands the skies."

"It was because I wanted to protect you."

He looked down at her quizzically. "I didn't know you

354

were in the mill house till I heard you call out Shango's name. Why were you there tonight, alone?''

''I was praying.'' She avoided his dark eyes, wishing she could say more. ''Praying that you would stop, before it was too late. I knew you could not succeed. I was afraid you would be killed.''

. He embraced her, then ran his wide hand through her wet, singed hair. ''Sometimes merely doing what must be done is its own victory. I'll not live a slave. Never.'' He held her again, tenderly, then turned away. ''Remember always to live and die with honor. Let no man ever forget what we tried to do here tonight.''

He was moving down the hill now, his machete in his hand.

''No!'' She was running after him, half-blinded by the rain. ''Don't try to fight any more. Leave. You can hide. We'll escape. . . .''

''A Yoruba does not hide from his enemies. I will not dishonor the compound of my father. I will stand and face the man who has wronged me.''

''No! Please!'' She was reaching to pull him back when a voice came out of the dark, from the pathway down below.

''Halt, by God!'' It was Benjamin Briggs, squinting through the downpour. ''So it's you. I might have known. You were behind this, I'll stake my life. Stop where you are, by Jesus, or I'll blow you to hell like the other two savages who came at my men.''

She found herself wondering if the musket would fire. The rain was still a torrent. Then she felt Atiba's hand shove her aside and saw his dark form hurtle down the trail toward the planter. Grasping his machete, he moved almost as a cat—bobbing, weaving, surefooted and deadly.

The rain was split by the crack of a musket discharge, and she saw him slip momentarily and twist sideways. His machete clattered into the dark as he struggled to regain his balance, but he had not slowed his attack. When he reached

Briggs, he easily ducked the swinging butt of the musket. Then his left hand closed about the planter's throat and together they went down in the mud, to the sound of Briggs' choked yells.

When she reached them, they were sprawled in the gully beside the path, now a muddy flood of water from the hill above. Atiba's right arm dangled uselessly, but he held the planter pinned against the mud with his knee, while his left hand closed against the throat. There were no more yells, only deathly silence.

"No! Don't!" She was screaming, her arms around Atiba's neck as she tried to pull him away.

He glanced up at her, dazed, and his grip on Briggs' throat loosened slightly. The planter lay gasping and choking in the rain.

"Dara . . . !" Atiba was looking past her and yelling a warning when the butt of the matchlock caught him across the chest. She fell with him as three straw-hatted indentures swarmed over them both.

"By God, I'll hang the savage with my own hands." Briggs was still gasping as he began to pull himself up out of the mud. He choked again and turned to vomit; then he struggled to his feet. "Tie the whoreson down. He's like a mad dog."

"He's been shot, Yor Worship." One of the indentures was studying the blood on his hands, from where he had been holding Atiba's shoulder. "Would you have us attend to this wound?"

"I shot the savage myself." Briggs glared at them. "No credit to the lot of you. Then he well nigh strangled me. He's still strong as a bull. Don't trouble with that shot wound. I'll not waste the swathing cloth." He paused again to cough and rub his throat. "He's going to have a noose around his neck as soon as the rain lets up."

Briggs walked over to where Atiba lay, his arms pinned against the ground and a pike against his chest. "May God damn you, sir. I just learned you managed to burn and ruin a good half the sugar in my curing house." He choked again and spat into the rain. Then he turned back. "Would you could understand what I'm saying, you savage. But mark this. Every black on this island's going to know it when I have you hanged, you can be sure. It'll put a stop to any more of these devilish plots, as I'm a Christian."

Serina felt her eyes brimming with tears. In trying to save him, she had brought about his death. But everything she had done had been out of devotion. Would he ever understand that? Still, perhaps there was time . . .

"Are you well, Master Briggs?" She turned to the planter. Her cinnamon fingers stroked lightly along his throat.

"Aye. And I suppose there's some thanks for you in it." He looked at her, puzzling at the wet, singed strands of hair across her face. "I presume the savage was thinking to make off with you, to use you for his carnal lusts, when I haply put a halt to the business."

"I have you to thank."

"Well, you were some help to me in the bargain, I'll own it. So there's an end on the matter." He glanced at Atiba, then back at her. "See to it these shiftless indentures tie him up like he was a bull. Wound or no, he's still a threat to life. To yours as well as mine."

Even as he spoke, a dark shadow seemed to drop out of the rain. She glanced up and just managed to recognize the form of Derin, his machete poised above his head like a scythe. It flashed in the lantern light as he brought it down against the arm of one of the indentures holding Atiba. The straw-hatted man screamed and doubled over.

What happened next was blurred, shrouded in the dark. Atiba was on his feet, flinging aside the other indentures. Then he seized his own machete out of the mud with his left hand and turned on Briggs. But before he could move, Derin jostled against him and grabbed his arm. There were sharp words in Yoruba and Atiba paused, a frozen silhouette poised above the planter.

"By Christ, I'll . . ." Briggs was drawing the long pistol from his belt when Atiba suddenly turned away.

The gun came up and fired, but the two Yoruba warriors were already gone, swallowed in the night.

"Well, go after them, God damn you." The planter was shouting at the huddled, terrified indentures. "Not a man on this plantation is going to sleep till both those heathens are hanged and quartered."

As the indentures gingerly started down the hill in the direction Atiba and Derin had gone, Briggs turned and, still coughing, headed purposefully up the pathway toward the remains of the mill room.

The burned-away roof had collapsed entirely, leaving the first sugar mill on Barbados open to the rain—its wide copper rollers sparkling like new.

Chapter Seventeen

"Heave, masters!" Winston was waist deep in the surf, throwing his shoulder against the line attached to the bow of the *Defiance*. "The sea's as high as it's likely to get. There'll never be a better time to set her afloat."

Joan Fuller stood on deck, by the bulwark along the waist of the ship, supporting herself with the mainmast shrouds as she peered down through the rain. She held her bonnet in her hand, leaving her yellow hair plastered across her face in watersoaked strands. At Winston's request, she had brought down one of her last kegs of kill-devil. It was waiting, safely lashed to the mainmast, a visible inducement to effort.

"Heave . . . ho." The cadence sounded down the line of seamen as they grunted and leaned into the chop, tugging on the slippery line. Incoming waves washed over the men, leaving them alternately choking and cursing, but the rise in sea level brought about by the storm meant the *Defiance* was already virtually afloat. Helped by the men it was slowly disengaging from the sandy mud; with each wave the bow would bob upward, then sink back a few inches farther into the bay.

"She's all but free, masters." Winston urged them on. "Heave. For your lives, by God." He glanced back at John Mewes and yelled through the rain, "How're the stores?"

Mewes spat out a mouthful of foam. "There's enough water and salt pork in the hold to get us up to Nevis Island, mayhaps. If the damned fleet doesn't blockade it first." He bobbed backward as a wave crashed against his face. "There's talk the whoresons could sail north after here."

"Aye, they may stand for Virginia when they have done with the Caribbees. But they'll likely put in at St. Christopher and Nevis first, just to make sure they humble every freeborn Englishman in the Americas." Winston tugged again and watched the *Defiance* slide another foot seaward. "But with any luck we'll be north before them." He pointed toward the dim mast lanterns of the English gunships offshore. "All we have to do is slip past those frigates across the bay."

The men heaved once more and the weathered bow dipped sideways. Then all at once, as though by the hand of nature, the *Defiance* was suddenly drifting in the surf. A cheer rose up, and Winston pushed his way within reach of the rope ladder dangling amidships. As he clambered over the bulwark Joan was waiting with congratulations.

"You did it. On my honor, I thought this rotted-out tub was beached for keeps." She bussed him on the cheek. "Though I fancy you might've lived longer if it'd stayed where it was."

Mewes pulled himself over the railing after Winston and plopped his feet down onto the wet deck. He winked at Joan and held out his arms. "No kiss for the quartermaster, yor ladyship? I was workin' too, by my life."

"Get on with you, you tub of lard." She swiped at him with the waterlogged bonnet she held. "You and the rest of this crew of layabouts might get a tot of kill-devil if you're lucky. Which is more than you deserve, considering how much some of you owe me already."

"Try heaving her out a little farther, masters." Winston was holding the whipstaff while he yelled from the quarterdeck. "She's coming about now. We'll drop anchor in a couple of fathoms, nothing more."

While the hull drifted out into the night and surf, Winston watched John Mewes kneel by the bulwark at the waist of the ship and begin to take soundings with a length of knotted rope.

"Two fathoms, Cap'n, by the looks of it. What do you think?"

"That's enough to drop anchor, John. I want to keep her in close. No sense alerting the Roundheads we're afloat."

Mewes shouted toward the portside bow and a seaman began to feed out the anchor cable. Winston watched as it rattled into the surf, then he made his way along the rainswept deck back to the starboard gallery at the stern and shoved another large anchor over the side. It splashed into the waves and disappeared, its cable whipping against the taffrail.

"That ought to keep her from drifting. There may be some maintopman out there in the fleet who'd take notice."

Whereas fully half the Commonwealth's ships had sailed for Oistins Bay to assist in the invasion, a few of the larger frigates had kept to station, their ordnance trained on the harbor.

"All aboard, masters. There's a tot of kill-devil waiting for every man, down by the mainmast." Winston was calling over the railing, toward the seamen now paddling through the dark along the side of the ship. "John's taking care of it. Any man who's thirsty, come topside. We'll christen the launch."

The seamen sounded their approval and began to scramble up. Many did not wait their turn to use the rope ladders. Instead they seized the rusty deadeyes that held the shrouds, found toeholds in the closed gunports, and pulled themselves up within reach of the gunwales. Winston watched approvingly as the shirtless hoard came swarming onto the deck with menacing ease. These were still his lads, he told himself with a smile. They could storm and seize a ship before most of its crew managed even to cock a musket. Good men to have on hand, given what lay ahead.

"When're you thinkin' you'll try for open sea?" Joan had

followed him up the slippery companionway to the quarter-deck. "There's a good half-dozen frigates hove-to out there, doubtless all with their bleedin' guns run out and primed. I'll wager they'd like nothing better than catchin' you to lee-ward."

"This squall's likely to blow out in a day or so, and when it does, we're going to pick a dark night, weigh anchor, and make a run for it. By then the Roundheads will probably be moving on Bridgetown, so we won't have a lot of time to dally about." He looked out toward the lights of the English fleet. "I'd almost as soon give it a try tonight. Damn this foul weather."

She studied the bobbing pinpoints at the horizon skepti-cally. "Do you really think you can get past them?"

He smiled. "Care to wager on it? I've had a special set of short sails made up, and if it's dark enough, I think we can probably slip right through. Otherwise, we'll just run out the guns and take them on."

Joan looked back. "You could be leaving just in time, I'll grant you. There're apt to be dark days ahead here. What do you think'll happen with this militia now?"

"Barbados' heroic freedom fighters? I'd say they'll be dis-armed and sent packing. Back to the cane and tobacco fields where they'd probably just as soon be anyway. The grand American revolution is finished. Tonight, when the militia should be moving everything they've got up to Oistins, they're off worrying about cane fires, letting the Roundheads get set to off-load their heavy guns. By the time the rains let up and there can be a real engagement, the English infantry'll have ordnance in place and there'll be nothing to meet them with. They can't be repulsed. It's over." He looked at her. "So the only thing left for me is to get out of here while I still can. And stand for Jamaica."

"That daft scheme!" She laughed ruefully and brushed the dripping hair from her face. "You'd be better off going up to

Bermuda for a while, or anywhere, till things cool off. You've not got the men to do anything else.''

''Maybe I can still collect a few of my indentures.''

''And maybe you'll see Puritans dancin' at a Papist wedding.'' She scoffed. ''Let me tell you something. Those indentures are going to scatter like a flock of hens the minute the militia's disbanded. They'll not risk their skin goin' off with you to storm that fortress over at Villa de la Vega. If you know what's good for you, you'll forget Jamaica.''

''Don't count me out yet. There's still another way to get the men I need.'' He walked to the railing and gazed out into the rain. ''I've been thinking I might try getting some help another place.''

''And where, pray, could that be?''

''You're not going to think much of what I have in mind.'' He caught her eye and realized she'd already guessed his plan.

''*That's* a fool's errand for sure.''

''Kindly don't go prating it about. The truth is, I'm not sure yet what I'll do. Who's to say?''

''You're a lying rogue, Hugh Winston. You've already made up your mind. But if you're not careful, you'll be in a worse bind than this. . . .''

''Beggin' yor pardon, Cap'n, it looks as if we've got a visitor.'' Mewes was moving up the dark companionway to the quarterdeck. He spat into the rain, then cast an uncomfortable glance toward Joan. ''Mayhaps you'd best come down and handle the orders.''

Winston turned and followed him onto the main deck. Through the dark a white horse could be seen prancing in the gusts of rain along the shore. A woman was in the saddle, waving silently at the ship, oblivious to the squall.

''Aye, permission to come aboard. Get her the longboat, John.'' He thumbed at the small pinnace dangling from the side of the ship. ''Just don't light a lantern.''

Mewes laughed. ''I'd give a hundred sovereigns to the man who could spark up a candle lantern in this weather!''

363

Winston looked up to see Joan slowly descending the companionway from the quarterdeck. They watched in silence as the longboat was lowered and oarsmen began rowing it the few yards to shore.

"Well, this is quite a sight, if I may say." Her voice was contemptuous as she broke the silence. Suddenly she began to brush at her hair, attempting to straighten out the tangles. "I've never known 'her ladyship' to venture out on a night like this. . . ." She turned and glared at Winston. "Though I've heard talk she managed to get herself aboard the *Defiance* once before in a storm."

"You've got big ears."

"Enough to keep track of your follies. Do you suppose your lads don't take occasion to talk when they've a bit of kill-devil in their bellies? You should be more discreet, or else pay them better."

"I pay them more than they're worth now."

"Well, they were most admirin' of your little conquest. Or was the conquest hers?"

"Joan, why don't you just let it rest?" He moved to the railing at midships and reached down to help Katherine up the rope ladder. "What's happened? This is the very devil of a night. . . ."

"Hugh . . ." She was about to throw her arms around him when she noticed Joan. She stopped dead still, then turned and nodded with cold formality. "Your servant . . . madam."

"Your ladyship's most obedient . . ." Joan curtsied back with a cordiality hewn from ice.

They examined each other a moment in silence. Then Katherine seemed to dismiss her as she turned back to Winston.

"Please. Won't you come back and help? just for tonight?"

He reached for her hand and felt it trembling. "Help you? What do you mean?" His voice quickened. "Don't tell me the Roundheads have already started marching on Bridge-town.''

"Not that we know of. But now that the rain's put out the cane fires, a few of the militia have started regrouping. With their horses." She squeezed his hand in her own. "Maybe we could still try an attack on the Oistins breastwork at dawn."

"You don't have a chance. Now that the rains have begun, you can't move up any cannon. The roads are like rivers. But *they've* got heavy ordnance. The Roundheads have doubtless got those cannons in the breastwork turned around now and covering the road. If we'd have marched last evening, we could've moved up some guns of our own, and then hit them at first light. Before they expected an attack. But now it's too late." He examined her sadly. Her face was drawn and her hair was plastered against her cheeks. "It's over, Katy. Barbados is lost."

"But you said you'd fight, even if you had nobody but your own men."

"Briggs and the rest of them managed to change my mind for me. Why should I risk anything? They won't."

She stood unmoving, still grasping his hand. "Then you're really leaving?"

"I am." He looked at her. "I still wish you'd decide to go with me. God knows . . ."

Suddenly she pulled down his face and kissed him on the lips, lingering as the taste of rain flooded her mouth. Finally she pulled away. "I can't think now. At least about that. But for God's sake please help us tonight. Let us use those flint-locks you've got here on the ship. They're dry. The Round-head infantry probably has mostly matchlocks, and they'll be wet. With your muskets maybe we can make up for the dif-ference in our numbers."

He examined her skeptically. "Just exactly whose idea is this, Katy?"

"Who do you suppose? Nobody else knows you've got them."

"Anthony Walrond knows." Winston laughed. "I'll say one thing. It would be perfect justice."

"Then use them to arm our militia. With your guns, maybe . . ."

"I'll be needing those flintlocks where I'm going."

Joan pushed forward with a scowl. "Give me leave to put you in mind, madam, that those muskets belong to Hugh. Not to the worthless militia on this island." She turned on Winston. "Don't be daft. You give those new flintlocks over to the militia and you'll never see half of them again. You know that as well as I do."

He stood studying the locked fo'c'sle in silence. "I'll grant you that. I'd be a perfect fool to let the militia get hold of them."

"Hugh, what happened to all your talk of honor?" Katherine drew back. "I thought you were going to fight to the last."

"I told you . . ." He paused as he gazed into the rain for a long moment. Finally he looked back. "I'd say there *is* one small chance left. If we went in with a few men, before it gets light, maybe we could spike the cannon in the breastwork. Then at least it would be an even battle."

"Would you try it?"

He took her hand, ignoring Joan's withering glare. "Maybe I do owe Anthony Walrond a little farewell party. In appreciation for his selling this island, and me with it, to the God damned Roundheads."

"Then you'll come?"

"How about this? If I can manage to get some of my lads over to Oistins before daybreak, we might try paying them a little surprise." He grinned. "It would be good practice for Jamaica."

"Then stay and help us fight. How can we just give up, when there's still a chance? They can't keep up their blockade forever. Then we'll be done with England, have a free nation here. . . ."

He shook his head in resignation, then turned up his face to feel the rain. He stood for a time, the two women watching him as the downpour washed across his cheeks. "There's no freedom on this island anymore. There may never be again. But maybe I do owe Anthony Walrond and his Windwards a lesson in honor." He looked back. "All right. But go back up to the compound. You'd best stay clear of this."

Before she could respond, he turned and signaled toward Mewes.

"John. Unlock the muskets and call all hands on deck."

Dalby Bedford was standing in the doorway of the make-shift tent, peering into the dark. He spotted Winston, trailed by a crowd of shirtless seamen walking up the road between the rows of rainwhipped palms.

"God's life. Is that who it looks to be?"

"What the plague! The knave had the brass to come back?" Colonel George Heathcott pushed his way through the milling crowd of militia officers and moved alongside Bedford to stare. "As though we hadn't enough confusion already."

The governor's plumed hat and doublet were soaked. While the storm had swept the island, he had taken command of the militia, keeping together a remnant of men and officers. But now, only two hours before dawn, the squall still showed no signs of abating. Even with the men who had returned, the ranks of the militia had been diminished to a fraction of its former strength—since many planters were still hunting down runaways, or had barricaded themselves and their families in their homes for safety. Several plantation houses along the west coast had been burned, and through the rain random gunfire could still be heard as slaves were being pursued. Though the rebellion had been routed, a few pockets of Africans, armed with machetes, remained at large.

The recapture of the slaves was now merely a matter of time. But that very time, Bedford realized, might represent the difference between victory and defeat.

"Those men with him are all carrying something." Heathcott squinted through the rain at the line of men trailing after Winston. "By God, I'd venture those could be muskets. Maybe he's managed to locate a few more matchlocks for us." He heaved a deep breath. "Though they'll be damned useless in this rain."

"Your servant, Captain." Bedford bowed lightly as Winston ducked under the raised flap at the entrance of the lean-to shelter. "Here to join us?"

"I thought we might come back over for a while." He glanced around at the scattering of officers in the tent. "Who wants to help me go down to the breastwork and see if we can spike whatever guns they've got? If we did that, maybe you could muster enough men to try storming the place when it gets light."

"You're apt to be met by five hundred men with pikes, sir, and Anthony Walrond at their head." Heathcott's voice was filled with dismay. "Three or four for every one we've got. We don't have the men to take and hold that breastwork now, not till some more of the militia get back."

"If those guns aren't spiked by dawn, you'd as well just go ahead and surrender and have done with it." He looked around the tent. "Mind if I let the boys come in out of the rain to prime their muskets?"

"Muskets?" Heathcott examined him. "You'll not be using matchlocks, not in this weather. I doubt a man could keep his matchcord lit long enough to take aim."

"I sure as hell don't plan to try taking the breastwork with nothing but pikes." Winston turned and gestured for the men to enter the tent. Dick Hawkins led the way, unshaven, shirtless, and carrying two oilcloth bundles. After him came Edwin Spurre, cursing the rain as he set down two bundles of his own. Over a dozen other seamen followed.

368

"This tent is for the command, sir." Heathcott advanced on Winston. "I don't know what authority you think you have to start bringing in your men."

"We can't prime muskets in the rain."

"Sir, you're no longer in charge here, and we've all had quite . . ." His glance fell on the bundle Spurre was unwrapping. The candle lantern cast a golden glow over a shiny new flintlock. The barrel was damascened in gold, and the stock was fine Italian walnut inlaid with mother of pearl. Both the serpentine cock and the heel plate on the stock were engraved and gilt. "Good God, where did that piece come from?"

"From my personal arsenal." Winston watched as Spurre slipped out the ramrod and began loading and priming the flintlock. Then he continued, "These muskets don't belong to your militia. They're just for my own men, here tonight."

"If you can keep them dry," Heathcott's voice quickened, "maybe you could . . ."

"They should be good for at least one round, before the lock gets damp." Winston turned to Heathcott. "They won't be expecting us now. So if your men can help us hold the breastwork while we spike those cannon, we might just manage it."

"And these guns?" Heathcott was still admiring the muskets.

"We won't use them any more than we have to." Winston walked down the line of officers. "There's apt to be some hand-to-hand fighting if their infantry gets wind of what's afoot and tries to rush the emplacement while we're still up there. How many of your militiamen have the stomach for that kind of assignment?"

The tent fell silent save for the drumbeat of rain. The officers all knew that to move on the breastwork now would be the ultimate test of their will to win. The question on every man's mind was whether their militia still possessed that will.

But the alternative was most likely a brief and ignominious defeat on the field, followed by unconditional surrender.

They gathered in a huddle at the rear of the tent, a cluster of black hats, while Winston's men continued priming the guns. "Damn'd well-made piece, this one." Edwin Spurre was admiring the gilded trigger of his musket. "I hope she shoots as fine as she feels." He looked up at Winston. "I think we can keep the powder pan dry enough if we take care. They've all got a cover that's been specially fitted."

Winston laughed. "Only the best for Sir Anthony. Let's make sure he finds out how much we appreciate the gun-smithing he paid for."

"It's a risk, sir. Damned if it's not." Heathcott broke from the huddle and approached Winston. "But with these flint-locks we might have an advantage. They'll not be expecting us now. Maybe we can find some men to back you up."

"We could use the help. But I only want volunteers." Winston surveyed the tent. "And they can't be a lot of un-tested farmers who'll panic and run if the Roundheads try and make a charge."

"Well and good." Bedford nodded, then turned to Heath-cott. "I'll be the first volunteer. We're running out of time."

Winston reached for a musket. "Then let's get on with it."

Rain now, all about them, engulfing them, the dense Carib-bean torrent that erases the edge between earth, sky, and sea. Winston felt as though they were swimming in it, the gusts wet against his face, soaking through his leather jerkin, awash in his boots. The earth seemed caught in a vast ephemeral river which oscillated like a pendulum between ocean and sky. In the Caribbees this water from the skies was different from anywhere else he had ever known. The heavens, like a brooding deity, first scorched the islands with a white-hot sun, then purged the heat with warm, remorseless tears.

Why had he come back to Oistins? To chance his life once

more in the service of liberty? The very thought brought a wry smile. He now realized there would *never* be liberty in this slaveowning corner of the Americas. Too much wealth was at stake for England to let go of this shiny new coin in Cromwell's exchequer. The Puritans who ruled England would keep Barbados at any cost, and they would see to it that slavery stayed.

No. Coming back now was a personal point. Principle. If you'd go back on your word, there was little else you wouldn't scruple to do as well.

Maybe freedom didn't have a chance here, but you fought the fight you were given. You didn't betray your cause, the way Anthony Walrond had.

"There look to be lighted linstocks up there, Cap'n. They're ready." Edwin Spurre nodded toward the tall outline of the breastwork up ahead. It was a heavy brick fortification designed to protect the gun emplacements against cannon fire from the sea. The flicker of lantern light revealed that the cannon had been rolled around, directed back toward the roadway, in open view.

"We've got to see those linstocks are never used." He paused and motioned for the men to circle around him. Their flintlocks were still swathed in oilcloth. "We need to give them a little surprise, masters. So hold your fire as long as you can. Anyway, we're apt to need every musket if the Windwards realize we're there and try to counterattack."

"Do you really think we can get up there, Cap'n?" Dick Hawkins carefully set down a large brown sack holding spikes, hammers, and grapples—the last used for boarding vessels at sea. "It's damned high."

"We're going to have to circle around and try taking it from the sea side, which is even higher. But that way they won't see us. Also, we can't have bandoliers rattling, so we've got to leave them here. Just take a couple of charge-holders in each pocket. There'll not be time for more anyway." He turned and examined the heavy brick of the breastwork. "Now look lively. Before they spot us."

Hawkins silently began lifting out the grapples—heavy barbed hooks that had been swathed with sailcloth so they would land soundlessly, each with fifty feet of line. Winston picked one up and checked the wrapping on the prongs. Would it catch and hold? Maybe between the raised battlements.

He watched as Hawkins passed the other grapples among the men, eighteen of them all together. Then they moved on through the night, circling around toward the seaward wall of the fortification.

Behind them the first contingent of volunteers from the Barbados militia waited in the shadows. As soon as the gunners were overpowered by Winston's men, they would advance and help hold the breastwork while the guns were being spiked.

In the rainy dark neither Winston nor his seamen noticed the small band of men, skin black as the night, who now edged forward silently through the shadows behind them.

They had arrived at the *Defiance* earlier that evening, only to discover it afloat, several yards at sea. Then they had watched in dismay as Winston led a band of seamen ashore in longboats, carrying the very muskets they had come to procure. Could it be the guns were already primed and ready to fire?

Prudently Atiba had insisted they hold back. They had followed through the rain, biding their time all the five mile trek to Oistins. Then they had waited patiently while Winston held council with the *branco* chiefs. Finally they had seen the muskets being primed . . . which meant they could have been safely seized all along!

But now time was running out. How to take the guns? It must be done quickly, while there still was dark to cover their escape into hiding. Atiba watched as Winston and the men quietly positioned themselves along the seaward side of the breastwork and began uncoiling the lines of their grapples. Suddenly he sensed what was to happen next.

Perhaps now there was a way to get the guns after all. . . .

"Wait. And be ready." He motioned the men back into the shadows of a palm grove. Then he darted through the rain.

Winston was circling the first grapple above his head, intended for the copestone along the top of the breastwork, when he heard a quiet Portuguese whisper at his ear.

"You will not succeed, senhor. The Inglês will hear your hooks when they strike against the stone."

"What the pox!" He whirled to see a tall black man standing behind him, a machete in his hand.

"A life for a life, senhor. Was that not what you said?" Atiba glanced around him. The seamen stared in wordless astonishment. "Do you wish to seize the great guns atop this fortress? Then let my men do it for you. This is best done the Yoruba way."

"Where the hell did *you* come from?" Winston's whisper was almost drowned in the rain.

"From out of the dark. Remember, my skin is black. Sometimes that is an advantage, even on an island owned by the white Inglês."

"Briggs will kill you if he catches you here."

Atiba laughed. "I could have killed *him* tonight, but I chose to wait. I want to do it the Inglês way. With a musket." He slipped the machete into his waistwrap. "I have come to make a trade."

"What do you mean?"

"Look around you." Atiba turned and gestured. Out of the palms emerged a menacing line of black men, all carrying cane machetes. "My men are here. We could kill all of you now, senhor, and simply take your muskets. But you once treated me as a brother, so I will barter with you fairly, as

373

though today were market day in Ife. I and my men will seize this *branco* fortress and make it an offering of friendship to you—rather than watch you be killed trying to take it yourself—in trade for these guns.'' He smiled grimly. ''A life for a life, do you recall?''

''The revolt you started is as good as finished, just like I warned you would happen.'' Winston peered through the rain. ''You won't be needing any muskets now.''

''Perhaps it is over. But we will not die as slaves. We will die as Yoruba. And many *branco* will die with us.''

''Not with my flintlocks, they won't.'' Winston examined him and noticed a dark stain of blood down his shoulder.

Atiba drew out his machete again and motioned the other men forward. ''Then see what happens when we use these instead.'' He turned the machete in his hand. ''It may change your mind.''

Before Winston could reply, he turned and whispered a few brisk phrases to the waiting men. They slipped their machetes into their waistwraps and in an instant were against the breastwork, scaling it.

As the seamen watched in disbelief, a host of dark figures moved surely, silently up the sloping stone wall of the breastwork. Their fingers and toes caught the crevices and joints in the stone with catlike agility as they moved toward the top.

''God's blood, Cap'n, what in hell's this about?'' Dick Hawkins moved next to Winston, still holding a grapple and line. ''Are these savages . . . ?''

''I'm damned if I know for sure. But I don't like it.'' His eyes were riveted on the line of black figures now blended against the stone of the breastwork. They had merged with the rain, all but invisible.

In what seemed only moments, Atiba had reached the parapet along the top of the breastwork, followed by his men. For an instant Winston caught the glint of machetes, reflecting the glow of the lighted linstocks, and then nothing.

"By God, no. There'll be no unnecessary killing." He flung his grapple upward, then gestured at the men. "Let's go topside, quick!"

The light clank of the grapple against the parapet was lost in the strangled cries of surprise from atop the breastwork. Then a few muted screams drifted down through the rain. The sounds died away almost as soon as they had begun, leaving only the gentle pounding of rain.

"It is yours, senhor." The Portuguese words came down as Atiba looked back over the side. "But come quickly. One of them escaped us. I fear he will sound a warning. There will surely be more *branco*, soon."

"Damn your eyes." Winston seized the line of his grapple, tested it, and began pulling himself up the face of the stone wall. There was the clank of grapples as the other men followed.

The scene atop the breastwork momentarily took his breath away. All the infantrymen on gunnery duty had had their throats cut, their bodies now sprawled haphazardly across the stonework. One gunner was even slumped across the breech of a demi-culverin, still clasping one of the lighted linstocks, its oil-soaked tip smoldering inconclusively in the rain. The Yoruba warriors stood among them, wiping blood from their machetes.

"Good Christ!" Winston exploded and turned on Atiba. "There was no need to kill all these men. You just had to disarm them."

"It is better." Atiba met his gaze. "They were *branco* warriors. Is it not a warrior's duty to be ready to die?"

"You bloodthirsty savage."

Atiba smiled. "So tell me, what are these great Inglês guns sitting all around us here meant to do? Save lives? Or kill men by the hundreds, men whose face you never have to see? My people do not make these. So who is the savage, my Inglês friend?"

"Damn you, there are rules of war."

"Ah yes. *You* are civilized." He slipped the machete into his waistwrap. "Someday you must explain to me these rules you have for civilized killing. Perhaps they are something like the 'rules' your Christians have devised to justify making my people slaves."

Winston looked at him a moment longer, then at the bodies lying around them. There was nothing to be done now. Best to get on with disabling the guns. "Dick, haul up that sack with the spikes and let's make quick work of this."

"Aye." Hawkins seized the line attached to his waist and walked to the edge of the parapet. At the other end, resting in the mud below, was the brown canvas bag containing the hammers and the spikes.

Moments later the air rang with the sound of metal against metal, as the seamen began hammering small, nail-like spikes into the touch-holes of each cannon. That was the signal for the Barbados militiamen to advance from the landward side of the breastwork, to provide defensive cover.

"A life for a life, senhor." Atiba moved next to Winston. "We served you. Now it is time for your part of the trade."

"You're not getting any of my flintlocks, if that's what you mean."

"Don't make us take them." Atiba dropped his hand to the handle of his machete.

"And don't make my boys show you how they can use them." Winston stood unmoving. "There's been killing enough here tonight."

"So you are not, after all, a man who keeps his word. You are merely another *branco*." He slowly began to draw the machete from his belt.

"I gave you no 'word.' And I wouldn't advise that . . ." Winston pushed back the side of his wet jerkin, clearing the pistols in his belt.

Out of the dark rain a line of Barbados planters carrying homemade pikes came clambering up the stone steps. Colonel Heathcott was in the lead. "Good job, Captain, by my life.'' He beamed from under his gray hat. ''We heard nary a peep. But you were too damned quick by half. Bedford's just getting the next lot of militia together now. He'll need . . .''

As he topped the last step, he stumbled over the fallen body of a Commonwealth infantryman. A tin helmet clattered across the stonework.

''God's blood! What . . .'' He peered through the half-light at the other bodies littering the platform, then glared at Winston. ''You massacred the lads!''

''We had some help.''

Heathcott stared past Winston, noticed Atiba, and stopped stone still. Then he glanced around and saw the cluster of Africans standing against the parapet, still holding machetes.

''Good God.'' He took a step backward and motioned toward his men. ''Form ranks. There're runaways up here. And they're armed.''

''Careful . . .'' Before Winston could finish, he heard a command in Yoruba and saw Atiba start forward with his machete.

''No, by God!'' Winston shouted in Portuguese. Before Atiba could move, he was holding a cocked pistol against the Yoruba's cheek. ''I said there's been enough bloodshed. Don't make me kill you to prove it.''

In the silence that followed there came a series of flashes from the dark down the shore, followed by dull pops. Two of the planters at the top of the stone steps groaned, twisted, and slumped against the stonework with bleeding flesh wounds. Then a second firing order sounded through the rain. It carried the unmistakable authority of Anthony Walrond.

''On the double, masters. The fireworks are set to begin.'' Winston turned and shouted toward the seamen, still hammering in the spikes. ''Spurre, get those flintlocks unwrapped and ready. It looks like Walrond has a few dry muskets of his own.''

''Aye, Cap'n.'' He signaled the seamen who had finished

their assigned tasks to join him, and together they took cover against the low parapet on the landward side of the breastwork. Heathcott and the planters, pikes at the ready, nervously moved behind them.

Winston felt a movement and turned to see Atiba twist away. He stepped aside just in time to avoid the lunge of his machete—then brought the barrel of the pistol down hard against the side of his skull. The Yoruba groaned and staggered back against the cannon nearest them. As he struggled to regain his balance, he knocked aside the body of the Commonwealth infantryman who lay sprawled across its barrel, the smoldering linstock still in his dead grasp. The man slid slowly down the wet side of the culverin, toward the breech. Finally he tumbled forward onto the stonework, releasing his grasp on the handle of the lighted linstock.

Later Winston remembered watching in paralyzed horror as the linstock clattered against the breech of the culverin, scattering sparks. The oil-soaked rag that had been its tip seemed to disintegrate as the handle slammed against the iron, and a fragment of burning rag fluttered against the shielded touch hole.

A flash shattered the night, as a tongue of flame torched upward. For a moment it illuminated the breastwork like midday.

In the stunned silence that followed there were yells of surprise from the far distance, in the direction of the English camp. No one had expected a cannon shot. Moments later, several rounds of musket fire erupted from the roadway below. The approaching Barbados militiamen had assumed they were being fired on from the breastwork. But now they had revealed their position. Almost immediately their fire was returned by the advance party of the Windward Regiment.

Suddenly one of the Yoruba waiting at the back of the breastwork shouted incomprehensibly, broke from the group, and began clambering over the parapet. There were more yells, and in moments the others were following him. Atiba, who had been knocked sprawling by the cannon's explosion, called for them to stay, but they seemed not to hear. In seconds they had vanished over the parapet and into the night.

"You betrayed us, senhor." He looked up at Winston. "You will pay for it with your life."

"Not tonight I won't." Winston was still holding the pistol, praying it was not too wet to fire.

"Not tonight. But soon." He shoved the machete unsteadily into his waistwrap. Winston noticed that he had difficulty rising, but he managed to pull himself up weakly. Then his strength appeared to revive. "Our war is not over." Amid the gunfire and confusion, he turned and slipped down the landward side of the breastwork. Winston watched as he disappeared into the rain.

"How many more left to spike, masters?" He yelled back toward the men with the hammers. As he spoke, more musket fire sounded from the plain below.

"We've got all but two, Cap'n." Hawkins shouted back through the rain. "These damned little demi-culverin. Our spikes are too big."

"Then the hell with them. We've done what we came to do." He motioned toward Heathcott. "Let's call it a night and make a run for it. Now."

"Fine job, I must say." Heathcott was smiling broadly as he motioned the cringing planters away from the wall. "We'll hold them yet."

While the seamen opened sporadic covering fire with their flintlocks, the militia began scrambling down the wet steps. When the column of Walrond's Windward Regiment now marching up from the seaside realized they were armed, it immediately broke ranks and scattered for cover. In moments Winston and Heathcott were leading their own men safely up the road toward the camp. They met the remainder of the Barbados militia midway, a bedraggled cluster in the downpour.

"You can turn back now, sirs." Heathcott saluted the lead

officer, who was kneeling over a form fallen in the sand. "You gave us good cover when we needed you, but now it's done. The ordnance is spiked. At sunup we'll drive the Roundheads back into the sea."

"Good Christ." The officer's voice was trembling as he looked up, rain streaming down his face. "We'd as well just sue for peace and have done with it."

"What?" Heathcott examined him. "What do you mean?"

"He was leading us. Dalby Bedford. The Windwards caught him in the chest when they opened fire." He seemed to choke on his dismay. "The island's no longer got a governor."

Chapter Eighteen

Above the wide hilltop the mid-morning rain had lightened momentarily to fine mist, a golden awning shading the horizon. A lone figure, hatless and wearing a muddy leather jerkin, moved slowly up the rutted path toward the brick compound reserved for the governor of Barbados. Behind him lay the green-mantled rolling hills of the island; beyond, shrouded in drizzle and fog, churned the once-placid Caribbean.

The roadway was strewn with palm fronds blown into haphazard patterns by the night's storm, and as he walked, a new gust of wind sang through the trees, trumpeting a mournful lament. Then a stripe of white cut across the new thunderheads in the west, and the sky started to darken once again. More rain would be coming soon, he told himself, yet more storm that would stretch into the night and mantle the island and sea.

He studied the sky, wistfully thinking over what had passed. Would that the squalls could wash all of it clean, the way a downpour purged the foul straw and offal from a cobblestone London street. But there was no making it right anymore. Now the only thing left was to try and start anew. In a place far away.

Would she understand that?

The gate of the compound was secured and locked, as though to shut out the world beyond. He pulled the clapper on the heavy brass bell and in its ring heard a foreboding finality.

"Sir?" The voice from inside the gate was nervous, fearful. He knew it was James, the Irish servant who had been with Katherine and the governor for a decade.

"Miss Bedford."

"By the saints, Captain Winston, is that you, sir? The mistress said you'd gone back over to Oistins."

"I just came from there."

"How's the fighting?" The voice revealed itself as belonging to a short, thin-haired man with watery eyes. "We've not heard from His Excellency since he sent that messenger down last night. Then after that Mistress . . ."

"Just take me to Miss Bedford." He quickly cut off what he realized could grow into an accounting of the entire household for the past fortnight.

How do I go about telling her, he asked himself. That it's the end of everything she had, everything she hoped for. That there's no future left here.

"Is she expecting you, Captain?" James' eyes narrowed as he pushed wide the heavy wooden door leading into the hallway. "I pray nothing's happened to . . ."

"She's not expecting me. Just tell her I've come."

"Aye, Yor Worship, as you please." He indicated a chair in the reception room, then turned to head off in the direction of the staircase.

Katherine was already advancing down the wide mahogany steps. She was dressed in a calico bodice and full skirt, her hair bunched into moist ringlets of its own making. Her bloodshot eyes told Winston she had not slept.

"Hugh, what is it? Why have you come back?" She searched his face in puzzlement. Then her eyes grew wild. "Oh God, what's happened?" She stumbled down the rest of the steps. "Tell me."

"Katy, there was some shooting . . . ."

And he told her, first that Dalby Bedford was dead, then how it happened. Next he explained that, since the island no longer had a seated governor, the Assembly had elected to accept in full the terms set forth by the admiral of the fleet. He told it as rapidly as he could, hoping somehow to lessen the pain. She listened calmly, her face betraying no emotion. Finally she dropped into a tall, bulky chair, and gazed around for a moment, as though bidding farewell to the room.

"Maybe it's better this way after all." She looked down. "Without the humiliation of the Tower and a public trial by Cromwell."

Winston watched her, marveling. There still was no hint of a tear. Nothing save her sad eyes bespoke her pain as she continued, "It's ironic, isn't it. Both of them. My mother, years ago, and now . . . Killed by a gun, when all they ever wanted for the world was peace." She tried to smile. "These are dangerous times to be about in the Americas, Captain. You're right to always keep those flintlocks in your belt." She turned away, and he knew she was crying. The servants had gathered, James and the two women, huddled by the staircase, unable to speak.

"Katy, I came as soon as I could to tell you. God only knows what's to happen now, but you can't stay here. They'll figure out in no time you've had a big hand in this. You'll likely be arrested."

"I'm not afraid of them, or Cromwell himself." She was still gazing at the wooden planks of the floor.

"Well, you ought to be." He walked over and knelt down next to her chair. "It's over. These planters we were fighting for gave the island away, so I say damned to them. There's more to the Americas than Barbados." He paused, and finally she turned to gaze at him. There were wet streaks down her cheeks. "Maybe now you'll come with me. We'll make a place somewhere else."

She looked into his eyes and silently bit her lip. It was

almost as though he had never truly seen her till this moment. His heart went out to her as he continued, "I want you with me. There's another island, Katy, if you're willing to try and help me take it."

"I don't . . ." She seemed unsure what she wanted to say. She looked at him a moment longer, then around at the room, the servants. Finally she gazed down again, still silent.

"Katy, I can't make you come. Nor can I promise it'll be easy. But you've got to decide now. There's no time to wait for . . . anything. We've both got to get out of here. I'm going to collect as many of my indentures as possible, then try and run the blockade tonight—rain, storm, no matter. Who knows if I'll make it, but it's my only hope." He rose to his feet. His muddy boots had left dark traces on the rug. "It's yours too, if you want it. Surely you know that."

Her voice came like a whisper as she looked up. "We tried, didn't we? Truly we did."

"You can't give liberty to the Americas if these Puritans only want it for themselves. It's got to be for everybody. . . . Remember what I said? They could have freed the Africans, in return for help, and they might have won. If I ever doubted that, God knows I don't anymore, not after what I saw last night. But they wanted slaves, and there's no mobilizing an island that's only half free. So they got what they deserve." He walked to the sideboard. A flask of brandy was there, with glasses; he lifted the bottle and wearily poured himself a shot. Then he turned and hoisted the glass. "We gave it our best, but we couldn't do it alone. Not here." He drank off the liquor and poured in more.

"Give me some of that." She motioned toward the bottle. He quickly filled another glass and placed it in her hands. The servants watched, astonished, as she downed it in one gulp, then turned back to Winston.

"How can I go just yet? There're his papers here, everything. What he did mustn't just be forgotten. He created a

384

democratic nation, an Assembly, all of it, here in the Americas. Someday . . .''

"Nobody gives a damn about that anymore." He strode over with the flask and refilled her glass. "You've got to get out of here. This is the first place they're apt to look for you. You can stay at Joan's place till we're ready to go."

"Joan?" She stared at him, disbelieving. "You mean Joan Fuller?"

"She's the only person left here I trust."

"She despises me. She always has."

"No more than you've despised her. So make an end on it."

"I . . ."

"Katy, there's no time to argue now. The damned Roundheads are going to be in Bridgetown by dark. I've got to go down to the ship, before the rain starts in again, and sort things out. We've got to finish lading and get ready to weigh anchor before it's too late."

He watched as she drank silently from the glass, her eyes faraway. Finally he continued, "If you want, I'll send Joan to help you pack up." He emptied the second glass of brandy, then set it back on the sideboard. When he turned back to her, he was half smiling. "I suppose I've been assuming you're going with me, just because I want you to so badly. Well?"

She looked again at the servants, then around the room. At last she turned to Winston. "Hold me."

He walked slowly to the chair and lifted her into his arms. He ran his hands through her wet hair, then brought up her lips. At last he spoke. "Does that mean yes?"

She nodded silently.

"Then I've got to go. Just pack what you think you'll want, but not too many silk skirts and bodices. You won't be needing them where we're going. Try and bring some of those riding breeches of yours."

385

She hugged him tighter. "I was just thinking of our 'little island.' When was that?"

"Yesterday. Just yesterday. But there're lots of islands in the Caribbean."

"Yesterday." She drew back and looked at him. "And tomorrow?"

"This time tomorrow we'll be at sea, or we'll be at the bottom of the bay out there." He kissed her one last time. "I'll send Joan quick as I can. So please hurry."

Before she could say more, he stalked out into the rain and was gone.

The sand along the shore of the bay was firm, beaten solid by the squall. The heavy thunderheads that threatened earlier had now blanked the sun, bringing new rain that swept along the darkened shore in hard strokes. Ahead through the gloom he could make out the outlines of his seamen, kegs of water balanced precariously on their shoulders, in an extended line from the thatched-roof warehouse by the careenage at the river mouth down to a longboat bobbing in the surf. After the raid on the Oistins breastwork, he had ordered them directly back to Bridgetown to finish lading. A streak of white cut across the sky, and in its shimmering light he could just make out the *Defiance,* safely anchored in the shallows, canvas furled, nodding with the swell.

Joan. She had said nothing when he asked her to go up and help Katherine. She'd merely glared her disapproval, while ordering the girls to bring her cloak. Joan was saving her thoughts for later, he knew. There'd be more on the subject of Katherine.

The only sounds now were the pounding of rain along the shore and the occasional distant rumble of thunder. He was so busy watching the men he failed to notice the figure in white emerge from the darkness and move toward his path.

When the form reached out for him, he whirled and dropped his hand to a pistol.

"Senhor, *desculpe.*"

The rain-mantled shadow curtsied, Portuguese style.

He realized it was a woman. Briggs' *mulata*. The one Joan seemed so fond of. Before he could reply, she seized his arm.

"*Faça o favor*, senhor, will you help us? I beg you." There was an icy urgency in her touch.

"What are you doing here?" He studied her, still startled. Her long black hair was coiled across her face in tangled strands, and there were dark new splotches down the front of her white shift.

"I'm afraid he'll die, senhor. And if he's captured . . ."

"Who?" Winston tried unsuccessfully to extract his arm from her grasp.

"I know he wanted to take the guns you have, but they were for us to fight for our freedom. He wished you no harm."

Good God, so she had been part of it too! He almost laughed aloud, thinking how Benjamin Briggs had been cozened by all his slaves, even his half-African mistress. "You mean that Yoruba, Atiba? Tell him he can go straight to hell. Do you have any idea what he had his men do last night?"

She looked up, puzzled, her eyes still pleading through the rain.

"No, I don't suppose you could." He shrugged. "It scarcely matters now. But his parting words were an offer to kill me, no more than a few hours ago. So I say damned to him."

"He is a man. No more than you, but no less. He was born free; yet now he is a slave. His people are slaves." She paused, and when she did, a distant roll of thunder melted into the rain. "He did what he had to do. For his people, for me."

"All he and his 'people' managed was to help the Commonwealth bring this island to its knees."

387

"How? Because he led the Yoruba in a revolt against slavery?" She gripped his arm even tighter. "If he helped defeat the planters, then I am glad. Perhaps it will be the end of slavery after all."

Winston smiled sadly. "It's only the beginning of that accursed trade. He might have stopped it—who knows?—if he'd won. But he lost. So that's the end of it. For him, for Barbados."

"But you can save him." She tugged Winston back as he tried to brush past her. "I know you are leaving. Take him with you."

"He belongs to Briggs." He glanced back. "Same as you do. There's nothing I can do about it. Right now, I doubt good master Briggs is of a mind to do anything but hang him."

"Then if his life has no value to anyone here, take him as a free man."

A web of white laced across the thunderhead. In its light he could just make out the tall masts of the *Defiance*, waving against the dark sky like emblems of freedom.

God damn you, Benjamin Briggs. God damn your island of slaveholders.

"Where is he?"

"Derin has hidden him, not too far from here. When Atiba fainted from the loss of blood, he brought him up there." She turned and pointed toward the dark bulk of the island. "In a grove of trees where the *branco* could not find him. Then he came to me for help."

"Who's this Derin?"

"One of the Yoruba men who was with him."

"Where're the others? There must've been a dozen or so over at Oistins this morning."

"Some were killed near there. The others were captured. Derin told me they were attacked by the militia. Atiba only escaped because he fainted and Derin carried him to safety. The others stayed to fight, to save him, and they were taken."

Her voice cracked. "I heard Master Briggs say the ones who were captured, Obewole and the others, would be burned alive tomorrow."

"Burned alive!"

"All the planters have agreed that is what they must do. It is to be made the punishment on Barbados for any slave who revolts, so the rest of the Africans will always fear the *branco.*"

"Such a thing would never be allowed on English soil."

"This is not your England, senhor. This is Barbados. Where slavery has become the lifeblood of all wealth. They will do it."

"Bedford would never allow . . ." He stopped, and felt his heart wrench. "Good Christ. Now there's no one to stop them. Damn these bloodthirsty Puritans." He turned to her. "Can you get him down here? Without being seen?"

"We will try."

"If you can do it, I'll take him."

"And Derin too?"

"In for a penny, in for a pound." His smile was bitter. "Pox on it. I'll take them both."

"Senhor." She dropped to her knees. "Tell me how I can thank you."

"Just be gone. Before my boys get wind of this." He pulled her to her feet and glanced toward the rain-swept line of seamen carrying water kegs. "They'll not fancy it, you can be sure. I've got worries enough as is, God knows."

"*Muito, muito obrigada,* senhor." She stood unmoving, tears streaming down her cheeks.

"Just go." He stepped around her and moved on down the shore, toward the moored longboat where the men were working. Now John Mewes was standing alongside, minimally supervising the seamen as they stacked kegs. Mingled with his own men were several of the Irish indentures.

"Damn this squall, Cap'n. We'll not be able to get underway till she lets up. It's no weather for a Christian to be at sea, that I promise you.''

''I think it's apt to ease up around nightfall.'' He checked the clouds again. ''What're we needing?''

''Once we get this laded, there'll be water aboard and to spare.'' He wiped the rain from his eyes and glanced at the sky. ''God knows the whole of the island's seen enough water to float to sea.'Tis salt pork we're wanting now, and biscuit.''

''Can we get any cassava flour?''

''There's scarcely any to be had. The island's half starved, Cap'n.''

''Did you check all the warehouses along here?''

''Aye, we invited ourselves in and rifled what we could find. But there's pitiful little left, save batches of moldy tobacco waitin' to be shipped.''

''Damn. Then we'll just have to sail with what we've got.'' Winston turned and stared down the shore. There had not been any provisions off-loaded from Europe since the fleet arrived. There were no ships in the harbor now, save the *Defiance* and the *Zeelander*.

The *Zeelander*.

''When's the last time you saw Ruyters?''

''This very mornin', as't happens. He came nosing by to enquire how it was we're afloat, and I told him it must've been the tide lifted her off.'' Mewes turned and peered through the rain toward the Dutch frigate. ''What're you thinking?''

''I'm thinking he still owes me a man, a Spaniard by the name of Vargas, which I've yet to collect.''

''That damned Butterbox'll be in no mood to accommodate you, I swear it.''

''All the same, we made a bargain. I want you and some of the boys to go over and settle it.'' He thumbed at the *Zeelander,* lodged in the sand not two hundred yards down the beach. ''In the meantime, I have to go back up to Joan's and collect . . . a few things. Why don't you try and find

Ruyters? Get that Spaniard, however you have to do it, and maybe see if he'll part with any of their biscuit.''

"Aye, I'll tend to it." He turned to go.

"And John . . ." Winston waved him back.

"Aye."

"We may be having some company before we weigh anchor. Remember that Yoruba we caught on board a few nights back?''

"Aye, I recollect the heathen well enough. I've not seen him since, thank God, though some of the lads claim there was one up at Oistins this mornin' who sounded a lot like him.''

"Same man. I've a mind to take him with us, and maybe another one. But don't say anything to the boys. Just let him on board if he shows up.''

"You're the captain. But I'd sooner have a viper between decks as that godless savage. They're sayin' he and a bunch of his kind gutted a good dozen Englishmen this mornin' like they was no better'n so many Spaniards.''

"Well, that's done and past. Just see he gets on board and the boys keep quiet about it.''

"They'll not be likin' it, by my life.''

"That's an order.''

"Aye." Mewes turned with a shrug, whistled for some of the seamen, then headed through the rain, down the shore toward the beached hulk of the *Zeelander*.

"She's here darlin'." Joan met him at the door. "In back, with the girls.''

"How is she?'' Winston threw off his wet cape and reached for the tankard of sack she was handing him.

"I think she's starting to understand he's dead now. I guess it just took a while. Now I think it's time you told me a few things yourself. Why're you taking her? Is't because you're worried the Roundheads might send her back home to be hanged?"

"Is that the reason you want to hear?"

"Damn your eyes, Hugh Winston. You're not in love with her, are you?"

He smiled and took a sip from the tankard.

"You'd best beware of her, love." She sighed. "That one's not for you. She's too independent, and I doubt she even knows what she's doin' half the time."

"And how about me? Think I know what I'm doing?" He pulled back a chair and straddled it.

"Doubtless not, given what you're plannin' next." She plopped into a chair. "But I've packed your things, you whoremaster. The girls're already sorry to see the lot of you leavin'. I think they've taken a fancy to a couple of your lads." She laughed. "But they'd have preferred you most of all. God knows, I've had to keep an eye on the jades day and night."

He turned and stared out in the direction of the rain. "Maybe you'll decide to come over someday and open shop on Jamaica. This place has bad times coming."

She leaned back and poured a tankard of sack for herself. "That's a fool's dream. But you're right about one thing. There're dark days in store here, not a doubt. Who knows how it'll settle out?"

The wind seemed to play against the doors of the tavern. Then they swung open and a sudden gust coursed through the room, spraying fine mist across the tables.

"Winston, damn me if I didn't figure I'd find you here." Benjamin Briggs pushed into the room, shook the rain from his wide hat, and reached for a chair. "I'm told you were the last to see that Yoruba of mine. That he tried to kill you this morning, much as he aimed to murder me."

"He was at Oistins, true enough." Winston glanced up.

"That's what I heard. They're claiming he and those savages of his brutally murdered some of Cromwell's infantry."

He shook his hat one last time and tossed it onto the table. "We've got to locate him. Maybe you have some idea where he is now?"

"He didn't trouble advising me of his intended whereabouts."

"Well, he's a true savage, by my soul. A peril to every Christian on this island." He sighed and looked at Winston. "I don't know whether you've heard, but the Roundheads have already started disarming our militia. We'll soon have no way to defend ourselves. I think I winged him last night, but that heathen is apt to come and kill us both if we don't hunt him down and finish the job while we've still got the chance." He lowered his voice. "I heard about those flint-locks of yours. I was hoping maybe you'd take some of your boys and we could go after him whilst things are still in a tangle over at Oistins."

Winston sat unmoving. "Remember what I told you the other day, about freeing these Africans? Well, now I say damned to you. You can manage your slaves any way you like, but it'll be without my flintlocks."

"That's scarcely an attitude that'll profit the either of us at the moment." Briggs signaled to Joan for a tankard of kill-devil. "Peculiar company you keep these days, Mistress Fuller. 'Twould seem the Captain here cares not tuppence for his own life. Well, so be it. I'll locate that savage without him if I needs must." He took a deep breath and gazed around the empty room. "But lest my ride down here be for naught, I'd as soon take the time right now and settle that bargain we made."

Joan poured the tankard and shoved it across the table to him. "You mean that woman you own?"

"Aye, the mulatto wench. I'm thinking I might go ahead and take your offer of a hundred pounds, and damned to her."

"What I said was eighty." Joan stared at him coldly.

"Aye, eighty, a hundred, who can recall a shilling here or

there." He took a swig. "What say we make it ninety then, and have an end to the business?"

Joan eyed him. "I said eighty, though I might consider eighty-five. But not a farthing more."

"You're a hard woman to trade with, on my honor." He took another draught from the tankard. "Then eighty-five it is, but only on condition we settle it here and now. In sterling. I'll not waste another day's feed on her."

Winston glanced at Joan, then back at Briggs. "Do you know where she is?"

The planter's eyes narrowed. "Up at my compound. Where else in God's name would she be?"

Winston took a drink and looked out the doorway, into the rain. "I heard talk she was seen down around here this morning. Maybe she's run off." He turned to Joan. "I'd encourage you to pay on delivery."

"Damn you, sir, our bargain's been struck." Briggs settled his tankard with a ring. "I never proposed delivering her with a coach and four horses."

Joan sat silently, listening. Finally she spoke. "You'd best not be thinkin' to try and swindle me. I'll advance you five pounds now, on account, but you'll not see a penny of the rest till she's in my care."

"As you will then." He turned and spat toward the corner. "She'll be here, word of honor."

Joan glanced again at Winston, then rose and disappeared through the shuttered doors leading into the back room.

After Briggs watched her depart, he turned toward Winston. "You, sir, have studied to plague me from the day you dropped anchor."

"I usually cut the deck before I play a hand of cards."

"Well, sir, I'll warrant Cromwell's got the deck now, for this hand at least. We'll see what you do about him."

"Cromwell can be damned. I'll manage my own affairs."

"As will we all, make no mistake." He took another drink. "Aye, we'll come out of this. We'll be selling sugar to the

Dutchmen again in a year's time, I swear it. They can't keep that fleet tied up here forever." He looked at Winston. "And when it's gone, you'd best be on your way too, sir. Mark it."

"I'll make note."

Joan moved back through the room. "Five pounds." She handed Briggs a small cloth bag. "Count it if you like. That makes her mine. You'll see the balance when she's safe in this room."

"You've got a trade." He took the bag and inventoried its contents with his thick fingers. "I'll let this tankard serve as a handshake." He drained the last of the liquor as he rose. As he clapped his soaking hat back onto his head, he moved next to where Winston sat. "And you, sir, would be advised to rethink helping me whilst there's time. That savage is apt to slit your throat for you soon enough if he's not tracked down."

"And then burned alive, like you're planning for the rest of them?"

Briggs stopped and glared. "That's none of your affair, sir. We're going to start doing what we must. How else are we to keep these Africans docile in future? Something's got to be done about these revolts."

He whirled abruptly and headed for the door. At that moment, the battered louvres swung inward and a harried figure appeared in the doorway, eyes frantic, disoriented. A few seconds passed before anyone recognized Jeremy Walrond. His silk doublet was wet and bedraggled, his cavalier's hat waterlogged and drooping over his face. Before he could move, Briggs' pistol was out and leveled at his breast.

"Not another step, you whoreson bastard, or I'll blow you to hell." His voice boomed above the sound of the storm. "Damn me if I shouldn't kill you on sight, except I wouldn't squander the powder and shot." He squinted through the open doorway. "Where's Anthony? I'd have him come forward and meet me like a man, the royalist miscreant."

Jeremy's face flooded with fear. "He's . . . he's been taken

395

on board the *Rainbowe*. I swear it." His voice seemed to crack. "By Powlett."

"By who?"

"A man named Powlett, the vice admiral. I think he's to be the new governor."

"Well, damned to them both." Briggs lowered the pistol guardedly, then shoved it back into his belt. "They're doubtless conspiring this very minute how best to squeeze every farthing of profit from our sugar trade."

"I . . . I don't know what's happening. They've made the Windwards as much as prisoners. Powlett's already disarmed the Regiment, and Colonel Morris is leading his infantry on the march to Bridgetown right now." He stepped gingerly in through the doorway. "I came down to try and find Miss Bedford. At the compound they said she might be . . ."

"I doubt Katherine has much time for you." Winston looked up from his chair. "So you'd best get on back to Oistins before I decide to start this little war all over again."

"Oh, for God's sake let the lad be. He's not even wearin, a sword," Joan interjected, then beckoned him forward. "Don't let this blusterin' lot frighten you, darlin'. Come on in and dry yourself off."

"I've got to warn Katherine." He edged nervously toward Joan, as though for protection. His voice was still quavering. "We didn't expect this. They'd agreed to terms. They said . . ."

"They lied." Winston drew out one of his pistols and laid it on the table before him. "And your gullible, ambitious royalist of a brother believed them. Haply, some others of us took our own precautions. Katherine's safe, so you can go on back to your Roundheads and tell them they'll never find her."

"But I meant her no harm. It was to be for the best, I swear it. I want her to know that." He settled at a table and lowered his face into his hands. "I never dreamed it would come to this." He looked up. "Who could have?"

" 'Tis no matter now." Joan moved to him, her voice kindly. "You're not to blame. 'Twas Sir Anthony that led the defection. It's always the old fools who cause the trouble. He's the one who should have known . . ."

"But you don't understand what really happened. I was the one who urged him to it, talked him into it. Because Admiral Calvert assured me none of this would happen."

"You planned this with Calvert!" Briggs roared. "With that damned Roundhead! You let him use you to cozen Walrond and the Windwards into defecting?"

Jeremy stifled a sob, then turned toward Joan, his blue eyes pleading. "Would you tell Katherine I just wanted to stop the killing. None of us ever dreamed . . ."

"Jeremy." Katherine was standing in the open doorway leading to the back. "Is it really true, what you just said?"

He stared at her in disbelief, and his voice failed for a second. Then suddenly the words poured out. "Katherine, you've got to get away." He started to rush to her, but something in her eyes stopped him. "Please listen. I think Powlett means to arrest you. I heard him talking about it. There's nothing we can do."

"You and Anthony've got the Windwards." She examined him with hard scorn. "I fancy you can do whatever you choose. Doubtless he'll have himself appointed governor now, just as he's probably been wanting all along."

"No! He never . . ." Jeremy's voice seemed to crack. Finally he continued, "A man named Powlett, the vice admiral, is going to be the new governor. Morris is marching here from Oistins right now. I only slipped away to warn you."

"I've been warned." She was turning back toward the doorway. "Goodbye, Jeremy. You always wanted to be somebody important here. Well, maybe you've managed it now. You've made your mark on our times. You gave the Americas back to England. Congratulations. Maybe Cromwell will declare himself king next and then grant you a knighthood."

"Katherine, I don't want it." He continued miserably,

"I'm so ashamed. I only came to ask you to forgive me. And to warn you that you've got to get away."

"I've heard that part already." She glanced back. "Now just leave."

"But what'll you do?" Again he started to move toward her, then drew back.

"It's none of your affair." She glared at him. "The better question is what you and Anthony'll do now? After you've betrayed us all. I thought you had more honor. I thought Anthony had more honor."

He stood for a moment, as though not comprehending what she had said. Then he moved forward and confronted her. "How can you talk of honor, in the same breath with Anthony! After what *you* did. Made a fool of him."

"Jeremy, you have known me long enough to know I do what I please. It was time Anthony learned that too."

"Well, he should have broken off the engagement weeks ago, that much I'll tell you. And he would have, save he thought you'd come to your senses. And start behaving honorably." He glanced at Winston. "I see he was wrong."

"I did come to my senses, Jeremy. Just in time. I'll take Hugh's honor over Anthony's any day." She turned and disappeared through the doorway.

Jeremy stared after her, then faced Winston. "Damn you. You think I don't know anything. You're the . . ."

"I think you'd best be gone." Winston rose slowly from his chair. "Give my regards to Sir Anthony. Tell him I expect to see him in hell. He pulled a musket ball from his pocket and tossed it to Jeremy. "And give him that, as thanks from me for turning this island and my ship over to the Roundheads. The next one he gets won't be handed to him . . ."

The doors of the tavern bulged open, and standing in the rain was an officer of the Commonwealth army. Behind him were three helmeted infantrymen holding flintlock muskets.

"Your servant, gentlemen." The man glanced around the room and noticed Joan. "And ladies. You've doubtless heard your militia has agreed to lay down its arms, and that includes even those who'd cravenly hide in a brothel rather than serve. For your own safety we're here to collect all weapons, till order can be restored. They'll be marked and returned to you in due time." He motioned the three infantrymen behind him to close ranks at the door. "We'll commence by taking down your names."

In the silence that followed nothing could be heard but the howl of wind and rain against the shutters. Dark had begun to settle outside now, and the room itself was lighted only by a single flickering candle, in a holder on the back wall. The officer walked to where Joan was seated and doffed his hat. "My name is Colonel Morris, madam. And you, I presume, are the . . ."

"You betrayed us!" Jeremy was almost shouting. "You said we could keep our muskets. That we could . . ."

"Master Walrond, is that you?" Morris turned and peered through the gloom. "Good Christ, lad. What are you doing here? You're not supposed to leave Oistins." He paused and inspected Jeremy. "I see you've not got a weapon, so I'll forget I came across you. But you've got to get on back over to Oistins and stay with the Windwards, or I'll not be responsible." He turned to Briggs. "And who might you be, sir?"

"My name, sir, is Benjamin Briggs. I am head of the Council of Barbados, and I promise you I will protest formally to Parliament over this incident. You've no right to barge in here and . . ."

"Just pass me that pistol and there'll be no trouble. It's hotheads like you that make this necessary." Morris reached into Briggs' belt and deftly extracted the long flintlock, its gilded stock glistening in the candlelight. He shook the powder out of the priming pan and handed it to one of the infantrymen. "The name with this one is to be . . ." He glanced back. "Briggs, sir, I believe you said?"

"Damn you. This treatment will not be countenanced. I

399

need that pistol." Briggs started to move forward, then glanced warily at the infantrymen holding flintlock muskets.

"We all regret it's necessary, just as much as you." Morris signaled to the three infantrymen standing behind him, their helmets reflecting the dull orange of the candles. "While I finish here, search the back room. And take care. There's apt to be a musket hiding behind a calico petticoat in a place like this."

Winston settled back onto his chair. "I wouldn't trouble with that if I were you. There're no other guns here. Except for mine."

Morris glanced at him, startled. Then he saw Winston's flintlock lying on the table. "You're not giving the orders here, whoever you are. And I'll kindly take that pistol."

"I'd prefer to keep it. So it'd be well if you'd just leave now, before there's trouble."

"That insubordinate remark, sir, has just gotten you put under arrest." Morris moved toward the table.

Winston was on his feet. The chair he had been sitting on tumbled across the floor. "I said you'd best be gone."

Before Morris could respond, a woman appeared at the rear doorway. "I'll save you all a search. I'm not afraid of Cromwell, and I'm surely not frightened of you."

"Katherine, no!" Jeremy's voice was pleading.

"And who might you be, madam?" Morris stared in surprise.

"My name is Katherine Bedford, sir. Which means, I suppose, that you'll want to arrest me too."

"Are you the daughter of Dalby Bedford?"

"He was my father. And the last lawfully selected governor this island is likely to know."

"Then I regret to say I do have orders to detain you. There are certain charges, madam, of aiding him in the instigation of this rebellion, that may need to be answered in London."

"Katherine!" Jeremy looked despairingly at her. "I warned you . . ."

"Is that why you're here, Master Walrond? To forewarn an accused criminal?" Morris turned to him. "Then I fear there may be charges against you too." He glanced at Briggs. "You can go, sir. But I'm afraid we'll have to hold your pistol for now, and take these others into custody."

"You're not taking Miss Bedford, or anybody, into custody." Winston pulled back his water-soaked jerkin to expose the pistol in his belt.

Morris stared at him. "And who, sir, are you?"

"Check your list of criminals for the name Winston." He stood unmoving. "I'm likely there too."

"Is that Hugh Winston, sir?" Morris' eyes narrowed, and he glanced nervously at the three men behind him holding muskets. Then he looked back. "We most certainly have orders for your arrest. You've been identified as the gunnery commander for the rebels here, to say nothing of charges lodged against you in England. My first priority is Miss Bedford, but I'll be pleased to do double duty and arrest you as well."

"Fine. Now, see that pistol?" Winston thumbed toward the table. "Look it over carefully. There're two barrels, both primed. It's part of a pair. The other one is in my belt. That's four pistol balls. The man who moves to arrest Miss Bedford gets the first. But if you make me start shooting, I'm apt to forget myself and not stop till I've killed you all. So why don't you leave now, Colonel Morris, and forget everything you saw here." He glanced back at Katherine. "I'm sure Miss Bedford is willing to forget she saw *you*. She's had a trying day."

"Damn your impudence, sir." Morris turned and gestured at the men behind him. "Go ahead and arrest her."

One of the helmeted infantrymen raised his flintlock and waved Katherine forward.

"No!" Jeremy shouted and lunged toward the soldier. "You can't! I never meant . . ."

The shot sounded like a crack of thunder in the close room.

Black smoke poured from the barrel of the musket, and Jeremy froze where he stood, a quizzical expression on his face. He turned to look back at Katherine, his eyes penitent, then wilted toward the floor, a patch of red spreading across his chest.

Almost simultaneous with the musket's discharge, the pistol in Winston's belt was already drawn and cocked. It spoke once, and the infantryman who had fired dropped, a trickle of red down his forehead. As the soldier behind him started to raise his own musket, the pistol gave a small click, rotating the barrel, and flared again. The second man staggered back against the wall, while his flintlock clattered unused to the floor.

Now the rickety table in front of Winston was sailing toward the door, and the pistol that had been lying on it was in his hand. The table caught the third infantryman in the groin as he attempted to raise his weapon and sent him sprawling backward. His musket rattled against the shutters, then dropped.

Morris looked back to see the muzzle of Winston's second flintlock leveled at his temple.

"Katy, let's go." Winston motioned her forward. "We'll probably have more company any minute now."

"You're no better than a murderer, sir." Morris finally recovered his voice.

"I didn't fire the first shot. But by God I'll be the one who fires the last, that I promise you." He glanced back. "Katy, I said let's go. Take whatever you want, but hurry."

"Hugh, they've killed Jeremy!" She stood unmoving, shock in her face.

"He wouldn't let me handle this my way." Winston kept his eyes on Morris. "But it's too late now."

"He tried to stop them. He did it for me." She was shaking. "Oh, Jeremy, why in God's name?"

"Katy, come on." Winston looked back. "Joan, get her things. We've got to move out of here, now."

Joan turned and pushed her way through the cluster of Irish girls standing fearfully in the rear doorway.

"You'll hang for this, sir." Morris eyed the pistol. The remaining infantryman still sat against the wall, his unfired musket on the floor beside him.

"The way you'd planned to hang Miss Bedford, no doubt." He motioned toward Briggs. "Care to collect those muskets for me?"

"I'll have no hand in this, sir." The planter did not move. "You've earned a noose for sure."

"I'll do it." Katherine stepped across Jeremy's body and assembled the three muskets of the infantrymen. She carried them back, then confronted Morris.

"You, sir, have helped steal the freedom of this island, of the Americas. It's impossible to tell you how much I despise you and all you stand for. I'd kill you myself if God had given me the courage. Maybe Hugh will do it for me."

"I'll see the both of you hanged, madam, or I'm not a Christian."

"I hope you try."

Joan emerged through the crowd, toting a large bundle. She laid it on a table by the door, then turned to Winston. "Here's what we got up at the compound this afternoon." She surveyed the three bodies sadly. "Master Jeremy was a fine lad. Maybe he's finally managed to make his brother proud of him; I'll wager it's all he ever really wanted." She straightened. "Good Christ, I hope they don't try and shut me down because of this."

"It wasn't your doing." Winston lifted the bundle with his free hand. "Katy, can you manage those muskets?"

"I'd carry them through hell."

"Then let's be gone." He waved the pistol at the infantryman sitting against the wall. "Get up. You and the colonel here are going to keep us company."

"Where do you think you can go?" Briggs still had not moved. "They'll comb the island for you."

"They'll look a long time before they find us on Barbados." He shoved the pistol against Morris' ribs. "Let's be off, Colonel."

"There'll be my men all about." Morris glared. "You'll not get far."

"We'll get far enough." He shifted the bundle under his arm.

"Darlin', Godspeed. I swear I'll miss you." Joan kissed him on the cheek, then turned to Katherine. "And mind you watch over him in that place he's headed for."

"Jamaica?"

"No. He knows where I mean." She looked again at Winston. "There's no worse spot in the Caribbean."

"Don't worry You'll hear from me." Winston kissed her back, then urged Morris forward.

"See that you stay alive." She followed them to the door. "And don't try anything too foolish."

"I always take care." He turned and bussed her on the cheek one last time. Then they were gone.

Chapter Nineteen

As Winston and Katherine led their prisoners slowly down the shore, the *Defiance* stood out against the dark sky, illuminated by flashes of lightning as it tugged at its anchor cables. The sea was up now, and Winston watched as her prow dipped into the trough of each swell, as though offering a curtsy. They had almost reached the water when he spotted John Mewes, waiting by the longboat.

"Ahoy, Cap'n," he sang out through the gusts of rain. "What're you doin'? Impressing Roundheads to sail with us now? We've already got near to fifty of your damn'd indentures."

"Are they on board?"

"Aye, them and all the rest. You're the last." He studied Katherine and Morris in confusion. "Though I'd not expected you'd be in such fine company."

"Then we weigh anchor."

"In this squall?" Mewes' voice was incredulous. "We can't put on any canvas now. It'd be ripped off the yards."

"We've got to. The Roundheads are already moving on Bridgetown. We'll try and use those new short sails." Winston urged Morris forward with his pistol, then turned back to Mewes. "Any sign of that African we talked about?"

"I've seen naught of him, and that's a fact." He peered

up the beach, hoping one last cursory check would suffice. Now that the rain had intensified, it was no longer possible to see the hills beyond. "But I did manage to get that Spaniard from Ruyters, the one named Vargas." He laughed. "Though I finally had to convince the ol' King of the Butterboxes to see things our way by bringin' over a few of the boys and some muskets."

"Good. He's on board now?"

"Safe as can be. An' happy enough to leave that damn'd Dutchman, truth to tell. Claimed he was sick to death of the putrid smell of the *Zeelander,* now that she's been turned into a slaver."

"Then to hell with the African. We can't wait any longer."

" 'Tis all to the good, if you want my thinkin'." Mewes reached up and adjusted Morris' helmet, then performed a mock salute. He watched in glee as the English commander's face flushed with rage. "You're not takin' these two damn'd Roundheads aboard, are you?"

"Damn you, sir." Morris ignored Mewes as he glared at Winston, then looked down at the pistol. He had seen a double-barrelled mechanism like this only once before—property of a Spanish diplomat in London, a dandy far more skilled dancing the bourrée than managing a weapon. But such a device in the hands of an obvious marksman like Winston; nothing could be more deadly. "There's been quite enough . . ."

"Get in the longboat."

"I'll do no such thing." Morris drew back. "I have no intention of going with you, wherever it is you think you're headed."

"I said get in. If you like it here so much, you can swim back after we weigh anchor." Winston tossed his bundle across the gunwale, seized Morris by his doublet, and sent him sprawling after it. Then he turned to the infantryman. "You get in as well."

Without a word the man clambered over the side. Winston

heaved a deep breath, then took the muskets Katherine was carrying and handed them to Mewes. "Katy, this is the last you're apt to see of Barbados for a long while."

"Please, let's don't talk about it." She seized her wet skirts and began to climb over the side, Winston steadying her with one hand. "I suppose I somehow thought I could have everything. But I guess I've learned differently."

He studied her in confusion for a moment, then turned and surveyed the dark shore one last time. "All right, John, prepare to cast off."

"Aye." Mewes loosened the bow line from its mooring and tossed it into the longboat. Together they shoved the bobbing craft and its passengers deeper into the surf.

"What's your name?" Winston motioned the infantryman forward as he lifted himself over the gunwales.

"MacEwen, Yor Worship." He took off his helmet and tossed it onto the boards. His hair was sandy, his face Scottish.

"Then take an oar, MacEwen. And heave to."

"Aye, Sor." The Scotsman ignored Morris' withering glare and quickly took his place.

"You can row too, Colonel." Winston waved the pistol. "Barbados is still a democracy, for at least a few more hours."

Morris said nothing, merely grimaced and reached for an oar.

Katherine laid her cheek against Winston's shoulder and looked wistfully back toward the shore. "Everything we made, the Commonwealth's going to take away now. Everything my father and I, and all the others, worked so hard for together."

He held her against him as they moved out through the surf and across the narrow band of water to the ship. In what seemed only moments the longboat edged beneath the quartergallery and the *Defiance* was hovering above them.

"John, have the boys drop that short sail and weigh anchor

as soon as we're aboard. This westerly off the coast should get us underway and past the blockade. We'll just keep her close hauled till we've doubled the Point, then run up some more canvas.''

"It'll be a miracle if we manage to take her by the Point in this sea, and in the dark besides." Mewes was poised in the bow of the longboat.

"When we get aboard, I'll take the helm. You just get the canvas on her.''

"Aye." He reached up and seized a notch beneath a gunport, pulling the longboat under the deadeyes that supported the mainmast shrouds. As he began mounting the rope ladder he tossed the line up through the rain.

Winston had taken Katherine's arm to help her up when he heard a buzz past his ear. Then, through the rain, came a faint pop, the report of a musket.

"God's blood!" He turned back to look. Dimly through the rain he could make out a line of helmeted infantrymen along the shore, muskets in hand. They were disorganized, without a commander, but standing alongside them and yelling orders was a heavy man in a wide black hat. Benjamin Briggs.

"He betrayed us! He brought them right down to the bay. I wonder what he's figuring to get in return? Doubtless a place in the new government. We've got to . . ."

Before he could finish, Katherine had caught his arm and was pointing over in the direction of the river mouth. "Hugh, wait. Do you see that? There's someone out there. In the surf. I thought I noticed it before.''

"More damned infantry?" He turned to stare. "They'd not try swimming after us. They'd wait for longboats.''

"I can't tell. It's over there, on the left. I think someone's trying to wade out.''

He squinted through the rain. A figure clad in white was waist deep in the surf, holding what seemed to be a large bundle.

"That's no Roundhead. I'll wager it's likely Briggs' *mulata*. Though she's just a little too late. I've a mind to leave her." He paused to watch as a wave washed over the figure and sent it staggering backward. Then another bullet sang past and he heard the shouts of Benjamin Briggs.

"Maybe I owe a certain planter one last service."

"Cap'n, we've got to get this tub to sea." Mewes was crouching behind the bulwarks of the *Defiance*. "Those damn'd Roundheads along the shore don't have many muskets yet, but they're apt to be gettin' reinforcements any time now. So if it's all the same, I don't think I'd encourage waitin' around all night."

"John, how are the anchors?"

"I've already weighed the heavy one up by the bow." He called down. "Say the word and we can just slip the cable on that little one at the stern."

"Maybe we've got time." He pushed the longboat back away from the side of the *Defiance*. As he reached for an oar, Morris threw down his helmet and dove into the swell. In moments the commander was swimming toward shore.

"Aye, he's gone, Yor Worship. He's a quick one, to be sure." The Scottish infantryman gave only a passing glance as he threw his weight against the oar. "You'll na be catching him, on my faith."

"And what about you?"

"With Yor Worship's leave, I'd as soon be stayin' on with you." He gave another powerful stroke with the oar. "Wherever you're bound, 'tis all one to me."

"What were you before? A seaman?"

"A landsman, Yor Worship, I'll own it. I was took in the battle of Dunbar and impressed into the Roundhead army, made to come out here to the Caribbees. But I've had a bellyful of these Roundheads and their stinking troop ships, I swear it. I kept my pigs better at home. I'd serve you like you was the king himself if you'd give me leave."

"MacEwen, wasn't it?"

"Aye, Yor Worship. At your service."

"Then heave to." Winston pulled at the other oar. Through the dark they could just make out the bobbing form, now neck deep in the surf. She was supporting the black arms of yet another body.

"Senhora!" Winston called through the rain.

The white-clad figure turned and stared blankly toward them. She seemed overcome with exhaustion, unsure even where she was.

"Espere um momento. We'll come to you." He was shouting now in Portuguese.

A musket ball sang off the side of the longboat as several infantrymen began advancing down the shore in their direction. The Scotsman hunkered beside the gunwales but did not miss a stroke of his oar as they neared the bobbing heads in the water.

"Here, senhora." Winston reached down and grasped the arms of the body Serina was holding. It was Atiba. While Katherine caught hold of her shoulders and pulled her over the gunwale, MacEwen helped Winston hoist the Yoruba, unconscious, onto the planking. He was still bleeding, his breath faint.

"He is almost dead, senhor. And they have killed Derin." Serina was half choked from the surf. "At first I was afraid to try bringing him. But then I thought of what would happen if they took him, and I knew I had . . ." She began mumbling incoherently as she bent over the slumped form of Atiba, her mouth against his, as though to urge breath back into him.

"Katy, the minute we're on board take them straight down to the cabin and see if you can get a little brandy into him. Maybe it'll do some good."

"I'll try, but I fear it's too late already. Let's just get underway." She turned to look at the deck of the *Defiance*, where a line of seamen had appeared with muskets.

The firing from the shore slowed now, as the infantry

410

melted back into the rain to avoid the barrage from the ship. By the time their longboat was hoisted up over the side and lashed midships, Morris had retreated to safety with his men.

While Mewes ordered the remaining anchor cable slipped and the mainsail dropped, Katherine ushered Serina through the companionway to the Great Cabin, followed by seamen carrying Atiba. Then the mast groaned against the wind, a seaman on the quarterdeck unlashed the helm, and in moments they had begun to pull away.

"That was easy." Mewes spat in the general direction of the scuppers, then hoisted up his belt as he watched the rain-swept shore begin to recede.

"Could be Morris is just saving us for the frigates." Winston was studying the bobbing mast lights off their portside bow. "He probably figures they heard the gunfire and will realize something's afoot."

"They've got their share of ordnance, that much I'll warrant. There's at least one two-decker still on station out there, the *Gloucester*. I sailed on her once, back when I first got impressed by the damn'd navy, twenty-odd years back. She's seen her years at sea, but she's got plenty of cannon between decks for all that."

"I think you'd better have the portside guns primed and ready to run out, just in case. But I figure once we get past the Point, we'll be clear. After that we can steer north and ride this coastal westerly right up to Speightstown, maybe heave-to there till the storm eases." He turned and headed down the deck. "I'm going aft to take the whipstaff. Get the yardmen aloft and damn the weather. I want the maintop and all braces manned."

"Aye, you never know." Mewes yelled the gunnery orders through the open hatch, then marched down the deck giving assignments.

Katherine was standing at the head of the companionway leading to the Great Cabin as Winston passed on his way to the quarterdeck. "I've put the African in your cabin, along

411

with the mulatto woman." She caught his arm as he headed up the steps. "She's delirious. And I think he's all but dead. He's got a bad musket wound in his shoulder."

"Even if he dies now, it'll be better than what Briggs and the planters had planned." He looked at her face and pushed aside a sudden desire to take her into his arms, just to know she was his at last. "But see if you can clean his wound with brandy. I'd hate to lose him now after all the trouble we went to bringing him aboard."

"Why *did* you do it, Hugh? After all, he tried to kill you once, on this very deck. I was here, remember."

"Who understands why we do anything? Maybe I like his brass. Maybe I don't even know the reason anymore."

He turned and headed up the steps.

Serina lifted his cheek against her own, the salt from her tears mingling with the sea water in his hair. The wound in his shoulder was open now, sending a trickle of blood glistening across his chest. His breathing was in spasms.

Shango, can you still hear me . . . ?

"Try washing his wound with this." Katherine was standing above her, in the dim light of the candle-lantern, holding a gray onion-flask of brandy.

"Why are you helping me, senhora?" Serina looked up, her words a blend of English and Portuguese. "You care nothing for him. Or for me."

"I . . . I want to." Katherine awkwardly pulled the cork from the bottle, and the fiery fumes of the brandy enveloped them.

"Because the senhor told you to do it. That is the real reason." She finally reached and took the bottle. "He is a good man. He risked his life for us. He did not need to. No other *branco* on this island would have."

"Then you can repay him by doing what he asked. He said to clean the wound."

Serina settled the bottle onto the decking beside the sleeping bunk, then bent over and kissed the clan marks on Atiba's dark cheek. As she did, the ship rolled awkwardly and a high wave dashed against the quartergallery. Quickly she seized the neck of the flask and secured it till they had righted.

"I think we will have to do it together."

"Together?"

"Never fear, senhora. Atiba's black skin will not smudge your white Inglês hands."

"I never thought it would." Katherine impulsively reached down and ripped off a portion of her skirt. Then she grabbed the flask and pulled back his arm. While Serina held his shoulder forward, she doused the wound with a stream of the brown liquor, then began to swab away the encrusted blood with the cloth. His skin felt like soft leather, supple to the touch, with hard ripples of muscles beneath.

The sting of the brandy brought an involuntary jerk. Atiba's eyes opened and he peered, startled, through the gloom.

"Don't try to move." Quickly Serina bent over him, whispering softly into his ear. "You are safe. You are on the *branco*'s ship."

He started to speak, but at that moment another wave crashed against the stern and the ship lurched sideways. Atiba's eyes flooded with alarm, and his lips formed a word.

"Dara . . ."

Serina laid her face next to his. "Don't talk. Please. Just rest now." She tried to give him a drink of the brandy, but his eyes refused it. Then more words came, faint and almost lost in the roar of the wind and the groaning of the ancient boards of the *Defiance*. Finally his breath seemed to dissolve as unconsciousness again drifted over him.

Katherine watched as Serina gently laid his head against the cushion on the bunk, then fell to her knees and began to pray, mumbling foreign words . . . not Portuguese. She found herself growing more and more uneasy; something about the two of them was troubling, almost unnatural. Finally she rose

413

and moved to watch the sea through the stern windows. Though the waves outside slammed ever more menacingly against the quartergallery, as the storm was worsening noticeably, she still longed for the wind in her face. Again she recalled her first night here with Hugh, when they had looked out through this very window together, in each other's arms. What would it be like to watch the sea from this gallery now, she wondered, when the ocean and winds were wild? She sighed and pulled open the latch.

What she saw took her breath away.

Off the portside, bearing down on them, was the outline of a tallmasted English warship with two gun decks.

Before she could move, there were shouts from the quarterdeck above, then the trampling of feet down the companionway leading to the waist of the ship. He'd seen it too, and ordered his gun crews to station.

She pulled back from the window as a wave splashed across her face, and a chill swept the room, numbing her fingers. She fumbled a moment trying to secure the latch, then gave up and turned to head for the door. If we're all to die, she told herself, I want to be up with Hugh, on the quarterdeck. Oh God, why now? After all we've been through?

As she passed the lantern, she noticed Serina, still bent over the African, still mumbling the strange words. . . .

"Do you know what's about to happen to us all!" The frustration was more than she could contain. "Come back over here and take a look."

When the mulatto merely stared at her with a distant, glazed expression, she strode to where she knelt and took her arm, pulling her erect. While she was leading her toward the open window, she heard a deep groaning rise up through the timbers of the frigate and knew the cannon were being run out. Winston had ordered a desperate gamble; a possible ordnance duel with a warship twice the burden of the *Defiance*. Moving the guns now, when the seas were high, only compounded their danger. If one broke loose from its tackles, it

414

could hurtle through the side of the ship, opening a gash that would surely take enough water to sink them in minutes.

"Do you see, senhora?" She directed Serina's gaze out the open windows. "If you want to pray, then pray that that man-of-war doesn't catch us. Your African may soon be dead anyway, along with you and me too."

"What . . . will they do?" The mulatto studied the approaching warship, her eyes only half seeing.

"I expect they'll pull alongside us if they can, then run out their guns and . . ." She felt her voice begin to quiver.

"Then I will pray."

"Please do that." She whirled in exasperation and quickly shoved her way out the door and into the companionway. As she mounted the slippery ladder to the quarterdeck, she felt John Mewes brush past in the rain, bellowing orders aloft. She looked up to see men perched along the yards, clinging to thin ropes in the blowing rain as they loosened the topgallants. The *Defiance* was putting on every inch of canvas, in weather where any knowing seaman would strike sail and heave-to.

"Good God, Katy, I wish you'd go back below decks. The *Gloucester* must have spied our sail when we doubled the Point." Winston's voice sounded through the rain. He was steering the ship all alone now, his shoulder against the whipstaff. Off the portside the English warship, a gray hulk with towering masts, was rapidly narrowing the distance between them.

"Hugh, I want to be up here, with you." She grabbed onto a shroud to keep her balance. "They're planning to try and sink us, aren't they?"

"Unless we heave-to. Which I have no intention of doing. So they'll have to do just that if they expect to stop us. And I'd say they have every intention of making the effort. Look." He pointed through the rain. Now the line of gunport covers along the upper gun deck were being raised. "They're making ready to start running out their eighteen-pounders."

415

"What can we do?"

"First put on all the canvas we've got. Then get our own guns in order. If we can't outrun them, we'll have to fight."

"Do you think we have a chance?" She studied the ship more closely. It seemed to have twice the sail of the *Defiance*, but then it was heavier and bulkier. Except for the *Rainbowe*, Cromwell had not sent his best warships to the Americas. This one could be as old as Hugh's.

"I've outrun a few men-of-war before. But not in weather like this."

"Then I want to stay up here. And that mulatto woman you took on board frightens me, almost as much as this."

"Then stay. For now. But if they get us in range, I want you below." He glanced aloft, where men clinging to the swaying yards had just secured the main tops'ls. As the storm worsened, more lightning flashed in the west, bringing prayers and curses from the seamen. "The weather's about as bad as it could be. I've never had the *Defiance* under full sail when it's been like this. I never want to again."

After the topgallants were unfurled and secured, they seemed to start picking up momentum. The *Gloucester* was still off their portside, but far enough astern that she could not use her guns. And she was no longer gaining.

"Maybe we can still outrun them?" She moved alongside Winston.

"There's a fair chance." He was holding the whipstaff on a steady course. "But they've not got all their canvas on yet. They know it's risky." He turned to study the warship and she saw the glimmer of hope in his eyes, but he quickly masked it. "In good weather, they could manage it. But with a storm like this, maybe not." He paused as the lightning flared again. "Still, if they decide to chance the rest of their sail . . ."

She settled herself against the binnacle to watch the *Gloucester*. Then she noticed the warship's tops'ls being unfurled. Winston saw it too. The next lightning flash revealed that the *Gloucester* had now begun to run out her upper row of guns, as the distance between them slowly began to narrow once more.

"Looks as if they're going to gamble what's left of their running rigging, Katy. I think you'd best be below."

"No, I . . ."

Winston turned and yelled toward the main deck, "John, pass the order. If they pull in range, tell Canninge to just fire at will whenever the portside guns bear. Same as when that revenue frigate *Royale* once tried to board us. Maybe he can cripple their gun deck long enough to try and lose them in the dark."

"Aye." A muted cry drifted back through the howl of rain.

"Hugh, I love you." She touched the sleeve of his jerkin. "I think I even know what it means now."

He looked at her, her hair tangled in the rain. "Katy, I love you enough to want you below. Besides, it's not quite time to say our farewells yet."

"I know what's next. They'll pull to windward of us and just fire away. They'll shoot away our rigging till we're helpless, and then they'll hole us till we take on enough water to go down."

"It's not going to be that easy. Don't forget we've got some ordnance of our own. Just pray they can't set theirs in this sea."

Lightning flashed once more, glistening off the row of cannon on the English warship. They had range now, and Katherine could see the glimmer of lighted linstocks through the open gunports.

"Gracious Lord, for what we are about to receive, make us truly thankful." John Mewes was mounting the quarterdeck to watch. "This looks to be it, Cap'n."

"Just keep on praying, John. And get back down on deck. I want every inch of sail on those yards."

"Aye, I'd like the same, save I don't know where exactly we've got any more to put on, unless I next hoist my own linen.'' He crossed himself, then headed down the companionway.

Suddenly a gun on the *Gloucester* flared, sending an eighteen-pound round shot through the upper sails of the *Defiance,* inches from the maintop. Then again, and this time the edge of the fo'c'sle ripped away, spraying splinters across the deck.

''John! Tell Canninge he'd better start firing the second his guns bear. And he'd best be damned quick on it too.'' Even as he spoke, a roar sounded from below and the deck tilted momentarily sideways. Katherine watched as a line of shot splintered into the planking along the side of the *Gloucester,* between her gun decks.

''Damn, he came close.'' Winston studied the damage. ''But not close enough.''

Again the lightning flashed, nearer now, a wide network across the heavens, and she saw the *Gloucester*'s captain standing on his own quarterdeck, nervously staring aloft at the storm.

''Katy, please go below. This is going to get very bad. If they catch this deck, there'll be splinters everywhere. Not to mention . . . ''

The *Gloucester*'s guns flamed again. She felt the deck tremble as an eighteen-pound shot slammed into the side of the *Defiance,* up near the bow.

''John, let's have some more of those prayers.'' Winston yelled down again. ''And while you're at it, tell Canninge to give them another round the second he's swabbed out. He's *got* to hurt that upper gun deck soon or we're apt to be in for a long night.''

''Hugh, can't we . . .'' She stopped as she saw a figure in a bloodstained white shift slowly moving up the companionway.

''Good Christ.'' He had seen it too. ''Katy, try and keep her the hell off the quarterdeck and out of the way.''

While he threw his shoulder against the whipstaff and began shouting more orders to Mewes on the main deck, Serina mounted the last step. She moved across the planking toward them, her eyes glazed, even more than before. "Come below, senhora." Katherine reached out for her. "You could be hurt."

The *mulata*'s hand shot up and seized her arm with an iron grip. Katherine felt her feet give way, and the next thing she knew she had been flung sideways against the hard rope shrouds.

"*E pada nibi!*" The voice was deep, chilling. Then she turned and advanced menacingly on Winston.

"God damn you!" He shoved her back, then reached to help Katherine. "Katy, are you all right? Just watch out for her. I wager she's gone mad after all that's happened. If we get time I'll have some of the boys come and take her below."

Again the *Gloucester*'s guns flared, and a whistle sang across the quarterdeck as the shot clipped the railing next to where they were standing. Serina stared wildly at the shattered rail, then at the English man-of-war. Her eyes seemed vacant, as though looking through all she saw.

"Good Christ, Katy, take a look at those skies." Winston felt a chill in his bowels as the lightning blossomed again. "The wind is changing; I can feel it. Something's happening. If we lose a yard, or tear a sail, they'll take us in a minute. All it needs is one quick shift, too much strain."

As if in response to his words, the hull shuddered, then pitched backward, and Katherine heard a dull crack from somewhere in the rigging.

"Christ." Winston was staring aloft, his face washed in the rain.

She followed his gaze. The mainmast had split, just below the maintop. The topsail had fallen forward, into the foremast, and had ripped through the foresail. A startled maintopman was dangling helplessly from the side of his round perch. Then something else cracked, and he tumbled toward the deck, landing in the middle of a crowd of terrified seamen huddled by the fo'c'sle door.

"I knew we couldn't bear full sail in this weather. We've just lost a good half of our canvas." He looked back. "You've got to go below now. Please. And see if you can somehow take that woman with you. We're in very bad trouble. If I was a religious man, I'd be on my knees praying right now."

The *Gloucester*'s guns spoke once more, and a shot clipped the quartergallery only feet below where they were, showering splinters upward through the air.

"Atiba!" Serina was staring down over the railing, toward the hole that had been ripped in the corner of the Great Cabin beneath them.

Then she looked out at the warship, and the hard voice rose again. *"Iwo ko lu oniran li oru o nlu u li ossan?"* Finally her eyes flared and she shouted through the storm, *"Shango. Oyinbo l'o je!"*

Once more the lightning came.

Later he wondered if he might have been praying after all. He remembered how the fork of fire slid down the mainmast of the *Gloucester*, then seemed to envelop the maintop, sending smoke billowing through the tops'ls above. Next it coiled about the mainmast shrouds.

In moments her main tops'l was aflame, as though she'd been caught with fire-arrows. Soon a tongue of the blaze flicked downward and ignited her main course. After that the shrouds began to smolder. Almost immediately her seamen began furling the other sails, and all open gunports were quickly slammed down to stop any shreds of burning canvas from accidentally reaching the gun deck. Next the helmsman threw his weight against the whipstaff to try and take her off the wind.

She was still underway, like a crippled fireship bearing down on them, and for a moment Winston thought they were in even greater danger than before. But then the *Gloucester*'s mainmast slowly toppled forward as the shrouds gave way, tearing into the other rigging, and she heeled. It was impossible to see what followed, because of the rain, but moments later burning spars were drifting across the waves.

"It was the hand of Providence, as I'm a Christian." John Mewes was mounting the quarterdeck, solemn and subdued. A crowd of stunned seamen were following him to gain a better view astern. "The Roundhead whoresons were tempting fate. They should've known better than puttin' to sea with topmasts like those in this damn'd weather. Heaven knows, I could have told them."

There was a murmur of assent from the others. They stood praising the beneficence of God and watched as the last burning mast disappeared into the rain.

After Winston had lashed the whipstaff in place and ordered the sails shortened, he collapsed against the binnacle.

"It was a miracle, Hugh." Katherine wrapped an arm about him. Her bodice was soaked with rain and sweat. "I think I was praying. When I'd all but forgotten how."

"I've heard of it happening, God knows. But I've never before seen it. Just think. If we'd had taller masts, we could well have caught it ourselves."

Now the mood was lightening, as congratulations began to pass among the men. It was only then Katherine noticed the white shift at their feet. The mulatto was crumpled beside the binnacle, still as death.

"John, have somebody come and take that woman below." Winston glanced down. "She looks to have fainted."

"Aye. I was near to faintin' myself, truth to tell."

Finally Winston pulled himself up and surveyed the seamen. "I say well done, masters, one and all. So let's all have a word of thanks to the Almighty . . . and see if we can locate a keg of brandy. This crew has earned it."

Katherine leaned against him as she watched the cheering men head for the main deck. "Where can we go now, Hugh?

421

There'll soon be a price on our heads in every English settlement from Virginia to Bermuda."

"From the shape of our rigging, I'd guess we're going nowhere for a day or so. We've got to heave-to till the weather lets up, and try to mend those sails. After that I figure we'd best steer north, hope to beat the fleet up to Nevis, where we can careen and maybe lay in some more victuals."

"And then are you really going to try your scheme about Jamaica? With just the men you've got here?"

"Not just yet. You're right about the men. We don't have enough now." He lowered his voice. "So I'm thinking we'll have to make another stop first."

"Where?"

"There's only one place I know of where we can still find what we'll be needing." He slipped his arm about her waist. "A little island off the north coast of Hispaniola."

"You don't mean Tortuga? The Cow-Killers . . ."

"Now Katy, there's no better time than now to start learning what they're called over there on that side of the Caribbean. I know the Englishmen here in the Caribbees call them the Cow-Killers, but over there we were always known by our French name."

"What's that?"

"Sort of an odd one. You see, since we cured our meat Indian-style, on those greenwood grills they called *boucans*, most seamen over there knew us as the *boucaniers*. And that's the name they kept when they started sailing against the Spaniards."

"You mean . . . ?"

"That's right. Try and remember it. Buccaneer."

Book Three
TORTUGA/JAMAICA

Chapter Twenty

The sun emerged from the distant edge of the sea, burning through the fine mist that hung on the horizon. Katherine was standing on the high quartergallery, by the railing at the stern, the better to savor the easterly breeze that tousled her hair and fluttered the cotton sleeves of her seaman's shirt. The quiet of the ship was all but complete, with only the rhythmic splash of waves against the bow and the occasional groan from the masts.

She loved being on deck to watch the dawn, out of the sweltering gloom of the Great Cabin. This morning, when the first light of day brightened the stern windows, she'd crept silently from their narrow bunk, leaving Hugh snoring contentedly. She'd made her way up to the quarterdeck, where John Mewes dozed beside the steering house where he was to monitor the weathered grey whipstaff, lashed secure on a course due west.

Now she gazed out over the swells, past the occasional whitecaps that dotted the blue, and tasted the cool, moist air. During the voyage she had learned how to read the cast of the sea, the sometimes fickle Caribbean winds, the hidden portent in the color of clouds and sun. She'd even begun practicing how to take latitude with the quadrant.

Suddenly a porpoise surfaced along the stern, then another, and together they began to pirouette in the wake of the ship like spirited colts. Was there any place else in the world, she wondered, quite like the Caribbean? She never tired of watching for the schools of flying fish that would burst from the sea's surface like flushed grouse, seemingly in chase of the great barracuda that sometimes flashed past the bow. And near the smaller islands, where shallow reefs turned the coastal waters azure, she had seen giant sea turtles, green leatherbacks and rusty-brown loggerheads, big as tubs and floating languorously on the surface.

The wildness of the islands and sea had begun to purge her mind, her memory. Fresh mornings like this had come to seem harbingers of a new life as well as a new day, even as the quick, golden-hued sunsets promised Hugh's warm embrace.

After Barbados they'd made sail for Nevis Island, and as they neared the small log-and-clapboard English settlement along its southern shore, the skies had finally become crystalline and dry, heralding the end of the autumn rainy season. They lingered in the island's reef-bound harbor almost three weeks while Winston careened the *Defiance* and stripped away her barnacles, scorched the lower planks with burning branches to kill shipworm, then caulked all her leaky seams with hemp and pitch. Finally he'd laded in extra barrels of salt beef, biscuit, and fresh water. They were all but ready to weigh anchor the day a Dutch merchantman put in with word that the Commonwealth fleet had begun preparations to depart Barbados.

Why so soon, they puzzled. Where were Cromwell's warships bound for now?

Wherever the fleet's next destination, it scarcely mattered. The American rebellion was finished. After word spread through Nevis and St. Christopher that Barbados had capitulated, all the planters' talk of defiance evaporated. If the largest English settlement in the Americas could not stand firm, they reasoned, what chance did the small ones have? A letter pledging fealty to Commons was dispatched to the fleet by the Assembly of those two sister islands. That step taken, they hoped Calvert would bypass them with his hungry army and sail directly for

Virginia, whose blustering royalists everyone now expected to also yield without a murmur.

Still, after news came that the troops were readying to move out, Katherine had agreed with Winston that they shouldn't chance being surprised at Nevis. Who could tell when the Commonwealth's warships might suddenly show themselves on the southern horizon? The next morning they weighed anchor, heading north for the first two hundred leagues, then steering due west. That had been six days ago. . . .

"You're lookin' lovely this morning, m'lady." John Mewes' groggy voice broke the silence as he started awake, then rose and stretched and ambled across the quarterdeck toward the bannister where she stood. "I'd say there she is, sure as I'm a Christian." He was pointing south, in the direction of the dim horizon, where a grey-green land mass had emerged above the dark waters. "The pride of the Spaniards."

"What is it, John?"

"Why, that's apt to be none other than Hispaniola, Yor Ladyship. Plain as a pikestaff. An' right on schedule." He bellied against the bannister and yawned. "Doesn't look to have budged an inch since last I set eyes on her."

She smiled. "Then that must mean we're nearing Tortuga. By the map, I remember it's just off the north coast, around latitude twenty."

"Aye, we'll likely be raisin' the old 'Turtle' any time now. Though in truth I'd as soon never see the place again."

"Why do you say that?"

" 'Tis home and hearth of the finest assembly of thieves as you're ever like to cross this side of Newgate prison. An' that's the fact of the matter."

"Are you trying to make me believe you've actually been there, John?" She regarded him carefully. John Mewes, she had come to realize, was never at a loss for a story to share—though his distinction between truth and fancy was often imprecise.

"Aye, 'twas some years past, as the sayin' goes. When the merchantman I was quartermaster on put in for a week to careen.'' He spat into the sea and hitched up the belt on his breeches.

"What exactly was it like?"

"A brig out of Portsmouth. A beamy two master, with damn'd seams that'd opened on us wide as a Dutch whore's cunny—beggin' Yor Ladyship's pardon—which is why we had to put in to caulk her . . ."

"Tortuga, John."

"Aye, the Turtle. Like I was sayin', she's the Sodom of the Indies, make no mistake. Fair enough from afar, I grant you, but try and put in, an' you'll find out soon enough she's natural home for the rogue who'd as soon do without uninvited company. That's why that nest of pirates has been there so long right under the very nose of the pox-rotted Spaniards. Mind you, she's scarcely more than twenty or thirty miles tip to tip, but the north side's a solid cliff, lookin' down on the breakers, whilst the other's just about nothing save shallow flats an' mangrove thickets. There's only one bay where you can put in with a frigate, a spot called Basse Terre, there on the south—that is, if you can steer through the reefs that line both sides of the channel goin' into it. But once you're anchored, 'tis a passing good harbor, for it all. Fine sandy bottom, with draft that'll take a seventy-gun brig.''

"So that's how the Cow-Killers . . . the buccaneers have managed to keep the island? There's only one spot the Spaniards could try and land infantry, and to get there you've got to go through a narrow passage in the reefs, easy to cover with cannon?"

"I'd say that's about the size of it. No bottom drops anchor at Tortuga unless those rogues say you aye." He turned and began to secure a loose piece of line dangling from the shroud supporting the mizzenmast. "Then too there's your matter of location. You see, m'lady, the island lays right athwart the Windward Passage, betwixt Hispaniola and Cuba, which is one of the Spaniards' main shippin' lanes. Couldn't be handier if you're thinkin' to lighten a Papist merchantman now and again. . . ."

Mewes' voice trailed off as he glanced up to see Winston emerge at the head of the companionway, half asleep and still shirtless under his jerkin. Following after him was Atiba, wearing a pair of ill-fitting seaman's breeches, his bare shoulders glistening in the sun's early glow. When he spotted Mewes, he gave a solemn bow, Yoruba style.

"*Ku abo*, senhor."

"Aye, *qu ava* it is." Mewes nodded back, then turned to Katherine. "Now, for your edification that means 'greetings,' or such like. Since I've been teachin' him English, I've been pickin' up a few of the finer points of that African gabble of his, what with my natural gift for language."

"God's life, you are learning fastly, Senhor Mewes." Atiba smiled. "And since you are scholaring my tongue so well, mayhaps I should cut some of our clan marks on your mug, like mine. It is a damnable great ceremony of my country."

"Pox on your 'damnable great ceremonies.' " Mewes busied himself with the shroud. "I'll just keep my fine face the way it is, and thank you kindly all the same."

Winston sleepily kissed Katherine on the forehead. She gave him a long hug, then pointed toward the south. "John claims that's Hispaniola."

"One and the same. The queen of the Greater Antilles. Take a good look, Katy. I used to hunt cattle in those very woods. That mountain range over in mid-island means we should raise Tortuga any time now." He turned and began unlashing the whipstaff, then motioned Atiba forward. "Want to try the helm for a while? To get the feel of her?"

"My damnable shoulder is good, senhor. I can set a course with this stick, or cut by a sword, as better than ever."

"We'll see soon enough." He watched Atiba grasp the long hardwood lever and test it. "I just may need you along to help me reason with my old friend Jacques."

"Hugh, tell me some more about what he's like." Katherine

took another look at the hazy outline of Hispaniola, then moved alongside them.

"Jacques le Basque?" Winston smiled and thought back. Nobody knew where Jacques was from, or who he was. They were all refugees from some other place, and most went by assumed names—even he had been known simply as "Anglais." "I'd guess he's French, but I never really knew all that much about him, though we hunted side by side for a good five years." He thumbed toward the green mountains. "But I can tell you one thing for sure: Jacques le Basque created a new society on northern Hispaniola, and Tortuga."

"What do you mean?"

"Katy, you talked about having an independent nation in the Americas, a place not under the thumb of Europe? Well, he made one right over there. The *boucaniers* were a nation of sorts—shipwrecked seamen, runaway indentures, half of them with jail or a noose waiting in one of the other settlements. But any man alive was welcome to come and go as he liked."

Katherine examined his lined face. "Hugh, you told me you once tried to kill Jacques over some misunderstanding. But you never explained exactly what it was about."

Winston fell silent and the only sound was the lap of waves against the bow. Maybe, he told himself, the time has come. He took a deep breath and turned to her. "Remember how I told you the Spaniards came and burned out the Providence Company's English settlement on Tortuga? As it happened, I was over on Hispaniola with Jacques at the time or I probably wouldn't be here now. Well, the Spaniards stayed around for a week or so, and troubled to hang some of Jacques's lads who happened in with a load of hides. When we found out about it, he called a big parlay over what we ought to do. All the hunters came—French, English, even some Dutchmen. Every man there hated the Spaniards, and we decided to pull together what cannon were left and fortify the harbor at Basse Terre, in case they got a mind to come back."

"And?"

"Then after some time went by Jacques got the idea we ought not just wait for them. That we'd best try and take the fight back. So he sent word around the north side of Hispaniola that any man who wanted to help should meet him on Tortuga. When everybody got there, he announced we needed to be organized, like the Spaniards. Then he stove open a keg of brandy and christened us *Les Frères de la Côte*, the Brotherhood of the Coast. After we'd all had a tankard or two, he explained he wanted to try and take a Spanish ship."

"You mean he sort of declared war on Spain?"

"As a matter of fact, that's how it turned out." He smiled. "Jacques said we'd hunted the Spaniards' cattle long enough; now we would hunt the whoreson Spaniards themselves. We'd sail under our old name of *boucanier*, and he swore that before we were through nobody would remember the time it only meant cow hunters. We'd make it the most dreaded word a Spaniard could hear."

John Mewes was squinting toward the west now, past the bowsprit. Abruptly he secured a last knot in the shroud, then headed down the companionway and past the seamen loitering by the mainmast.

"And that was the beginning? When the Cow-Killers became sea rovers and pirates?" For some reason the story made her vaguely uneasy. "You were actually there? A part of it?"

"I was there." Winston paused to watch Mewes.

"So then you . . . joined them?"

"No particular reason not to. The damned Spaniards had just murdered some of ours, Katy, not to mention about six hundred English settlers. I figured why not give them a taste back? Besides, it looked to be the start of a grand adventure. We got together as many arms as we could muster, muskets and axes, and put to sea. Us against the Spaniards . . ."

"Cap'n, care to come forward an' have a look?" Mewes was pointing at the dark green hump that had just appeared on the horizon. "That looks to be her, if I'm not amiss."

Winston turned to study the sea ahead of them. Just above the surface of the sea was the tip of a large hump, deep green like a leatherback turtle.

"Aye. Maybe you'd best order all hands to station for the afternoon watch, John." He reached back and kissed Katherine lightly. "Katy, the rest of this little tale will have to wait. We've got to get ready now. In truth, I don't exactly know how pleased my old friend Jacques is going to be seeing me again after all these years."

As she watched him head down the companionway, she felt a curious mixture of excitement and unease. Now, all at once, she was wondering if she really did want to know what Hugh had been like back then. Perhaps, she told herself, there are some things better just forgotten.

"*Bon soir,* Capitaine." A young man carrying a candle-lantern was standing at the water's edge to greet their longboat as Winston, John Mewes, and Atiba, backed by five seamen with flintlocks, rowed in to the shallows. "Tibaut de Fontenay, *à votre service, Messieurs.* We spotted your mast lights from up at the *Forte.* Since you seemed to know the reefs, we assumed you had been here before. So you are welcome."

He appeared to be in his early twenties and was attired lavishly—a plumed hat topped his long curls, his long velvet waistcoat was parted rakishly to display an immaculate white cravat, and high, glistening boots shaped his calves. The dull glow of the lantern illuminated an almost obsequious grin.

Around them the dark outlines of a dozen frigates nodded in the light swell, while lines of foam, sparkling in the moonlight, chased up the shore. The *Defiance* had been the last vessel to navigate Basse Terre's narrow channel of reefs before the quick Caribbean dusk descended.

"The name is Winston. Master of the *Defiance.*" He slid over the gunwale of the longboat and waded through the light surf. "Late of Barbados and Nevis."

432

"Bienvenue." The man examined him briefly, then smiled again as he extended his hand and quickly shifted to heavily-accented English. "Your affairs, Capitaine, are of course no concern to us here. Any man who comes in peace is welcome at La Tortue, in the name of His Majesty, King Louis Quatorze of France."

"What the devil!" Winston drew back his hand and stared up at the lantern-lit assemblage of taverns along the shore. "Tortuga is French now?"

"Mais oui, for the better part of a year. The *gouverneur* of St. Christophe—the French side—found it necessary to dispatch armed frigates and take this island under his authority. The Anglais *engagés* planting here were sent on their way; they are fortunate we did not do worse. But ships of all nations are always invited to trade for our fine hides, brasil wood for making dye, and the most succulent *viande fumèe* you will taste this side of Paris." He bowed lightly, debonairly. "Or Londres. We also have a wide assortment of items in Spanish gold for sale here—and we have just received a shipload of lovely mademoiselles from Marseilles to replace the diseased English whores who had come near to ruining this port's reputation."

"We don't need any provisions, and we don't have time for any entertainment this stop. The *Defiance* is just passing through, bound for the Windward Passage. I'd thought to put in for tonight and have a brandy with an old friend. Jacques le Basque. Know if he's around?"

"My master?" The man quickly raised his lantern to scrutinize Winston's face. "He does not normally receive visitors at the *Forte,* but you may send him your regards through me. I will be happy to tell him a Capitaine Winston . . ."

"What in hell are you talking about? What 'fort' is that?"

"Forte de la Roche, 'the fort on the rock,' up there." He turned to point through the dark. On a hill overlooking the harbor a row of torches blazed, illuminating a battery of eighteen-pound culverin set above a high stone breastwork.

"When was *that* built? It wasn't here before."

433

"Only last year, Capitaine. Part of our new fortifications. It is the residence of our *commandant de place.*"

"Your *commandant* . . ." Winston stopped dead still. "You've got a governor here now?"

"*Oui.*" He smiled. "In fact, you are fortunate. He is none other than your friend Jacques. He was appointed to the post last year by the Chevalier de Poncy of St. Christophe, administrator of all our French settlements in the Caribbean." He examined the men in the longboat, his glance anxiously lingering on Atiba, who had a shiny new cutlass secured at his waist. "May I take it you knew Jacques well?"

"I knew him well enough in the old days, back before he arranged to have himself appointed governor. But then I see times have changed."

"Many things have changed here, Capitaine."

"I'll say they have." Winston signaled for Atiba to climb out of the longboat. "But my friend and I are going up to this 'Forte' and pay a visit to Commandant le Basque, and you can save your messages and diplomatic papers. He knows who I am."

De Fontenay stiffened, not quite sure how to reply. As he did, a band of seamen emerged out of the dark and came jostling down the sandy shore toward them, carrying candle-lanterns and tankards and singing an English chantey with convivial relish.

> ". . . We took aboard the Captain's daughter,
> And gave her fire 'twixt wind and water . . ."

Several were in pairs, their arms about each other's shoulders. All were garbed in a flamboyant hodgepodge of European fashions—gold rings and medallions, stolen from the passengers of Spanish merchant frigates, glistened in the lantern light. Most wore fine leather sea boots; a few were barefoot.

The man at their head was carrying a large keg. When he

spotted the bobbing longboat, he motioned the procession to a halt, tossed the keg onto the sand, and sang out an invitation.

"Welcome to you, masters. There's a virgin pipe of Spanish brandy here we're expectin' to violate. We'd not take it amiss if you'd help us to our work."

He drew a pistol from his belt and swung its gold-trimmed butt against the wooden stopper in the bunghole, knocking it inward.

"*No*, Monsieur. *Merci. Bien des remerciements.*" De Fontenay's voice betrayed a faint quaver. "I regret we have no time. I and my good friend, the Anglais here . . ."

"I wasn't asking *you* to drink, you arse-sucking French pimp." The man with the pistol scowled as he recognized de Fontenay. "I'd not spare you the sweat off my bollocks if you were adyin' of thirst." He turned toward Winston. "But you and your lads are welcome, sir, whoever you might be. I'll wager no honest Englishman ever declined a cup in good company. My name is Guy Bartholomew, and if you know anything of this place, you'll not have to be told I'm master of the *Swiftsure*, the finest brig in this port."

Winston examined him in the flickering light. Yes, it was Guy Bartholomew all right. He'd been one of the original *boucaniers*, and he'd hated Jacques from the first.

"Permit me to introduce Capitaine Winston of the *Defiance*, Messieurs." De Fontenay tried to ignore Bartholomew's pistol. "He has asked me personally to . . ."

"Winston? The *Defiance*? God's wounds." Bartholomew doffed his black hat. "Let me drink to your good health, Captain." He paused to fill his tankard with the dark brown liquid spilling from the keg, then hoisted it in an impromptu toast.

"You don't remember me from before, Bartholomew? Back on Hispaniola?"

The *boucanier* stared at him drunkenly. "No, sir. I can't rightly say as I do. But yours is a name known well enough in this part of the world, that's for certain. You wouldn't be planning to do a bit of sailing from this port, would you now? 'Twould be a pleasure to have you amongst us."

"Monsieur," De Fontenay was edging on up the hill, "Capitaine Winston is a personal friend of our *commandant*, and we must . . ."

"A friend of Jacques?" Bartholomew studied Winston's face. "I'd not believe any such damn'd lies and calumnies of an honest Englishman like you, sir."

"I knew him many years past, Bartholomew. I hope he remembers me better than you do. Though I'm not sure he still considers me a friend after our little falling out."

"Well, sir, I can tell you this much. Things have changed mightily since the old days. Back then he only stole from the pox-eaten Spaniards. Now he and that French bastard de Poncy rob us all. They take a piece of all the Spaniards' booty we bring in, and then Jacques demands another ten percent for himself, as his 'landing fee.' He even levies a duty on all the hides the hunters bring over from Hispaniola to sell."

De Fontenay glared. "There must always be taxes, anywhere. Jacques is *commandant* now, and the Chevalier de Poncy has . . ."

"Commandant?" Bartholomew snorted. "My lads have another name for him, sir. If he ever dared come down here and meet us, the Englishmen in this port would draw lots to see who got the pleasure of cutting his throat. He knows we can't sail from any other settlement. It's only because he's got those guns up there at the fort, covering the bay, and all his damned guards, that he's not been done away with long before now." He turned back to Winston. "The bastard's made himself a dungeon up there beneath the rock, that he calls Purgatory. Go against him and that's where you end up. Few men have walked out of it alive, I'll tell you that."

De Fontenay shifted uneasily and toyed with a curl. "Purgatory will not be there forever, I promise you."

"So you say. But you may just wind up there yourself one day soon, sir, and then we'll likely hear you piping a different tune. Even though you are his *matelot*, which I'll warrant might more properly be called his whore.''

"What I am to Jacques is no affair of yours.''

"Aye, I suppose the goings-on in the fort are not meant to be known to the honest ships' masters in this port. But we still have eyes, sir, for all that. I know you're hoping that after Jacques is gone, that Frenchman de Poncy will make you *commandant* of this place, this stinking piss-hole. Just because the Code of the *boucaniers* makes you Jacques' heir. But it'll not happen, sir, by my life. Never.''

"Monsieur, enough. *Suffit!*'' De Fontenay spat out the words, then turned back to Winston. "Shall we proceed up to the Forte?'' He gestured toward the hill ahead. "Or do you intend to stay and spend the night talking with these Anglais *cochons?*''

"My friend, do beware of that old bastard.'' Bartholomew caught Winston's arm, and his voice grew cautionary. "God Almighty, I could tell you such tales. He's daft as a loon these days. I'd be gone from this place in a minute if I could just figure how.''

"He tried to kill me once, Master Bartholomew, in a little episode you might recall if you set your mind to it. But I'm still around.'' Winston nodded farewell, then turned back toward the longboat. John Mewes sat nervously waiting, a flintlock across his lap. "John, take her on back and wait for us. Atiba's coming with me. And no shore leave for anybody till morning.''

"Aye.'' Mewes eyed the drunken seamen as he shoved off. "See you mind yourself, Cap'n. I'll expect you back by sunrise or I'm sendin' the lads to get you.''

"Till then.'' Winston gestured Atiba to move alongside him, then turned back to De Fontenay. "Shall we go.''

"*Avec plaisir*, Capitaine. These Anglais who sail for us can be most *dangereux* when they have had so much brandy.'' The young Frenchman paused as he glanced uncertainly at Atiba. The tall African towered by Winston's side. "Will your . . . *gentilhomme de service* be accompanying you?''

"He's with me."

"*Bon.*" He cleared his throat. "As you wish."

He lifted his lantern and, leaving Bartholomew's men singing on the shore, headed up the muddy, torch-lit roadway leading between the cluster of taverns that comprised the heart of Basse Terre's commercial center.

"How long has it been since you last visited us, Capitaine?" De Fontenay glanced back. "I have been *matelot* to Jacques for almost three years, but I don't recall the pleasure of welcoming you before this evening."

"It's been a few years. Back before Jacques became governor."

"Was this your home once, senhor?" Atiba was examining the shopfronts along the street, many displaying piles of silks and jewelry once belonging to the passengers on Spanish merchantmen. Along either side, patched-together taverns and brothels spilled their cacophony of songs, curses, and raucous fiddle music into the muddy paths that were streets.

Winston laughed. "Well, it was scarcely like *this*. There used to be thatched huts along here and piles of hides and smoked beef ready for barter. All you could find to drink in those days was a tankard of cheap kill-devil. But the main difference is the fort up there, which is a noticeable improvement over that rusty set of culverin we used to have down along the shore."

"I gather it must have been a very long time ago, Monsieur, that you were last here." De Fontenay was moving hurriedly past the rickety taverns, heading straight for the palm-lined road leading up the hill to the fort.

"Probably some ten years or so."

"Then I wonder if Jacques will still remember you."

Winston laughed. "I expect he does."

De Fontenay started purposefully up the road. About six hundred yards from the shoreline the steep slope of a hill began. The climb was long and tortuous, and the young Frenchman was breathing heavily by the time they were halfway up.

"This place is damnable strong, senhor. Very hard to attack, even with guns." Atiba shifted the cutlass in his belt and peered up the hill, toward the line of torches. He was moving easily, his bare feet molding to the rough rock steps.

"It could never be stormed from down below, that much is sure." Winston glanced back. "But we're not here to try and take this place. He can keep Tortuga and bleed it dry for all I care. I'll just settle for some of those men I saw tonight. If they want to part company with him . . ."

"Those whoresons are not lads who fight. They are drunkards."

"They can fight as well as they drink." Winston smiled. "Don't let the brandy fool you."

"Your *brancos* are a damnable curiosity, senhor." He grunted. "I am waiting to see how my peoples here live, the slaves."

"The *boucaniers* don't cut cane, so they don't have slaves."

"Then mayhaps I will drink with them."

"You'd best hold that till after we're finished with Jacques, my friend." Winston glanced up toward the fort. "Just keep your cutlass handy."

They had reached the curving row of steps that led through the arched gateway of the fortress. Above them a steep wall of cut stone rose up against the dark sky, and across the top, illuminated by torches, was the row of culverin. Sentries armed with flintlocks, in helmets and flamboyant Spanish coats, barred the gateway till de Fontenay waved them aside. Then guards inside unbolted the iron gate and they moved up the final stairway.

Winston realized the fort had been built on a natural plateau, with terraces inside the walls which would permit several hundred musketmen to fire unseen down on the settlement below. From somewhere in the back he could hear the gurgle of a spring—meaning a supply of fresh water, one of the first requirements of a good fortress.

Jacques had found a natural redoubt and fortified it brilliantly. All the settlement and the harbor now were under his guns. Only the mountain behind, a steep precipice, had any vantage over Forte de la Roche.

"Senhor, what is that?" Atiba was pointing toward the massive boulder, some fifty feet wide and thirty feet high, that rested in the center of the yard as though dropped there by the hand of God.

Winston studied it, puzzling, then noticed a platform atop the rock, with several cannon projecting out. A row of brick steps led halfway up the side, then ended abruptly. When they reached the base, de Fontenay turned back.

"The citadel above us is Jacques's personal residence, what he likes to call his 'dovecote.' It will be necessary for you to wait here while I ask him to lower the ladder."

"The ladder?"

"*Mais oui*, a security measure. No one is allowed up there without his consent."

He called up, identified himself, and after a pause the first rungs of a heavy iron ladder appeared through an opening in the platform. Slowly it began to be lowered toward the last step at the top of the stair.

Again de Fontenay hesitated. "Perhaps it might be best if I go first, Messieurs. Jacques is not fond of surprises."

"He never was." Winston motioned for Atiba to stay close.

De Fontenay hung his lantern on a brass spike at the side of the stairs, then turned and lightly ascended the rungs. From the platform above, two musketmen covered his approach with flint-locks. He saluted them, then disappeared.

As Winston waited, Atiba at his side, he heard a faint human voice, a low moaning sound, coming from somewhere near their feet. He looked down and noticed a doorway at the base of the rock, leading into what appeared to be an excavated chamber. The door was of thick hewn logs with only a small grate in its center.

Was that, he wondered, the dungeon Bartholomew called Purgatory?

Suddenly he felt an overwhelming sense of anger and betrayal at what Jacques had become. Whatever else he might have been, this was the man whose name once stood for freedom. And now . . .

He was turning to head down and inspect Purgatory first-hand when a welcome sounded from the platform above.

"*Mon ami! Bienvenue,* Anglais. *Mon Dieu, il y a très long-temps!* A good ten years, *n'est-ce pas?*" A bearded face peered down, while a deep voice roared with pleasure. "Perhaps you've finally learned something about how to shoot after all this time. Come up and let me have a look at you."

"And maybe you've improved your aim, Jacques. Your last pistol ball didn't get you a hide." Winston turned back and reached for the ladder.

"*Oui,* truly it did not, Anglais. How near did I come?" He extended a rough hand as Winston emerged.

"Close enough." Winston stepped onto the platform of the citadel.

In the flickering torchlight he recognized the old leader of the *boucaniers,* now grown noticeably heavier; his thick beard, once black as onyx, was liberally threaded with white. He sported a ruffled doublet of red silk and had stuffed his dark calico breeches into bucket-top sea boots of fine Spanish leather. The gold rings on several fingers glistened with jewels, and the squint in his eyes was deep and malevolent.

Le Basque embraced Winston, then drew back and studied his scar. "*Mon Dieu,* so I came closer than I thought. *Mes condoléances.* I must have been sleepy that morning. I'd fully intended to take your head."

"How about some of your French brandy, you old *bâtard?* For me and my friend. By the look of things, I'd say you can afford it."

"*Vraiment.* Brandy for the Anglais . . . and his friend." The *boucanier* nodded warily as he saw Atiba appear at the top of the ladder. After a moment's pause, he laughed again, throatily. "Truly I can afford *anything.* The old days are over. I'm rich. Many a Spaniard has paid for what they did to us back then."

He turned and barked an order to de Fontenay. The young man bowed, then moved smoothly through the heavy oak doors leading into Jacques's residence. "You know, I still hear of you from time to time, Anglais. But never before have we seen you here, *n'est-ce pas?* How have you been?"

"Well enough. I see you've been busy yourself." Winston glanced up at the brickwork house Jacques had erected above the center of the rock. It was a true citadel. Along the edge of the platform, looking out, a row of nine-pound demi-culverin had been installed. "But what's this talk you chased off the English planters?"

"They annoyed me. You know that never was wise. So I decided to be rid of them. Besides, it's better this way. A few were permitted to stay on and sail for me, but La Tortue must be French." He reached for a tankard from the tray de Fontenay was offering. "I persuaded our *gouverneur* up on St. Christophe to send down a few frigates to help me secure this place."

"Is that why you keep men in a dungeon up here? We never had such things in the old days."

"My little Purgatory?" He handed the tankard to Winston, then offered one to Atiba. The Yoruba eyed him coldly and waved it away. Jacques shrugged, taking a sip himself before continuing. "Surely you understand the need for discipline. If these men disobey me, they must be dealt with. Otherwise, no one remembers who is in charge of this place."

"I thought we'd planned to just punish the Spaniards, not each other."

"But we are, Anglais, we *are*. Remember when I declared they would someday soil their breeches whenever they heard the word *'boucanier'*? Well, it's come true. They swear using my name. Half the time the craven bastards are too terrified to cock a musket when my men board one of their merchant frigates." He smiled. "Everything we wanted back then has come to pass. Sweet revenge." He reached and absently drew a finger down de Fontenay's arm. "But tell me, Anglais, have you got a woman these days? Or a *matelot?*" He studied Atiba.

"An Englishwoman is sailing with me. She's down on the *Defi*ance."

"The *Defiance?*"

"My Spanish brig."

"*Oui,* but of course. I heard how you acquired it." He laughed and stroked his beard. "*Alors,* tomorrow you must bring this *Anglaise* of yours up and let me meet her. Show her how your old friend has made his way in the world."

"That depends. I thought we'd empty a tankard or two tonight and talk a bit."

"*Bon.* Nothing better." He signaled to de Fontenay for a refill, and the young man quickly stepped forward with the flask. "Tonight we remember old times."

Winston laughed. "Could be there're a few things about the old days we'd best let be. So maybe I'll just work on this fine brandy of yours and hear how you're getting along these days with our good friends the Spaniards."

"Ah, *Anglais,* we get on very well. I have garroted easily a hundred of those bastards for every one of ours they killed back then, and taken enough cargo to buy a kingdom. You know, if their Nuevo Espana Armada, the one that ships home silver from their mines in Mexico, is a week overdue making the Canary Islands, the King of Spain and all his creditors from Italy to France cannot shit for worrying I might have taken it. Someday, my friend, I will."

"Good. I'll drink to it." Winston lifted his tankard. "To the Spaniards."

Jacques laughed. "*Oui.* And may they always be around to keep me rich."

"On that subject, old friend, I had a little project in mind. I was thinking maybe I'd borrow a few of your lads and stage a raid on a certain Spanish settlement."

"*Anglais,* why would you want to bother? Believe me when I tell you there's not a town on the Main I could not take tomorrow if I choose. But they're mostly worthless." He drank again, then rose and strolled over to the edge of the platform.

443

Below, mast lights were speckled across the harbor, and music drifted up from the glowing tavern windows. "By the time you get into one, the Spaniards have carried everything they own into the forest and emptied the place."

"I'll grant you that. But did you ever consider taking one of their islands? Say . . . Jamaica?"

"*Mon ami*, the rewards of an endeavor must justify the risk." Jacques strolled back and settled heavily into a deep leather chair. "What's over there? Besides their militia?"

"They've got a fortress and a town, Villa de la Vega, and there's bound to be a bit of coin, maybe even some plate. But the harbor's the real . . ."

"*Oui, peut-être.* Perhaps there's a *sou* or two to be had there somewhere. But why trouble yourself with a damned militia when there're merchantmen plying the Windward Passage day in and day out, up to their gunwales with plate, pearls from their oyster beds down at Margarita, even silks shipped overland from those Manila galleons that put in at Acapulco . . . ?"

"You know an English captain named Jackson took that fortress a few years back, and ransomed it for twenty thousand pieces-of-eight? That's a hundred and sixty thousand *reals.*"

"Anglais, I also know very well they have a battery of guns in that fort, covering the harbor. It wouldn't be all that simple to storm."

"As it happens, I've taken on a pilot who knows that harbor better than you know the one right down below, and I'm thinking I might sail over and see it." Winston took another swallow. "You're welcome to send along some men if you like. I'll split any metal money and plate with them."

"Forget it, Anglais. None of these men will . . ."

"Wait a minute, Jacques. You don't own them. That was never the way. So if some of these lads decide to sail with me, that's their own affair."

"My friend, why do you think I am the *commandant de place* if I do not command? Have you seen those culverin just below us, trained on the bay? No frigate enters Basse Terre—or leaves

444

it against my will. Even yours, *mon ami*. Don't lose sight of that.''

"I thought you were getting smarter than you used to be, Jacques."

"Don't try and challenge me again, Anglais." Jacques's hand had edged slowly toward the pistol in his belt, but then he glanced at Atiba and hesitated. "Though it's not my habit to kill a man while he's drinking my brandy." He smiled suddenly, breaking the tension, and leaned back. "It might injure my reputation for hospitality."

"When I'm in the fortress overlooking Jamaica Bay one day soon, I'll try and remember to drink your health."

"You really think you can do it, don't you?" He sobered and studied Winston.

"It's too easy not to. But I told you we could take it as partners, together."

"Anglais, I'm not a fool. You don't have the men to manage it alone. So you're hoping I'll give you some of mine."

"I don't want you to 'give' me anything, you old whoremaster. I said we would take it together."

"Forget it. I have better things to do." He smiled. "But all the same, it's always good to see an old friend again. Stay a while, Anglais. What if tomorrow night we feasted like the old days, *boucanier* style? Why not show your *femme* how we used to live?"

"Jacques, we've got victuals on the *Defiance.*"

"Is that what you think of me?" He sighed. "That I would forgo this chance to relive old times? Bring this *petite* Anglaise of yours up and let her meet your old *ami*. I knew you before you were sure which end of a musket to prime. I watched you bring down your first wild boar. And now, when I welcome you and yours with open arms, you scorn my generosity."

"We're not finished with this matter of the Spaniards, my friend."

"*Certainement.* Perhaps I will give it some consideration. We can think about it tomorrow night, while we all share some

445

brandy and dine on *barbacoa*, same as the old days. As long as I breathe, nothing else will ever taste quite so good." He motioned for de Fontenay to lower the iron ladder. "We will remember the way we used to live. In truth, I even think I miss it at times. Life was simpler then."

"Things don't seem so simple around here any more, Jacques."

"But we can remember, my friend. Humility. It nourishes the soul."

"To old times then, Jacques." He drained his tankard and signaled for Atiba. "Tomorrow."

"Oui, Anglais. *A demain.* And my regards to your friend here with the cutlass." He smiled as he watched them start down the ladder. "But why don't you ask him to stay down there tomorrow? I must be getting old, because that sword of his is starting to make me nervous. And we wouldn't want anything to upset our little *fête*, now would we, *mon frère?"*

Katherine stood at the bannister amidships, Serina by her side, and studied the glimmer of lights along the shore, swaying clusters of candle-lanterns as seamen passed back and forth in longboats between the brothels of Tortuga and their ships.

The buccaneers. They lived in a world like none she had ever seen. As the shouts, curses, songs, and snatches of music drifted out over the gentle surf, she had to remind herself that this raffish settlement was the home of brigands unwelcome in any other place. Yet from her vantage now, they seemed like harmless, jovial children.

Still, anchored alongside the *Defiance* were some of the most heavily armed brigantines in the New World—no bottom here carried fewer than thirty guns. The men, too, were murderers, who killed Spanish civilians as readily as infantry. Jacques le Basque presided over the most dreaded naval force in the New World. He had done more to endanger Spain's fragile economy than all the Protestant countries together. If they grew any stronger, the few hundred men on this tiny island might well so disrupt Spain's vital lifeline of silver from the Americas as to bankrupt what once had been Europe's mightiest empire.

The report of a pistol sounded from somewhere along the shore, followed by yells of glee and more shots. Several men in Spanish finery had begun firing into the night to signal the commencement of an impromptu celebration. As they marched around a keg of liquor, a cluster of women, prostitutes from the taverns, shrieked in drunken encouragement and joined in the melee.

"This place is very frightening, senhora." Serina shivered and edged next to Katherine. Her hair was tied in a kerchief, African style, as it had been for all the voyage. "I have never seen *branco* like these. They seem so crazy, so violent."

"Just be thankful we're not Spaniards, or we'd find out just how violent they really are."

"Remember I once lived in Brazil. We heard stories about this place."

" 'Tis quite a sight, Yor Ladyships." John Mewes had ambled over to the railing, beside them, to watch for Winston. "The damnedest crew of rogues and knaves you're ever like to make acquaintance with. Things've come to a sad pass that we've got to try recruitin' some of this lot to sail with us."

"Do you think they're safe ashore, John?"

"Aye, Yor Ladyship, on that matter I'd not trouble yourself unduly." Mewes fingered the musket he was holding. "You should've seen him once down at Curaçao, when a gang o' Dutch shippers didn't like the cheap price we was askin' for a load of kill-devil that'd fallen our way over at . . . I forget where. Threatened to board and scuttle us. So the Captain and me decided we'd hoist a couple of nine-pound demi's up on deck and stage a little gunnery exercise on a buoy floatin' there on the windward side o' the harbor. After we'd laid it with a couple of rounds, blew it to hell, next thing you know the Butterboxes . . ."

"John, what's that light over there? Isn't that him?"

Mewes paused and stared. At the shoreline opposite their anchorage a lantern was flashing.

"Aye, m'lady. That's the signal, sure enough." He smiled. "Didn't I tell you there'd be nothing to worry over." With an exhale of relief, he quickly turned and ordered the longboat lowered, assigning four men to the oars and another four to bring flintlocks.

The longboat lingered briefly in the surf at the shore, and moments later Winston and Atiba were headed back toward the ship.

"It seems they are safe, senhora." Serina was still watching with worried eyes. "Perhaps these *branco* are better than those on Barbados."

"Well, I don't think they have slaves, if that's what you mean. But that's about all you can say for them."

A few moments later the longboat bumped against the side of the *Defiance,* and Winston was pulling himself over the bulwarks, followed by Atiba.

"Katy, break out the tankards. I think we can deal with Jacques." He offered her a hug. "He's gone half mad—taken over the island and run off the English settlers. But there're plenty of English *boucaniers* here who'd like nothing better than to sail from somewhere else."

"Did he agree to help us?"

"Of course not. You've got to know him. It's just what I expected. When I brought up our little idea, he naturally refused point-blank. But he knows there're men here who'll join us if they like. Which means that tomorrow he'll claim it was his idea all along, then demand the biggest part of what we take for himself."

"Tomorrow?"

"I'm going back up to the fort, around sunset, to sort out details."

"I wish you wouldn't." She took his hand. "Why don't we just get whatever men we can manage and leave?"

448

"That'd mean a fight." He kissed her lightly. "Don't worry. I'll handle Jacques. We just have to keep our wits."

"Well then, I want to go with you."

"As a matter of fact he did ask you to come. But that's out of the question."

"It's just as dangerous for you as for me. If you're going back, then so am I."

"Katy, no . . ."

"Hugh, we've done everything together this far. So if you want to get men from this place, then I'll help you. And if that means I have to flatter this insane criminal, so be it."

He regarded her thoughtfully, then smiled. "Well, in truth I'm not sure a woman can still turn his head, but I suppose you can give it a try."

Serina approached them and reached to touch Winston's hand. "Senhor, was your council of war a success?"

"I think so. All things in time."

"The *branco* in this place are very strange. Is it true they do not have slaves?"

"Slaves, no. Though they do have a kind of servant here, but even that's different from Barbados."

"How so, senhor?"

"Well, there've never been many women around this place. So in the old days a *boucanier* might acquire a *matelot*, to be his companion, and over the years the *matelots* got to be more like younger brothers than indentures. They have legal rights of inheritance, for instance, since most *boucaniers* have no family. A *boucanier* and his *matelot* are legally entitled to the other's property if one of them dies." He looked back toward the shore. "Also, no man has more than one *matelot*. In fact, if a *boucanier* does marry a woman, his *matelot* has conjugal rights to her too."

"But, senhor, if the younger man, the *matelot*, inherits everything, what is to keep him from just killing the older man? To gain his freedom, and also the other man's property?"

"Honor." He shrugged and leaned back against the railing,

inhaling the dense air of the island. He lingered pensively for a moment, then turned to Katherine. "Katy, do remember this isn't just any port. Some of those men out there have been known to shoot somebody for no more cause than a tankard of brandy. And underneath it all, Jacques is just like the rest. It's when he's most cordial that you'd best beware."

"I still want to go." She moved next to him. "I'm going to meet face-to-face with this madman who once tried to kill you."

Chapter Twenty-one

The ochre half-light of dusk was settling over the island, lending a warm tint to the deep green of the hillside forests surrounding Forte de la Roche. In the central yard of the fortress, directly beneath le Basque's "dovecote," his uniformed guards loitered alongside the row of heavy culverin, watching the mast lights of anchored frigates and brigantines nod beneath the cloudless sky.

Tibaut de Fontenay had taken no note of the beauty of the evening. He was busy tending the old-fashioned *boucan* Jacques had ordered constructed just behind the cannon. Though he stood on the windward side, he still coughed occasionally from the smoke that threaded upward, over the "dovecote" and toward the hill above. The *boucan* itself consisted of a rectangular wooden frame supporting a greenwood grill, set atop four forked posts. Over the frame and grill a thatchwork of banana leaves had been erected to hold in the piquant smoke of the smoldering naseberry branches beneath. Several haunches of beef lay flat on the grill, and now the fire was coating them with a succulent red veneer. It was the traditional Taino Indian method of cooking and preserving meat, *barbacoa*, that had been adopted intact by the *boucaniers* decades before.

Jacques leaned against the railing at the edge of the platform above, pewter tankard in hand, contentedly stroking his salt-and-pepper beard as he gazed out over the harbor and the multihued sunset that washed his domain in misty ambers. Finally, he turned with a murmur of satisfaction and beckoned for Katherine to join him. She glanced uneasily toward Winston, then moved to his side.

"The aroma of the *boucan,* Mademoiselle, was always the signal the day was ending." He pointed across the wide bay, toward the green mountains of Hispaniola. "Were we over there tonight, with the hunters, we would still be scraping the last of the hides now, while our *boucan* finished curing the day's kill for storing in our banana-leaf *ajoupa.*" He smiled warmly, then glanced down to see if her tankard required attention. "Though, of course, we never had such a charming *Anglaise* to leaven our rude company."

"I should have thought, Monsieur le Basque, you might have preferred a Frenchwoman." Katherine studied him, trying to imagine the time when he and Hugh had roamed the forests together. Jacques le Basque, for all his rough exterior, conveyed an unsettling sensuality. She sensed his desire for her as he stood alongside, and when he brushed her hand, she caught herself trembling involuntarily.

"You do me an injustice, Mademoiselle, to suggest I would even attempt passing such a judgment." He laughed. "For me, womankind is like a garden, whose flowers each have their own beauty. Where is the man who could be so dull as to waste a single moment comparing the deep hue of the rose to the delicate pale of the lily. The petals of each are soft, they both open invitingly at the touch."

"Do they always open so easily, Monsieur le Basque?"

"Please, you must call me Jacques." He brushed back a wisp of her hair and paused to admire her face in the light of the sunset. "It is ever a man's duty to awaken the beauty that lies sleeping in a woman's body. Too many exquisite creatures never realize how truly lovely they are."

"Do those lovely creatures include handsome boys as

452

well?'' She glanced down at de Fontenay, his long curls lying tangled across his delicate shoulders.

Jacques drank thoughtfully from his tankard. ''Mademoiselle, there is something of beauty in all God's work. What can a man know of wine if he samples only one vineyard?''

''A woman might say, Jacques, it depends on whether you prefer flowers, or wine.''

''*Touché*, Mademoiselle. But some of us have a taste for all of life. Our years here are so brief.''

As she stood beside him, she became conscious again of the short-barreled flintlock—borrowed from Winston's sea chest, without his knowing it—she had secreted in the waist of her petticoat, just below her low-cut bodice. Now it seemed so foolish. Why had Hugh painted Jacques as erratic and dangerous? Could it be because the old *boucanier* had managed to better him in that pistol duel they once had, and he'd never quite lived it down? Maybe that was why he never seemed to get around to explaining what really happened that time.

''Then perhaps you'll tell me how many of those years you spent hunting.'' She abruptly turned and gestured toward the hazy shoreline across the bay. Seen through the smoke of the *boucan* below, Hispaniola's forests seemed endless, impenetrable. ''Over there, on the big island?''

''Ah, Mademoiselle, thinking back now it seems like forever. Perhaps it *was* almost that long.'' He laughed genially, then glanced toward Winston, standing at the other end of the platform, and called out, ''Anglais, shall we tell your lovely mademoiselle something about the way we lived back in the old days?''

''You can tell her anything you please, Jacques, just take care it's true.'' Winston was studying the fleet of ships in the bay below. ''Remember this is our evening for straight talk.''

''Then I will try not to make it sound too romantic.'' Jacques chuckled and turned back. ''Since the Anglais insists I must be precise, I should begin by admitting it was a some-

453

what difficult existence, Mademoiselle. We'd go afield for weeks at a time, usually six or eight of us together in a party— to protect ourselves should we blunder across some of the Spaniards' lancers, cavalry who roamed the island trying to be rid of us. In truth, we scarcely knew where we would bed down from one day to the next. . . ."

Winston was only half listening as he studied the musket-men in the yard below. There seemed to be a restlessness, perhaps even a tension, about them. Was it the *boucan?* The bother of the smoke? Or was it something more? Some treachery in the making? He told himself to stay alert, that this was no time to be lulled by Jacques's famed courtliness. It could have been a big mistake not to bring Atiba, in spite of Jacques's demand he be left.

"On most days we would rise at dawn, prime our muskets, then move out to scout for game. Usually one of us went ahead with the dogs. Before the Anglais came to live with us, that perilous assignment normally fell to me, since I had the best aim." He lifted the onion-flask of French brandy from the side of the veranda and replenished her tankard with a smooth flourish. "When you stalk the wild bull, the *taureau sauvage,* you'd best be able to bring him down with the first shot, or hope there's a stout tree nearby to climb." He smiled and thumbed toward Winston. "But after the Anglais joined us, we soon all agreed he should have the honor of going first with the dogs. We had discovered he was a born marksman." He toasted Winston with his tankard. "When the dogs had a wild bull at bay, the Anglais would dispatch it with his musket. Afterwards, one of our men would stay to butcher it and take the hide while the rest of us would move on, following him."

"Then what?" She never knew before that Winston had actually been the leader of the hunt, their marksman.

"Well, Mademoiselle, after the Anglais had bagged a bull for every man, we'd bring all the meat and hides back to the base camp, the *rendezvous.* Then we would put up a *boucan,* like the one down there below us now, and begin smoking the meat while we finished scraping the hides." He smiled through his graying beard. "You would scarcely have recognized the Anglais, or me, in those days, Mademoiselle. Half the time our breeches were so caked with blood they looked like we'd been tarred." He glanced back at the island. "By nightfall the *barbacoa* would be finished, and we would eat some, then salt the rest and put it away in an *ajoupa*, together with the hides. Finally, we'd bed down beside the fire of the *boucan,* to smoke away the mosquitoes, sleeping in those canvas sacks we used to keep off ants. Then, at first light of dawn, we rose to go out again."

"And then you would sell your . . . *barbacoa* and hides here on Tortuga?"

"Exactly, Mademoiselle. I see my old friend the Anglais has already told you something of those days." He smiled and caught her eye. "Yes, often as not we'd come back over here and barter with the ships that put in to refit. But then sometimes we'd just sell them over there. When we had a load, we would start watching for a sail, and if we saw a ship nearing the coast, we'd paddle out in our canoes . . ."

"Canoes?" She felt the night grow chill. Suddenly a memory from long ago welled up again, bearded men firing on their ship, her mother falling. . . .

"Oui, Mademoiselle. Dugout canoes. In truth they're all we had those days. We made them by hollowing out the heart of a tree, burning it away, just like the Indians on Hispaniola used to do." He sipped his brandy, then motioned toward Winston. "They were quite seaworthy, *n'est-ce pas?* Enough so we actually used them on our first raid." He turned back. "Though after that we naturally had Spanish ships."

"And where . . . was your first raid, Monsieur le Basque?" She felt her grip tighten involuntarily on the pewter handle of her tankard.

"Did the Anglais never tell you about that little episode, Mademoiselle?" He laughed sarcastically. "No, perhaps it is not something he chooses to remember. Though at the time we thought we could depend on him. I have explained to you that no man among us could shoot as well as he. We wanted him to fire the first shot, as he did when we were hunting. Truly we had high hopes for him." Jacques drank again, a broad silhouette against the panorama of the sunset.

"He told me how you got together to fight the Spaniards, but . . ."

"Did he? *Bon.*" He paused to check the *boucan* below them, then the men. Finally he shrugged and turned back. "It was the start of the legend of the *boucaniers*, Mademoiselle. And you can take pride that the Anglais was part of it. Few men are still alive now to tell that tale."

"What happened to the others, Jacques?" Winston's voice hardened as he moved next to one of the nine-pound cannon. "I seem to remember there were almost thirty of us. Guy Bartholomew was on that raid, for one. I saw him down below last night. I knew a lot of those men well."

"*Oui*, you had many friends. But after you . . . left us, a few unfortunate incidents transpired."

Winston tensed. "Did the ship . . . ?"

"I discovered what can occur when there is not proper organization, Anglais. But now I am getting ahead of our story. Surely you remember the island we had encamped on. Well, we waited on that cursed sand spit several weeks more, hoping there would be another prize. But alas, we saw nothing, *rien*. Then finally one day around noon, when it was so hot you could scarcely breathe, we spied a Spanish sail—far at sea. By then all our supplies were down. We were desperate. So we launched our canoes and put to sea, with a vow we would seize the ship or perish trying."

"And you took it?" Winston had set down his tankard on the railing and was listening intently.

"*Mais oui.* But of course. Desperate men rarely fail. Later we learned that when the captain saw our canoes approaching he scoffed, saying what could a few dugouts do against his

456

guns. He paid for that misjudgment with his life. We waited till dark, then stormed her. The ship was ours in minutes.''

"Congratulations.''

"Not so quickly, Anglais. Unfortunately, all did not go smoothly after that. Perhaps it's just as well you were no longer with us, *mon ami*. Naturally, we threw all the Spaniards overboard, crew and passengers. And then we sailed her back here, to Basse Terre. A three-hundred-ton brigantine. There was some plate aboard—perhaps the *capitaine* was hoarding it—and considerable coin among the passengers. But when we dropped anchor here, a misunderstanding arose over how it all was to be divided.'' He sighed. "There were problems. I regret to say it led to bloodshed.''

"What do you mean?'' Winston glared at him. "I thought we'd agreed to split all prizes equally.''

He smiled patiently. "Anglais, think about it. How could such a thing be? I was the commander; my position had certain requirements. And to make sure the same question did not arise again, I created Articles for us to sail under, giving more to the ship's master. They specify in advance what portion goes to every man, from the maintop to the keel . . . though the commander and officers naturally must receive a larger share . . .''

"And what about now?'' Winston interrupted. "Now that you Frenchmen have taken over Tortuga? I hear there's a new way to split any prizes the men bring in. Which includes you and Chevalier de Poncy.''

"*Oui*, conditions have changed slightly. But the men all understand that.''

"They understand these French culverin up here. *Mes compliments*. It must be very profitable for you and him.''

"But we have much responsibility here.'' He gestured toward the settlement below them. "I have many men under my authority.''

"So now that you've taken over this place and become *commandant*, it's not really like it used to be, when everybody worked for himself. Now there's a French administration. And that means extortion, though I suppose you call it taxes."

"*Naturellement.*" He paused to watch as de Fontenay walked to the edge of the parapet and glanced up at the mountain behind the fort. "But tonight we were to recall those old, happy days, Anglais, before the burden of all this governing descended on my unworthy shoulders. Your *jolie* mademoiselle seems to take such interest in what happened back then."

"I'd like to hear about what happened while Hugh was on that raid with you. You said he was to fire the first shot."

"*Oui.*" Jacques laughed. "And he did indeed pull the first trigger. I was truly sad to part with him at what was to be our moment of glory. But we had differences, I regret to say, that made it necessary . . ."

"What do you mean?" She was watching Hugh's uneasiness as he glanced around the fort, suspecting he'd probably just as soon this story wasn't told.

"We had carefully laid a trap to lure in a ship, Mademoiselle. Up in the Grand Caicos, using a fire on the shore."

"Where?"

"Some islands north of here. Where the Spaniards stop every year." Jacques continued evenly, "And our plan seemed to be working brilliantly. What's more, the Anglais here was given the honor of the first bullet." He sipped from his tankard. "But when a prize blundered into it, the affair turned bloody. Some of my men were killed, and I seem to recall a woman on the ship. I regret to say the Anglais was responsible."

"Hugh, what . . . did . . . you . . . do?" She heard her tankard drop onto the boards.

"To his credit, I will admit he at least helped us bait the hook, Mademoiselle." Jacques smiled. "Did you not, Anglais?"

"That I did. Except it caught an English fish, instead of a Spaniard."

Good Christ, no! Katherine sucked in her breath. The coldhearted bastard. I *am* glad I brought a pistol. Except it'll not be for Jacques le Basque. "I think you two had best spare me the rest of your heroic little tale, before I . . ."

"But, Mademoiselle, the Anglais was our finest marksman. He could bring down a wild boar at three hundred paces." He toasted Winston with a long draught from his tankard. "Don't forget I had trained him well. We *wanted* him to fire the first shot. You should at least take pride in that, even if the rest does not redound entirely to his credit."

"Hugh, you'd better tell me the truth. Right now." She moved toward him, almost quivering with rage. She felt her hand close about the grip of her pistol as she stood facing Winston, his scarred face impassive. "Did you fire on the ship?"

"Mademoiselle, what does it matter now? All that is past, correct?" Jacques smiled as he strolled over. "Tonight the Anglais and I are once more *Frères de la Côte,* brothers in the honorable order of *boucaniers.*" He patted Winston's shoulder. "That is still true, *n'est-ce pas?* And together we will mount the greatest raid ever—on the Spanish island of Jamaica."

Winston was still puzzling over Katherine's sudden anger when he finally realized what Jacques had said.

So, he thought, the old *bâtard* wants to give me the men after all. Just as I'd figured. Now it's time to talk details.

"Together, Jacques. But remember I'm the one who has the pilot, the man who can get us into the harbor. So that means I set the terms." He sipped from his tankard, feeling the brandy burn its way down. "And since you seem to like it here so much, I'll keep the port for myself, and we'll just draw up some of those Articles of yours about how we manage the rest."

"But of course, Anglais. I've already been thinking. Perhaps we can handle it this way: you keep whatever you find in the fortress, and my men will take the spoils from the town.''

"Wait a minute. The town's apt to have the most booty, you know that, Jacques.''

"Anglais, how can we possibly foretell such a thing in advance? Already I am assuming a risk . . .''

Jacques smiled and turned to look down at the bay. As he moved, the railing he had been standing beside exploded, spewing slivers of mastic wood into the evening air. When he glanced back, startled, a faint pop sounded from the direction of the hill behind the fort.

Time froze as a look of angry realization spread through the old *boucanier's* eyes. He checked the iron ladder, still lowered, then yelled for the guards below to light the linstocks for the cannon and ready their muskets.

"Katy, take cover." Winston seized her arm and she felt him pull her against the side of the house, out of sight of the hill above. "Maybe Commandant le Basque is not quite so popular with some of his lads as he seems to think.''

"I can very well take care of myself, Captain. Right now I've a mind to kill you both." She wrenched her arm away and moved down the side of the citadel.

"Katy, what . . . ?" As Winston stared at her, uncomprehending, another musket ball from the dark above splattered into the post beside Jacques. He bellowed a curse, then drew the pistol from his belt and stepped into the protection of the roof. When he did, one of the guards from below, wearing a black hat and jerkin, appeared at the top of the iron ladder leading up from the courtyard. Jacques yelled for him to hurry.

"Damn you, *vite*, there's some fool up the hill with a musket . . .''

Before he could finish, the man raised a long flintlock pistol and fired.

The ball ripped away part of the ornate lace along one side

of Jacques's collar. Almost before the spurt of flame had died away, Jacques's own pistol was cocked. He casually took aim and shot the guard squarely in the face. The man slumped across the edge of the opening, then slid backward and out of sight.

"Anglais." He turned back coolly. "Tonight you have just had the privilege of seeing me remind these *cochons* who controls this island."

Even as he spoke, the curly head of de Fontenay appeared through the opening. When Jacques saw him, he beckoned him forward. "Come on, and pull it up after you. Too many killings will upset my guests' dinner."

The young Frenchman stepped slowly onto the platform, then slipped his right hand into his ornate doublet and lifted out a pistol. He examined it for a moment before reaching down with his left and extracting another.

"I said to pull up the ladder, damn you. That's an order."

De Fontenay began to back along the railing, all the while staring at Jacques with eyes fearful and uncertain. Finally he summoned the courage to speak.

"You are a *bête,* Jacques, truly a beast." His voice trembled, and glistening droplets of sweat had begun to bead on his smooth forehead. "We are going to open Purgatory and release the men you have down there. Give me the keys, or I will kill you myself, I swear it."

"You'd do well to put those guns away, you little *fou.* Before I become annoyed." Jacques glared at him a moment, then turned toward Winston, his voice even. "Anglais, kindly pass me one of your pistols. Or I will be forced to kill this little *putain* and all the rest with my own bare hands. I would regret having to soil them."

"You'd best settle this yourself, Jacques. I keep my pistols. Besides, maybe you *should* open that new dungeon of yours. We never needed anything like that in the old days."

"Damn you, Anglais." His voice hardened. "I said give me a gun."

461

At that moment, another guard from below appeared at the opening. With a curse, Jacques stepped over and shoved a heavy boot into his face, sending the startled man sprawling backward. Then he seized the iron ladder and drew it up, beyond reach of those below. He ignored de Fontenay as he turned back to Winston.

"Are you defying me too, Anglais? *Bon.* Because before this night is over, I have full intention of settling our accounts."

"Jacques, *mon ami!*" Winston laughed. "Here all this time I thought we were going to be *frères* again." He sobered. "Though I would prefer going in partners with a commander who can manage his own men."

"You mean this little one?" He thumbed at de Fontenay. "Believe me when I tell you he does not have the courage of . . ."

Now de Fontenay was raising the pistol in his right hand, shakily. "I said to give us the keys, Jacques. You have gone too far."

"You will not live that long, my little *matelot,* to order me what to do." Jacques feigned a menacing step toward him. Startled, de Fontenay edged backward, and Jacques erupted with laughter, then turned back to Winston. "You see, Anglais? Cowards are all the same. Remember when *you* wanted to kill me? You were point-blank, and you failed. Now this little *putain* has the same idea." He seized Winston's jerkin. "Give me one of your guns, Anglais, or I will take it with my own hands."

"*No!*" At the other end of the citadel Katherine stood holding the pistol she had brought. She was gripping it with both hands, rock steady, aimed at them. Slowly she moved down the porch. "I'd like to just be rid of you both. Which one of you should I kill?"

The old *boucanier* stared at her as she approached, then at Winston. "Your Anglaise has gone mad."

"*I* was on that English ship you two are so proud of attacking." She directed the flintlock toward Winston. "Hugh, the woman you remember killing—she was my mother."

The night flared with the report of a pistol, and Jacques flinched in surprise. He glanced down curiously at the splotch of red blossoming against the side of his silk shirt, then looked up at de Fontenay.

"That was a serious mistake, my little *ami*. One you will not live long enough to regret."

The smoking pistol de Fontenay held dropped noisily onto the boards at his feet, while he raised the other. "I said give to me the keys, Jacques. Or I will kill you, I swear it."

"You think I can be killed? By you? *Jamais.*" He laughed, then suddenly reached out and wrenched away the pistol Katherine was holding, shoving her aside. With a smile he aimed it directly at de Fontenay's chest. "Now, *mon ami . . .*"

There was a dead click, then silence. It had misfired.

"I don't want this, Jacques, truly." De Fontenay started to tremble, and abruptly the other pistol he held exploded with a pink arrow of flame.

"Anglais . . ." Jacques jerked lightly, a second splotch of red spreading across his pale shirt. Then he dropped to one knee with a curse.

De Fontenay stepped hesitantly forward. "Perhaps now you will understand, *mon maître,* what kind of man I can be."

He watched in disbelief as Jacques slowly slumped forward across the boards at his feet. Then he edged closer to where the old *boucanier* lay, reached down and ripped away a ring of heavy keys secured to his belt. He held them a moment in triumph before he looked down again, suddenly incredulous. "*Mon Dieu,* he is dead."

With a cry of remorse he crouched over the lifeless figure and lovingly touched the bloodstained beard. Finally he remembered himself and glanced up at Winston. "It seems I have finished what you began. He told me today how you two quarreled once. He cared nothing for us, you or me, friend or lover." He hesitated, and his eyes appeared to plead. "What do we do now?"

Winston was still staring at Katherine, his mind flooded with dismay at the anger in her eyes. At last he seemed to hear de Fontenay and turned back. "Since you've got his keys, you might as well go ahead and throw them down. I assume you mean to open the dungeon."

"*Oui*. He had begun to lock men there just on his whim. Yesterday he even imprisoned a . . . special friend of mine. It was too much." He walked to the edge of the platform and flung the ring of keys down toward the pavement of the fort.

As the ring of metal against stone cut through the silence, he yelled out, "Purgatory is no more. Jacques le Basque is in hell." He abruptly turned and shoved down the ladder. In the courtyard below, pandemonium erupted.

At once a cannon blazed into the night. Then a second, and a third. Moments later, jubilant musket fire sounded up from the direction of the settlement as men poured into the streets, torches and lanterns blazing.

"Good God, Katy, I don't know what you've been thinking, but we'd best talk about it later. Right now we've got to get out of here." Winston walked hesitantly to where she stood. "Somebody's apt to get a mind to fire this place."

"No, I don't . . ."

"Katy, *come on*." He grabbed her arm.

De Fontenay was still at the railing along the edge of the platform, as though not yet fully comprehending the enormity of his act. Below him a string of prisoners, still shackled, was being led from the dungeon beneath the "dovecote."

Winston forcibly guided Katherine down the ladder and onto the stone steps below. Now guards had already begun dismantling the *boucan* with the butts of their muskets, sending sparks sailing upward into the night air.

Then the iron gateway of the fortress burst open and a mob of seamen began pouring through, waving pistols and cheering. Finally one of them spotted Winston on the steps and pressed through the crowd.

"God's blood, is it true?"

Winston looked down and recognized Guy Bartholomew.

"Jacques is dead."

"An' they're all claiming you did it. That you came up here and killed the bastard. The very thing we all wanted, and you managed it." He reached up and pumped Winston's hand. "Maybe now I can stand you a drink. For my money, I say you should be new *commandant* of this piss-hole, by virtue of ridding the place of him."

"I didn't kill him, Bartholomew. That 'honor' goes to his *matelot.*"

The excited seaman scarcely paused. " 'Tis no matter, sir. That little whore is nothing. I know one thing; every Englishman here'll sail for you, or I'm not a Christian."

"Maybe we can call some of the ships' masters together and see what they want to do."

"You can name the time, sir. And I'll tell you this: there're going to be a few changes around here, that I can warrant." He turned to look at the other men, several of whom were offering flasks of brandy to the prisoners. Around them, the French guards had remembered Jacques's store of liquor and were shoving past, headed up the ladder. In moments they were flinging down flasks of brandy.

Bartholomew turned and gazed down toward the collection of mast lights below them. "There's scarcely an Englishman here who'd not have left that whoreson's service long ago, save there's no place else but Tortuga the likes of us can drop anchor. But now with him gone we can . . ."

"Until further notice, this island is going to be under *my* administration, as representative of the Chevalier de Poncy, *gouverneur* of St. Christophe." De Fontenay had appeared at the top of the steps and begun to shout over the tumult in the yard. His curls fluttered in the wind as he called for quiet. "By the Code of the *boucaniers*, the *Telle Étoit la Coutume de la Côte,* I am Jacques's legal heir. Which means I can claim the office of acting *commandant de place* . . .''

Bartholomew yelled up at him. "You can claim whatever you like, you pimp. But no Englishman'll sail for you, an' that's a fact. We'll spike these cannon if you're thinking to try any of the old tricks. It's a new day, by all that's holy.''

"What do you mean?" De Fontenay glanced down.

"I mean from this day forth we'll sail for whatever master we've a mind to.''

De Fontenay called to Winston. "You saw who killed him, Monsieur. Tell them." He looked back toward Bartholomew. "This man knew Jacques better than any of you. His friend, the Anglais, from the very first days of the *boucaniers*. He will tell you the Code makes me . . .''

"Anglais!" Bartholomew stared at Winston a moment, then a smile erupted across his hard face. "Good God, I do believe it is. You've aged mightily, lad, on my honor. Please take no offense I didn't recognize you before.''

"It's been a long time.''

"God's blood, none of us ever knew your Christian name. We all thought you dead after you and Jacques had that little shooting spree." He grasped Winston's hand. "Do you have any idea how proud we were of you? I tell you we all saw it when you pulled a pistol on that bastard. You may not know it, sir, but it was because of you his band of French rogues didn't rape that English frigate. All the Englishmen amongst us wanted to stop it, but we had no chance." He laughed. "In truth, sir, that was the start of all our troubles here. We never got along with the damn'd Frenchmen after that, Articles or no.

"Hugh, what's he saying?" Katherine was staring at him.

"What do you mean?''

"Is it true you *stopped* Jacques and his men from taking our ship? The one you were talking about tonight?''

"The idea was we were only to kill Spaniards. No Englishman had done anything to us. It wouldn't have been hon-

466

orable. When Jacques didn't agree with me on that point, things got a little unpleasant. That's when somebody started firing on the ship.''

"Aye, the damn'd Frenchmen," Bartholomew interjected. ''I was there, sir.''

"I'm sorry the rest of us didn't manage to warn you in time." Winston slipped his arm around her.

Suddenly she wanted to smother him in her arms. "But do you realize you must have saved my life? They would have killed us all.''

"They doubtless would have. Eventually." He reached over and kissed her, then drew back and examined her. "Katy, I have a confession to make. I think I can still remember watching you. When I was in the longboat, trying to reach the ship. I think I fell in love with you that morning. With that brave girl who stood there at the railing, musket balls flying. I never forgot it, in all the years. My God, to think it was *you.*'' He held her against him for a moment, then lifted up her face. "Which also means I have you and yours to thank for trying to kill me, when I wanted to get out to where you were.''

"The captain just assumed you were one of *them*. I heard him talk about it after. Nobody had any idea . . .'' She hugged him. "You and your 'honor.' You changed my life.''

"You and that ship sure as hell changed *mine*. After I fell in love with you, I damned near died of thirst in that leaky longboat. And then Ruyters . . .''

"Capitaine, please tell them I was the one who shot Jacques. That I am now *commandant de place.*'' De Fontenay interrupted, his voice pleading. "That I have the authority to order them . . .''

"You're not ordering anything, by Jesus. I'm about to put an end to any more French orders here and now." Bartholomew seized a burning stick from the fire in the *boucan* and flung it upward, onto the veranda of the "dovecote."

A cheer went up from the English seamen clustered around,

and before Jacques's French guards could stop them, they were flinging torches and flaming logs up into the citadel.

"Messieurs, no. Please! *Je vous en prie. Non!*" De Fontenay stared up in horror.

Tongues of flame began to lick at the edge of the platform. Some of the guards dropped their muskets and yelled to get buckets of water from the spring behind the rock. Then they thought better of it and started edging gingerly toward the iron gates leading out of the fortress and down the hill.

The other guards who had been rifling the liquor came scurrying down the ladder, jostling de Fontenay aside. As Winston urged Katherine toward the gates, the young *matelot* was still lingering forlornly on the steps, gazing up at the burning "dovecote." Finally, the last to leave Forte de la Roche, he sadly turned and made his way out.

"Senhor, what is happening here?" Atiba was racing up the steps leading to the gate, carrying his cutlass. "I swam to shore and came fastly as I could."

"There's been a little revolution up here, my friend. And I'll tell you something else. There's likely to be some gunpowder in that citadel. For those demi-culverin. I don't have any idea how many kegs he had, but knowing Jacques, there was enough." He took Katherine's hand. "It's the end for this place, that much you can be sure."

"Hugh, what about the plan to use his men?" She turned back to look.

"We'll just have to see how things here are going to settle out now. Maybe it's not over yet."

They moved onto the tree-lined pathway. The night air was sharp, fragrant. Above the glow of the fire, the moon hung like a lantern in the tropical sky.

"You know, I never trusted him for a minute. Truly I didn't." She slipped her arm around Winston's jerkin. "I realize now he was planning to somehow try and kill us both tonight. Thank heaven it's over. Why don't we just get out of here while we still can?"

468

"Well, sir, it's a new day." Guy Bartholomew emerged out of the crowd, his smile illuminated by the glow of the blaze. "An' I've been talkin' with some of my lads. Why don't we just have done with these damn'd Frenchmen and claim this island?" He gleefully rubbed at the stubble on his chin. "No Englishman here's goin' to line the pockets of a Frenchman ever again, that I'll promise you."

"You can try and make Tortuga English if you like, but you won't be sailing with me if you do."

"What do you mean, sir?" Bartholomew stood puzzling. "This is our best chance ever to take hold and keep this place. An' there's precious few other islands where we can headquarter."

"I know one that has a better harbor. And a better fortress guarding it"

"Where might that be?"

"Ever think of Jamaica?"

"Jamaica, sir?" He glanced up confusedly. "But that belongs to the pox-eaten Spaniards."

"Not after we take it away from them it won't. And when we do, any English privateer who wants can use the harbor there."

"Now, sir." Bartholomew stopped. "Tryin' to seize Jamaica's another matter entirely. We thought you were the man to help us take charge of this little enterprise here of pillagin' the cursed Spaniards' shipping. You didn't say you're plannin' to try stealin' a whole *island* from the whoresons."

"I'm not just planning, my friend." Winston moved on ahead, Atiba by his side. "God willing, I'm damned sure going to do it."

"It's a bold notion, that I'll grant you." He examined Winston skeptically, then grinned as he followed after. "God's life, that'd be the biggest prize any Englishman in the Caribbean ever tried."

"I think it can be done."

"Well, I'll be plain with you, sir. I don't know how many

469

men here'll be willing to risk their hide on such a venture. I hear the Spaniards've got a militia over there, maybe a thousand strong. 'Tis even said they've got some cavalry.''

"Then all you Englishmen here can stay on and sail for the next *commandant* Chevalier de Poncy finds to send down and take over. He'll hold La Tortue for France, don't you think otherwise. All those commissions didn't stay in Jacques's pocket, you can be sure. He's bound to have passed a share up to the Frenchmen on St. Christopher.''

"We'll not permit it, sir. We'll not let the Frenchmen have it back.''

"How do you figure on stopping them? This fortress'll take weeks to put into any kind of shape again, and de Poncy's sure to post a fleet down the minute he hears of this. I'd say this place'll have no choice but stay French.''

"Aye, I'm beginnin' to get the thrust of your thinkin'.'' He gazed ruefully back up at the burning fort. "If that should happen, and I grant you there's some likelihood it just might, then there's apt to be damned little future here for a God-fearin' Englishman. So either we keep on sailin' for some other French bastard or we find ourselves another harbor.''

"That's how I read the situation now.'' Winston continued on down the hill. "So why don't we hold a vote amongst the men and see, Master Bartholomew? Maybe a few of them are game to try making a whole new place.''

Chapter Twenty-two

A cricket sang from somewhere within the dark crevices of the stone wall surrounding the two men, a sharp, shrill cadence in the night. To the older it was a welcome sign all was well; the younger gave it no heed, as again he bent over and hit his steel against the flint, sending sparks flying into the wind. Finally he cursed in Spanish and paused to pull his goatskin jerkin closer.

Hipolito de Valera had not expected this roofless hilltop outpost would catch the full force of the breeze that rolled in off the bay. He paused for another gust to die away, then struck the flint once more. A shower of sparks scattered across the small pile of dry grass and twigs by the wall, and then slowly, tentatively the tinder began to glow. When at last it was blazing, he tossed on a large handful of twigs and leaned back to watch.

In the uneven glow of the fire his face was soft, with an aquiline nose and dark Castilian eyes. He was from the sparsely settled north, where his father don Alfonso de Valera had planted forty-five acres of grape arbor in the mountains. Winemaking was forbidden in the Spanish Americas, but taxes on Spanish wines were high and Spain was far away.

"¡Tenga cuidado! The flame must be kept low. It has to be heated slowly." Juan Jose Pereira was, as he had already observed several times previously this night, more knowing of the world. His lined cheeks were leather-dark from a lifetime of riding in the harsh Jamaican sun for the cattle-rancher who owned the largest *hato* on the Liguanea Plain. Perhaps the youngest son of a vineyard owner might understand the best day to pick grapes for the claret, but such a raw youth would know nothing of the correct preparation of chocolate.

Juan Jose monitored the blaze for a time, and then—his hands moving with the deft assurance of the ancient *conquistadores*—carefully retrieved a worn leather bag from his pocket and dropped a brown lump into the brass kettle now hanging above the fire. He next added two green tabasco peppers, followed by a portion of goat's milk from his canteen. Finally he stirred in a careful quantity of *muscavado* sugar—procured for him informally by his sister's son Carlos, who operated the boiling house of a sugar plantation in the Guanaboa Vale, one of only seven on the island with a horse-drawn mill for crushing the cane.

As he watched the thick mixture begin to simmer, he motioned for the younger man to climb back up the stone stairway to the top of their outpost, the *vigia* overlooking the harbor of Jamaica Bay. Dawn was four hours away, but their vigil for mast lights must be kept, even when there was nothing but the half moon to watch.

In truth Juan Jose did not mind his occasional night of duty for the militia, especially here on the mountain. He liked the stars, the cool air so unlike his sweltering thatched hut on the plain, and the implicit confirmation his eyes were still as keen as they had been the morning he was baptized, over fifty years ago.

The aroma of the chocolate swirled up into the watchtower above, and in the moonlight its dusky perfume sent Hipolito's thoughts soaring.

Elvita. Wouldn't it be paradise if *she* were here tonight, instead of a crusty old *vaquero* like Juan Jose? He thought again of her almond eyes, which he sometimes caught glancing at him during the Mass . . . though always averted with a pretense of modesty when his own look returned their desire.

He sat musing over what his father would say when he informed him he was hopelessly in love with Elvita de Loaisa. Undoubtedly don Alfonso would immediately point out that her father Garcia de Loaisa had only twenty acres of lowland cotton in cultivation: what dowry would such a lazy family bring?

What to do? Just to think about her, while the moon . . .

"Your chocolate." Juan Jose was standing beside him holding out a pewter bowl, from which a tiny wisp of steam trailed upward to be captured in the breeze. The old man watched him take it, then, holding his own portion, settled back against the stone bench.

"You were gazing at the moon, my son." He crossed himself, then began to sip noisily. "The spot to watch is over there, at the tip of the Cayo de Carena." Now he was pointing south. "Any *protestante* fleet that would attack us must first sail around the Point."

The old man consumed the rest of his chocolate quickly, then licked the rim of the bowl and laid it aside. Its spicy sweetness was good, true enough, one of the joys of the Spanish Americas, but now he wanted something stronger. Unobtrusively he rummaged through the pocket of his coat till he located his flask of pimento brandy. He extracted the cork with his teeth, then pensively drew twice on the bottle before rising to stare out over the stone balustrade.

Below them on the right lay Jamaica Bay, placid and empty, with the sandy cay called Cayo de Carena defining its farthest perimeter. The cay, he had always thought, was where the Passage Fort really should be. But their governor, don Francisco de Castilla, claimed there was no money to build a second one. All the same, spreading below him was the finest harbor in the New World—when Jamaica had no more than three thousand souls, maybe four, on the whole island. Did not even the giant *galeones*, on their way north from Carte-gena, find it easy to put in here to trade? Their arrival was, in fact, always the event of the year, the time when Jamaica's hides and pig lard were readied for Havana, in exchange for fresh supplies of wine, olive oil, wheat flour, even cloth from home. Don Fernando, owner of the *hato*, always made cer-tain his hides were cured and bundled for the *galeones* by late spring.

But don Fernando's leather business was of scant concern to Juan Jose. What use had he for white lace from Seville? He pulled again at the flask, its brandy sharp and pungent, and let his eyes wander to the green plain on his left, now washed in moonlight. *That* was the Jamaica he cared about, where everything he required could be grown right in the earth. Cotton for the women to spin, beef and cassava to eat, wine and cacao and cane-brandy for drinking, tobacco to soothe his soul. . . .

He suddenly remembered he had left his pipe in the leather knapsack, down below. But now he would wait a bit. Think-ing of a pleasure made it even sweeter . . . Just as he knew young Hipolito was dreaming still of some country señorita. When a young man could not attend to what he was told for longer than a minute, it could only be first love.

As he stood musing, his glance fell on Caguaya, the Pas-sage Fort, half a mile to the left, along the Rio Cobre river that flowed down from Villa de la Vega. The fort boasted ten great guns, and it was manned by militia day and night. If any strange ship entered the bay, Caguaya would be signaled from here at the *vigia*, using two large bells donated by the Church, and the fort's cannon would be readied as a precau-tion. He studied it for a time, pleased it was there. Its guns would kill any heretic *luterano* who came to steal.

The pipe. He glanced over at Hipolito, now making a show of watching the Point at Cayo de Carena, and briefly enter-tained sending him down for it. Then he decided the climb would be good for his legs, would help him keep his breath—

which he needed for his Saturday night trysts with Margarita, don Fernando's head cook. Though, Mother of God, she had lungs enough for them both. He chuckled to himself and took a last pull on the fiery brandy before collecting the pewter bowls to start down the stairs. "My *pipa*. Don't fall asleep gazing at the moon while I'm below."

The young man blushed in the dark and busily studied the horizon. Juan Jose stood watching him for a moment, wondering if *he* had been that transparent thirty-some years past, then turned and began descending the steps, his boots ringing hard against the stone.

The knapsack was at the side wall, near the door, and as he bent over to begin searching for the clay stem of his pipe he caught the movement of a shadow along the stone lintel. Suddenly it stopped.

"*¿Que pasa?*" He froze and waited for an answer.

Silence. Now the shadow was motionless.

His musket, and Hipolito's, were both leaning against the far wall, near the stairs. Then he remembered . . .

Slowly, with infinite care, he slipped open the buckle on the knapsack and felt for his knife, the one with the long blade he used for skinning. His fingers closed about its bone handle, and he carefully drew it from its sheath. He raised up quietly and smoothly, as though stalking a skittish calf, and edged against the wall. The shadow moved again, tentatively, and then a massive black form was outlined against the doorway.

Un negro!

Whose could it be? There were no more than forty or fifty slaves on the whole of Jamaica, brought years ago to work on the plantations. But the cane fields were far away, west of Rio Minho and inland. The only *negro* you ever saw this far east was an occasional domestic.

Perhaps he was a runaway? There was a band of Maroons, free *negros,* now living in the mountains. But they kept to themselves. They did not come down onto the plain to steal.

The black man stood staring at him. He did not move, merely watched as though completely unafraid.

Then Juan Jose saw the glint of a wide blade, a cutlass, in the moonlight. This was no thief. Who was he? What could he want?

"Señor, stop." He raised his knife. "You are not permitted . . ."

The *negro* moved through the doorway, as though not understanding. His blade was rising, slowly.

Juan Jose took a deep breath and lunged.

He was floating, enfolded in Margarita's soft bosom, while the world turned gradually sideways. Then he felt a pain in his knee as it struck against the stone—oddly, that was his first sensation, and he wondered fleetingly if it would still be stiff when he mounted his mare in the morning. Next he noticed a dull ache in the side of his neck, not sharp but warm from the blood. He felt the knife slip away, clattering onto the stone paving beyond his reach, and then he saw the moon, clear and crisp, suspended above him in the open sky. Next to it hovered Hipolito, his frightened eyes gazing down from the head of the stair. The eyes held dark brown for a second, then turned red, then black.

"*Meu Deus*, you have killed him!" A woman's voice pierced the dark. She was speaking in Portuguese as she moved through the door behind the tall *negro*.

Hipolito watched in terrified silence, too afraid even to breathe. Behind the *negro* and the woman were four other men, whispering in Inglés, muskets poised. He realized both the guns were still down below, and besides, how could . . .

"The whoreson tried to murder me with his damnable knife." The man drew up the cutlass and wiped its blood against the leather coat of Juan Jose, sprawled at his feet.

"We were not to kill unless necessary. Those were your orders."

The *negro* motioned for quiet and casually stepped over the body, headed for the stairs.

Mother of God, *no!* Hipolito drew back, wanting to cry out, to flee. But then he realized he was cornered, like an animal.

Now the *negro* was mounting the stairs, still holding the sword, the woman directly behind him.

Why, he wondered, had a woman come with them. These could not be ordinary thieves; they must be *corsario luterano*, heretic Protestant *flibustero* of the sea. Why hadn't he seen their ship? They must have put in at Esquebel, the little bay down the western shore, then come up by the trail. It was five miles, a quick climb if you knew the way.

But how could they have known the road leading up to the *vigia?* And if these were here, how many more were now readying to attack the fort at Caguaya, just to the north? The bells . . . !

He backed slowly toward the small tower and felt blindly for the rope. But now the huge figure blotted out the moon as it moved toward him. Fearfully he watched the shadow glide across the paving, inching nearer, a stone at a time. Then he noticed the wind blowing through his hair, tousling it across his face, and he would have pushed it back save he was unable to move. He could taste his own fear now, like a small copper *tlaco* in his mouth.

The man was raising his sword. Where was the rope! Mother of God!

"*Não.*" The woman had seized the *negro*'s arm, was pulling him back. Hipolito could almost decipher her Pòrtuguese as she continued, "*Suficiente.* No more killing."

Hipolito stepped away from the bell tower. "Senor, *por favor* . . ."

The man had paused, trying to shake aside the woman. Then he said something, like a hard curse.

Hipolito felt his knees turn to warm butter and he dropped

forward, across the stones. He was crying now, his body shivering from the hard, cold paving against his face.

"Just tie him." The woman's voice came again. "He is only a boy."

The man's voice responded, in the strange language, and Hipolito thought he could feel the sword against his neck. He had always imagined he would someday die proudly, would honor Elvita by his courage, and now here he was, cringing on his belly. They would find him like this. The men in the vineyards would joke he had groveled before the Protestant *ladrones* like a dog.

"I will stay and watch him, and this place. Leave me two muskets." The woman spoke once more, then called out in Inglés. There were more footsteps on the stairs as the other men clambered up.

"Why damn me, 'tis naught but a lad," a voice said in Inglés, "sent to do a man's work."

"He's all they'd need to spy us, have no fear. I'll wager 'twould be no great matter to warn the fort. Which is what he'll be doin' if we . . .

"Señor, how do you signal the fort?" The woman was speaking now, in Spanish, as she seized Hipolito's face and pulled him up. "Speak quickly, or I will let them kill you."

Hipolito gestured vaguely toward the two bells hanging in the tower behind.

"Take out the clappers, then tie him." The woman's voice came again, now in Inglés. "The rest of you ready the lanterns."

The dugout canoes had already been launched, bobbing alongside the two frigates anchored on the sea side of the Cayo de Carena. Directly ahead of them lay the Point, overlooking the entry to Jamaica Bay.

Katherine felt the gold inlay of the musket's barrel, cold and hard against her fingertips, and tried to still her pulse as

478

she peered through the dim moonlight. Up the companion-way, on the quarterdeck, Winston was deep in a final parlay with Guy Bartholomew of the *Swiftsure*. Like all the seamen, they kept casting anxious glances toward a spot on the shore across the bay, just below the *vigia*, where the advance party would signal the all-clear with lanterns.

The last month had not been an easy time. After the death of Jacques le Basque, Tortuga was plunged into turmoil for a fortnight, with the English and French *boucaniers* at Basse Terre quarreling violently over the island's future. There had nearly been war. Finally Bartholomew and almost a hundred and fifty seamen had elected to join Winston in his attempt to seize a new English privateering base at Jamaica. But they also demanded the right to hold Villa de la Vega for ransom, as Jackson had done so many years before. It was the dream of riches that appealed to them most, every man suddenly fancying himself a second Croesus. Finally Winston and Bartholomew had drawn up Articles specifying the division of spoils, in the tradition of the *boucaniers*.

After that, two more weeks had passed in final prepara-tions, as muskets and kegs of powder were stockpiled. To have sufficient landing craft they had bartered butts of kill-devil with the Cow-Killers on Hispaniola for ten wide dugout canoes—all over six feet across and able to transport fifteen to twenty men. With the dugouts aboard and lashed securely along the main deck of the two ships, the assault was ready.

They set sail as a flurry of rumors from other islands began reaching the buccaneer stronghold. The most disquieting was that a French fleet of armed warships had already been dis-patched south by the Chevalier de Poncy of St. Christopher, who intended to restore his dominion over Tortuga and ap-point a new French *commandant* de place.

Yet another story, spreading among the Spanish planters on Hispaniola, was that an English armada had tried to in-vade the city of Santo Domingo on the southern coast, but was repulsed ingloriously, with hundreds lost.

The story of the French fleet further alarmed the English buccaneers, and almost two dozen more offered to join the Jamaica expedition. The Spanish tale of a failed assault on Santo Domingo was quickly dismissed. It was merely another in a long history of excuses put forward by the *audiencia* of that city to explain its failure to attack Tortuga. There would never have been a better time to storm the island, but once again the cowardly Spaniards had managed to find a reason for allowing the *boucaniers* to go unmolested, claiming all their forces were needed to defend the capital.

The morning of their departure arrived brisk and clear, and by mid-afternoon they had already made Cape Nicholao, at the northwest tip of Hispaniola. Since the Windward Passage lay just ahead, they shortened sail, holding their course west by southwest till dark, when they elected to heave-to and wait for morning, lest they overshoot. At dawn they were back underway, and just before nightfall, as planned, they had sighted Point Morant on the eastern tip of Jamaica. Winston ordered the first stage of the assault to commence.

The frigates made way along the southern coast till they neared the Point of the Cayo de Carena, the wide cay at the entry to Jamaica Bay. Then, while the *Swiftsure* kept station to watch for any turtling craft that might sound the alarm, Winston hoisted the *Defiance*'s new sails and headed on past the Point, directly along the coast. The attack plan called for an advance party to proceed overland from the rear and surprise the *vigia* on the hill overlooking the bay, using a map prepared by their Spanish pilot, Armando Vargas. Winston appointed Atiba to lead the men; Serina went with them as translator.

They had gone ashore two hours before midnight, giving them four hours to secure the *vigia* before the attack was launched. A signal of three lanterns on the shore below the *vigia* would signify all-clear. After they had disappeared up the trail and into the salt savannah, the *Defiance* rejoined the *Swiftsure*, at which time Winston ordered the fo'c'sle unlocked and flintlocks distributed, together with bandoliers of powder and shot. While the men checked and primed their muskets, Winston ordered extra barrels of powder and shot loaded into the dugouts, along with pikes and half-pikes.

Now the men stirred impatiently on the decks, new flint-locks glistening in the moonlight, anxious for their first feel of Spanish gold. . . .

Katherine pushed through the crowd and headed up the companionway toward the quarterdeck. Winston had just dismissed Bartholomew, sending him back to the *Swiftsure* to oversee final assignments of his own men and arms. The old *boucanier* was still chuckling over something Winston had said as she met him on the companionway.

"See you take care with that musket now, m'lady." He doffed his dark hat with a wink as he stepped past. "She's apt to go off when you'd least expect."

She smiled and nodded, then smoothly drew back the hammer on the breech with an ominous click as she looked up.

"Then tell me, Guy, is this what makes it fire?"

"God's blood, m'lady." Bartholomew scurried quickly past, then glanced uncertainly over his shoulder as he slid across the bannister and started down the swaying rope ladder, headed for the shallop moored below.

"Hugh, how long do you expect before the signal?"

"It'd best be soon. If not, we won't have time to cross the bay before daylight." He peered through the dark, toward the hill. "We've got to clear the harbor and reach the mouth of the Rio Cobre while it's still dark, or they'll see us from the Passage Fort."

"How far up the river is the fort?"

"Vargas claims it's only about a quarter mile." He glanced back toward the hill. "But once we make the river, their cannon won't be able to touch us. It's only when we're exposed crossing the bay that we need worry."

"What about the militia there when we try to storm it?"

"Vargas claims that if they're not expecting trouble, it'll

be lightly manned. After we take it, we'll have their cannon, together with the ordnance we've already got. There's nothing else on the island save a few matchlock muskets.''

"And their cavalry.''

"All they'll have is lances, or pikes.'' He slipped his arm around her waist. "No, Katy, after we seize Passage Fort, the Spaniards can never get us out of here, from land or sea. Jamaica will be ours, because this harbor will belong to us.''

"You make it sound too easy by half.'' She leaned against him, wishing she could fully share his confidence. "But if we do manage to take the fort, what about Villa de la Vega?''

"The town'll have to surrender, sooner or later. They'll have no harbor. And this island can't survive without one.''

She sighed and glanced back toward the shore. In the moonlight the blue mountains of Jamaica towered silently above the bay. Would those mountains some day stand for freedom in the Caribbean, the way Tortuga once did . . . ?

She sensed Winston's body tense and glanced up. He was gazing across the bay toward the shore, where a dim light had suddenly appeared. Then another, and another.

"Katy, I've waited a long, long time for this. Thinking about it, planning it. All along I always figured I'd be doing it alone. But your being here . . .'' He seemed to lose the words as he held her against him. "Tonight we're about to do something, together, that'll change the Americas forever.''

The oars bit into the swell and the dark waters of the bay slapped against the bark-covered prow, an ancient cadence he remembered from that long voyage north, ten years past. Where had all the years gone?

Behind him was a line of dugouts, a deadly procession of armed, grim-faced seamen. All men of Tortuga, not one among them still welcome in any English, French, or Dutch settlement.

Was it possible to start over with men like these? A new nation?

"*Mira,*" Vargas whispered over the rhythm of the oars. His dark eyes were glistening as he pointed toward the entry to the harbor, a wide strait that lay between the Point of the Cayo de Carena and the mainland. Around them the light surf sparkled in the moonlight. "Is not this *puerto* the finest in all the Caribbean?" He smiled back at Winston, showing a row of tobacco-stained teeth. "No storm reaches here. The smallest craft can anchor safely, even in a *huracán.*"

"It's just like I figured. So the spot to situate our cannon really *is* right there on the Point. Do that and nobody could ever get into the bay."

Vargas laughed. "*Si,* that is true. If they had guns here, we could never get past. But Jamaica is a poor island. The Passage Fort over on the river has always been able to slow an assault long enough for them to empty the town. Then their women and children are safe. What else do they have worth stealing?"

"Hugh, is this the location you were talking to John about?" Katherine was studying the wide and sandy Point.

"The very place. That's why I had him stay with the *Defiance* and keep some of the lads."

"I hope he can do it."

"He'll wait till sun-up, till after we take the fort. But this cay is the place to be, mark it."

"You are right, señor," Vargas continued as they steered on around the Point. "I have often wondered myself why there was no port city out here. Perhaps it is because this island has nothing but stupid *agricultores.*"

Their tiny armada of dugouts glided quickly across the strait, then hugged the shore, headed toward the mouth of the Rio Cobre. Now they were directly under the *vigia.*

As they rowed past, five figures suddenly emerged from the trees and began wading toward them. Winston immediately signaled the dugouts to put in.

Atiba was grinning as he hoisted himself over the side. "It was simple." He settled among the seamen. "There were only two whoreson Spaniards."

"Where's Serina?" Katherine scanned the empty shoreline. "Did anything happen?"

"When a woman is allowed to sit in council with warriors, there are always damnable complications." Atiba reached and helped one of the English seamen in. "She would not have us act as men and kill the whoresons both. So she is still up there on the mountain, holding a musket."

"You're not a better man if you murder their militia." Katherine scowled at him. "After you take a place, you only need hold it."

"That is the weak way of a woman, senhora." He glanced toward the hill as again their oars flashed in the moonlight. "It is not the warrior way."

Winston grimaced, but said nothing, knowing the killing could be far from over.

In only minutes they had skirted the bay and were approaching the river mouth. As their dugouts veered into the Rio Cobre, the whitecaps gave way to placid ripples. The tide had just begun running out, and the surface of the water was flawless, reflecting back the half-moon. Now they were surrounded by palms, and beyond, dense forests. Since the rainy season was past, the river itself had grown shallow, with wide sand bars to navigate. But a quarter mile farther and they would be beneath the fort.

"Jamaica, at last." Winston grinned and dipped a hand into the cool river.

Katherine gazed up at the Passage Fort, now a sharp silhouette in the moonlight. It had turrets at each corner and a wide breastwork, from which a row of eighteen-pound culverin projected, hard fingers against the sky. "I just pray our welcome celebration isn't too well attended."

As they rowed slowly up the river, the first traces of dawn were beginning to show in the east. She realized their attack would have to come quickly now. Even though the *vigia* had been silenced, sentries would doubtless be posted around the fort. There still could be a bloody fight with small arms if they were spotted in time for the Spaniards to martial the militia inside. Let one sentry sound the alarm and all surprise would be lost.

"I think we'd best beach somewhere along here." Bartholomew was sounding with an oar. The river was growing increasingly sandy and shallow. "She's down to no more'n half a fathom."

"Besides that, it's starting to get light now." Winston nodded concurrence. "Much farther and they might spy us. Signal the lads behind to put."

"Aye." He turned and motioned with his oar. Quickly and silently the dugouts veered into the banks and the men began climbing over the sides. As they waded through the mud, each carrying a flintlock musket and a pike, they dragged the dugouts ashore and into the brush.

"All right, masters." Winston walked down the line as they began to form ranks. "We want to try taking this place without alerting the whole island. If we can do that, then the Spaniards'll not have time to evacuate the town. Remember anything we take in either place will be divided according to the Articles drawn. Any man who doesn't share what he finds will be judged by the rest, and may God have mercy on him." He turned and gazed up the hill. There was a single trail leading through the forest. "So look lively, masters. Let's make quick work of this."

As they headed up the incline, the men carefully holding their bandoliers to prevent rattling, they could clearly see the fort above the trees. Now lights began to flicker along the front of the breastwork, torches. Next, excited voices began to filter down, faint in the morning air.

Armando Vargas had moved alongside Winston, his eyes narrow beneath his helmet and his weathered face grim. He listened a moment longer, then whispered, "I fear something may have gone wrong, señor."

"What are they saying?" Winston was checking the prime on his pistols.

"I think I hear orders to run out the cannon." He paused to listen. "Could they have spotted our masts over at the *cayo?* It is getting light now. Or perhaps an alert was sounded by the *vigia* after all." He glared pointedly back toward Atiba. "Perhaps it was not so secure as we were told."

Behind them the seamen had begun readying their flint-locks. Though they appeared disorganized, they handled their muskets with practiced ease. They were not raw recruits like Barbados' militia; these were fighting men with long experience.

They continued quickly and silently up the path. Now the moon had begun to grow pale with the approach of day, and as they neared the rear of the fortress they could see the details of its stonework. The outside walls were only slightly higher than a man's head, easy enough to scale with grapples if need be.

As they emerged at the edge of the clearing, Winston suddenly realized that the heavy wooden door at the rear of the fort was already ajar.

Good Christ, we can just walk in.

He turned and signaled for the men to group. "It's time, masters. Vargas thinks they may have spotted our masts, over at the Point, and started to ready the guns." His voice was just above a whisper. "In any case, we'll need to move fast. I'll lead, with my lads. After we're inside, the rest of you hit it with a second wave. We'll rush the sentries, then take any guards. After that we'll attend to the gunners, who like as not won't be armed."

Suddenly more shouts from inside the fort drifted across the clearing. Vargas motioned for quiet, then glanced at Winston. "I hear one of them saying that they must send for the cavalry."

486

"Why?"

He paused. "I don't know what is happening, but they are very frightened in there, señor."

"Good God, if they get word back to the town, it's the end of any booty."

"Hugh, I don't like this." Katherine stared toward the fortress. There were no guards to be seen, no sentries. Everyone was inside, shouting. "Maybe it's some kind of ruse. Something has gone terribly wrong."

"To tell the truth, I don't like it either." He cocked his pistol and motioned the men forward. "Let's take it, masters."

Some fifty yards separated them from the open door as they began their dash forward across the clearing. Now they could hear the sound of cannon trucks rolling over paving stone as the guns were being set.

Only a few more feet remained. Would the door stay open? Why had there been no musket fire?

As Winston bounded up the stone steps leading to the door, hewn oak with iron brackets, still no alarm rose up, only shouts from the direction of the cannon at the front of the breastwork. He seized the handle and heaved it wide, then waved the others after him. Atiba was already at his side, cutlass drawn.

Now they were racing down the dark stone corridor, a gothic arch above their heads, its racks of muskets untouched.

My God, he thought, they're not even going to be armed. Only a few feet more . . .

A deafening explosion sounded from the front, then a second and a third. Black smoke boiled up as a yell arose from the direction of the cannon. The guns of the fort had been fired.

When they emerged at the end of the corridor and into the smoky yard, Spanish militiamen were already rolling back the ordnance to reload. The gunners froze and looked on dumbfounded.

"¡Inglés Demonio!" One of them suddenly found his voice and yelled out, then threw himself face down on the paving stones. One after another, all the others followed. In moments only one man remained standing, a tall officer in a silver helmet. Winston realized he must be the gunnery commander.

He drew his sword, a long Toledo-steel blade, and stood defiantly facing Winston and the line of musketmen.

"No." Winston waved his pistol. "It's no use."

The commander paused, then stepped back and cursed his prostrate militiamen. Finally, with a look of infinite humiliation, he slowly slipped the sword back into its scabbard.

A cheer went up from the seamen, and several turned to head for the inner chambers of the fortress, to start the search for booty. Now the second wave of the attack force was pouring through the corridor.

"Katy, it's over." Winston beckoned her to him and and boxed ceremoniously. "Jamaica is . . ."

The yard erupted as the copestone of the turret at the corner exploded, raining chips of hard limestone around them.

"Great God, we're taking fire from down below." He stood a moment in disbelief. Around him startled seamen began to scurry for cover.

Even as he spoke, another round of cannon shot slammed into the front of the breastwork, shaking the flagstone under their feet.

"Who the hell's in charge down there? There were no orders to fire on the fort . . ."

Another round of cannon shot crashed into the stone facing above them.

"Masters, take cover. There'll be hell to pay for this, I promise you." He suddenly recalled that Mewes had been left in command down below. "If John's ordered the ships into the bay and opened fire, I'll skin him alive."

"Aye, and with this commotion, I'll wager their damned cavalry lancers will be on their way soon enough to give us a welcome." Bartholomew was standing alongside him. "I'd say we'd best secure that door back there and make ready to stand them off."

"Order it done." Winston moved past the gunners and headed toward the front of the breastwork, Katherine at his side. As they approached the Spanish commander, he backed away, then bowed nervously and addressed them in broken English.

"You may receive my sword, señor, in return for the lives of my men. I am Capitan Juan Vicente de Padilla, and I offer you unconditional surrender. Please run up your flag and signal your gunships."

"We've got no flag." Winston stared at him. "Yet. But we will soon enough."

"What do you mean, *mi capitán?* You are Inglés." His dark eyes acquired a puzzled expression. "Of course you have a flag. It is the one on your ships, down in the bay."

"Hugh, what's he talking about? Has John run up English colors?" Katherine strode quickly past the smoking cannon to the edge of the breastwork and leaned over the side.

Below, the bay was lightening in the early dawn. She stood a moment, then turned back and motioned Winston to join her. Her face was in shock. He shoved his pistol into his belt and walked to her side.

Headed across the bay, guns run out, was a long line of warships. Nearest the shore, and already launching longboats of Roundhead infantry, were the *Rainbowe* and the *Marsten Moor*—the red and white Cross of St. George fluttering from their mizzenmasts.

Chapter Twenty-three

"Heaven help us. To think the Lord Protector's proud Western Design has been reduced to assaulting this worthless backwater." Edmond Calvert's voice trailed off gloomily as he examined the blue-green mountains of Jamaica. Then he turned to face Colonel Richard Morris, standing beside him on the quarterdeck. "No silver mines, no plantations, doubtless nothing save wild hogs and crocodiles."

"Well, sir, at least this time the navy has landed my men where we'd planned." Morris was studying the Passage Fort that loomed above them. Amidships, moored longboats were being loaded with helmeted infantry, muskets at the ready. "Their culverin seem to have quieted. If the town's no better defended, there should be scant difficulty making this place ours."

"That, sir, was precisely what you were saying when we first sighted Santo Domingo, scarcely more than a fortnight past—before those craven stalwarts you'd call an army were chased back into the sea."

Morris' eyes narrowed. "When the accounting for Hispaniola is finish'd, sir, that debacle will be credited to the incompetence of the English navy."

"All the same, you'd best take your stouthearted band of cowards and see what you can manage here." Calvert dismissed the commander with a perfunctory salute. Rancor no longer served any end; what was lost was lost.

What had been forfeited, he knew, was England's best chance ever to seize a portion of Spain's vast New World wealth. Oliver Cromwell's ambitious Western Design had foundered hopelessly on the sun-scorched shores of Hispaniola.

He reflected again on the confident instructions in his secret commission, authorized by the Lord Protector himself and approved by his new Council of State only four months earlier.

The Western Design of His Highness is intended to gain for England that part of the West Indies now in the possession of the Spaniard, for the effecting thereof we shall communicate to you what hath been under our Consideration.

Your first objective is to seize certain of the Spaniards' Islands, and particularly Hispaniola. Said Island hath no considerable place in the South part thereof but the City of Santo Domingo, and that not being heavily fortified may doubtless be possest without much difficulty, which being done, that whole Island will be brought under Obedience.

From thence, after your Landing there, send force for the taking of Havana, which lies in the Island of Cuba, which is the back door of the West Indies, and will obstruct the passing of the Spaniards' Plate Fleet into Europe.

Having secured these Islands, proceed immediately to Cartegena, which we would make the Seat of the intended *Design,* and from which England will be Master of the Spaniards' Treasure which comes from Peru by the way of Panama in the South Seas to Porto Bello or Nombre de Dios in the North Sea . . .

How presumptuous it all seemed from this vantage. Worse still, the Council of State had not even bothered taking notice of Jamaica, an under-defended wilderness now their only chance to seize *anything* held by the Spaniards.

Most depressing of all, Cromwell would surely be loath to spend a shilling on the men and arms needed to hold such a dubious prize. Meaning the Spaniards would simply come and reclaim it the minute the fleet set sail.

Surely, he told himself, Cromwell was aware they had shipped out without nearly enough trained men to attack Spanish holdings. Even his Council of State realized as much. But they had nourished the delusion that, once Barbados was bludgeoned back into the Commonwealth, its planters would dutifully offer up whatever first-rate men, arms, and cavalry were needed for the campaign.

What the Council of State had not conceived was how indifferent those islanders would be to the territorial ambitions of Oliver Cromwell. Barbados' planters, it turned out, wanted nothing to do with a conquest of the Spanish Americas; to them, more English-held lands in the New World only meant the likelihood of more acres planted in sugar one day, to compete with the trade they hoped to monopolize. Consequently, Morris' Barbados recruits consisted almost wholly of runaway indentures eluding their owners and their creditors, a collection of profane, debauched rogues whose only boldness lay in doing mischief.

Sugar and slaves. They might well have undermined Barbados' brief try for independence; but they also meant there would be no more English lands in the Americas.

Calvert's heart grew heavy as he remembered how their careful strategy for taking Hispaniola had been wrecked. They had decided to avoid the uncharted harbor of Santo Domingo and land five miles down the coast. But by a mischance of wind on their stern, it was thirty. Then Morris had disembarked his troops with scarcely any water or victuals. All the first day, however, he had marched unopposed, his Puritan infantrymen even pausing to vandalize Papist churches along the way, using idols of the Virgin for musket practice.

The Spaniards, however, had a plan of their own. They had been busy burning all the savannahs farther ahead to drive away the cattle, leaving a path of scorched ground. Soon Morris' supplies were exhausted and hunger began to set in; whereupon his infantry started stealing the horses of the cavalry, roasting and devouring them so ravenously the Spaniards reportedly thought horsemeat must be some kind of English delicacy.

Then came another catastrophe. For sport, the army burned some thatched huts belonging to Hispaniola's notorious Cow-Killers. Soon a gang of vengeful hunters had massed in the woods along the army's path and begun sniping with their long-barrelled muskets. After that, whenever fireflies appeared in the evenings, the English sentries, never before having seen such creatures, mistook them for the burning matchcord of the Cow-Killers' muskets and began firing into the night, causing general panic and men trampled to death in flight. Also, the rattling claws of the night-foraging Caribbean land crabs would sound to the nervous English infantry like the clank of the Cow-Killers' bandoliers. An alarm would raise—"the Cow-Killers"—and soldiers would run blindly into the forests and deadly swamps trying to flee.

When they finally reached Santo Domingo, Morris and his demoralized men gamely tried to rush and scale the walls, whereupon the Spaniards simply fired down with cannon and slew hundreds. Driven back, Morris claimed his retreat was merely "tactical." But when he tried again, the Spanish cavalry rode out and lanced countless more in a general rout, only turning back when they tired of killing. It was the most humiliating defeat any English army had ever received—suffered at the hands of the supposedly craven Spaniards, and the wandering Cow-Killers, of Hispaniola.

Back at sea, they realized the foolhardiness of an attempt on Havana or Cartegena, so the choice they were confronted with was to return to England empty-handed and face Cromwell's outrage, or perhaps try some easier Spanish prize. That was when they hit on the idea of Jamaica—admittedly a smaller island than Hispaniola and of scant consequence to Spain, but a place known for its slight defenses. They immediately weighed anchor and made sail for Jamaica Bay. . . .

"Well, sir, I take it the shooting's over for now. Mayhaps this time your rabble army will see fit to stand and fight like Englishmen." Edging his way cautiously up the smoky companionway, in black hat and cotton doublet, was one of the few Barbados planters who had offered to join the expedition. He glanced at the sunlit fortress, then stared at the green hills beyond. "Though from the looks of the place, I'd judge it's scarcely worth the waste of a round of shot. 'Twould seem to be damn'd near as wild as Barbados the day I first set foot on her."

"I think Colonel Morris knows his duty, sir." Calvert's tone grew official. "And I presume some of this land could readily be put into cultivation."

Why, Calvert puzzled, had the planter come? He'd not offered to assist the infantry. No, most probably he volunteered in hopes of commandeering the choicest Spanish plantations on Hispaniola all for himself. Or perhaps he merely couldn't countenance the thought he'd been denied a seat on Barbados' new Council. Yes, that was more likely the case. Why else would a sugar grower as notoriously successful as Benjamin Briggs have decided to come with them?

"Cultivation!" Briggs turned on him. "I see you know little enough about running a plantation, sir. Where's the labor you'd need?"

"Perhaps some of these infantry will choose to stay and settle. With the Spaniards all about, this island's going to require . . ."

"This set of layabouts? I doubt one in a hundred could tell a cassava root from a yam, assuming he had the industry to hoe one up." Briggs moved to the railing and surveyed the wide plain spreading up from the harbor. "This batch'd not be worth tuppence the dozen for clearing stumps and planting."

. . . But, he found himself thinking, maybe things would be different if you went about it properly. And brought in some Africans. Enough strapping blacks and some of these savannahs might well be set to production. And if not along here, then maybe upland. The hills look as green as Barbados was thirty years ago. Could it be I was wise to come after all? Damn Hispaniola. This place could be the ideal spot to prove what I've always believed.

Aye, he told himself. Barbados showed there's a fortune to be made with sugar. But what's really called for is land, lots of it; and half the good plots there're still held by damn'd ten-acre freeholders. The New World is the place where a man has to think in larger terms. So what if I sold off those Barbados acres, packed up the sugarmill and brought it *here*, cut a deal with the Dutchmen for a string of quality Nigers on long credit . . . ?

All we need do is send these few Spaniards packing, and this island could well be a gold mine.

"If you'll pardon me, Mister Briggs, I'll have to be going ashore now." Calvert nodded, then turned for the companionway.

"As you will, sir." Briggs glanced back at the island. "And if it's all the same, I think I'll be joining you. To take the measure of this fish we've snagged and see what we've got."

"You might do better to wait, Mister Briggs, till we've gained a clear surrender from the Spaniards."

"Well, sir, I don't see any Spaniards lurking about there on the plain." He headed down the companionway after Calvert. "I'm the civilian here, which means I've got responsibilities of my own."

* * *

"Hugh, are we going to just stand here and let these bastards rob us?" Katherine was angrily gripping her musket. *"We* took this fort, not Morris and his Roundheads."

Winston stood staring at the warships, his mind churning. Why the hell were they *here?* Cromwell had better things to do with his navy than harass a few Spanish planters.

Whatever they want, he vowed to himself, they'll damn well have to fight for it.

" 'Tis the most cursed sight I e'er laid eyes on." Guy Bartholomew had moved beside them. "Mayhaps that rumor about some fleet trying Santo Domingo was all too true. An' when they fail'd at that, they decided to pillage Jamaica instead."

Next to him was Timothy Farrell, spouting Irish oaths down on the ships. "Aye, by the Holy Virgin, but whatever happen'd, I'll wager you this—it's the last we're like to see of any ransom for the town." His eyes were desolate. "The damn'd English'll be havin' it all. They've never heard of dividing a thing fair and square, that I promise you."

"Well, they can't squeeze a town that's empty." Winston turned to Bartholomew. "So why don't we start by giving this navy a little token of our thanks. Set these Spaniards free to go back and help clear out Villa de la Vega. By the time the damn'd Roundheads get there, there'll be nothing to find save empty huts."

"Well, sir, it's a thought, I'll grant you. Else we could try and get over there first ourselves, to see if there's any gold left to be had. These Spaniards' Romanish churches are usually good for a few trinkets." The *boucanier* looked down again. A line of longboats was now edging across the bay below, headed for the shore beneath the fort. He glanced back at his men. "What say you, lads?"

"There's no point to it, Cap'n, as I'm a Christian." One of the grizzled *boucaniers* behind him spoke up. "There're lads here aplenty who've sailed for the English navy in their time, an' I'm one of 'em. You can be sure we'd never get

496

past those frigates with any Spanish gold. All we'd get is a rope if we tried riflin' the town now, or holdin' it for ransom. When an honest tar borrows a brass watch fob, he's hang'd for theft; when the generals steal a whole country, it's called the spoils of war. No sir, I've had all the acquaintance I expect to with so-called English law. I warrant the best thing we can do now is try getting out of here whilst we can, and let the whoresons have what they came to find. We took this place once, by God, and we can well do it again.''

There was a murmur of concurrence from the others. Some experienced seamen were already eyeing the stone corridor, reflecting on the English navy's frequent practice of impressing any able-bodied man within reach whenever it needed replacements.

"Well, sir, there's some merit in what you say." Bartholomew nodded thoughtfully. "Maybe the wisest course right now is to try and get some canvas on our brigs before this navy starts to nose about our anchorage over at the other side of the *cayo.*"

"That's the best, make nae mistake." The Scotsman MacEwen interjected nervously. "An' if these Spaniards care to trouble keeping the damn'd Roundheads entertained whilst we're doin' it, then I'd gladly hand them back every gunner here, with a skein of matchcord in the trade. Whatever's in the town can be damn'd.''

"Then it's done." Winston motioned for the Spanish commander. Captain Juan Vicente de Padilla advanced hesitantly, renewed alarm in his dark eyes.

"Do you wish to receive my sword now, *capitán?*"

"No, you can keep it, and get the hell out of here. Go on back to Villa de la Vega and let your governor know the English navy's invaded.''

"*Capitán,* I do not understand your meaning." He stood puzzling. "Your speech is Inglés, but you are not part of those *galeones* down below?"

"We're not English. And I can promise you this island

hasn't heard the last of us." Winston thumbed toward the corridor. "Now you'd best be out of here. I don't know how long those Roundheads expect to tarry."

With a bow of supreme relief, Captain de Padilla turned and summoned his men. In moments the Spanish gunners were jostling toward the corridor, each wanting to be the first to evacuate his family and wealth from Villa de la Vega.

"In God's name, Hugh, don't tell me you're thinking to just hand over this fort!" Katherine was still watching the shore below, where infantrymen were now forming ranks to begin marching up the slope. "I, for one, intend to stand and fight as long as there's powder and shot."

"Don't worry, *we've* got the heavy guns. And their damned warships are under them." He signaled to Tom Canninge, master gunner of the *Defiance*. "Have the boys prime and run out these culverin. We need to be ready."

"Good as done." Canninge shouted an order, and his men hurriedly began hauling the tackles left lying on the stone pavement by the Spanish gunners, rolling back the iron cannon to reload.

By now the infantry had begun advancing up the hill. Winston watched them long enough through the sparse trees to recognize Richard Morris at their head.

So we meet again, you Roundhead bastard. But this time *I* start out holding the ordnance.

"Masters, cover us with your muskets." He motioned for Katherine and together they started for the corridor. The hallway had grown lighter now, a pale gold in the early light of dawn. At the far end the heavy oak door had been left ajar by the departing Spanish gunners.

As they stepped into the sunshine, Atiba suddenly appeared beside them, concern on his face. "Senhor, I think it is no longer safe at the damnable *vigia* on the hill. I must go back up there now."

"All right." Winston waved him on. "But see you're quick on it."

"I am a man of the mountains. When I wish, I can travel faster than a Spaniard with a horse." He began to sprint across the clearing, headed for the trees.

"Katy, hang on to this." Winston drew one of the pistols from his belt and handed it to her. "We'll talk first, but if we have to shoot, the main thing is to bring down Morris. That ought to scatter them."

As they rounded the corner of the fort, Colonel Richard Morris emerged through the trees opposite, leading a column of infantry. The commander froze when he saw them. He was raising his musket, preparing to give order to fire, when his face softened into a disbelieving grin.

"God's blood. Nobody told me *you'd* decided to join up with this assault." He examined them a moment longer, then glanced up at the breastwork, where a line of seamen had appeared, holding flintlocks. He stared a moment in confusion before looking back at Winston. "I suppose congratulations are in order. We had no idea 'twas you and your men who'd silenced their guns. You've doubtless saved us a hot ordnance battle. Bloody fine job, I must say." He lowered his musket and strode warily forward. "What have you done with all the Spaniards?"

"They're gone now." Winston's hand was on the pistol in his belt.

"Then the place is ours!" Morris turned and motioned the infantrymen forward. "Damned odd I didn't notice your . . . frigate in amongst our sail. We could've used you at Hispaniola." He tried to smile. "I'd say, sir, that an extra month's pay for you and your lads is in order, even though I take it you joined us late. I'll see to it myself."

"You can save your eighteen shillings, Colonel. We plan to hold this fort, and maybe the island to go with it. But you're free to rifle the town if you think you can still find anything."

"You plan to hold *what*, sir?" Morris took a cautious step backward.

"Where you're standing. It's called Jamaica. We got here first and we intend to keep however much of it strikes our fancy."

"Well, sir, that's most irregular. I see you've still got all the brass I recall." He gripped the barrel of his musket. "I've already offered you a bonus for exceptional valor. But if you're thinking now to try and rebel against my command here, what you're more likely to earn is a rope around your neck."

Winston turned and yelled up to Canninge. "Tom, ready the guns and when I give the order, lay a few rounds across the quarterdeck of the *Rainbowe* anchored down there. Maybe it'll encourage Colonel Morris to reexamine the situation."

"Good God!" Morris paled. "Is this some kind of jest?"

"You can take whatever you want from the Spaniards. But this harbor's mine. That is, if you'd prefer keeping Cromwell's flagship afloat."

"This harbor?"

"That's right. We're keeping the harbor. And this fortress, till such time as we come to an understanding."

While Morris stared up again at the row of cannon, behind him the last contingent of infantry began to emerge through the trees. Leading it was Admiral Edmond Calvert, and beside him strode a heavyset man in a wide, dark hat. They moved through the row of silver-helmeted infantrymen, who parted deferentially for the admiral, headed toward Morris. They were halfway across the clearing before Benjamin Briggs noticed Katherine and Winston.

"What in the name of hell!" He stopped abruptly. "Have the both of you come back to be hanged like you merit?"

"I'd take care what you say, Master Briggs." Winston looked down the slope. "My lads up there might mistake your good humor."

Briggs glanced up uncertainly at the breastwork, then back.

"I'd like to know what lawless undertaking it is brings *you* two to this forsaken place?"

500

"You might try answering the same question."

"I'm here to look to English interests."

"I assume that means your personal interests. So we're probably here for much the same reason."

"I take it you two gentlemen are previously acquainted." Calvert moved cautiously forward. "Whatever your past cordiality, there'll be ample time to manage the disposition of this place after it's ours. We're dividing the skin before we've caught the fox. Besides, it's the Lord Protector who'll . . ."

There was a shout from the breastwork above, and Calvert paused to look up. Tom Canninge was standing beside one of the grey iron culverin, waving down at Winston.

"Cap'n, there's a mass of horsemen coming up the road from the town."

"Are they looking to counterattack?"

The gunner paused and studied the road. "From here I'd say not. They're travelin' slow, more just walkin' their mounts. An' there're a few blacks with them, who look to be carryin' some kind of hammock."

Now Morris was gazing warily down the road toward Villa de la Vega. He consulted briefly with Calvert, then ordered his men to take cover in the scattering of trees across the clearing.

Coming toward them was a row of Spanish horsemen, with long lances and silver-trimmed saddles, their mounts prancing deferentially behind a slow-moving cluster of men, all attired in the latest Seville finery. In the lead was an open litter, shaded from the sun by a velvet awning, with the poles at each of its four corners held shoulder high by an aged Negro wearing a blue silk loincloth.

Katherine heard a rustle at her elbow and turned to see the admiral bowing. "Edmond Calvert, madam, your servant." He quickly glanced again at the Spanish before continuing. "Colonel Morris just advised me you are Dalby Bedford's daughter. Please allow me to offer my condolences."

She nodded lightly and said nothing, merely tightening her

grip on the pistol she held. Calvert examined her a moment, then addressed Winston. "And I'm told that you, sir, were gunnery commander for Barbados."

Winston inspected him in silence.

Calvert cleared his throat. "Well, sir, if that's indeed who you are, I most certainly have cause to know you for a first-rate seaman. I take it you somehow managed to outsail the *Gloucester.*" He continued guardedly. "You were a wanted man then, but after what's happened today, I think allowances can be made. In truth, I'd like to offer you a commission here and now if you'd care to serve under me."

"Accept my thanks, but I'm not looking for recruitment." Winston nodded, then turned back to study the approaching cavalry. "The 'commission' I plan to take is right here. And that's the two of us. Miss Bedford and I expect to make Jamaica home base."

Calvert smiled as he continued. "Well, sir, if you're thinking now you want to stay, there'll surely be a place for you here. I'll take odds the Spaniards are not going to let us commandeer this island without soon posting a fleet to try and recover it. Which means we've got to look to some defenses right away, possibly move a few of the culverin from the *Rainbowe* and *Marsten Moor* up here to the breastwork. There's plenty to . . ."

"What are you saying!" Katherine stared at him. "That you're going to try and *hold* Jamaica?"

"For England." He sobered. "I agree with you it'll not be an easy task, madam, but we expect to do our best, I give you my solemn word. Yes, indeed. And if you and the men with you care to assist us, I will so recommend it to His Highness. I fear we'll be wanting experienced gunners here, and soon."

While Katherine stood speechless, Benjamin Briggs edged next to them and whispered toward Calvert, "Admiral, you don't suppose we'd best look to our defenses, till we've found out what these damn'd Spaniards are about?"

"This can only be one thing, Mister Briggs. Some kind of attempt to try and negotiate." Calvert examined the procession again as it neared the edge of the clearing. "Not even Spaniards attack from a palanquin."

Now the approaching file was slowing to a halt. While the horsemen reined in to wait in the sunshine, one of the men who had been walking alongside the litter began to converse solemnly with a shadowed figure beneath its awning. Finally he reached in and received a long silk-wrapped bundle, then stepped around the bearers and headed toward them.

He was wearing a velvet waistcoat and plumed hat, and as he approached the four figures standing by the breastwork, he appeared momentarily disoriented. His olive skin looked sallow in the early light and his heavy moustache drooped. Finally he stopped a few feet away and addressed them collectively.

"I am Antonio de Medina, lieutenant-general to our governor, don Francisco de Castilla, who has come to meet you. He regrets that his indisposition does not permit him to tender you his sword from his own hand." He paused and glanced back at the litter. An arm emerged feebly and waved him on. "His Excellency has been fully advised of the situation, and he is here personally to enquire your business. If it is ransom you wish to claim, he would have me remind you we are but a poor people, possessing little wealth save our honesty and good name."

"I am Admiral Edmond Calvert, and I receive his greeting in the name of England's Lord Protector." Calvert was studying the shrouded litter with puzzlement. "Furthermore, you may advise don Francisco de Castilla that we've not come for ransom. We're here to claim this island in the name of His Highness Oliver Cromwell. For England."

"Señor, I do not understand." Medina's brow wrinkled. "Inglés *galeones* such as yours have come in times past, and we have always raised the ransom they required, no matter how difficult for us. We will . . ."

503

"This time, sir, it's going to be a different arrangement." Briggs stepped forward. "He's telling you we're here to stay. Pass that along to your governor."

"But you cannot just claim this island, señor." Medina examined Briggs with disbelief. "It has belonged to Spain for a hundred and forty years."

"Where's your bill of sale, by God? We say it belongs to whoever's got the brass to seize hold of it. Spaniards took half the Americas from the heathen; now it's England's turn."

"But this island was granted to our king by His Holiness the Pope, in Rome."

"Aye, your Pope's ever been free to dispense lands he never owned in the first place." Briggs smiled broadly. "I seem to recall back in King Harry's time he offered England to anybody who'd invade us, but none of your Papist kings troubled to take up his gift." He sobered. "This island's English, as of today, and damned to your Purple Whore of Rome."

"Señor, *protestante* blasphemies will not . . ."

"Take care, Master Briggs." Winston's voice cut between them. "Don't be so quick to assume England has it. At the moment it looks like this fortress belongs to me and my men."

"Well, sir, if you're thinking to try and steal something from this place, which now belongs to England, I'd be pleased to hear how you expect to manage it."

"I don't care to steal a thing. I've already got what I want. While we've been talking, my lads down on the *Defiance* were off-loading culverin there at the Cayo de Carena. On the Point. As of now, any bottom that tries to enter, or leave, this harbor is going to have to sail under them. So the harbor's mine, including what's in it at the moment. Not to mention this fort as well."

"Perhaps you'd best tell me what you have in mind, sir." Calvert glanced up at the breastwork, its iron cannon now all directed on the anchored ships below.

"We might consider an arrangement." Winston paused, then looked down at the bay.

"What do you mean?"

"These men sailing with me are *boucaniers*, Cow-Killers to you, and we need this harbor. In future, we intend sailing from Jamaica, from right over there, at the Point. There'll be a freeport there, for anybody who wants to join with us."

"Are you saying you mean to settle down there on the Point, with these buccaneers?" Calvert was trying to comprehend what he was hearing. Could it be that, along with Jamaica, Cromwell was going to get armed ships, manned by the only men in the Caribbean feared by the Spaniards, for nothing?

Perhaps it might even mean Jamaica could be kept. The Western Design might end up with something after all . . .

"Well, sir, in truth, this island's going to be needing all the fighting men it can muster if it's to defend itself from the Spaniards." Calvert turned to Briggs. "If these buccaneers of his want to headquarter here, it could well be a godsend."

"You'd countenance turning over the safety of this place to a band of rogues?" Briggs' face began to grow dark with a realization. "Hold a minute, sir. Are you meanin' to suggest Cromwell won't trouble providing this island with naval protection?"

"His Highness will doubtless act in what he considers to be England's best interest, Mister Briggs, but I fear he'll not be too anxious to expend revenues fortifying and patrolling an empty Spanish island. I wouldn't expect to see the English navy around here, if that's what you're thinking."

"But this island's got to have defenses. It's not the same as Barbados. Over there we were hundreds of leagues to windward. And the Spaniards never cared about it in the first place. But Jamaica's different. It's right on the Windward Passage. You've got to keep an armed fleet and some fortifications here or the Spaniards'll just come and take the place back whenever they have a mind."

505

"Then you'd best start thinking about how you'd plan to arrange for it." Calvert turned back to Medina. "Kindly advise His Excellency I wish to speak with him directly."

The lieutenant-general bowed and nervously returned to the litter. After consulting inside for a moment, he ordered the bearers to move it forward.

What they saw was a small, shriveled man, bald and all but consumed with venereal pox. He carefully shaded his yellow eyes from the morning sun as he peered out.

"As I have said, Excellency, we are pleased to acknowledge your welcome," Calvert addressed him. "For the time we will abstain from sacking Villa de la Vega, in return for which courtesy you will immediately supply our fleet with three hundred head of fat cattle for feeding our men, together with cassava bread and other comestibles as we may require."

After a quick exchange, Medina looked back, troubled. "His Excellency replies he has no choice but to comply."

"Fine. But I'm not quite finished. Be it also known without any mistaking that we have hereby taken charge of the island of Jamaica. I expect to send you the terms to sign tomorrow morning, officially surrendering it to England."

Winston stepped forward and faced Medina. "You can also advise His Excellency there'll be another item in the terms. Those slaves standing there, and all others on the island, are going to be made free men."

"Señor, all the *negros* on this island have already been set free, by His Excellency's proclamation this very morning. To help us resist. Do you think we are fools? Our *negros* are *católico*. They and our Maroons will stand with us if we have to drive you *protestante* heretics from this island."

"Maroons?" Calvert studied him.

"*Si,* that is the name of the free *negros* who live here, in the mountains." He approached Calvert. "And know this, Inglés. They are no longer alone. The king of Spain will not let you steal this island, and we will not either. Even now,

506

our people in Villa de la Vega have taken all their belongings and left for the mountains also. We will wage war on you from there forever if need be. You may try to steal this island, against the laws of God, but if you do, our people will empty their *hatos* and drive their cattle into the hills. Your army will starve. This island will become your coffin, we promise you."

"That remains to be seen, sir." Calvert inspected him coldly. "If you don't choose to honor our terms and provide meat for this army, then we'll just take what we please."

"Then we bid you good day." Medina moved back to confer with the governor. After a moment, the bearers hoisted the litter, turned, and headed back down the road, trailed by the prancing horses of the cavalry.

Calvert watched, unease in his eyes, as they moved out. "In truth, I'm beginning to fear this may turn out to be as bloody as Hispaniola. If these Spaniards scorn our terms of surrender and take to the hills, it could be years before Jamaica is safe for English settlement."

Behind them the infantrymen had begun to emerge from the woods across the clearing, led by Morris. Next Guy Bartholomew appeared around the side of the fortress, his face strained and haggard in the morning light. He watched puzzling as the Spanish procession disappeared into the distance, then turned to Winston.

"What's all the talk been about?"

"There's going to be a war here, and soon. And we don't want any part of it. So right now we'd best head back over to the Point. That spot's going to be ours, or hell will hear the reason why. John's been off-loading my culverin and he should have the guns in place by now. We don't need these cannon any more. Get your lads and let's be gone."

"I'd just as soon be out of here, I'll tell you that. I don't fancy the looks of this, sir, not one bit." With an exhale of relief, Bartholomew signaled up to the breastwork, then headed back. "God be praised."

As Winston waved him on, he spotted Atiba approaching

across the clearing, Serina at his side. The Yoruba still had his cutlass at his waist, and Serina, her white shift torn and stained from the underbrush, was now carrying a Spanish flintlock. When she saw Briggs, she hesitated a second, startled, then advanced on him.

"My damn'd Niger!" The planter abruptly recognized them and started to reach for his pistol. "The very one who tried to kill me, then made off with my *mulata* . . ."

Serina lifted her musket and cocked it, not missing a step. "Leave your gun where it is, Master Briggs, unless you want me to kill you. He is free now."

"He's a damn'd runaway." Briggs halted. "And I take it you're in with him now. Well, I'll not be having the two of you loose on this island, that much I promise you."

Serina strode directly to where he stood. "I am free now too." Her voice was unwavering. "You can never take me back, if that's what you have come here to do."

"We'll damn'd well see about that. I laid out good money for the both . . ."

"There are many free *preto* on this island. To be black here does not mean I have to be slave. It is not like an Inglês settlement. I have learned that already. The Spaniard at the *vigia* told me there is a free nation of my people here."

Atiba had moved beside her, gripping the handle of his cutlass. "I do not know why you have come, whoreson *branco,* but there will be war against you, like there was on Barbados, if you ever try to enslave any of my peoples living in this place."

"There'll be slaves here and plenty, sirrah. No runaway black is going to tell an Englishman how to manage his affairs. Aye, there'll be war, you may depend on it, till every runaway is hanged and quartered. And that includes you in particular . . ."

He was suddenly interrupted by a barrage of firing from the woods behind them, and with a curse he whirled to stare. From out of the trees a line of Spanish militia was emerging,

508

together with a column of blacks, all bearing muskets. They wore tall helmets and knelt in ranks as they methodically began firing on the English infantry. Briggs paused a second, then ducked and bolted.

"Hugh, we've got to get out of here. *Now.*" Katherine seized his arm and started to pull him into the shelter of the breastwork.

Shouts rose up, while helmets and breastplates jangled across the clearing as the English infantrymen began to scatter. Morris immediately cocked his musket and returned fire, bringing down a Spanish musketman, then yelled for his men to find cover. In moments the morning air had grown opaque with dark smoke, as the infantry hurriedly retreated to the trees on the opposite side of the clearing and began piling up makeshift barricades of brush.

"Senhor, I think the damnable war has already begun," Atiba yelled to Winston as he followed Serina around the corner of the breastwork.

"That it has, and I for one don't want any part of it." He looked back. "Katy, what do you say we just take our people and get on down to the Point? Let Morris try and fight them over the rest."

She laughed, coughing from the smoke. "They can *all* be damned. I'm not even sure whose side I want to be on anymore."

While Briggs and Calvert huddled with Morris behind the barricade being set up by the English infantrymen, the four of them quickly made their way around the side of the fort, out of the shooting. Bartholomew was waiting by the oak door, the seamen crowded around. Now the fortress was empty, while a musket battle between the Spanish and the English raged across the clearing on its opposite side.

"I've told the lads," he shouted above the din. "They're just as pleased to be out of here, that I'll warrant you, now that we've lost all chance to surprise the town. I'd say we're ready to get back over to the Point and see what it is we've managed to come up with.''

''Good.'' Winston motioned them forward.

As he led them down the trail, Katherine at his side, he felt a tug at his sleeve and turned to see Atiba.

''I think we will not be going with you, my friend.'' The Yoruba was grim. ''Dara says if there is to be a war against the Inglês *branco* here, then we must join it. This time I believe a woman's counsel is wise.''

''You'd get tangled up in this fray?''

''It could be a damnable long war, I think. Perhaps much years. But I would meet these free people of my blood, these Maroons.''

''But we're going to take the harbor here. You could . . .''

''I am not a man of the sea, my friend. My people are of the forest. That is what I know and where I want to be. And that is where I will fight the Inglês, as long as I have breath.''

''Well, see you take care. This may get very bad.'' Winston studied him. ''We're headed down to the Point. You'll always be welcome.''

''Then I wish you fortune. Your path may not be easy either. These damnable Inglês may try to come and take it away from you.''

''If they do, then they don't know what a battle is. We're going to make a free place here yet. And mark it, there'll come a day when slaveholders like Briggs will be a blot on the name of England and the Americas. All anybody will want to remember from these times will be the buccaneers.''

''That is a fine ambition.'' He smiled, then glanced down at Serina. ''I wonder what becomes of this island now, with all of us on it.''

''I will tell you.'' She shifted her musket. ''We are going to bring these Inglês to their knees. Someday they will come to us begging.'' She reached up and kissed Katherine, then lightly touched Winston's hand. Finally she prodded Atiba forward, and in moments they were gone, through the trees.

"Hugh, I'm not at all sure I like this." Katherine moved next to him as they continued on down the hill toward the dugouts. Bartholomew was ahead of them now, leading the *boucaniers*. "I thought we were going to capture an island. But all we've ended up with is just a piece of it, a harbor, and all these criminals."

"Katy, what did you once say about thinking you could have it all?"

"I said I'd learned better. That sometimes you've got to settle for what's possible." She looked up at him. "But you know I wasn't the only one who had a dream. Maybe you wanted a different kind of independence, but you had some pretty grand ideas all the same."

"What I wanted was to take Jamaica and make it a free place, but after what's happened today nobody's going to get this island for a long, long time."

She looked up to see the river coming into view through the trees, a glittering ribbon in the early sun. "Then why don't we just make something of what we have, down there on the Point. For ourselves."

He slipped an arm around her and drew her against him.

"Shall we give it a try?"

London

Report of the Council of Foreign Plantations to the Lords of Trade of the Privy Council Board concerning the Condition of the Americas, with Recommendations for Furtherance of the Interests of our Merchants.

. . . Having described Barbados, Virginia, Maryland, and New England, we will now address the Condition of Jamaica subsequent to the demise of the late (and unlamented) Oliver Cromwell and the Restoration of His Royal Majesty, Charles Stuart II, to the Throne of England.

Unlike Barbados, which now has 28,515 Black slaves and whose lands command three times the price of the most Fertile acres in England, the Island of Jamaica has yet to enjoy prosperous Development for Sugar. Although its production may someday be expected to Surpass even that of Barbados (by virtue of its greater Size), it has ever been vexatious to Govern, and certain Recommendations intended to ammend this Condition are here set forth.

It is well remembered that after Jamaica was seized from the Spaniards, the Admiral and Infantry Commander (who shall not be cruelly named here) were both imprisoned in the Tower by Oliver Cromwell as Reward for their malfeasance in the *Western Design*. Furthermore, the English infantry first garrisoned there soon proved themselves base, slothful Rogues, who would neither dig nor plant, and in short time many sought to defect to the Spaniards for want of rations. These same Spaniards thereafter barbarously scattered their cattle, reducing the English to eating dogs and snakes, whereupon over two-thirds eventually starved and died.

The Spaniards did then repair to the mountains of that Island with their Negroes, where together they waged war for many years against all English forces sent against them, before at last retiring to live amongst their fellow Papists on Cuba. After that time, Oliver Cromwell made offer of Free acres, under the authority of his Great Seal, to any Protestant in England who would travel thither for purposes of settlement, but to scant effect. His appeal to New Englanders to come and plant was in like manner scorned.

Thus for many years Jamaica has remained a great Thorn in the side of England. Even so, we believe that certain Possibilities of this Island may soon compensate the Expense of maintaining it until now.

The Reason may be taken as follows. It has long been understood that the Aspect of our American settlements most profitable to England is the Trade they have engendered for our Merchants. Foremost among the Commodities required are Laborers for their Plantations, a Demand we are at last equipp'd to supply. The Royal African Company (in which His Majesty King Charles II and all the Court are fortunate Subscribers) has been formed and a string of English slaving Fortresses has now been established on the Guinea coast. The Company has thus far shipped 60,753 Africans to the Americas, of which a full 46,396 survived to be Marketed, and its most recent yearly dividend to English subscribers was near to 300%. A prized coin of pure West African gold, appropriately name'd the Guinea, has been authorized by His Majesty to commemorate our Success in this remunerative new Business.

Now that the Assemblies of Virginia and Maryland happily have passed Acts encouraging the Usefulness of Negro slaves in North America, we may expect this Trade to thrive abundantly, in light of the Fact that Blacks on English plantations do commonly Perish more readily than they breed.

Furthermore, the noblest Plantation in the New World could well one day be the Island of Jamaica, owing to its abundance of fertile acres, if two Conditions thwarting its full Development can be addressed.

The first being a band of escaped Blacks and Mullatoes, known to the Spaniards as Maroons, who make bold to inhabit the mountains of said Island as a Godless, separate Nation. Having no moral sense, and not respecting the laws and customs of Civil nations, they daily grow more insolent and threatening to the Christian planters, brazenly exhorting their own Blacks to disobedience and revolt. By their Endeavors they have prevented many valuable tracts of land from being cultivated, to the great prejudice of His Majesty's revenue. All attempts to quell and reduce these Blacks (said to live as though still in Africa, with their own Practices of worship) have availed but little, by virtue of their unassailable redoubts, a Condition happily not possible on the small island of Barbados. Our records reveal that some 240,000 pounds Sterling have thus far been expended in fruitless efforts to bring them under submission. Yet they must be destroyed or brought in on some terms, else they will remain a great Discouragement to the settling of a people on the Island.

It is now concluded that, since all English regiments sent against them have failed to subdue these Maroons (who fall upon and kill any who go near their mountain strongholds), efforts must be attempted in another Direction. Accordingly we would instruct the Governor of the Island, Sir Benjamin Briggs, to offer terms of Treaty to their leader, a heathenish

Black reported to be called by the name Etiba, whereby each Nation may henceforth exist in Harmony.

The other Condition subverting full English control of the island is the Town that thrives at the Entrance to Jamaica Bay, a place called Cayo de Carena by the Spaniards and now known, in honor of the Restoration of His Majesty, as *Port Royal*. Said Port scarcely upholds its name, being beholden to none save whom it will. It is home to those Rovers of the sea calling themselves Buccaneers, a willful breed of men formerly of Tortuga, who are without Religion or Loyalty. Travelling whither they choose, they daily wreak depredations upon the shipping of the Spaniard (taking pieces-of-eight in the tens of millions) and have made the Kingdom of the Sea their only allegiance.

Unlike our own Failure to settle prosperous Plantations on Jamaica, this port has enjoyed great Success (of a certain Kind). No city founded in the New World has grown more quickly than this place, nor achieved a like degree of Wealth. It is now more populous than any English town in the Americas save Boston—and it has realized a position of Importance equalled only by its infamous Reputation. In chase of the stolen Spanish riches that daily pour in upon its streets, merchants will pay more for footage along its front than in the heart of London. Having scarce supply of water, its residents do drink mainly strong liquors, and our Census has shown there are not now resident in this Port ten men to every Tippling House, with the greatest number of licenses (we are advis'd) having been issued to a certain lewd Woman once of Barbados, who has now repaired thither to the great advancement of her Bawdy Trade.

Although this Port has tarnished the Name of England by its headquartering of these insolent Buccaneers, it is yet doubtful whether the Island would still be in His Majesty's possession were it not for the Fear they strike in the heart of the Spaniards, who would otherwise long since have Reclaimed it.

The chiefest of these Rovers, an Englishman known to all, has wrought much ill upon the Spaniards (and on the Hollanders, during our recent war), for which Service to England (and *Himself*) he is now conceived by His Majesty as a Gentleman of considerable parts, though he has acted in diverse ways to obstruct our quelling of the island's meddlesome Maroons.

Accordingly, His Majesty has made known to the Council his Desire that we strive to enlist this Buccaneer's good offices in persuading his Rovers (including a notorious Woman, equally well known, said to be his Wife, who doth also sail with these Marauders) to uphold English jurisdiction of the Island and its Port. Should this Design fall out as desir'd, His Majesty has hopes that (by setting, as he would have it privately, these Knights of the Blade in charge of his Purse) he can employ them to good effect.

In furtherance of this end, it is His Majesty's pleasure that we, in this coming year, recall Sir Benjamin Briggs (whose honesty His Majesty has oft thought Problemmatical) and make effort to induce this Buccaneer to assume the post of Governor of Jamaica.

Afterword

In the foregoing I have attempted to distill the wine of history into something more like a brandy, while still retaining as much authentic flavor as possible. Many of the episodes in the novel are fictionalized renderings of actual events, albeit condensed, and the majority of individuals depicted also were drawn from life. The action spans several years, from the first major slave auction on Barbados, thought to have occurred slightly before mid-century, to the English seizure of Jamaica in 1655. The structure of race and economics in England's Caribbean colonies changed dramatically in those short years, a social transformation on a scale quite unlike any other I can recall. The execution of King Charles and the Barbados war of independence also took place during that crucial time.

All documents, letters, and broadsides cited here are essentially verbatim save the two directly involving Hugh Winston. Of the people, there naturally were many more involved than a single novel could encompass. Hugh Winston is a composite of various persons and viewpoints of that age (such as Thomas Tryon), ending of course with the famous buccaneer Sir Henry Morgan, later appointed Governor of Jamaica in recognition of his success pillaging Spanish treasure. Governor Dalby Bedford is a combination of Governor Philip Bell and his successor Francis, Lord Willoughby. (Neither was actually killed in the Barbados revolution. The revolt collapsed when, after defectors had welcomed Parliament's forces ashore, five days of rain immobilized the planters, whereupon a stray English cannon ball knocked down the door of a plantation house where the island's militia commanders were gathered and laid out one of the sentries, demoralizing them into surrender.) Katherine Bedford was inspired by Governor Bell's wife, "in whome by reason of her quick and industrious spirit lay a great stroak of the government." Benjamin Briggs is an embodiment of many early settlers; his installation of the first sugar mill on the island and his construction of a walled compound for protection recall James Drax and Drax Hall, and his later career is not unlike that of Thomas Modyford, a prosperous Barbados planter who later became governor of Jamaica.

Anthony and Jeremy Walrond are vaguely reminiscent of the prominent royalists Humphrey and George Walrond. Edmond Calvert was drawn for some portions of the story from Sir George Ayscue and for others from Admiral William Penn. Richard Morris is a combination of Captain William Morris and General Robert Venables, and James Powlett recalls Vice Admiral Michael Pack. Most of the Council and Assembly members appearing here were actually in those bodies, and my Joan Fuller is homage to a celebrated Bridgetown brothel proprietor of the same name; of them all, I sincerely hope I have done most justice to her memory.

Jacques le Basque was modeled on various early *boucaniers*—beginning with Pierre le Grand, the first to seize a Spanish ship (using dugouts), and ending with the much-hated French buccaneer-king Le Vasseur, who built Forte de la Roche and its "dovecote." Tibaut de Fontenay was the latter's nephew, who murdered him much as described over the matter of a shared mistress.

Although Serina, as mulatto "bed-warmer" to Benjamin Briggs, had no specific prototype at that early time (a condition soon to change, much to the dismay of English wives at home), Atiba was inspired by a Gold Coast slave named Coffe who led an unsuccessful revolt on Barbados in the seventeenth century, intending to establish a black nation along African lines. As punishment he and several others were "burned alive, being chained at the stake." When advised of his sentence, he reportedly declared, "If you roast me today, you cannot roast me tomorrow." A contemporary broadside depicting the affair retailed briskly in London. Atiba's subsequent career, as a Maroon leader with whom the English eventually were forced to negotiate, also had various historical models, including the fearsome Cudjoe, head of a warlike nation of free Negroes still terrifying English planters on Jamaica almost eighty years after it was seized.

Very few physical artifacts survive from those years. On Barbados one can see Drax Hall, on which Briggs Hall was closely modeled, and little else. On Tortuga, this writer chopped his way through the jungle and located the site of Le Vasseur's Forte de la Roche and "dovecote." A bit of digging uncovered some stonework of the fort's outer wall, but all that remained of the "dovecote" was a single plaster step, almost three and a half centuries old, once part of its lower staircase and now lodged in the gnarled root of a Banyan tree growing against the huge rock atop which it was built. On Jamaica there seems to be nothing left, save a few relics from the heyday of Port Royal. Only the people of those islands, children of a vast African diaspora, remain as living legacy of Europe's sweet tooth in the seventeenth century.

The story here was pieced together from many original sources, for which thanks is due the superb Library and Rare Book Room of Columbia University, the Rare Book Room of the New York Public Library, the Archives of Barbados, and the Institute of Jamaica, Kingston. For information on Yoruba culture and practices, still very much alive in Brazil and parts of the Caribbean, I am grateful to Dr. John Mason of the Yoruba Theological Seminary, the Caribbean Cultural Center of New York, and friends in Haiti who have over the years exposed me to Haitian *vodun*. For information on Tortuga and the *boucaniers*, including some vital research on Forte de la Roche, I am indebted to the archeologist Daniel Koski-Karell; and for their hospitality to an enquiring novelist I thank *Les Frères des Ecoles chrétiennes*, Christian Brothers missionaries on the Isle de la Tortue, Haiti. I am also grateful to Dr. Gary Puckrein, author of *Little England*, for his insights concerning the role slavery played in Barbados' ill-starred attempt at independence.

Those friends who have endured all or portions of this manuscript, pen in hand, and provided valuable criticisms and suggestions include, in alphabetical order—Norman and Susan Fainstein, Joanna Field, Joyce Hawley, Julie Hoover, Ronald Miller, Ann Prideaux, Gary Prideaux, and Peter Radetsky. Without them this could never have been completed. I am also beholden to my agent, Virginia Barber, and to my editor, Anne Hukill Yeager, for their tireless encouragement and assistance.